Alice's
Neck

Books by
BARBARA NOVAK

American Painting of
the 19th Century

Nature and Culture

Alice's Neck

Alice's Neck

Barbara Novak

TICKNOR
& FIELDS

New York

1987

Library of Congress Cataloging-in-Publication Data

Novak, Barbara.
    Alice's neck.

    I. Title.
PS3564.0886A79   1987   813'.54   87-10028
ISBN 0-89919-539-3

Printed in the United States of America

P 10 9 8 7 6 5 4 3 2 1

For

AUGUSTA KAUFMAN

Men are so necessarily mad,
that not to be mad would
amount to another form
of madness.

— Pascal

I

It's a great huge game of chess that's being played — all over the world — if this is the world at all, you know. Oh, what fun it is! How I wish I was one of them! I wouldn't mind being a Pawn, if only I might join — though of course I should like to be a Queen, best.

— Through the Looking-Glass

I

IT WAS ANNA'S MOVE. Sitting in front of the small portable chessboard, balancing it on the lap of her dressing gown, her two selves were playing chess as the sunlight from Fifth Avenue streamed into the patients' recreation room at Mount Sinai. She had been hospitalized in this dreary place for three weeks. They put electric in her head. The attendant wanted to play with her, but she didn't want him. Her two selves were perfectly capable of playing chess on their own. They said she was crazy. Crazy was when you didn't have a self. She had at least two, and at this moment, the red queen hit the seventh square. Everything happened at seven.

At seven she was orphaned. At seventeen she willingly surrendered her virginity. In the seventy-ninth year of the twentieth century she went to Harvard. On the seventh day of the seventh month of the year that began in academic '79 she landed here. Her room here was on the seventh floor. I must research that when I get out, she said to her other self, sitting invisibly opposite at the other side of the chessboard. Surely there are all sorts of numerological and mystical meanings I'm missing. Research that, she said to herself sternly, moving the red queen out of the seventh square.

Reassured by her other self that the research would take place some time soon, whenever (that is, with a bit of luck) they decided she was no longer in-sane, but sane (how strange, that word, she stopped to consider, it should be out-sane. In-sane meant in sanity. In sanity not insanity. Just a space, that's all), when they decided that, those doctors who looked at her and shook their heads and kept her locked up with all those crazy people, when they decided that, she would research it. Seven. Research seven.

What did the doctors who were observing Anna Bernstein within the antiseptic precincts of the mental hospital on the premises of Mount Sinai on upper Madison Avenue near Spanish Harlem see?

A pale face that looked only temporarily so, as though the blood had been drained out the night before by a vampire. Blue eyes, long straight blonde hair, properly Wasped, refuted by the ethnic name. Tallish, with a long swanlike neck. Bony. Thin. In proper clothes, other than the present rather badly tea-stained dressing gown, mannequinlike. Good cheekbones. Never without her copy of Lewis Carroll. Identification phenomenon. Difficult case. Not quite simple manic depressive, some schizophrenic tendencies. Strange breakdown. Simple student stress? Only children's books on her bookshelves: Grimm, Milne, Carroll, Lear. Never carried anything but the Carroll with her. Slept with it on her pillow. New kind of security blanket. Played chess with herself every morning, always following the same game described by Carroll in the *Looking-Glass*.

— Said Dr. Linnell: Good-looking wench.

— Said Dr. Gotthard: Not quite a nymphet but very young still. Young and tender. Just past Lolita, a bit overripe.

— Said Dr. Linnell: Inverts reality. Wrong side of the mirror constantly. Must be dyslexic. Probably flunked out at Harvard.

— Said Dr. Gotthard: Wrong as usual, *cher* colleague. It was love.

— Said Dr. Linnell: Hardly that alone.

In her moments of lucidity, and there were still many of them, Anna Bernstein was given to taking stock. Inventorying her life, such as it had been. Trying hard to remember. To remember, verb, produced memories, noun. In that more concrete, rather than active form, nouns battered themselves against the inside of her skull. Some of them hurt. Others were soothing, soft-edged, and silky. She couldn't seem to sort them out, never knew which would land first. In her seventh year, when songwriters wrote about seventh heaven, her parents were killed in a car accident. From Long Island, she was sent to live with her grandmother in Brooklyn.

Her parents had gone (she hoped) to seventh heaven. She hoped too she would meet them there later. Much later. But first she had to be a good girl and grow up and live her life. Everyone, said her grandmother, in broken English that Anna couldn't quite understand so well at first, everyone had to live their life. Then when they had done that, they could catch up to the people they loved who had gone on ahead.

Anna, aged seven, one long blonde braid like a China-man's queue down her straight back, wanted to know, as her grandmother pulled her hair tight each morning, why they didn't wait.

— Sometimes you got to leave sooner. Her grandmother shrugged, setting her soft mouth sternly. You can't control the timetable.

— Who controls the timetable? asked Anna, aged seven, more than once.

But Grandma never answered her, just sent her out to play with her cousins. There were lots of cousins, distant ones, and lots of games. Grandma couldn't read English, so there were few books. Anna, aged seven, had to make do with the ones at P.S. 83 Brooklyn. No one read *Alice* to her, and despite an interim education at Erasmus Hall High School and Brooklyn College, improbable as it seems, she didn't discover Lewis Carroll until she reached Widener Library in 1979. Cambridge did not look like Brooklyn.

Brooklyn was filled with tall brick buildings that belied the names of its main streets: Flatbush Avenue, Ocean Parkway.

Where were the flat bushes and oceans? Anna would ask her grandmother. Sometimes she would look for the flat bushes in Prospect Park.

— Oh, Grandma — look, it's flat, I found one.

But Grandma would shake her head and say no, that was not one. That was not why it was called Flatbush Avenue. It was called Flatbush Avenue because it was the main street, with lots of shops.

Grandma's reasoning perplexed young Anna, and older Anna, more semiologically aware, used to reflect back on it in Cambridge. She spent a whole week, not long after her arrival, reading through histories of Brooklyn in Widener Library, looking for the source of Flatbush. Flatbush, she discovered, was originally a town near Breuckelen and New Utrecht, not far from Flatlands (at first called Amersfoort). Flatbush was at first called Medwoud, Midwout, or Midwood. Breuckelen itself meant marshland, and looked like Breuckelen in Holland. But Anna couldn't find the Flat Bush. Her concern for it at that earlier point in her life, when she began to discover places on her walks through Brooklyn with her grandmother, had resulted in her first real research project. Systematically, around the age of eight or nine, she would examine carefully each and every shrub in Prospect Park, cataloguing its morphological characteristics: looking for the flat head. Would it, she sometimes wondered, be a flat head? Or would it, rather, be flat up and down? How much was flat enough to be considered flat? The quest for the Flat Bush, literal as it was, was an important quest for the older as well as the younger Anna. It told her something about the nature of knowledge. It led her into questions, and the search for answers. Where is the truth? What is accurate? How many experimental attempts must be made? What evidence do you accept? Many times, another young Anna might have compromised or rationalized. That bush is flat enough, her cousins would often sigh, lifting their eyebrows at her strange games. Look, Anna, isn't that bush flat enough? But this young Anna, determined, resolute, ever the truth

seeker, uncompromising, just shook her head. It was not yet the Flat Bush.

Cambridge
July 29, 1980

Ms. Anna Bernstein
Klingenstein Clinical Center
Mount Sinai Hospital
100th Street and Madison Avenue
New York, N.Y. 10029

Dear Anna,

So sorry I have not been able to get down to New York. My publisher is keeping me very busy with my book on Millais, and I've been copyedited by a tyrant of a young girl who thinks she knows more than a full professor where the commas go. She doesn't, of course, but even telling her how *wrong* she is takes up so much time. Then they are fighting with me about color — these people always promise more than they can deliver. And as I've told you — after working five years on the book, I won't see any real money anyway. Thank God the work itself offers its own compensations.

Enough of me, dear girl. How are you feeling? I hope very much that we — you and I — didn't cause this tiny mishap you have had. Try to remember that our relationship had its own virtue, and even if my wife did find out, there was no reason to feel you had lost me forever. You are still my student; I still look forward to seeing you sitting brightly in my Ruskin seminar next semester. So you see, all is not lost, and you will have the deep affection of your great and good friend,

Victor

Cambridge
July 29, 1980

Ms. Anna Bernstein
Klingenstein Clinical Center
Mount Sinai Hospital
New York, N.Y.

Dear Anna–

I thought you looked very much better when I dropped in to see you last week. Really pretty — though still a little pale. I'm sure that's as much due to the medication they have you on as anything else. Remember, kiddie, you're a survivor. Take it from an old Darwinian — you'll make it. You, my girl, are surely one of the fittest. Don't quite know what caused it all, but I'm glad I found you when I did, and if you are going to give me your undying gratitude forever because I saved your life, I'll take it — I'll take it. Then maybe you'll be willing to shack up with me exclusively, and continue *The Descent of Man*. Forgive me for dwelling on the great man at such length, but I've just finished another essay on his cross-fertilization of orchids and I'm full of him. My thesis adviser was very pleased with it. Says I'm coming along, whatever that means. More important, honey bun — *you* come along. Whatever caused it, it wasn't worth it. My God, you're twenty-one years old. You've got a life expectancy, lucky woman, just because you're not male, of about fifty-five more years.

Will run down to see you again as soon as possible. I'm sorry in a way that they transferred you from Mount Auburn to Mount Sinai, but I know you feel better closer to home even if your grandmother isn't well enough to visit. And I'll get by as often as I can.

Your loyal friend
and willing lover,

Andrew

July 29, 1980

Ms. Anna Bernstein
Mount Sinai
New York

Dear Anna —

I love you. I love you. Marry me. Marry me.

Kurt

❧❧❧❧

Who were these people whose letters from Cambridge were delivered all at once, three days after the mailing date, to Anna Bernstein on the psychiatric floor of Mount Sinai in New York? Anna read them in the order in which they are here given. The last seemed, to an attendant watching, to have caused some pain. She crumpled it, and discarded it quickly. Then moved another queen into the eighth square.

❧❧❧❧

Victor Allingame. Professor of Art History at the Fogg Art Museum at Harvard; specialty: Pre-Raphaelite painting. Married, four children, one rather unprepossessing wife, with the appropriate number of ducks decorating her home: bordering the dado in the dining room, adorning the mantel, embossing the place mats, lacquered forever in place for easy cleaning. The typical faculty wife, it might be said, who wears little makeup, dresses in 1980 in styles of the fifties, and has brought to the marriage not only the matching lineage of suitable DAR credentials, but an ancestry that includes three senators, one Vice President, one Secretary of the Treasury (and, if truth be known, several blackguard plantation owners in Virginia who beat their slaves). Victor Allingame himself, of course, is pure New England — Puritan ancestors stretching back to Increase and Cotton Mather themselves. Perhaps this is why, when he and Anna made love, he insisted there be just the tiniest quotient of S-M in it. Hard for the descendant of such Puritans to enjoy it thoroughly without some kind of self-inflicted punishment.

Andrew Hanson. Graduate student in Natural History. Ph.D. in progress on the re-evaluation of the possible validity of catastrophic ideas in the light of post-Darwinian discoveries about evolution and time. Pet collector, owner of three cats, Samantha, Red, and Bony, one dog, an obnoxious spoiled poodle named Lucinda, retrieved from an old mistress who had discarded her along with the affair, a blue parakeet named Lettie, and a black rabbit named Celeste. Loyal friend, confidant, willing bed companion, lender of books and bibliographies, movie pal, neighbor at 2 Trowbridge Street.

Kurt Hahn. Artist and art historian. Ph.D. in progress on Emil Nolde. Mother born in Germany, daughter of a prominent German bureaucrat who fled to Argentina when the war was lost. Father, Nevada cattle rancher and alfalfa farmer stationed in Germany after the war. Raised in Nevada. Paintings, in 1980, just beginning to attract notice from New York–based critics looking for figurative and expressionist work. Apostle Gallery, Boylston Street. Western in manner: distinguished on the Harvard campus by cowboy shirts, boots, jeans, and an old cowboy hat given him by one of his daddy's buddies at a rodeo. Lover and suitor.

Cambridge did not look like Brooklyn. Closing her eyes, Anna called up images: the college green with the tall stately trees flanking the path to Widener, with its equally stately classical portico. The hub of Harvard Square, spreading out to link the red-bricked college buildings with the wooden frames of the old Brattle Street mansions. Brattle Street, with its white picket fences and yellow Longfellow House, not far from Henry James's old residence at number 20 Quincy Street, which received votive calls from Anna whenever she could make them. Here he stood, here he visited, here, at number 85 Brattle, John Singer Sargent breakfasted, Hiawatha, Hiawatha, the associations of New England were quickly learned, quickly adopted after Anna's landing from Brooklyn, for landing it was — a new country, a new world. Yet, coming from Brooklyn, from Grandma with her broken English, to the resonant dialects of Harvard Yard, Anna had gradually felt herself spread-eagled between two cultures, as much alienated as linked. Her own biography, following our listing after those of the above-mentioned letter writers, would have read:

> Anna Bernstein. Daughter of Robert and Ellen Bernstein (deceased) of Glen Cove, Long Island. Only child. Granddaughter of Gittel Cohen, formerly of Lomza, Poland. Many relatives deceased at Auschwitz, Poland. Others resident in various parts of Brooklyn. No genealogical roots traceable, beyond grandmother's father, village blacksmith, who had a red beard. Ph.D. in progress on Caspar David Friedrich, nineteenth-century German artist.

The Anna Bernstein currently resident on the seventh floor of Mount Sinai's psychiatric hospital was not the same Anna Bernstein who arrived at Harvard almost a year earlier. That Anna Bernstein had, within a week of establishing residence on Trowbridge Street, begun a diary, which now accompanied her along with the children's books to Mount Sinai. In this volume, simple and blackbound, with blank pages, of the type used by artists as sketchbooks, she wrote not only daily thoughts and events, but quotes from reading that caught her fancy. These were not, however, correlated or chronologized in any orderly way, so that an unsuspecting and indeed prying reader would be confused, not to say undone, by the temporal palimpsest that presented itself to the eye — in different-colored pens, pencils, in and around the margins, later observations overlapping carelessly with those prior, and so on. Anna Bernstein herself, of course, might have been expected to know just what came where and when, much as the owner of a very messy desk knows what bits of letters and notes are where in the various piles of documents that occlude its surface, except that her own sense of past, present, and future had, ever since her parents' death and her own now long-since removal to Brooklyn, been curiously confused.

Since it does not matter, either to Anna or to us, therefore, where we open the diary, let us simply open it with the kind of randomness that bespeaks total calculation and see what we get.

Undated, in red ink:

Where or what is history?
Celeste leaves rabbit shit all over Andrew's apartment.
Haven't seen any flat bushes in Cambridge yet.
Ruskin was really an unmitigated bastard to Effie.

The most readily accessible of these, Andrew Hanson, was, at this moment, sitting in a carrel at Widener Library, thinking about orchid propagation, and idly comparing the petals of the orchid, fragile, pink, sensual, to a woman's vagina. These thoughts alternated intermittently with thoughts of Anna Bernstein when she first arrived at Harvard. They met through Celeste. That is, the paper sack in which Andrew Hanson was disposing of Celeste's droppings was dropped by him accidentally outside Anna Bernstein's door and burst. While he was trying to recapture each of the small round pellets in the corridor, Anna Bernstein opened the door of her new apartment, stepped out, and slid on several of them, sprawling on the floor of number 2 Trowbridge Street very unhappily but, with all due credit to her, silently. Andrew Hanson picked her up, disposed of the remaining pellets, and formed a friendship.

Discovering that Anna Bernstein was from Brooklyn, Andrew Hanson, himself from Wisconsin, was even more intrigued, because he had never known anyone from Brooklyn. In Andrew's eyes, Anna was exotic. Her long thin neck seemed extraordinarily sensual, like a flower stem, from which hung not only a sweet, regular-featured face with almond eyes and small, temperate nose, but long straight Rapunzel-like hair. She had never been out of Brooklyn before, except earlier in her life when she had lived with her family on Long Island. That experience, however, had been misted over by the death of her parents, so that, as she told him over their initial cup of Lipton tea in his apartment, accompanied by his menagerie, with friendly Celeste in her lap and plants crawling over and around them in the sunlight, it always seemed to her as though, if real, it had happened to her in another life, another incarnation. Anna believed, he quickly discovered, in reincarnation. She had read all about it when she was fifteen.

— The only thing is, she said, I've never understood why it always happens to a child in a village in India, who tells his parents that he used to live in a neighboring village, and can lead them by the hand to his old family, and tell them the names of all the aunts and cousins and so on. But it never seems to happen to Arnie Goldstein of Ocean Parkway, Brooklyn. I've never been able to understand selective reincarnation, have you? Is life so cheap in India that when you're born, you automatically get a second chance?

Andrew was quick to decide that Anna, for all the gaps in her education and development, had a very interesting head. She was a special kind of enfant-savant. When she discovered something, she tried to follow it through. She read everything she could. She researched. Research for Anna was a kind of primitive self-education that had gone on since she landed with Grandma and realized that Grandma's reading was exclusively limited to Isaac Bashevis Singer in the *Jewish Daily Forward*. The Yiddish letters seemed beautiful to Anna but might have been Egyptian hieroglyphics.

— Grandma is not illiterate, you understand, she told Andrew. She reads Hebrew and Yiddish and Polish and Russian. But in Brooklyn, all she read was the *Jewish Daily Forward*. Yiddish is almost a dead language, I think, like

Latin. Grandma spoke it so much I picked up a few words, but I could never read it. So what I got was some sporadic education from my teachers, but I only really learned what I latched on to myself.

At fifteen, she had latched on to Vedic literature and the Bhagavad-Gita. But it was Andrew who told her she looked to him like Tenniel's illustration of Alice, and later brought her to the entries for Charles Dodgson and Lewis Carroll in Widener Library.

Anna Bernstein, to cement their new friendship, went to bed with Andrew that same afternoon. This was not because she was either immoral or liberated, but because she was touched by his kindness and hospitality and wanted to reciprocate in some way. It has been said by someone who knew her intimately (and partook of *her* generosity) that Isadora Duncan invited a man to bed as she would offer him a cup of tea. Anna Bernstein did this in much the same way. Whatever sense of morality or ethical behavior she had was shaped early by her parents and then by Grandma, who had, however, neglected to discuss this particular with her, possibly out of shyness, and possibly out of the feeling that Anna could be trusted to intuit proper behavior in any specific situation from Grandma's general behavioral rule: Be kind.

Thus, Andrew Hanson was early treated to the experience of Anna's long lithe legs, to the firm glories of her young bosom, to the womanly amplitude of her hips. Anna, on the other hand, returned to her own apartment next door with the pleasurable awareness of having acquired a new friend and champion at Harvard. Having reinforced the relationship in a way that seemed to her thoroughly proper, she felt free to rely on her new friend for all kinds of things: initial directions to various university offices and buildings, library assistance, coins for the laundromat, late-night companionship at the Wursthaus, weekend excursions to Concord and Marblehead, occasional jaunts to the Museum of Fine Arts, walks along the Charles.

Andrew, reflecting on it now, was the first to admit that

none of this had been in any way burdensome. Anna's youth and innocence, despite the deep scar of the early parental loss, were appealingly supplemented at the outset by her constant delight in discovery at Harvard. Harvard was indeed to her the other side of the looking glass, and if it was also a Wonderland, in which she found not a white rabbit but black Celeste, it was no less wondrous in her eyes. Anna approached Harvard with the same habit of mind with which she had searched earlier for the flat bush. Her obsessive curiosity and lucid intelligence had won her admission to the Fogg to begin with. So Harvard, to Anna, was to be researched, and along with it Cambridge, the Boston area, and much of New England. Andrew Hanson, willing bystander and observer, new friend and lover, could go along for the ride.

Thus too, Victor Allingame, Harvard professor, traditional New Englander, descendant of Cotton Mather, became, when he entered into the saga of Anna Bernstein at Harvard, an integral part of her research and education, as well as an important part of the puzzle Anna's story presents to us. Victor Allingame spotted Anna Bernstein not long after Andrew Hanson did. She was sitting, it turned out, at the back of his classroom, and he noticed her, after a slide lecture on Burne-Jones, in that split second when the lights flipped on. Engrossed still in recording his carefully chosen words, she sat with her blonde hair half covering her face while students rose around and beside her, hurriedly circumventing the rapt obstacle she presented to their passage. This absorbed apparition seemed not to belong to the same century as the others. In the heat of early autumn, she was draped in something white, all white, and lacy, with broad puffed sleeves, and a flounce at the hem. She wore no makeup, and her pale complexion reinforced the anachronism.

Victor Allingame was enchanted. She was like one of the figures in the paintings that had just graced the screen. She was a blonde *belle dame sans merci*. She was out of Tennyson, or Rossetti. Who was she? How had he been fortunate enough to attract her to his classroom? (Victor Allingame had, indeed, attracted many other interesting young ladies to his classroom over the past twenty-five years.) If his marital conscience suffered at all over the tiny dalliances he established, he comforted himself that they were crucial muses for his scholarly invention. When, especially, they carried with them not only youth, but almost, it seemed, a message from the past, they could hardly be denied. Victor Allingame always invested himself thoroughly in everything that involved him. What, he wondered with delight, would it seem like to have a contemporary relationship with a modern woman who looked as though she had lived a hundred years earlier, in another time and culture? Would one set off the other as a foil, as in a slide comparison? Could one tease out, so to speak, the basic cultural and temporal factors of each part of the equation more faithfully, with such a sample for guidance? Had Victor Allingame been another kind of man, we might describe him as licking his lips. What Victor Allingame *did* do was approach Anna Bernstein and gallantly offer his assistance.

Anna Bernstein, who had finished recording the professor's words, and was now embarked on a list of groceries she must buy on the way home, paused at Breakstone's sweet butter and two milks and looked up, startled, at the gentleman who had been so kindly instructing her for the preceding hour.

Anna Bernstein smiled and thanked him, but no she did not need assistance.

Victor Allingame, nonplussed, decided to pursue the matter further.

— Surely I can tell you something more about Burne-Jones that might be helpful. He was a good friend of Ruskin's you know, stood up with him at the Whistler trial.

Anna was, at this, finally diverted from her shopping list. Switching her head from Ivory detergent and Kleenex, she said,

— Oh. Then he was on the wrong side. Whistler was totally right, don't you think?

Now it was Victor Allingame's turn to be startled. Was this young vision indeed someone out of a past age? She spoke so knowledgeably, with such authority, that anyone hearing her would assume she had been there.

— Where, may I ask, did you learn so much about the Whistler trial, young lady?

— There was an exhibition, at the Brooklyn Museum. About a year ago. It had a great catalogue. Transcript of the trial. All about the pot of paint in the public's face, and knocking off a painting in nothing flat.

— And you feel Whistler was right?

— The knowledge of a lifetime. I loved that.

— But Ruskin, my dear, was one of the greatest of the world's connoisseurs.

Now Anna Bernstein seemed a bit at sea.

— I don't really know Ruskin, she said doubtfully. I haven't read him.

Victor Allingame had regained his advantage. Just a young thing, with spotty knowledge at best. He could teach her a lot. Introduce her to Ruskin. Open that whole world to her. Give her a genuine familiarity with an age she resembled only superficially. Interesting project, he thought to himself, to see if he could fill the head of this young thing, from Brooklyn, of all places, with genuine Pre-Raphaelite thoughts. Imagine making her Pre-Raphaelite inside as well as out. That was the wonderful thing about teaching — you could change heads, alter minds, fill in all the little lacunae. You could mold others to your own image. À la Pygmalion.

Victor Allingame, drawing himself up to his full lean six-foot-two height, and looking down his long thin aristocratic and somewhat equine nose at Anna, was not in any real way malevolent, nor were his motives. Victor Allingame was prone to making special efforts with some of his more promising students. Anna Bernstein was beginning to look to him, with her silken blonde hair and elegantly slender bone structure, as though she was very promising.

— Next time, young lady, er, Miss . . .

— Bernstein, Anna Bernstein, came the quick response.

God, how unlikely, thought Victor Allingame. A Rossetti named Anna Bernstein, from Brooklyn.

— Next time, Miss Bernstein, I'll supply you with a Ruskin bibliography.

Anna Bernstein murmured her polite thanks, and without seeming to recognize the profound effect she, or rather her appearance, had had on Victor Allingame, gathered her books together and exited from his classroom, intent on her various shopping chores. Without waiting, however, for her benefactor to supply her with his reading list, she was led by her natural curiosity to look up Ruskin in Widener Library that afternoon, and soon formed what was to be a lifelong friendship with his long-suffering wife, Effie.

Anna's initial encounters with Andrew Hanson and Victor Allingame established two of her three important relation- ships at Harvard, and occupied the first month or so of her time at Cambridge. Andrew Hanson was always readily available, as suggested, for late-night talks at the Wurst- haus. Anna, intrigued by the thick, luscious knockwurst, developed a craving for eating one or sometimes two of these in the evening after Widener Library closed, and would enlist Andrew Hanson as a companion on her forays. With or without sauerkraut was always the biggest decision, for she liked it both ways, and so, small as the decision was, a choice had to be made, and was made with as much inquiry into the particular state of her feelings and desires at that moment as might have been done with a much weight- ier problem.

— Which is it tonight, with or without? Andrew would tease, laughing at her with his brown eyes and slouching, with his dark beard and moustache, rather like a desperado in his chair.

Anna would sit up straight, by contrast, to her whole height and make the decision with monumental gravity. The waitress, yet another student, would wait patiently, already used to this nightly ritual, her gritty hair indicating her lack of personal time for self-care.

This night it was with, and the curling golden fronds of sauerkraut decorating the wurst were welcomed when they arrived with little orgasmic shrieks.

— My God, Anna, said Andrew affectionately, it's only sauerkraut.

Yet there must, in the eyes of the absurd gods who handle human affairs, have indeed been a larger meaning here, for the orgasmic reception of the sauerkraut was en route to another orgasmic reception, of far greater importance for Anna's life, symbolized, if we will, by the pickled vegetable itself — a prelude to a preoccupation with things German that was to grow as Anna settled, for her thesis topic, on the nineteenth-century German artist Caspar David Friedrich, and to her romantic preoccupation with the young man she was to meet this fateful night, at an adjoining table at the Wursthaus, who was now leaning over and, in her moment of orgasmic delight, requesting, in an almost somber way, the mustard.

When Kurt Hahn requested the mustard, Anna looked at him perplexed. Partly, it must have been that he was unlike anyone she had ever seen. What she saw might not have seemed so unusual to anyone but Anna, for what she saw might really have been Kurt Hahn seen uniquely through her eyes. Whatever the explanation, Kurt Hahn, bedecked in blue cowboy shirt, carved Western boots, jeans, and a battered gray felt cowboy hat, turned and mellowed in color by time, dust, rain, heat, sweat, and animal contact, was, to Anna's eyes (as the saying goes), a "sight to behold."

More, even, than his dress, which proclaimed him to be someone not native to New England, Kurt Hahn's person affected Anna. Kurt Hahn was not really handsome, in the conventional sense, but his hazel eyes, etched at the edges with smiles, and his tan trimness, as of someone who rarely ventured indoors, struck Anna at that moment profoundly. Small wisps of straight blond hair poked out from under the patinated head covering. If Anna Bernstein had seemed to Victor Allingame an apparition from the past, Kurt Hahn seemed to Anna Bernstein like someone who had traversed space instantaneously. Kurt Hahn did not, she was sure, belong in New England. Kurt Hahn should have been out in some Western desert, kicking his Western boots at rattlesnakes, drinking water out of his canteen, muttering about how it had heated up past potability, spitting it out on the arid sand. Kurt Hahn, to Anna, was at that moment too hot and thirsty to be using mustard.

— The mustard is much too hot for you, right now, she said sympathetically. Why don't you wait till you cool off?

Kurt Hahn, comfortably seated in the Wursthaus, having just come in from the cool autumn evening, was now just as startled by Anna as she had been by him.

— Come on, lady, he muttered unhappily, all I want is the mustard.

And then, suddenly annoyed, at a lower but still audible level,

— All right, I'll ask the fucking waitress for the mustard. Fucking Eastern snobs won't even give you mustard, for God's sake.

Andrew Hanson, observing all this, recovered himself sufficiently at this point to hand Kurt Hahn the mustard in what he hoped was a conciliatory way. He did not know why Anna had refused, had just sat there looking at Kurt Hahn with a stunned and preoccupied expression on her face. But Kurt Hahn was discomfited at what could only seem a discourtesy on Anna's part, and Andrew had a strong sense of justice. All Kurt Hahn wanted was the mustard, and that was fair enough. In no way did he seem menacing, nor had he asked for the mustard in a boorish way. Anna had already used the mustard, as had Andrew himself, so there was no real reason for her to refuse Kurt Hahn, unless she wanted another wurst, and in that case, she could request the mustard back. It was, after all, what people did in a place like the Wursthaus, and in many such restaurants, as we well know. When you ask someone to pass the mustard, and ask in a friendly and courteous way, you do not expect to be told to cool off first. What could Anna possibly have meant? Andrew Hanson looked at Anna quizzically. Anna was still looking, however, in a rather stunned way at Kurt Hahn. Kurt Hahn was spreading his frankfurter with the mustard, mumbling something and shaking his head.

Kurt Hahn ate his frankfurter with what must have seemed, to anyone watching, unusual relish. Anna watched out of the corner of her eye, still bemused. Kurt Hahn then ordered another, and since the mustard had remained undisturbed in the corner of his table, near but not in any way infringing on the surface of theirs, he was within his rights, as they all saw it, to use it freely again. Of course, it might have been polite and friendly to have offered it back, once he had availed himself of it the first time, but Kurt Hahn, normally a polite man, was too bothered to have thought of this. For the truth is, Kurt Hahn was not that happy at Harvard. Kurt Hahn was having difficulty exchanging Western style for Harvard style. And though eccentricity was surely tolerated, no, more than tolerated, encouraged, at Harvard, Kurt Hahn's cowboy eccentricities were often tittered at. Kurt Hahn himself was too macho to stand tittering.

It was, perhaps, this macho to which Anna Bernstein, with that infallible extra sense women have for this quality, responded. It was not the kind of macho that thinks the woman's place is in the home, and refuses to take out the garbage. It was rather the charismatic kind, in short, the romance-novel kind, and Anna Bernstein had, never having encountered it before, reacted instantly.

It was after his second frankfurter that Anna Bernstein began to recover. Then, with great care, she summoned the waitress, ordered yet another knockwurst for herself, and very politely addressed Kurt Hahn:

— I'll take it back now.

This rather ambiguous sentence was accompanied by a smile so sweet that Kurt Hahn almost melted like Little Black Sambo's tigers around the tree.

Nonetheless, he handed the mustard back sullenly, refusing, once injured, to be seduced by a soft manner. But Anna had strong qualities of persistence. She beamed at him once more. Advance, conquer. The innocent laser struck and dissolved. He was quickly hers. Conversation began, small tidbits of information were exchanged — both were at the Fogg, both working on German art and culture; why, after all they were schoolmates, there was a bond; the human version of bird and animal pair-bonding could begin. Andrew Hanson, the natural historian, participating in and at the same time observing all this, was reluctant to lose his lovely new friend, of whom he had become very fond, more fond than he had admitted, even to himself. Andrew Hanson was very careful to keep the conversation à trois. Cleverly realizing he could not prevent a friendship forming between Anna Bernstein and Kurt Hahn, he allowed the entry to be made through his own generous welcome of the latter to the original twosome. Thus, a three-way friendship was established, which, for some time to come, would keep the inevitable pair-bonding of Anna Bernstein and Kurt Hahn at bay.

❧ 2 ❧

DR. GOTTHARD, generally a professional gentleman, was
finding Anna Bernstein more and more interesting in a
nonprofessional way. Anna had progressed to the point
where her dressing gown was unstained, and had begun to
comb her long blonde hair neatly around her shoulders. Her
copy of *Alice*, as always, sat in her lap.

— I thought, my dear, that your specialty at Harvard was
German nineteenth-century painting.

— Yes.

— Then, are you a little girl, always carrying your copy of
Alice?

— No. She sighed, and looked up at Dr. Gotthard with
exasperation. I never was a little girl.

— Tell me about your parents.

— They're dead. They've been dead always, it seems. I
can hardly remember when they weren't dead. Look, Dr.
Gotthard. You may not believe this, but just because I'm
here, and read Lewis Carroll all the time, doesn't mean I'm
crazy.

Silence.

— What does it mean?

After a still longer pause:

— My mother was very beautiful. She had blonde hair
too. We lived in a big wooden house.

— Were you happy?

— Why do you doctors always assume that we're crazy because of unhappy childhoods? As far as I can remember, and I can remember very little, we were all happy.

. — Then it must have been a great trauma for you when they died.

Anna shrugged.

— I went to Grandma in Brooklyn. I love Grandma, she's been wonderful to me. She loves me very much.

— But it was a change.

Silence. Then: ˙

— It was a change.

— How?

— Grandma was Jewish.

Dr. Gotthard avoided raising his eyebrows.

— Weren't your parents Jewish?

— My parents were American.

— Jewish and American.

— American.

— I don't understand. Couldn't they be both?

— They didn't speak Yiddish, they spoke English. They never went to a synagogue, as far as I know. They didn't practice any religion that I could see. We always celebrated Christmas and Thanksgiving and the Fourth of July. Nobody was Jewish on Long Island.

— Nobody?

— Nobody I knew or noticed.

— Then you became Jewish when you moved to Brooklyn?

Anna laughed at Dr. Gotthard.

— No. She chortled gleefully. No, I became Jewish yesterday.

— Yesterday?

— Yesterday.

Dr. Gotthard could get no more from Anna that day. She sat in her chair, the sunlight streaming into the patients' recreation room and onto her golden hair, and opened her copy of *Alice*. For a while she read silently, laughing and chuckling to herself, seemingly unaware of his presence. Finally she remembered him, and carefully raised her voice so that he could hear too:

"Very true," said the Duchess: "flamingoes and mustard both bite. And the moral of that is — 'Birds of a feather flock together.' "

"Only mustard isn't a bird," Alice remarked.

"Right, as usual," said the Duchess: "what a clear way you have of putting things!"

"It's a mineral, I think," said Alice.

"Of course it is," said the Duchess, who seemed ready to agree to everything Alice said: "there's a large mustard-mine near here. And the moral of that is — 'The more there is of mine, the less there is of yours.' "

"Oh, I know!" exclaimed Alice, who had not attended to this last remark. "It's a vegetable. It doesn't look like one, but it is."

"I quite agree with you," said the Duchess; "and the moral of that is — 'Be what you would seem to be' — or, if you'd like it put more simply — 'Never imagine yourself not to be otherwise than what it might appear to others that what you were or might have been was not otherwise than what you had been would have appeared to them to be otherwise.' "

Dr. Gotthard left the room daunted by Anna and Lewis Carroll. All those identity problems. But then, he ruminated, Lewis Carroll himself didn't know who he was — Charles Dodgson, that's who he was. Dr. Gotthard had a difficult problem for someone who worked in a psychiatric clinic — he was impatient with multiple identities. Dr. Gotthard was committed to health and wholeness. Unfortunately, this caused him to consider any deviation from his *a priori* concept of health and wholeness unhealthy, unwhole, and potentially mad. Lewis Carroll and his nymphets. Alice Liddell indeed. All those naked children posing for him with their mothers present. Dirty old man. What was Anna's unhealthy preoccupation with a dirty old man?

Anna, on the other hand, having successfully disposed of Dr. Gotthard, allowed her mind to dwell on the passage she had just read aloud. How had Lewis Carroll known her so well in 1862? How had he known when he wrote the Alice books and propelled them into posterity that she would be waiting for them? How could he have known about the meeting with Kurt Hahn, symbolized as if by some religious icon by a mustard pot in the Wursthaus? How could he have known about the riddle of imagining yourself not to be otherwise than what it might appear to others that what you were or might have been was not otherwise than what you had been would have appeared to them to be otherwise? What if she had said to Dr. Gotthard, as Alice had said to the Caterpillar: "I can't explain *myself*, I'm afraid, Sir. Because I'm not myself you see."

— I don't see, Dr. Gotthard would have said, as did the Caterpillar in 1862.

— I'm afraid I can't put it more clearly, Anna would have replied, as had Alice very politely, for I can't understand it myself, to begin with, and being so many different sizes in a day is very confusing.

Anna's many different sizes, she thought, had begun to become apparent soon after the entry of Kurt Hahn into her life, and, it must be said, into Andrew's as well. For Kurt Hahn, in adding his notable presence to that of the neighborly pair, also added substantially to the way they passed their days. Such times often began by breakfasting all together under the hanging fern plants in the windowed nook of Anna's studio. These repasts were deliberately inverted, aimed at turning the day upside down: fried chicken and french fries reheated from Colonel Sanders; hot dogs retrieved from forays to the Wursthaus the night before; ice cream and chocolate cake, pizza with anchovies.

There was a clear predilection for junk foods, for these were attractive and illicit.

For Anna this companionship was both enlarging and somewhat awesome. She had never had such friends before. At home, and even at college in Brooklyn, she had always lived simply with Grandma. There were casual friendships and contacts with Brooklyn cousins and acquaintances. She had commuted to college. But now, now with her two companions she daily crossed the green expanse of Harvard Yard — Harvard, founded by John Harvard, according to the *Encyclopaedia Britannica* "an immigrant Puritan minister to America, a bachelor and master of arts of Emmanuel College, Cambridge," which early on had this legend carved on its gates: "After God had carried us safe to *New-England* and wee had builded our houses, provided necessaries for our liveli-hood, rear'd convenient places for Gods worship and settled the Civill Government; One of the next things we longed for, and looked after was to advance *Learning*, and perpetuate it to Posterity; dreading to leave an illiterate Ministry to the Churches, when our present Ministers shall lie in the Dust."

God and learning and two companions at Harvard. Anna, who to her deep regret had never had close women friends other than Grandma, her best friend, now had two dear male friends. In her enthusiasm for Harvard, she quickly made herself a part of it, in simple, almost childlike ways. Often in the mornings, Andrew Hanson and Kurt Hahn would find her still in the Harvard sweatshirt she had slept in, her Coop book bag prominently propped near the bed. Their morning coffee mugs were stamped with the Harvard crest. The alien feelings developed only slowly, as did the irredeemable passion for Kurt Hahn.

❧✦❧

Anna, seated in the patients' recreation room, was always distressed when she tried to remember. But only when she remembered, she was sure, could she straighten things out and fit the puzzle back together. Something had gone wrong. She had lost her way in the puzzle, but if she followed the Alice books carefully enough, the way might become clear. For what she didn't tell Dr. Gotthard was that Lewis Carroll, *his* dirty old man, was *her* mentor. Oh, she knew all about him and Alice Liddell. Dr. Gotthard looked at Anna herself with much the same kind of ideas in his head — she could see them swirling as though his forehead were made of glass. And after all, had she not learned that that had been Ruskin's problem? Poor Effie.

❧❦❧

It was November when Victor Allingame, having limited his prior contacts with Anna to small flirtatious cups of coffee after class, decided to enlarge upon their acquaintance. Anna's autodidactic familiarity with Ruskin and Effie, whose second husband, the Pre-Raphaelite John Everett Millais, was the subject of Victor Allingame's book, made his task even easier.

All the time that Andrew and Kurt and Anna had been forming the friendship that stemmed from the mustard pot incident, Victor Allingame had been slowly contemplating and savoring the idea of the Conquest and Education of Anna Bernstein.

That conquest and education Victor Allingame thought a moral necessity. With all the self-righteous conviction with which men enter wars, blind to his own self-interestedness and to the resulting expansion of his own ego, he took it as his duty to make Anna Bernstein his sexual and intellectual protégée, the better to control her inner development. God and learning at Harvard, to Victor Allingame, took the form of sexual Calvinism, and anything he did to, with, or for Anna, out of his own superior experience and wisdom, would be to her benefit. He would be good for Anna Bernstein.

Victor Allingame invited Anna to Thanksgiving dinner with his family, an invitation crucial to the adventures of Anna Bernstein at Harvard that were to end on the seventh floor of Mount Sinai in the seventh month of the following year. The invitation involved a matter barely touched on earlier: History, in this instance personal history, amplified by hereditary history, that is, genealogy.

Victor Allingame took genealogy very seriously. His pedigree was always on show (and in sharing it we are sharing knowledge common to his set). His mother, an important administrative figure in the DAR, whose approximately two hundred thousand members trace themselves back to the Revolution, was a member too of the Colonial Dames of America, a more exclusive group, who trace themselves back to the officers and officials of the pre-Revolutionary period, and of the still more exclusive Colonial Dames XVII Century, who trace themselves back to officials in office prior to 1699. The ancestral portraits hanging in Victor Allingame's home were done not only by anonymous limners traipsing through New England in pre-Revolutionary days, but by many of the great American portraitists who followed, from John Singleton Copley through John Singer Sargent, a century later.

Quite apart from the art historical interest of the portraits, which both the Fogg Museum and the Museum of Fine Arts in Boston had been covetously eyeing for years (much to the pleasure of Victor Allingame's wife, who enjoyed all the special previews, dinners, and exhibitions at these institutions to which they were always cordially invited), Victor Allingame's American ancestors gravely measured the years of his Americanness. They established definitively that he was truly American by blood and breeding, as royal as democratic America could aspire to. And quite apart from manners and snobbery, which these things might also connote, such portraits announced Victor Allingame, he fully believed, to be an important part of the culture, the tradition, they represented. They gave him, in some way, the *right* to an American past, a scarcer and richer commodity in a country where present and future are more readily available.

Had someone suggested to him that Anna Bernstein was,

like him, a member of a Chosen People, or that God had chosen the Jews before He chose the Americans, and that she had close to six thousand years of seniority, he would not have understood.

♪♫♪♫♪

In Lewis Carroll's *Symbolic Logic*, which Anna, having discovered it in Widener Library, systematically read (keeping a copy beside her bed on Trowbridge Street under the mug with the Harvard crest), we read (Book VIII, Chapter I, 7, No. 32):

> *Warmth relieves pain;*
> *Nothing, that does not relieve pain, is useful in*
> *   toothache.*
> *Warmth is useful in toothache.*

Pain grew imperceptibly over Anna's Harvard year. It was so frequently offset by warmth that she was often unconscious of its presence. For the warmth of her new companionship, in the cool New England autumn, came both from the constant presence of friends, which she had never experienced before, and from constant intellectual exchanges.

Ironically, the warmth not only relieved the pain, but was in part responsible for it. Or rather, the sources of the warmth were also by their very existence catalytic to her pain. Thus, warmth and pain were growing steadily, though in a roughly balanced way, in Anna Bernstein. But so rich was the warmth that the pain was hardly recognized until it was almost unbearable. How could she, indeed, have realized that the intellectual stimulus afforded by her new Harvard friends could generate such an intense personal and emotional self-analysis? Or that that analysis, once begun, would lead her into such a labyrinth of knowledge that it would be impossible for her to let go until she had, like Theseus, unraveled the world?

For that was the problem. The secrets of the universe

were wound up like a ball of knitting wool. Anna had picked off the beginning end, which had started to wind through all the complex tunnels of human existence. The clues were in the books in Widener, and beyond books, in the street outside, and beyond the street in the world, and beyond the world, in the universe, and back from now into history, not only recorded history but pre-history, and somehow Anna's introduction to God and learning at Harvard meant she couldn't let go, not yet, maybe not ever, till she had solved all the puzzles. But this in itself was not so threatening as was her discovery, suddenly, that she had to find her *place* in all this.

In Anna's diary, recorded in blue ink:

Just at this moment Alice felt a very curious sensation, which puzzled her a good deal until she made out what it was: she was beginning to grow larger again. . . .

"I wish you wouldn't squeeze so," said the Dormouse, who was sitting next to her. "I can hardly breathe."

"I ca'n't help it," said Alice very meekly: "I'm growing."

"You've no right to grow here," said the Dormouse.

"Don't talk nonsense," said Alice more boldly: "you know you're growing too."

"Yes, but I grow at a reasonable pace," said the Dormouse: "not in that ridiculous fashion."

❧❦❧

Victor Allingame's invitation to Anna was not amicably accepted by her two warm companions when they learned of it.

— Thanksgiving with *that* creep, snarled Andrew. Come home with me to Milwaukee.

He sat Celeste in his lap, while Lucinda pranced up and down on her back paws, trying to unseat the rabbit.

— Andrew, give me Celeste, said Anna, cuddling the

black rabbit in her arms. One day Lucinda will eat her up out of jealousy.

— Lucinda's just a spoiled, overpetted bitch, observed Kurt from the other end of the room, where he had been working with some Nolde reproductions. Come home with me to Nevada, we can get lost in the desert together.

Thanks to Andrew's vigilance, Kurt and Anna had hardly been alone together. Kurt had tried to arrange a separate date, a movie, even a walk, but Anna had felt such loyalty to Andrew's feelings, she always included him, almost automatically:

— We couldn't see *Being There* without Andrew, it wouldn't be nice. He'd be hurt. How can we go see *Flying Down to Rio* without Andrew? He adores Astaire and Rogers. Yes, it's a lovely day for a walk on the Charles, I'll get Andrew.

Anna of course knew well enough what Kurt Hahn had in mind. But she was uneasy about what she might feel if left alone with him. Andrew Hanson was her protective armor. Andrew Hanson was her shield. For if truth be known, Kurt Hahn had smitten Anna from the first moment of the mustard, and she welcomed what she clearly perceived as Andrew Hanson's deliberate interference.

Now, she looked at both of them over the long table in Andrew Hanson's room, where each now was ostensibly working at his own pursuits, and said:

— Grandma is going to my cousin's. I'd rather stay here. And Thanksgiving at Professor Allingame's should be pure New England. I'll learn something.

Andrew and Kurt looked at each other. The magic word for Anna was *learning*. Anna was determined, they knew, to discover the secrets of the universe. Anna would not rest until, like some voracious mythological monster, she had swallowed the world.

It was now two weeks before Thanksgiving. Anna Bernstein had spent the last month happily unraveling the world at Widener Library, her pleasure in books increasing daily.

Never overwhelmed by their sheer quantity, never set back by multitudes of facts or ideas, she did, indeed, consume anything printed that crossed her path. She could spend, surreptitiously munching on granola bars, as much as eight or even ten hours of a fine autumn Cambridge day curled in her carrel, with books on the desk, floor, beneath, behind, *literally* stacked and rearranged according to the strange logic of her own intelligence. For a projected thesis on Caspar David Friedrich's art, Anna was studying all of German nineteenth-century culture: history, literature, politics, fairy tales, philosophy, science, religion. Thus Heine, Goethe, Schiller, Schelling, Humboldt, Novalis, the Brothers Grimm, became crucial friends, keys to the puzzle of Friedrich. Since she was studying Pre-Raphaelite art with Victor Allingame, she was also studying English art and culture, with Effie Ruskin a special favorite. Effie, whose mother had not told her what to do, Effie, who appealed to Ruskin as Alice Liddell had appealed to Lewis Carroll; yet she had provoked him not to write an *Alice* but to align himself with his parents against her. Poor Effie, whose only fault was to be a woman, not a little girl. Lewis Carroll and Grimm, then, through extensions from Effie and Caspar David Friedrich, were an integral part of Anna's research. If some small part of her still listened for her lost mother's voice reading aloud to her in her cozy pre-Brooklyn bed on Long Island as she drowsed dreaming of fairies and princes, she did not acknowledge this overtly. There were also the small bookish tributes she paid to her new friends. Andrew Hanson's interests were represented in the irregular piles that surrounded Anna's carrel by several key works of Darwin, especially *The Voyage of the Beagle,* which appealed to Anna for the aura of its title, and *The Descent of Man,* which remained for Anna, throughout that pivotal year, a *summa* of knowledge that would — indeed must — offer a major clue to human existence, no matter how superseded over the succeeding hundred years. And since Kurt Hahn was working on the painting of the modern German Emil Nolde, Anna had begun to compile a small group of books on

contemporary German culture that she had not yet, however, begun to read.

Sometimes, Andrew and Kurt were able to lure her out for
walks along the Charles. Then they would watch with
proprietary delight as the slim fair-haired creature, more
graceful than she knew, strolled along the river's edge,
asking yet more questions about the buildings that dotted
the Boston skyline at the other side, looking, as Victor
Allingame had already observed, as if she had stepped out
of an earlier period. This she achieved in the hippie style of
a slightly earlier epoch, with long cotton Indian dresses, less
expensive but more fragilely graceful than clothes from the
department stores, in plain white or with flowered prints
and designs on them, light gauzelike things, which she
warmed up for the coming winter with heavy ethnic sweaters from Mexico and Uruguay and wool stockings. With
Kurt Hahn in his cowboy hat and Andrew Hanson, increasingly heavy-bearded, they made an interesting trio.

On one such day, Anna and Kurt Hahn finally found
themselves alone.

Andrew had gone to Washington to find, in the Library of
Congress, a few rare books and manuscripts unavailable at
Harvard. Anna was animal-sitting in Andrew's apartment,
feeding Lettie, the parakeet, keeping peace between Celeste
and Lucinda, talking soothingly to the aloof cats, who for all
their arrogance missed Andrew and welcomed her second-
best company. Andrew had left unexpectedly, muttering to
Anna about how if he didn't go now it would have to be
after Thanksgiving. It was Friday, none of them had classes,
and Kurt dropped in, as so often, for breakfast, bringing a
roast chicken from a Cambridge deli. He and Anna sat in the
sunny breakfast nook, looked at each other, and suddenly
had nothing to say.

For all the shared camaraderie *à trois*, Anna and Kurt did
not yet know each other. This was not Kurt's fault, nor even
really Andrew's, but Anna's, for Kurt filled Anna with a
trepidation she did not admit even to herself. She found him

more attractive than any man she had known. She saw his
eyes, with their cartography of lines at the edges, in her
sleep, in the darkened classroom of Victor Allingame, while
Rossetti or Millais or Holman Hunt was on the screen. She
found him gay and profound, gallant in his strange Western
way, vulnerable, and more than anything, important to her.
This awareness had struck her from the beginning, and then
grown alarmingly throughout their three-sided friendship.
It was alarming because Anna had never felt it before. She
had had small flirtations. She had, since her deflowering at
seventeen, slept amiably on occasion with several young
men. She was, as we know, already sleeping companion-
ably, in the friendly fashion of a good neighbor, with
Andrew Hanson. But Kurt Hahn offered a problem she had
never dealt with before. Frightened, longing suddenly for
her lost mother, Anna Bernstein did not know how to deal
with this. Until this very moment in the sunny windowed
nook of Andrew Hanson's apartment, she simply avoided it
as much as possible.

Anna's distress now revealed itself, perhaps somewhat
improbably, in what amounted to almost total speechless-
ness. Together, she and Kurt demolished the small fowl,
and since there was little conversation other than may I have
the salt please, or I love the wings, or do you like the thigh,
no I neither, or it's beautifully crisp isn't it, there was, for
each of them, a strange sensual delight in the taste and
aroma of this just-cooked creature, as though it were an
exotic game bird, recently downed by Kurt Hahn with his
bow and arrow. Anna looked to Kurt, in the sunlight, even
more fair, like someone out of a chivalric tale, or one of the
exquisite heroines of the Brothers Grimm, a Rapunzel, a
Cinderella, a Sleeping Beauty, awakening to dine with her
love on things that fly in the air, symbols of spirit.

Had Kurt Hahn been informed of the idealizing distor-
tions of his sentiments at this moment, he would not have
been convinced. Anna Bernstein was a golden angel. His
mother had read to him of such creatures on nights when he
could not, really would not sleep, wanting to hear just one

more version of the triumph of good over evil, of the victory of hero and heroine, of the frog who was now a prince, of the giant slain by the small child. These thoughts were early compounded for him by his Western boyhood. For though his mother had brought her German heritage with her, his father had transported her, not long after the war, from Berlin to Nevada, and in that Western desert, Kurt Hahn had joined American myths to his European heritage. As a Westerner, he was no more immune to those myths than Americans from other parts of the country. He was John Wayne or Gary Cooper, walking down the center of the town, alone, pistol drawn. He was a Louis L'Amour hero, a sheep farmer saving his ranch from devastation by the bad guys. He shot a rattlesnake, two inches away from Anna's foot, right between the eyes. He was offering her water after she lost her way in the desert.

Anna, for her part, took the small helpings from Kurt Hahn as he replenished her plate. But she felt that if she dared to speak to him, she would break some spell, whether his or hers, or one that they shared, she did not know.

So it was of course Kurt Hahn, not Anna, who suggested, since it was a gentle day, that they stroll along the Charles, and it was Kurt Hahn, walking beside the river with Anna, who kept talking, with a strange exhilarated light in his eyes, about the Boston skyline at the other side, pointing out to Anna the various sights — the glass Hancock Tower, which had lost its windows, and which close up, though they couldn't see it from where they were, reflected perfectly not only the entire sky, clouds and all, but Henry Hobson Richardson's brownstoned Trinity Church, to which he and Anna should go someday soon so that she could see the La Farge stained-glass windows, and also they would then cross over Copley Square and walk past the new fountain and into the main library by McKim, Mead, and White, where Puvis de Chavannes had painted his classical idylls under piercing blue-skied landscapes. And there too, on the skyline, could Anna see it, look look where I'm pointing, see over there, is the golden dome of the State House. Like

Europe really; but Boston, though Kurt Hahn disliked many aspects of it, *was* like Europe, with its wooden Paul Revere house and the early cemetery near Park Street, not as old as what his mother had come from, not nearly as old as the land she had gone to, but at least with *some* sense of obligation to time.

Kurt Hahn then poured into Anna, mute and receptive vessel for his thoughts and dreams, something of his history as a recent mutant bred out of both Europe and America, but not just any America — Western America, and not just any Europe — Germany. To bring Goethe and Schelling to the Nevada desert was not easy, but his mother had tried. She had brought her whole library with her across the ocean, not only the nineteenth-century idealists but the earlier mystics — Eckhart, Böhme. When Kurt, born just outside of Reno, was still an uncomprehending infant, she had sung German lullabies to him. When he was a bit older, she read him the Grimm Brothers in German, translating each sentence in heavily accented English as she went along, so that he became bilingual on fairy tales. His father, whose family, also originally German, had settled in Nevada in the 1860s, coming across the Loveland Trail in wagons and attacked by Paiutes en route, was the descendant of one survivor, a woman, saved by an Indian who raped her. She went to live with him and his tribe in the southern part of Nevada and California and had three children by him. So Kurt had some Indian in him as well, and as his mother introduced him to the German mystics, his father told him Indian tales — how they hunted, how they fought, what some of their rituals meant, how they felt about nature and time and death.

Anna, receiving all this, catching the modulations of greater or lesser enthusiasm in Kurt's voice, observing his Western sprawl, wrist dangling casually, one knee bent to the sky as they sat along the riverside on the cool grass and looked across the Charles River to the golden dome of the State House, was more hopelessly lost than ever. For Kurt Hahn was both the most attractive man she had ever met and one of the most articulate, and Anna could now fall in love not only with a body, but with a mind and soul. Nothing was said on this occasion about Kurt Hahn's maternal grandfather, who now lived in Argentina. Kurt Hahn was talking about the good Germany. Anna herself was devoting her time to these very ideas in the Widener stacks, entering each day into the mystical silences of Caspar David Friedrich, traversing his Bohemian landscapes, joining his people contemplating the moon, his monk by the sea, absorbing his flat islands of Rügen. She was not thinking of her own maternal grandfather, whose brothers and sisters had turned to smoke at Auschwitz, but only of Kurt Hahn's voice and words, drifting over her like one of Friedrich's mists as they walked slowly and thoughtfully back to Trowbridge Street.

When Kurt and Anna arrived at Anna's apartment, Anna, whose dress had been muddied a bit along the shore of the Charles, decided to change. Stopping at Andrew's to pick up Lucinda, who was now anxious to go out for her own walk, she opted first for a bath, and settled into the tub almost as a defense, both to recover from the strong sentiment she was feeling and to allow all she had just experienced literally to "soak in." But after a few minutes of tepid quiet soaking it was perhaps only natural that she was receptive to the tentative opening of the door by Kurt Hahn, who, seeing Anna in the large, old-fashioned porcelain tub, looking, with her hair pinned up, like one of the pink ladies in the court of Francis I at Fontainebleau, with her nipples exposed like small ripe berries, abandoned any pretense of courtly hesitation and, hardly stopping to strip himself of his customary Western regalia, simply tossing aside hat and boots, joined her with a great splash. This explosion, accompanied as it was by shrieks of laughter from them both, but especially from Anna, brought Lucinda, still pettish and fretting, but thoroughly willing to enter into the fun, at a running dash to join the two lovers in the narrow enclosure.

It was in this somewhat bizarre situation that Anna and

Kurt Hahn finally made love, wetly, giggling, with Lucinda turning it into a momentary *ménage à trois*. Not an orgy in the customary sense, but carried further, finally, to Anna's dry bed, minus Lucinda, where they spent the rest of the day, rising only to munch on some left-over chicken wings, and, briefly, to feed the bird, cats, and rabbit next door in Andrew Hanson's rooms. Lucinda, having been present at the first moment of consummation, was privileged to stay on the floor at the foot of the bed, feeding illicitly on chicken bones and guarding the lovers like the dogs on courtly sarcophagi.

Andrew Hanson sat with Anna in the visiting room at Mount Sinai. One of the orderlies had just placed the daisies he had brought in a hideous yellow plastic vase. The room too was yellow, prescribed by a decorator with a degree in psychology who thought it would help the manic depressives, some of whom had been pushed by the electric treatments Anna so hated from depressive to manic states.

— Thank you, Andrew, said Anna primly. Daisies are wonderful, aren't they?

— They are when they aren't sitting in an awful vase, said Andrew with annoyance. They don't go out of their way to make things pleasant here.

Anna looked around the room, straining to perceive it with Andrew's eyes. There was the stuffed yellow sofa, where she sometimes sat with the other patients to watch TV. There was the smaller yellow chair, where she often played chess with herself. There was the reproduction on the wall of van Gogh's yellow sunflowers in a yellow vase on a yellow ground. Did mental hospitals think crazy people could enjoy only crazy art? Van Gogh hadn't cut off his ear because he was crazy but because he was angry. Where is the line between madness and anger? Research that, she told herself sternly, research that. And research yellow, too, yellow must be for some reason. It's all yellow here.

— They try to be nice, she said soothingly. I don't really mind, Andrew. What I really mind, she strained forward to whisper to him, is that they're all crazy here. Even the attendants. It's hard to find someone to talk to.

"In that direction," the Cat said, waving its right paw round, "lives a Hatter: and in that direction," waving the other paw, "lives a March Hare. Visit either you like: they're both mad."

"But I don't want to go among mad people," Alice remarked.

"Oh, you ca'n't help that," said the Cat: "we're all mad here. I'm mad. You're mad."

"How do you know I'm mad?" said Alice.

"You must be," said the Cat, "or you wouldn't have come here."

— When are you coming out? Andrew asked solicitously, leaning toward Anna to push back a strand of blonde hair. They've kept your apartment for you. They haven't rented it to anyone. And I'm watering your plants. They're doing very well with me, he said with mock smugness.

Anna was feeling a bit confused that day. She thought she had had some more electric. She didn't remember. She couldn't seem to remember the plants, but Andrew mustn't know this, because if he did he would think she belonged here.

— The geraniums, she said. How nice. I hope they're still blooming. And how is the orchid plant doing?

Since there were neither geraniums nor orchids in Anna's rooms at Trowbridge Street, Andrew felt a bit bewildered. Anna had seemed quite lucid till this moment. He didn't feel for a second that she was truly mad anyway, just a hurt, confused kid. He didn't want to upset her any more.

— The orchids have two new blooms. Isn't that great?

— Well, they're probably getting more sun. You've moved them into your place?

— Yes, said Andrew, though I have to watch that Celeste doesn't eat them.

Celeste? Anna thought quickly. Celeste must be Andrew's wife. I'd forgotten that he had a wife. But if he hasn't, then who's Celeste?

— How is Celeste feeling? she asked politely. Have you taken her to any films or concerts recently? What's been showing at the Brattle?

Andrew Hanson could not imagine why he should take a rabbit to the Brattle Theater, but he simply muttered, in some polite confusion, that he had been too busy with his research to do much. Since that research had to do with Darwin and the cross-fertilization of orchids, Anna's reference to the orchid plant was not so far off. Somewhere in her head little boxes with memory data were opening up, albeit under the wrong stimulus. She was like a computer malfunctioning. Her mental circuits, shocked by the strong electric currents, were fizzing and sparking, failing and faltering.

Anna, looking at Andrew Hanson, and hoping he did not notice her own confusion, was following through on what she hoped was a profitable train of thought: Andrew's wife Celeste.

— You should try to take her out more. Women like to be taken places. If you sit in the library all day, and she has nothing to do, she'll get restless and start having an affair.

Andrew Hanson couldn't see Celeste having an affair, since she was the only rabbit in the house. Lucinda was a bitch, and he did not know about the possibility of a lesbian affair between a poodle and a rabbit. Two of the cats, Red and Bony, were male. Was that more feasible? A female rabbit and a tomcat? Such a coupling, thought Andrew Hanson, might turn out to be even more interesting, since at least with a male and female to start it all, there might be a possibility of propagation. Rabbits after all were so fertile. Could Celeste give birth to a new hybrid form?

Andrew Hanson looked at Anna. He had always loved her, had always considered her brilliant, even as she overstuffed her mind with the contents of Widener Library. But now her madness was leading her God only knew where. Anna's mind, on the other hand, was now tracking on the subject of wives. One wife she could remember quite clearly, vividly. Victor Allingame's wife.

Her name was Bitsy. That is to say, that was all Victor Allingame ever called her. Surely there was something else on her birth certificate, maybe Betsy or Betty or Elizabeth Victoria, but it was typical of the Allingame style, to which Anna was so ceremoniously introduced at Thanksgiving, that she should be known simply as Bitsy. Bitsy Allingame, who with her relentlessly classic Wasp New England style had entered Anna's story on that festive occasion.

Thanksgiving had followed upon the bathtub incident with Kurt Hahn relatively quickly. Kurt and Andrew had gone, as planned, to Nevada and Wisconsin respectively, Kurt refusing to leave until he had Anna's solemn promise that she would visit Nevada at Christmas.

In Anna's diary, only one listing appears to relate to Victor Allingame's invitation. Written in red ink:

Bitsy saw us under the turkey.

3

WHEN ANNA was a little girl, she had written a composition at P.S. 83 Brooklyn about how it felt to be a turkey on Thanksgiving. When she was older, she had a friend who refused to eat anything that flew. She had meant to research the idea of the bird as symbol of spirit, but had not yet gotten to it. Why, Anna wondered, did they kill the symbol of spirit to celebrate Thanksgiving? Was it simply to remind all Americans that Christmas was coming? Because, of course, that is what had happened to Thanksgiving in America. It had become the official day marking the Christmas preparations. Once Thanksgiving had happened, all the department stores started keeping longer shopping hours, counting down the days before Christmas, in a modern commercial variant on the partridge in a pear tree. Only the turkeys, not the partridges, would be dead, because it would be the day after, and who knew how many turkeys were slaughtered in this particular massacre to commemorate thanks? Like participants in an ancient savage ritual, Americans had chosen to slaughter turkeys to show their gratitude. Anna had never considered this especially civilized, to sacrifice the turkey as Abraham had wanted to sacrifice Isaac. But there, at least, the Lord had stayed his hand. The turkeys were not as fortunate. Anna decided to research the real history and meaning of Thanksgiving in

Widener Library several days before the sacrificial celebration.

In Widener Anna discovered that it all began, evidently, in 1621, when Governor Bradford commemorated the Pilgrim harvest with a three-day holiday. The Pilgrims were not really called Pilgrims then, and no one actually called them Pilgrims until two centuries later. They were called Old Comers, and then Forefathers.

These old comers or forefathers had been looking for religious freedom in America, much as Grandma had, who had come because of the pogroms, and had been glad not to be in Europe because of Hitler, though she had wept for years and years about the family at Auschwitz.

But these old comers, some of whom had gone to Holland and not liked it there, went to Plymouth in 1620, and the next year William Bradford (who left behind a manuscript that was copied into old church records and quoted as late as 1793 by someone called the Reverend Chandler Robbins in a memorial sermon, in which he referred to the "saints" who left Holland as "pilgrimes") declared a holiday. After the manuscript was found and the word *pilgrimes* discovered in it in 1793 everyone liked the idea, so in 1819 the Pilgrim Society was formed and Daniel Webster spoke at a bicentennial celebration the next year and said, "We have come to this Rock to record here our homage to our Pilgrim Fathers." So that's how they became Pilgrims, and someone who was there in 1621, whose name was Edward Winslow, was so excited about the holiday that he wrote home about it in December and told how Governor Bradford, "our harvest being gotten in . . . sent four men on fowling," and how "They four in one day killed as much fowl, as, with a little help beside, served the Company almost a week." And how the Indians were invited and went out and killed five deer, which they contributed to the party.

So it was clear to Anna that there was carnage from the very beginning, that the trick was to go out and kill fowl and deer, neither side being more considerate of God's living creatures than the other, as vegetarians might say, though

admittedly, she thought, there is an argument for survival
and for killing only for food, without waste, which is always
made by carnivores, who nonetheless, if they have any
conscience at all, often wish they had the morality, will
power, or metabolism to be vegetarians.

From Sir James George Frazer's *Golden Bough,* Anna soon
learned that there were also much deeper and more universal meanings to the killing of the turkey. The Thanksgiving
turkey, so carefully roasted with great pomp and ceremony
by modern American housewives according to recipes laid
out in countless cookbooks and periodicals, stuffed vari-
ously with apples, oranges, nuts, rice, etc., and browned in
foil, parchment, or cheesecloth at 300° or 350° or 400° or 450°
in the oven, depending on the methodology and the calculated time per pound, was the most distant descendant not
only of Governor Bradford's fowl, but of the ancient corn
god Osiris, whose death and resurrection rites ensured not
only the recurrent fertility of the fields but eternal life itself.
Connections and relays like this intoxicated Anna, and she
never knew where to stop.

The corn-god ceremony could be found, she discovered,
in various shapes and forms, in various mythological guises
all over the world. Sometimes it was symbolized by a small
effigy of the god molded of earth and corn. But a human
victim, as representative of the corn spirit, could also be
sacrificed, torn into bits and scattered over the fields to
fertilize them. Sometimes the victim was strangled, sometimes squeezed to death, sometimes cut up alive, sometimes
dragged along the fields, sometimes burned slowly till he or
she cried out, to supply more rain. Ultimately killing the
representative of the god, and eating him or her, would
ensure that divine properties were ingested. So the Thanksgiving turkey was the descendant too of some corn spirit,
some Osiris, some divinity, and had become a sacrifice of
that god, to that god, for that god.

Anna's only wonder was that the Old Comer Pilgrim
Fathers and their Indian guests had not decided to eat each
other, as well as the fowl and deer they killed, for in ancient

ritual customs and world mythology, the interchange between human, animal, and symbolic sacrifice was extraordinarily active and close-knit. One step sideways and one
could become a sacrificial lamb or goat, and be committed to
the fire, like the human scapegoat of the harvest festival of
Thargelia, in Greece, beaten on the genitals to release his
reproductive energies and sacrificed as the god of vegetation
on a pyre of forest trees. Somewhere in Anna's mind,
innocently tracing the history of Thanksgiving, the idea of
human sacrifice by fire began to reverberate.

Andrew Hanson, sitting with Anna in the yellow room with
the yellow chairs, the flowers in the yellow vase, the yellow
print of yellow flowers by van Gogh on the wall, suddenly
found he could not reach her. She had a tendency to retreat
mentally and emotionally since coming here among the
manic depressives and suicides *manqués*. These were being
treated with old-fashioned electroconvulsive shock treatments and new chemical inhibitants that were supposed to
reverse stress-induced depression.

Stress — the things that happened to any human being in
the course of a lifetime, or a daytime, the things that
included not only death of a loved one, but moving your
house, or getting a divorce, or having an exam, or being in
love, or having too many commitments, or a difficult boss,
or being too fat or too thin, or having too much money or,
more often, too little, or not liking your life, or fearing your
death, or hearing too much noise from airplanes or the
sounds of children, usually other people's, playing — stress
could cause what Anna had, and they could shock or inject
it out of you.

Of course, had they been members of some primitive
tribe, they might have painted their bodies and danced
around her and called to the gods to get the demons out. To
Andrew Hanson, used to dealing with animal descent and
flower propagation, for whom the human species was a

relatively new development on the *scala naturae*, all gods were equal anyway. But he had noticed toward the end of that school year that Anna's awareness of the situation of the Jewish God in the Western world had seemed to change. Andrew Hanson, no longer able to reach Anna, kissed her tenderly on the cheek and left, promising to return next week.

Anna had returned to Bitsy Allingame. She sat in her yellow chair with patients and doctors stirring about her, and remembered Bitsy Allingame on Thanksgiving Day, Bitsy Allingame, tall, thin, aristocratic, who greeted her at the door looking as though she still had a tennis racquet in her hand, though actually she held a knife. This was not because she meant Anna any harm. She had been roused by the doorbell out of the intricate process of cutting radishes into small rosettes, and came to the door reflexively, holding the relevant half-rosed radish in the other hand. Bitsy Allingame had been investing maximum intensity in the radish cutting, and was too deeply involved to stop and think that greeting a guest at the door with a knife in your hand might be interpreted as an unfriendly act. Bitsy Allingame put her all into everything she did: shopping at the supermarket, playing tennis and golf, buying clothes for the children, vacationing in Bermuda, writing to the family, gardening, bird watching, flower arranging, collecting Lily Pulitzer clothes and mint coins, serving on the Ladies Committee of the Museum of Fine Arts, working with the Friends of the Fogg, keeping minutes for the local historical society and the branch of the DAR of which she was secretary, giving faculty-wife teas.

When Bitsy Allingame had any time left over from these pursuits, she worked on her genealogical tree. She was making a work of art out of it. She was doing an enormous, complex, and demanding crewel tree for the bed she shared with Victor Allingame, and that bed, when finished, now covered only by a rather predictable antique quilt, would boast Bitsy and Victor's genealogical tree, with little balloons all over it, and branches dashing here and there, done in early Pennsylvania Dutch fraktur style, though of course the Puritan ancestors of Bitsy and Victor Allingame had had nothing but contempt for their Quaker counterparts, who had closer access to that style. That style was now, however, fittingly called Early American, and as such Bitsy had first-priority access to it. All over the tree, in purple, blue, red, orange, yellow, and green and all sorts of variations thereof, were the names and dates of ancestors.

That tree would grace the bed of Victor and Bitsy Allingame, would lie between the four posters and above the ruffled lace dust flounce, would be lovingly taken off and deposited on the antique bureau before Victor and Bitsy Allingame crawled into bed to watch the TV they had reluctantly allowed to enter the house for the children's sake, and then guiltily, with great Puritanical trepidation and soul searching, allowed to follow them into the bedroom for those late nights when one or the other or both could not quite sleep, though Victor would not allow it to keep him from his serious research, nor Bitsy Allingame to extend her wakefulness because tomorrow was a committee day. That tree, with its ancestors and dates, its reminders of past couplings, might even, Bitsy Allingame thought in her heart of hearts, restore Bitsy and Victor Allingame's own coupling activity, for she had noticed for the past few years that this had become less and less frequent, that she had become much more a golf chum or a tennis companion to Victor than even she, who had always felt a ladylike distaste for sex, would really have liked. Perhaps, she had been thinking, she would turn all the balloons into hearts. Then, allowing her fancy to expand, she might buy some new curtains, white organza, with tiny red hearts all over them, and she would buy some red heart-shaped pillows to plunk over the spread as well. A lover's environment, suitably embossed with the ancestral crests of lineage.

For as Bitsy Allingame knew very well, lineage was all, and her own lineage, pure and wholesome in its derivations, was one of her most important contributions to the Allingame household. Bitsy's blue blood matched Victor's down to the last nuanced shade.

◦⊰⊱◦

Though Anna had not been able to remember the plants, and had mistaken Celeste's identity in her encounter with Andrew just a few minutes earlier (indeed she did not even remember that Andrew had visited and left), her memory of Thanksgiving Day at Bitsy Allingame's home was reasonably intact and, as far as it went, quite accurate.

Bitsy Allingame stood in the doorway of the yellow wooden house on Brattle Street with the knife in one hand and the half-finished radish in the other, and smiled, albeit a bit patronizingly, at Anna Bernstein.

— Miss Bernstein, she said, shifting the belt of her tweed shirtwaist dress a bit self-consciously, is it not?

Arching her nose as high to the Cambridge heaven as it would go, since she had been doing her morning exercises religiously to encourage her modest chin, and hoping that she had more chin than she had had two hours ago (now that she saw that her guest was quite young and lovely), she continued:

— Victor's little friend, how nice. We're both in browns, proper for Thanksgiving, aren't we? Is that Indian? she asked, referring to the garment that peeked out from under the heavy sweater, and reminding herself that she must get rid of that horrid Indian thing her daughter had just brought home. They have such interesting patterns, haven't they?

Then, remembering that they were still standing in the doorway, which, like the windows, was trimmed in white, matching the Longfellow House down the block and offering from the street a most tasteful aspect, especially in spring and summer, when flanked by Bitsy's assiduously cared-for flowers, she said,

— Won't you come in?

and ceremoniously led the way into the center hall.

Anna Bernstein said the one thing that seemed to her most appropriate for the occasion:

— Thank you,

and followed Bitsy Allingame into the paneled interior of the central hallway, which, as in so many of these older homes, was dominated by the sweep of stairway. The hallway was lined with old engravings, in fruitwood frames, all lit by tiny candle-shaped sconces, even now in early afternoon. Anna was ushered first into the parlor, a strangely stiff room, with deep Williamsburg green walls, sparsely furnished with rather primitive early colonial pieces, giving the impression more of wood than of softness, an impression heightened by the unlikely presence of one stuffed yellow chintz couch, stamped with big purple flowers, in its center. Flanking the couch were those small hard chairs and moldy-looking table which had first given the impression of woodiness and which, Bitsy Allingame announced proudly, dated back to some of Victor's earliest American ancestors. Since Anna did not, at this point, understand the real relevance of this remark, it fell unnoticed. She was still waiting for Bitsy Allingame to drop the knife, which by now, poised by Bitsy Allingame midway in the air, had hit several strangely menacing angles as she gestured first at one piece and then another, and named its significant provenance. That such provenance *was* significant, there can be no doubt, for its importance was marked by Bitsy Allingame's slightly lifted tone of voice. Bitsy Allingame was reeling off the names of a good many family figures, clearly important ones, that Anna had never heard of, during the seemingly obligatory tour of the parlor, and then of the library, which was lined with British horse prints and shelves of books on art and history. Anna liked that room, though she could have done without the horses. It had a different warmth to it, provided by the presence of the books themselves, with their variegated tones and textures. Bitsy Allingame, not aware that Anna was noting titles to pursue when she got back to Widener, was prattling on about Great-Great-Great-Aunt Lucinda (which only managed to call up for Anna the image of Andrew's Lucinda at the foot of the bed as she and Kurt Hahn made love that first day) and was still gesturing with her knife when Victor Allingame entered the room.

— Anna, my dear.

He greeted her with the pleased warmth of an old relative, giving her an avuncular embrace, at the same time saying pointedly to Bitsy,

— The Indian attack is over, my dear.

Bitsy Allingame stopped in midsentence, as though, at this moment, some Indian had indeed shot his arrow into her ever-earnest heart. For Bitsy Allingame was not so opaque as to miss the tone of Victor's remark, or as not to feel shamed and unbearably gauche as she stood, still clutching her knife and radish.

Anna, who had registered Bitsy Allingame's condescension all through the genealogical enumeration of the parlor and library, could not help feeling sorry for her. Victor Allingame's manner to his wife was hardly the same as the one he had displayed to Anna over a few cups of coffee.

Now Victor Allingame linked his arm under Anna's and took over the tour himself.

— You're the first. Perfect. I can show you around. I hope Bitsy hasn't spoiled it by telling it all wrong at the outset.

Anna, unaware of what "it" could be, simply smiled at Victor Allingame, and feeling once more a twinge of sympathy for poor Bitsy, who still held knife and radish in hand, smiled at her too and said,

— Mrs. Allingame has been very generous, and I should apologize for taking up so much of her time when she probably is so busy in the kitchen.

Bitsy, who had lost even more of her chin than she started with that morning, stood, her mouth slightly open. Victor had *hurt her feelings, yet again,* and the girl was *so young and pretty* and her heart replied *yet again,* and she had had such high hopes for the crewel bedspread, but the bedspread, affirming her indissoluble link with Victor Allingame by reason of genealogical bond, of blood and breeding and family and all the important things, the bedspread would now (she knew, she knew, she had had it happen with Victor before), the bedspread would now have to compete with Anna Bernstein. Bitsy finally was obliged to say,

— Yes, if you will excuse me, Miss Bernstein, I must just run in and see how the bird is doing.

Victor Allingame, dismissing the bird, its aroma (which was beginning to waft through the house), and Bitsy herself, was leading Anna into yet another room.

— I'm glad I got here in time. Bitsy would have spoiled it, I know, he said once again.

Anna, still enjoying the anticipation that the aroma had begun to stir (her digestive juices whispering to each other about the forthcoming feast, for there was the scent not only of turkey but of sweet potato and pumpkin pie), forced herself to concentrate on Victor Allingame's spirited accompaniment to their slow passage. Victor Allingame's conversation, like Bitsy's, was also ancestral, for one of his ancestors, the already-mentioned Edward Winslow, had participated in the initial Thanksgiving feast, and Victor Allingame had, right here, in this colonial desk in the small room off the library, the letter itself.

Anna was spared the minute perusal of this venerated document, preserved as it was in a wooden box of colonial vintage, used, according to legend, to carry Revolutionary dispatches from the field, and now treated as if it were a shrine, a reliquary filled with the bones of a Puritan saint. Victor Allingame, impatient to bring Anna to greater heights of experience than that offered even by this unique missive, could not trouble to read out the antiquated hand and spelling, though of course he knew it quite by heart, and could have recited it at any given moment.

He wanted to direct Anna into another part of this mysteriously expanding house, which was suddenly revealing all kinds of corridors and adjacent rooms she had not expected. These had been added to the early colonial original by succeeding generations of Allingames so that the result resembled nothing so much as a kind of Victorian-colonial labyrinth, each room garishly colored in some Early American hue carefully researched by Bitsy Allingame on duty-days at the DAR.

The next room, ruby red, was virtually empty save for a huge golden harp in the center, and a small upright piano in the far corner.

— The music room, Anna said brightly.

— Yes of course, my dear.

Victor Allingame flushed with pleasure.

— Muffie plays.

— Muffie?

— My eldest daughter.

Victor Allingame was about to say, She's a year or so older than you, and thought better of it.

— She's at Oxford this year. I pick away at it a bit myself, he added modestly. Nothing much. We all play something. When we have our next musicale, you must come. We often have faculty and friends join us.

— I'd love to, answered Anna, with some wonder.

She had not encountered such home musicales in Brooklyn, and Grandma had not been especially musical. Indeed, when she thought about it, she felt very ignorant about music.

— Yes, she repeated with more genuine feeling, I'd love to.

Victor Allingame's music room had unexpectedly gained more points than his ancestral references. But he hardly allowed himself time to savor this, for he had headier heights in mind. He steered Anna through the music room into yet another, painted deep, almost azure blue. This room, devoid of furniture, was very long. Though not wide, it was not quite a corridor. It remained, in fact, a long room.

The room, the pride of Victor Allingame's life, was filled not with furniture but with paintings, reinforcing the vertical space of the azure walls themselves. On these walls were Victor Allingame's ancestors, who dominated the Allingame household with the elements of Past they embodied, their physiognomic peculiarities genetically revealing — the Allingame nose, the Allingame brow. Here was not only Time but History, sociological and political and even philosophical history. Here, indeed, was much of the history of the United States of America, within the 20 x 40 inches of Alexander Allingame, 1845, or the 30 x 45 inches of Gabriella Allingame, 1880, or the 20 x 30 inches of Nebuchadnezzar Brown, 1695.

Perhaps there was really nothing very unusual in Victor Allingame's obvious ancestral pride, though his manner, when expressing it, may have been a bit odd. His face flushed, his voice quivered, his hand went to his brow and ruffled his hair.

— Copley, of course, he said, pointing to a fat colonial dame, dressed in a glistening yellow satin gown, with a bowl of cherries on a burnished wooden table before her. Stuart, he said, proceeding to the next, a face only, of a rather haggard-looking gentleman, who turned out to be the Allingame ancestor who had signed the Declaration of Independence.

Anna through all this had been politely and agreeably appreciative, saying very little. (Indeed she had said very little since being met at the door by Bitsy Allingame with knife and radish.) She commented enthusiastically on the lace ruffles of the fat lady's sleeve. She looked closely at Stuart's painterly bravura and murmured it worthy of Gainsborough. She paused over a rather elegant lady, swathed in a taffeta gown, by John Singer Sargent. But Victor Allingame's manner was now so odd as to compromise any deep impression this wealth of art and history might have made on Anna. For Victor Allingame was, it appeared, *building up to something*, and for all his willingness to stop and comment about each great masterpiece, great on two counts — executed by America's finest artists *and* representing History Incarnate — he seemed impatient, as though, indeed, the best was yet to come.

This, it turned out, was precisely the case, for having stopped at each successive framed image on each of the long walls of the room without ever pausing long enough for

Anna to savor any of them individually, he led her ultimately to the far wall, where a single painting dominated
the extended vista.

This painting had attracted Anna from a distance when
she first entered, but Victor Allingame had clearly avoided it
till this last moment. For how else could it become, as it
clearly was, his *pièce de résistance?* It was a primitive render-
ing of a man in a dark suit with a white jabot, dressed,
clearly, like an early Puritan. It was flat and somber,
executed by some anonymous limner around 1690. It was
not nearly as important a painting from a qualitative point of
view as the Copley or the Stuart, or even the Sargent, whose
lady in taffeta was one of his more superficial efforts. It was
important for the person himself depicted. This was the
ancestor of whom Victor Allingame was most proud, who
had provoked those noticeable manifestations as he prepared to introduce him to Anna — COTTON MATHER.

The exalted name was uttered with such unadulterated
pride that Victor Allingame seemed visibly to puff up, much
as the source of the brown aroma reaching their nostrils
from the distant kitchen might have puffed its feathers on
some earlier prideful occasion.

⁂

Anna, sitting in the yellow room at Mount Sinai and
recalling that day, found herself idly opening her copy of
Alice, which lay beside her on the yellow chair like a faithful
dog, to precisely the right page.

*"So I wasn't dreaming after all," she said to herself,
"unless — unless, we're all part of the same dream. Only I
do hope it's my dream, and not the Red King's! I don't like
belonging to another person's dream," she went on in a
rather complaining tone: "I've a great mind to go and wake
him, and see what happens!"*

⁂

When Victor Allingame uttered the name of Cotton Mather, he revealed to Anna something of his dream. What had Anna Bernstein known about Victor Allingame's dream when he spoke the magic name? Her research in Widener Library had partly prepared her for Cotton Mather. Though other names on Victor Allingame's genealogical tree were new to her, Cotton Mather was someone she encountered everywhere. Perry Miller had written of him, and Sacvan Bercovitch, who had written at length about "the formal and conceptual implications of the approach that eventuates in Mather's *Magnalia Christi Americana.*" Cotton Mather, born, she had confirmed from the gold frame in Victor Allingame's blue Ancestor Room, in 1663–died 1728, was the son of Increase and the grandson of Richard Mather and John Cotton. Increase, she remembered, was himself a significant figure, since he became President of Harvard College in 1685 and, though forced to resign in 1701, had written before then some important sermons, one of the most famous being *A Discourse Concerning the Uncertainty of the Times of Men,* which he delivered at Harvard in 1697, after two undergraduates ice skating on Fresh Pond were drowned.

Such a title could clearly be as applicable in 1979 as in 1697, even more, she thought, since modern man could more than match his Puritan forebears under the cloud of Indian warheads with darker, more global nuclear warheads. Though death being death, she supposed, each individual death must feel like total wipe-out for the one involved, whether everyone else goes or not.

Cotton Mather and his daddy Increase had been such important Puritans they had provoked broadside verses not unlike Lewis Carroll's. A contemporary comment about the Mathers and the Brattle Street Church went:

Relations are Rattles with Brattle and Brattle,
Lord Bro'r mayn't command,

But Mather and Mather had rather had rather
The good old way should stand.

Cotton Mather had been unceasingly prolific, and Anna had
avidly noted his statistics. He had written over a hundred
biographies. He wrote a biography of his daddy. He wrote
a life of John Winthrop called *Nehemias Americanus*. He left
endless diaries, in which he made much of Old Testament
heroes, including Nehemiah, who was "a personal type" of
Jesus, just as the church was a "spiritual Israel" and
America a New Jerusalem.

Anna had been amazed at how important the Old Testament had been for the Puritans. Cotton Mather was an
important figure in the witchcraft trials; Cotton Mather had
had something, just *what* Anna was not quite sure, to do
with the executions of such people as Goodwife Cory.
Cotton Mather was against the devil in New England, and
against the Indians as well. Cotton Mather was constantly
invoking the Old Testament. Anna was not sure this meant
that he was for the Jews, that is, for such Jews as Anna
Bernstein, or those others who went, if not to the stake,
then to the ovens.

Cotton Mather had been very aware of the Chosen People
of the New Jerusalem just as he had been very aware of the
chosen status of the Old Testament Jews. Sacvan Bercovitch, who was Anna's best source for this, had said, "In its
original form, typology was a hermeneutical mode of connecting the Old Testament to the New in terms of the life of
Jesus. It interpreted the Israelite saints, individually, and
the progress of Israel, collectively, as a foreshadowing of the
gospel revelation." Anna read this several times.

Anna kept getting mixed up, especially sitting in the yellow
chair in the yellow room at Mount Sinai. Sacvan Bercovitch
had not been referring to the new Israel, created in part to
accommodate all the unburned Jews. Sacvan Bercovitch had
simply been referring to Cotton Mather and biblical Israel,
the one with a Nehemiah who could stand as a type for

Governor Winthrop, when he became the exemplary American, the exemplary Christian, who like the Children of Israel goes out into the "vast and roaring Wilderness," and is "bruised with many pressures, humbled under many overbearing difficulties," before he can "possess that good land which abounded with all prosperity," flowing with milk and honey.

Anyway, Cotton Mather had foreseen "the Holy City, in America," as "America — a City the Street whereof will be Pure Gold." Now *that* connected very clearly for Anna with Grandma, because she remembered Grandma saying that Grandpa had come to America expecting that the streets would be "lined with gold." Grandpa Cohen and Cotton Mather had that in common. Grandpa Cohen and Cotton Mather were both looking for gold in America.

And beyond that, hadn't Anna told herself when she came to this place that kept mixing her head up, hadn't she written in her diary that she must research seven? And hadn't she noticed when she was reading about Cotton Mather in Widener Library before going to Victor Allingame's home on the very same street, Brattle Street, that housed the church in the verse, hadn't she noticed that Cotton Mather also had a thing about sevens? Hadn't he said, in fact, that the greatest of the prophetic visions proceed successively by Sevens? How about the sevenfold proclamation to the upright children of Abraham and the seven trumpets of the Apocalypse? And now Anna, thinking about sevens, could add to that, from somewhere in her reading, she wasn't quite sure where, the seven steps of the Tower of Babel (the eighth of course being Heaven) and the seven pillars of Wisdom identified by Hebrew mystics with the seven days of Creation and the seven days of the week. She opened her diary, found the entry for seven, and found that somehow, from somewhere else, she had noted:

JIEVOAO. An early SEVEN-letter form for the Blessed Name of the Holy One of Israel, which only the High Priest (according to someone, Robert Graves perhaps) could utter once a year and under his breath in the Holy of Holies, and which could not be committed to writing.

So God, as usual, got into it, and didn't even want it to be said. God had an incredible need for privacy, she thought. He made it very hard to get to know Him. But it was surely clear now that Anna's red queen, like Alice's, got stuck in the seventh square for a reason.

4

VICTOR ALLINGAME stood before Anna Bernstein and waited for her reaction to his illustrious ancestor. Anna did not know, at the moment, whether it would be polite to talk about the witch hunting, nor did she feel it discreet to say that, as a Jew, she was heartened that Cotton Mather seemed to care so much about the Old Testament. Somehow, though she wasn't quite sure why, she felt that this was not what Victor Allingame wanted to hear just then.

But suddenly, looking at the portrait of Cotton Mather, she knew, she knew just what Victor Allingame expected her to say. Victor Allingame expected her to say,

— There's really a very marked family resemblance.

Victor Allingame beamed. Victor Allingame turned even redder. Victor Allingame puffed up even more. For Anna's well-trained eye had discerned exactly what he wanted her to discern — that he resembled his famous ancestor, that most historic and illustrious American, that great figure from whom so much of American culture had sprung — its morality, its historic mission, its chosen character, its Godly benedictions, its heavenly permissions. What had become known as the Allingame brow, the Allingame nose, even the Allingame chin — Anna could see them all in the carefully limned portrait before her, as well as on the puffy pleased face of Victor Allingame himself.

Cotton Mather, who had had three wives and fathered fifteen children, only two of whom survived him; who got mad at Harvard and suggested to Elihu Yale that he fund another college in Connecticut; whose *Memorable Providences Relating to Witchcraft and Possessions* (1689) was, Anna thought, still worth reading as a book that had helped stir up the witchcraft hysteria; who had, as a Harvard alumnus A.B. 1678, supported the gallows death for witchcraft of a fellow alumnus, the Reverend George Burroughs, A.B. 1670; who was admired by Benjamin Franklin largely for his *Do Good* book; who campaigned for smallpox inoculation, and believed in his own Godly mission to lead America to the paths of righteousness, had left to Victor Allingame his brow, his nose, and his chin.

That nose, brow, and chin, in their present incarnation, were now glowing with satisfaction and pride and directing Anna toward the dining room as the doorbell rang. Others were beginning to arrive: three of the four Allingame children, singularly nondescript, so that Anna, sitting in her yellow chair in New York City, could not quite visualize them, dressed, she was sure, in standard New England dress, two girls of teen age in baggy sweaters and plaid skirts, one still younger boy, who did not look like Cotton Mather, wearing jeans and a plaid flannel shirt; two Harvard professors, of English and Geology, and their wives, not very different from Bitsy, named Buzzy and Harriet.

Everyone at Thanksgiving dinner that day had New England ancestors who had been in on or close to the original feast, except Anna Bernstein. Yet Anna, unable to envision any ancestor beyond Grandma, who had barely known her own parents, did not feel especially deprived. Curiosity dominated her mood that day, and the insular homogeneity of the group was, at that moment, in no way threatening. She was Anna Bernstein, that was enough. It was early in the academic year, and things had not progressed enough in any direction for it to be much otherwise. She was, if anything, newer and more freshly American than all the Old Americans at the table, for she was still filled with the immigrant's dream, with Grandma's optimism about what God and learning at Harvard might do for her, with her early assimilated American identity from her parents' home in a Long Island suburb. She was, it is true, not in any way connected with the original Old Comers. But as a New Comer she felt well able to participate in the American Dream. She was truly Adamic, or better, perhaps, Eve-ic, and all things were possible, once she had swallowed the learning in Widener Library.

Thus the snobbery of the Allingame household thoroughly escaped her. She could hardly be diminished by it. She barely recognized it. Past ancestry and blood had never been held up to her as special virtues.

✹✷✹✷✷

Anna was no longer in the yellow room. She thought they had given her something. She was in bed. She lay there trying to remember where she had been, mixing Victor Allingame and Cotton Mather together under the same broad-brimmed Puritan hat. Bitsy Allingame kept running in and out. The knife had turned into a turkey feather, the radish now a rose. Then suddenly there was Ruskin, as photographed by Lewis Carroll, and Effie's children, after she'd married Millais, and another photograph by Carroll which was to form one of the illustrations of Victor Allingame's new book. Victor Allingame/Cotton Mather was looking very sternly at Ruskin, who kept protesting that he hadn't touched her, he hadn't wanted to, he only liked little girls, and Effie was crying and asking what was wrong with her, and Ruskin's Rose La Touche, with whom he had fallen in love when she was ten, was dancing with Victor Allingame/Cotton Mather and now she was wearing the Puritan hat. Suddenly Effie and Anna both were at the stake, being burned for witchcraft, and Lewis Carroll was scolding them for having grown up, and then Cotton Mather was scolding them for not being Puritans. Then she was no longer outside, but in a burning room, with ancestor portraits on the walls around her, melting with the heat. It seemed like this room. She felt hot, hotter still. She screamed for a nurse. Someone came and gave her something else. She slept for a while, mercifully dreamless.

When she awoke, she reached for the copy of Carroll's *Symbolic Logic* that Andrew, hoping to be helpful, had left for her. Opening it at random to "Book XIV, Some Further Problems to be Solved by the Methods of Part II, problem 81," she read:

1. *No invalids are unromantic civilians;*
2. *All architects are dreamy enthusiasts;*
3. *No lovers are unpoetical;*
4. *No military men are dreamy;*
5. *All romantic enthusiasts are in love;*
6. *None live on muffins except unpoetical invalids.*

Univ. "persons"; a = architects; b = dreamy; c = enthusiasts; d = invalids; e = living on, &c; h = lovers; k = military; l = poetical; m = romantic.

Perversely, Anna refused that day to eat anything but muffins.

❦

The truth of the matter is that Anna Bernstein, the only student honored on that occasion by an invitation to Thanksgiving dinner at Victor Allingame's, had sat between Victor Allingame and the Professor of Geology, and happily devoured a Thanksgiving turkey that tasted brown.

— You're working with Victor on the Pre-Raphaelites? asked the geologist, taking in, as he munched on a large wing of the now almost decimated corn-spirit sacrifice, Anna's silken hair and gauzed Indian dress.

— Yes. I loved getting to know Effie.

— Effie?

— Ruskin's wife. Since Professor Allingame is writing a book on John Everett Millais, who married her after she left

Ruskin, it gives me a chance to get into the Ruskin literature.
She had such a hard time of it, poor dear. I was so glad
when Millais found her and took her away.

The geologist smiled, with some condescension, and
asked,

— Is that female solidarity, or did she really have a rough
time?

— Ruskin, declared Anna, in a suddenly loud, almost
violent voice, was a monster.

Anna said this so vehemently that the other voices at the
table subsided completely. Bitsy Allingame hurriedly passed
the sweet potatoes down from her end of the table, and one
of the children giggled.

— He never fucked her you know, said Anna in exactly
the same number of decibels. I don't think he could. God
knows why he wanted her in the first place.

Bitsy Allingame blushed. Really, the girl was a menace.
Clearly all she thought about was sex. Bitsy would be in for
trouble with Victor, she knew it now. Oh dear, and the
crewel ancestor spread was almost finished, almost all
filled in, missing only a handful of great-aunts near the
bottom.

Victor Allingame, turning from his partner, found Anna's
conversation of greater interest.

— Turner wouldn't have made it, I don't think, in anything like the same way without Ruskin.

Anna narrowed her eyes at Victor Allingame.

— His greatness as a critic doesn't excuse his behavior as
a man, as a human being.

— Oh, is this a feminist issue?

— His parents were especially awful to her.

Victor Allingame shrugged, and piled some cranberry
sauce onto his turkey breast.

— Oh, the usual in-law trouble, I'm sure.

— In-law trouble! Anna — generally low-voiced, polite,
soft-spoken, noncommittal — almost shouted. They were
all against her.

Victor Allingame wondered if lovely Anna Bernstein of

the long blonde silky Pre-Raphaelite hair, the unlikely dream from Brooklyn from an earlier century, was perhaps just the slightest bit paranoid.

— Where do you get your information, Miss Bernstein? What is your source?

Anna Bernstein could clearly see the book in her carrel at Widener Library. It was small and rather thin. It had been edited by Effie's grandson, the Admiral, based on her unpublished letters home. It had a maroon cover.

— I can't remember his name, but he was her grandson.

— Prejudiced, snorted Victor Allingame, who had not, admittedly, in all his research on English art and criticism, taken the trouble to read this unique volume, though he knew of its existence. Family gossip.

Anna looked at Victor Allingame, who had, not so much earlier, made a terrific fuss about family pride and ancestry, and was now making so little of family evidence and documents.

— Once Effie's mother wrote to Rose La Touche's mother, she broke off with him too.

— Poor Ruskin. Victor Allingame sighed. Effie's malign resentment followed him throughout his life.

— But Millais, your hero, married her, said Anna in astonishment. *He* must have loved her.

— Feminine wiles, said Victor. She should never have said the things she said about Ruskin afterward.

— But for six years, Anna now pleaded, troubled, upset for her dear friend Effie, whose pains, sorrows, inadequacies, small ignorances, had touched a core in her. Effie's mother had told her nothing about sex, as Anna's dead mother had not. Effie was afraid to write home and ask whether her unconsummated marriage was normal. For six years, Anna said, she lived in an abnormal situation. Ruskin went to his parents' home every morning and left her sitting there alone until after dinner. He found her naked body ugly. He made her feel dirty, simply because she was a woman. He only liked little girls.

Victor Allingame looked at Anna Bernstein and thought

her indeed a mix of little and big, a delightful mix. Like Dr. Gotthard later, he recognized the unconscious coquettishness with which she carried her near-nymphet beauty. Had he recalled Carroll's photographs, he would have recognized the same quality in the famous photograph of Alice Liddell as beggar girl at age six. But Anna was, after all, just twenty-one and deliciously ripe. Victor Allingame decided to have Anna for Thanksgiving dessert.

First, however, she was preceded by pumpkin pie, and glaciers, for the geologist, wearied by so much talk of a subject on which he had little expertise, launched into a discourse of his own. Responding to a relatively innocent remark by Anna about her friend Andrew's interest in catastrophism, he continued through the fruit and cheese course while consuming several large bunches of purple autumn grapes, looking rather like a fat Silenus out of a painting by Jordaens — who should not, Anna thought, have been eating grapes which contained so much fructose anyway — and then through the rather tart pumpkin pie, on top of which Bitsy had resourcefully plunked some Häagen-Dazs vanilla ice cream.

— Werner had the right idea.

— Werner?

Anna had not encountered Werner.

The geologist was delighted. This little Anna Bernstein from Brooklyn, this twenty-one-year-old chit, had been making him feel inadequate, since he had never been able to take the time from the Jurassic and Triassic to look into things like art and literature, and would not even be here at dinner at the home of an art history colleague had they not served on several committees together; they really had little in common, though their wives were well acquainted from the DAR and their children played tennis together. He had remarked, in passing, to Victor Allingame that for various personal family reasons, having to do with children scattered here and there and not able or inclined to come home, he and his wife would be having turkey *à deux* this year. And since Thanksgiving is the kind of American holiday when you gather to your bosom all those who cannot gather families of their own, because it is nothing if not a family holiday, and there is nothing so American as a family occasion, it was only natural for Victor Allingame to say, Oh do join us, Bitsy would love to have you. And so the geologist, who would not have reminded Anna of Silenus had he not loved to eat, and would not have called to mind Jordaens did he not eat with rather crude gusto, was delighted to come.

— Werner, my dear, he happily responded, was a late eighteenth-century catastrophist, who believed that all world changes came about through major natural occurrences, or catastrophes, like floods or earthquakes or volcanic erup-tions. His full name, he said, pedantic throttle now out, was Abraham Gottlob Werner, Professor of Mineralogy at Frei-burg. He was the founder of Neptunist geology, though he preferred to call it geognosy.

One whole bunch of purple grapes, weighing easily a pound or more on the scale at the fruit market, was consumed at this relatively brief initial stage, with Anna from her side and Victor Allingame from his, watching with almost mesmerized fascination; the geologist, whose face was already red, grew redder still from their infusion, popping them off their stems into his mouth with small juicy spurts misting delicately into the surrounding air so that Anna, smelling the juice, autumnal and fresh, wondered if indeed the Bacchanalian rites had some of this rich earthy quality.

This fat grape-eating god, however, was throwing all his organic eloquence into the mineral world of rocks and mountains. Millions and millions and millions of years. Precambrian. Paleozoic. Mesozoic. Cenozoic. Paleocene, Eocene. Oligocene. Miocene. Pliocene. Pleistocene. Holo-cene. Starting more than four billion years away, he was coming closer and closer in time, until by the eighteenth century there were geologists who could understand all these layers of earth, layers of lives, layers of deaths, first of fishes, then of birds, then of apes, and then of men. Darwin finally came along and displaced ideas like catastrophism with evolution, but Harvard's own Agassiz, who was great on glaciers, and who married Elizabeth Cary Agassiz, first President of Radcliffe, so it was all in the family, literally, Agassiz, who was actually something of a racist, because he said God had wanted the white yellow brown black red distinctions since He had thought them up, Agassiz defended catastrophism and the Bible and was very popular in Boston.

Anna began to be intrigued. She turned her attention away from the second pound of grapes, now following the first in rhythmic spurts into the oral orifice of the fat god, and started to listen carefully. She must research some of this. This was strong stuff. It would help her to understand Time. It would help her to talk intelligently to Andrew. Where was her notebook? Where had it slipped to? She felt with her toe under the table and found it, she thought, deep under the turkey, still on the table during the dessert course. No way of getting to it politely at this moment without submerging under the tablecloth, which she was too shy to do. She commanded herself to remember all these wonderful sources and concentrated. Hutton, Lyell, uniformitarianism, Huxley. She must look it all up. She must learn the vocabulary: fossils, folds, faults, crusts, plates, sutures, fathometers, magnetometers.

The turkey, still sitting in its central location, had been largely reduced to mere bone with odd bits of flesh adhering. This skeleton, itself not unlike a prehistoric fossil uncovered from some mud flat, should, reasonably, have been removed from the table when the dessert courses appeared.

But Bitsy Allingame had not had her normal help in the kitchen today, because Moira O'Donnell's father was ill and she had had to go home unexpectedly. So the turkey remained there because Bitsy and the two young girls in plaid skirts had cleared the table themselves, and no one had thought to take it away. Since Bitsy Allingame had used a wooden duck decoy festooned with autumn leaves as a centerpiece, the fowl sacrifice, which had been picked clean by the celebrant company, made an interesting counterfoil, with its stark skeletal whiteness, to the painted artifice of the duck. God's fowl and man's fowl, Anna thought. Or Darwin's fowl, rather than God's, if you will.

The remains of the turkey, then, graced the center of the table as the talk turned to fire and ice and the manner of the world's ending.

— Ice, said the geologist definitively. Another Ice Age is clearly on the way. No way out of it.

— Why not nuclear holocaust? asked Anna, very serious now. That could happen any time, politicians being what they are, while your Ice Age, as you yourself admit, could take another several thousand years.

— God, not man, will end the world, said Bitsy Allingame from her end of the table.

— But what if He chooses to let us blow ourselves up? asked Anna politely, for Bitsy Allingame had hardly deigned to say two words to her until now, and she didn't want to discourage the dialogue.

— When He could stop it? asked Bitsy incredulously. God, my dear, she said, sitting very erect, God is good.

Bitsy Allingame, Anna felt, had spoken of God as if she had just nominated Him Chairman of the Board. Anna wondered if she herself could ever be on such good terms with God that she could not only know what He was thinking, but attest to His character. Judging from what she had gathered this evening, everyone in the Boston-Cambridge area seemed to know what God was thinking. Louis Agassiz of Harvard had built his whole scientific theory on the premise that God had simply thought the world up, the whole thing, at the very beginning, and separated species that way, and races — very difficult to explain to the colored peoples of the world, who could hardly believe so completely in white supremacy and God's implied whiteness. And Cotton Mather, Victor Allingame's Doppelgänger, had thought he knew just what God was thinking when he figured out who was chosen and who was clearly a witch, destined for the gallows or the stake. God's biases, which, were all this true, preceded even the beginning, made Him sound very unpleasant to Anna.

There was, however, little room at the table for Free Will at present. Only for yet another bowl of Häagen-Dazs ice cream, duly downed by the fat god. Then, people started floating away, except of course for the fat god (who was almost carried out), leaning heavily on his wife's shoulder. Bitsy Allingame made her excuses to Anna, who had been restrained from leaving by an almost furtive hand, belonging to Victor Allingame, on her shoulder. Bitsy Allingame had to drive the children to a friend's house in Framingham, where they would spend the rest of the holiday. Bitsy Allingame would not be long, how nice of Anna to have come.

So Anna Bernstein and Victor Allingame found themselves alone in the dining room, and when Anna remembered her notebook under the table and started to look for it, Victor Allingame joined her there, and there they remained, since Victor Allingame was indeed having Anna for dessert as planned, under the skeletal homage to the corn spirit, until Bitsy Allingame returned and called, Anyone, anyone home, from the next room.

"Curiouser and curiouser!" cried Alice. . . . "Now I'm opening out like the largest telescope that ever was! Good-bye, feet!" (for when she looked down at her feet, they seemed to be almost out of sight, they were getting so far off).

꧁✿꧂

Kurt Hahn and Andrew Hanson were very eager to hear, on their return, about Anna's Thanksgiving. She did not think to tell them about the manner in which she had thanked Victor Allingame for her Thanksgiving invitation. Anna Bernstein had allowed Victor Allingame his dessert for the same reason she had so gifted Andrew Hanson. Thanks were personal, a matter of individual manners, and Anna would have found it as tacky to mention it to the others as to announce that she had written a thank-you note to Bitsy Allingame, which, incidentally, she had done the very next day. Whether Bitsy Allingame had indeed seen them under the turkey or whether this idea was simply a misconception on Anna's part, we do not know.

Since Anna saw fucking as a mode of etiquette, how did her coupling with Victor Allingame and Andrew Hanson differ from that with Kurt Hahn? It differed a great deal, although neither of the two others would have understood this. Each thought himself singularly blessed with Anna's love, and even if he knew of the others, found Anna's method of lovemaking so personally satisfying, so pure, so endearing, as to be quite convinced that only when involving himself did it really matter.

Thus Anna on Thanksgiving Day acquired another lover for a sum total of three, but she had only one love. Something even more important had happened to her that day, however, something that would affect her all the way to the yellow room at Mount Sinai, and could even, in retrospect, be said to have started the events, occurring not so much outside as inside Anna, that led to her being there. Anna Bernstein had made contact with the idea of ancestors and past, specifically an American past.

Victor Allingame's snobbery about his genealogical origins did not yet affect Anna, for never having been exposed to snobbery, she did not recognize it. She also had never thought about an individual or personal past and the way in which that touched an American past. Once this occurred, her own Edenic sense of being an American was jostled by the realization that she was, quite literally, a latecomer to Paradise, and that others could trace their origins to those Old Comers who were actually the first comers, and that the tracing itself — being able to say, Richard begat Increase begat Cotton begat ultimately Victor Allingame three hundred years later, and to find all the leaves on the family tree of Bitsy Allingame's crewel bedspread — was of ultimate importance. For some, this would have been important in terms of superiority and rank. For Anna it was far more profound. It was the being able to *touch* a past. This obsession, then, was gradually added to her many others.

Andrew Hanson, perfectly happy to have started from a fish or an alga, would have argued with her. But Anna's feet, like Alice's, were getting farther and farther away. A process had begun that would, given all the circumstances still to unravel, end in the yellow room.

— He goes way way back, Andrew, Anna told him at breakfast a few days after Thanksgiving. Back to the Old Comers, to Cotton Mather. To the very beginning of America. And he can trace everyone in his family who preceded him, from then to now. So he knows how he happened to be.

Andrew looked at Anna, sitting in the sunlight, plants twining around her, eating an English muffin with Celeste in her lap, and poured her some tea out of a cracked earthenware pot.

— We all happened to be in the same way. Our parents fucked us into existence, squeamish as some might be about that.

Anna shook her head impatiently.

— Oh Andrew, stop teasing. You know what I mean. He knows who he is.

Andrew Hanson was annoyed. Anna had been to dinner with a bunch of New England snobs and had suddenly become *socially* conscious. Harvard, with its Old Boy network, had that potential, and not even its professors were exempt. It didn't matter how many children of immigrants or how many minorities, whether tokens or through-dint-of-hard-work-or-natural-intelligence qualified, were allowed by the Admissions Committee to pass through the Gates of God and Learning, the Old Comers still ended up at the top of the ladder, even if their children *were* only C students.

— Come on, Anna, said Andrew Hanson, himself the product of hard-working immigrant grandparents from Norway. *We're* the American Dream. Only second generation and we're already getting the best education in the country. Just because we're smart enough, not because we go back to those witch burners in the seventeeth century.

Kurt, who had just entered, supported him.

— Anna, I'm surprised at you. Caring about that kind of superficial junk.

— It's not junk, said Anna, feeling beleaguered. I don't care about the country clubs and the DAR. It's something else they have, something I didn't think about till now. They're Americans, and when someone talks about the Declaration of Independence they have a great-great-great-grandfather who signed it, or who fought in 'seventy-six or in 1812, or who served in Lincoln's Cabinet, or was a friend of Emily Dickinson's, or lived next door to Hawthorne in Salem, or went on walks with Thoreau.

— So? Kurt Hahn shrugged, pouring himself some tea. Who the fuck cares?

— *I* care! Anna almost shouted. They know their *history*. Where is my history? I'm an American, I want to share its past. I have no other history. I can't trace back, I don't want to trace back. Grandma used to tell me stories about Poland. I don't want Poland to be my past. They hated the Jews worse than the Germans there. That can't be my past.

Kurt Hahn and Andrew Hanson were uncomfortable. It was the first time any sense of difference had arisen among them. Anna had never cared before about personal histories; she had carried her own history lightly. She had not made them in any way self-conscious about their own origins. Now suddenly another element, courtesy of Victor Allingame, had entered.

Kurt Hahn, only recently German, was especially taken aback as he thought of his boyhood in Nevada, raised by his German mother. He had been offered Goethe and Schelling as his heritage. Not Hitler. Despite his maternal grandfather in Argentina, whom he had never met. His mother had rarely talked about him, except to say he had been kind to her as a child, and then had to go away.

— Come, Anna, said Kurt Hahn, let's walk across the Yard.

Andrew Hanson, fortunately for Kurt Hahn, had to stay and finish some writing, so, for the first time with Andrew back in town, Kurt Hahn and Anna had a morning walk alone across Harvard Yard, where it was quite apparent that, as elsewhere, the corn spirit's preface to the season of Good-Will-to-Men, that curious mix of department store ads and Jesus, had been followed by an almost frenzied rush of wind-up and preparation.

Anna and Kurt Hahn, walking past the bare trees of early December, could feel the hurry in the air. Students walked more quickly, shouts between them sounding harassed: meet you at the Wursthaus, when are you giving your seminar report, did you hear that lecture last night, I'm late for class, I'm late, I'm late. Something of that acceleration communicated itself to the two lovers, and this, added to the interjection of self-consciousness that Thanksgiving at Victor Allingame's had promulgated, made their walk slightly strained. Yet these mild disquiets were easily absorbed by the larger atmosphere of their mutual feeling. Anna Bernstein and Kurt Hahn were falling deeply into the morass of feeling, sentiment, sensitivity, dependency, and obsession that has been the source of so many novels and poems and songs. Had Anna Bernstein been able to distance herself from her growing sentiments, she might, as was her indelible habit, have tried to research them. Love. Research love. Research how it comes upon you, stealthily, unsuspected, until the perceived glint of an eye, a smile, or the turn of a head suddenly elicits strange, unnatural behavior; how the popular songs are suddenly true: sleepless fantasies and reveries, strange litanies in which the beloved's name is endlessly repeated on diverse pieces of paper with other work at hand, breathlessness when the loved one's voice is heard, even when transformed by the electrical circuitry of the telephone. How this love disease, once contracted, is not even immediately diagnosed by either victim or carrier.

In this instance, there was no single victim or carrier, for this love was not unrequited. Both Anna and Kurt were each victim and carrier simultaneously, although the rate at which each was falling could be calculated as differing somewhat.

Kurt was falling faster. Kurt Hahn, who had always prided himself on his macho, signaled by the sort of swaggering Gary Cooper/John Wayne way he walked and wore his cowboy hat. Kurt Hahn, who had always thought that fuck them and leave them was the best policy with girls, though his softer sensitivities had made him receptive to the nobler sentiments of Goethe. Kurt Hahn was agonizing over Anna precisely like Goethe's Werther.

Yet there was something in Anna's manner that cautioned him not to reveal himself too fully or too soon. Anna was still behaving like a comrade, hardly willing to admit that she had a favorite among her three lovers, not wishing to bestow more upon one than on another, trying to count her coupling with Kurt Hahn on that magical day *au bain* with Lucinda as yet another signal of Harvard friendship, quick to include Victor Allingame (Cotton Mather, genealogical obsessions, and all) among her intimates, as though the safety in numbers would somehow definitively ward off the threat, the danger of Kurt Hahn. For dangerous he was, in ways Anna could not even have suspected at that early point in the school year. But her special intuitive graces caught and responded to some of those perilous intimations.

Thus they talked that day not of their own love, but of the Thanksgiving just past, not of course of coupling under the turkey with Victor Allingame, but of the significance of the Thanksgiving ritual.

— To be part of a tradition, said Anna, continuing the thoughts she had been expressing earlier, and matching her stride to Kurt's, so that even in walking together they moved as one, is an exceptional kind of belonging.

— I don't see that it matters that much, one way or the other, said Kurt with a shrug. We exist *now*. It's important for scholarship, naturally, and I care about it abstractly to see where the past was, but for me the past is past.

— No, said Anna firmly, her eyes clouded over in a new way. The past is present and future. It's all part of the same chain if you belong to it. We're links on the chain. And you can't have now without then and when.

— But the tradition you saw at Allingame's, said Kurt with exasperation, isn't history. It's snobbery. Who gives a fuck about his Calvinist ancestors? A bunch of witch-burning bigots, that's all they were.

— But they were here, said Anna, gesturing around Harvard Yard at the tree branches stark against a gray sky, at the students scurrying across the zigzag paths. They were here first. They began it all. They started something. And if you're part of their chain, when you exist in time, you carry them along with you, and everything that happened, and you become so much more than just yourself.

Kurt shook his head, hardly able to resist declaring his love for Anna in the middle of Harvard Yard, to get ridiculously down on his knees in the sparse autumn grass, to ask her to marry him, tell Victor Allingame to bug off, for he suspected, without actually knowing, her courtesies to the others. Anna was wrapped in a heavy dark brown Peruvian sweater under which her gauze dress billowed lightly in the wind, like a butterfly left over from summer. Anna was beautiful and golden. Anna was his Rapunzel, the golden girl out of the Grimms' stories his mother read to him as he fell asleep.

— Yourself is enough for me, Anna, said Kurt Hahn, restraining his more amorous instincts toward self-declaration. We're here now, that's what matters. Those links you talk about are invisible, they can't be touched or seen or felt. They don't matter.

Anna looked at Kurt, at her Kurt, this Kurt for whom her feelings of love were growing so rapidly that the expansion and acceleration could be measured instant by instant.

— You must understand. I can't believe we would really disagree on this. You're an art historian. History is important to you.

— But history and tradition are not necessarily the same.

— They're almost indissoluble, said Anna.

— Not really. Maybe it's just a semantic problem. But history to me is an abstract record. We study it because as we trace it along, we can learn from it. *They* did it that way, and that explains what *they* were about, and then maybe we learn from them, not to make their mistakes, or to take on the best of their values or whatever it is they have to teach us. But tradition, tradition is a hidebound set of rules and conventions that makes people inflexible.

— But that's just one reading of it, said Anna, anxious now to explain to Kurt Hahn what she really meant. You could read it that way if you wanted to. But supposing you read tradition as a kind of pattern, something that helps give shape to history.

— History is already shaped by the historians. They take the chaotic mass that time offers us, what Worringer called actuality, not reality, and they don't get it all anyway, they only get what's left after attrition has set in, what comes down in artifacts, or documents, or works of art, and then they shape that, as best they can, through each historian's own point of view. Some historians just give you the raw material. But some of the others are likely to synthesize, if you're lucky, or overinterpret if you're unlucky, so who in hell knows what to trust anyway?

— But forget about whether or not you can believe it, said Anna impatiently. I know there's no absolute truth. But say you have a relatively believable view of history. It's still a very complicated thing. And traditions trace paths through that. Repetitions and continuities. And each history has its own traditions. And those paths give history its face, like the lines on an old person's skin. They give it its character. And if you belong to those lines, you absorb some of that character. If not, who are you? What do you belong to?

— You belong to yourself, you have your own character. Your own life shapes your character. You don't have to depend on absorbing it by belonging to a tradition — who your ancestors were, whether you can belong to the DAR, or any of that. You have your life to live, and each life is precious in itself, Anna, and your life, your life, Anna my darling (he tried to say it lightly), is very very precious.

— Yes, said Anna morosely, but where is my tradition?

They had circled back to the steps of the Fogg Museum.

— Anna, someone called from the direction of the Yard behind them. Anna, wait, I'll go in with you.

Anna Bernstein and Kurt Hahn turned to see a tall, slim, dark-haired girl half running, half floating to join them. Her name was Joanna Wilkens.

Anna had never been very good at making women friends. This was not because she disliked them or preferred men, but because she was so shy that anyone who wanted to befriend her had to make the first move, and men, due to their physical attraction to her, were more apt to do this than were women, who, Anna sometimes found, met her with some resentment. They distrusted her unworldliness, often misreading it as calculated to arouse in the male beast a primordial protectiveness.

Joanna Wilkens, however, had very exceptional powers of perception, which enabled her to respond to Anna with some understanding of what she was really about. This may, indeed, have been more evident to Joanna Wilkens than to Anna herself (who was getting increasingly confused on this very point) or to the three lovers, each of whom, in the manner of lovers, saw Anna as he wished to see her, or even to us, at this moment, since we are based essentially in the yellow room, trying hard, along with Anna, to muddle our way through electric shock and antidepressant drugs back to a point in time that, steadily receding, has lost its original clarity.

Joanna Wilkens was herself a product of New England, of much the same vintage as Victor Allingame, though her family had followed, on her father's side, Governor Hooker into Connecticut, while her mother came from one of the first settlements in Virginia. Her father's family had always been in banking or in some aspect of money, and her parents had long since despaired of Joanna's unwillingness to join the Junior League, to come out as a debutante, to do volunteer work with her mother at the local offices of the DAR. Rather, Joanna was so unlike them, so unconscious of her family traditions and obligations, of family *pride*, in fact, that she often seemed to them not to be their child at all, and Mrs. Wilkens (though she would never admit it to a living soul) sometimes wondered if perhaps in the hospital one of the nurses had put the wrong identification bracelet on the wrong baby.

There was, however, one ancestor to whom Joanna Wilkens was very devoted for reasons thoroughly removed from those either of her parents or of Bitsy Allingame. The Wilkens family had produced a spiritualist medium named Euphemia, a great-great-aunt of Joanna's on her father's side. The daughter of a Massachusetts sea captain, she became renowned for her psychic powers, her gifts of automatic writing, healing, and inspirational speaking, especially in New York, where she was a prominent figure in the Society for the Diffusion of Spiritual Knowledge.

An enthusiastic proselytizer for the spiritualist cause, Euphemia traveled all over the United States of America and throughout Canada, England, New Zealand, and Australia. She was a dear friend of Madame Blavatsky, and helped her to formulate the precepts of the Theosophical Society, though the Great Madame herself would surely have attributed all of that to divine inspiration.

The author of many books and treatises on spiritualism, among them *American Spiritualism* (Boston, 1875), *Occult Mysteries* (New York, 1879), *The Enigma of the Universe* (London, 1886), as a child she had also been a talented musician and when she became a spiritualist she was fortunate enough to be visited by Mozart, who dictated to her in automatic writing some unpublished music of his own, which she then published under the *nom de plume* Jonas Skeffington. On a visit to England, she encountered John Ruskin (with his own Effie long in the background), who displayed some small interest in spiritualism and immortality until he proved to himself it was probably true, at which point he was no longer concerned.

Joanna Wilkens had first made contact with Anna when Ruskin's name came up in Victor Allingame's class, and she leaned over to Anna, seated beside her, to murmur,

— He was a friend of Aunt Euphemia's.

This comment, uttered in the darkness, with Millais's drawing of Effie on the screen and a portrait of Ruskin by Charles Moore beside her, struck Anna for a number of reasons. First, though she had hardly thought of it, Effie was itself a contraction of Euphemia. Second, here was someone else who seemed interested in Ruskin as a real person, and even though Anna could never never forgive him for what he had done to *her* Euphemia, her Effie, it was quite remarkable to find another student in the room who thought of Ruskin as a human being instead of as a disembodied writer of endlessly confusing critical tracts.

Anna Bernstein strained in the darkness, using the half light of the lantern to see the girl beside her, and made out somebody dressed in typical New England style, rather like Bitsy Allingame, tweedy and sweatery, with a book bag on the floor at her feet, and straight black hair pulled back with a small barrette. Joanna Wilkens, however, was hardly as usual as she looked, and her eccentricities became more apparent to Anna as the friendship, established at this very moment of revelation of mutual interest, grew stronger. For Joanna Wilkens had herself joined a spiritualist group and had dreams, stretching far beyond art history, that included following Great-Great-Aunt Euphemia into the cloudy realms of Summer Land.

So Joanna Wilkens's interruption of Anna Bernstein's earnest conversation with Kurt Hahn at the steps of the Fogg Museum was not unwelcome, despite the urgent need of the lovers to continue talking to each other. Kurt Hahn left the ladies to go back to Widener. Anna and her new friend dawdled into another of Victor Allingame's classes.

Entry in Anna's diary, undated, in green ink:

". . . *You can be the White Queen's Pawn, if you like, as Lily's too young to play: and you're in the Second Square to begin with: when you get to the Eighth Square you'll be a Queen —*" *Just at this moment, somehow or other, they began to run.*

Alice never could quite make out, in thinking it over afterwards, how it was that they began: all she remembers is, that they were running hand in hand, and the Queen went so fast that it was all she could do to keep up with her: and still the Queen kept crying "Faster! Faster!" but Alice felt she could not *go faster, though she had no breath left to say so.*

The most curious part of the thing was, that the trees and the other things round them never changed their places at all: however fast they went, they never seemed to pass anything. . . .

"Are we nearly there?" Alice managed to pant out at last.

"Nearly there!" the Queen repeated. "Why, we passed it ten minutes ago! Faster!" . . . Just as Alice was getting quite exhausted they stopped, and she found herself sitting on the ground, breathless and giddy.

The Queen propped her up against a tree and said kindly, "You may rest a little, now."

Alice looked round her in great surprise. "Why, I do believe we've been under this tree the whole time! Everything's just as it was!"

"Of course it is," said the Queen. "What would you have it?"

"Well, in our *country," said Alice, still panting a little, "you'd generally get to somewhere else — if you ran very fast for a long time as we've been doing."*

"A slow sort of country!" said the Queen. "Now, here, you see, it takes all the running you can do, to keep in the same place. If you want to get somewhere else, you must run at least twice as fast as that!"

Anna was sitting again in the yellow room, playing chess, as usual with nobody.

"I see nobody on the road," said Alice.
"I only wish I had such eyes," the King remarked in a fretful tone. "To be able to see Nobody! And at that distance too!"

She was playing chess, and thinking about how fast everything had been. Like Alice, she was out of breath just thinking about it. First there was Andrew Hanson, but he had been followed by Kurt Hahn and the mustard, and then there were Victor and Bitsy Allingame and the turkey, and then there was Joanna. But along with Joanna, somehow, had come another world, for Joanna wasn't just here, she was also there, and Anna had had to run very fast just to stay *here*. *There* was almost too much for her, and as she would tell the red queen, I refuse to run twice as fast just to get somewhere else, running as fast as I ran is quite enough thank you.

To the others sitting in the yellow room — a young girl who had taken an overdose of pills because she had been dropped by her boyfriend for someone else; a fifteen-year-old boy who had tried to hang himself because he failed an exam, but it wasn't the exam really, but his parents' perfectionism, and they were right, he couldn't do anything right, the rope had broken; an old lady whose children had placed her in a rest home, where she overdosed on arthritis painkiller because she missed her house, and her dead husband, and her independence — Anna's playing chess with Nobody and talking to the Red Queen seemed a bit odd. Perhaps this is because the manic depressives who are unsuccessful in terminating their own lives are not necessarily mad in the conventional sense of the word, but mad (in society's eyes of course) only in regard to life and death. (Surely it is possible to be mad in one part and perfectly sane in some others.) Thus, their eyes were not good enough to see Nobody playing chess with Anna, and they thought her quite strange to be talking to the Red Queen.

Anna was talking to the Red Queen, however, for a very good reason. Joanna had taken her *there,* and everything had begun to seem much too fast and had added to her sense that she must, she really must rest.

Dr. Gotthard asked her about it:

— You mean she was a spiritualist?

— Her Great-Great-Aunt Euphemia was a famous one. Anna nodded, moving the red queen to yet another square.

— But she was a spiritualist herself? Was she into the occult?

Anna tried to think.

— Oh yes. She had gotten there. You see, there was Harvard and Cotton Mather and Ruskin and Effie, and Effie was hardly much more grown up than Alice, and of course Lewis Carroll loved to do the photographs of little girls without any clothes on, if the mothers would give permission, but he felt if the mothers insisted on staying that meant they didn't trust him, and he was insulted. Now, they're all dead, of course, a long time, but Joanna knew how to get there. I think her aunt was a role model. Yes. Yes certainly. These days, you know, women have to have role models. It's part of our liberation.

— Do you have a role model, Anna? Dr. Gotthard asked gently.

The tears glistened in Anna's eyes.

— My mother was my role model, but she left so soon. I was only seven. I haven't had a role model since I was seven, though Grandma tried very hard, you understand, but Grandma wasn't American, she was much much much later than Cotton Mather, and that makes a big difference.

— To whom?

Anna looked at Dr. Gotthard blankly.

— Why to me, of course.

She moved a pawn and captured a knight.

— Kurt was the knight, you see. And Grandma was

Jewish. Grandma had no connection with Cotton Mather.
And I spoke to Mother about it.
     — When?
     — When Joanna brought me to the séance.

5

DR. GOTTHARD could not find out just then how deeply Anna had been drawn into occult experience, or what it had meant to her, or how it had contributed to the situation in which he found her. Joanna had brought Anna to a Spiritualist Church meeting, a simple billet reading, shortly after their encounter on the steps of the Fogg right after Thanksgiving, and then proceeded, throughout the spring semester, to bring her to various Spiritualist festivities. The séance Anna referred to occurred closer to the end of the spring semester. But Anna had found the initial billet reading quite magical.

It was conducted by a young pretty girl wearing a blindfold, in a small auditorium rented by the American Spiritualist Church from another, more accepted religious group, which used the hall for teaching and lectures. It held about a hundred people. They lined up to await acceptance of their tickets of admission, for which each made a small donation to the church. Anna had gotten into a conversation with a woman in front of her who was talking about past lives.

— My six-year-old son was a rabbi in the seventeenth century.

— Oh?

— I adopted him when he was a baby, and I thought it would be a good idea to find out about his past lives.

— Yes, it would be.

— I just had an out-of-body experience, a few minutes ago. I was out on the roof. It's tiring, waiting this way. I wish they would open the doors and let us sit down.

The woman turned impatiently away and faced the door, tapping her foot nervously.

Anna wondered about the six-year-old seventeenth-century rabbi. Did he start chanting in Hebrew at his mother when she came in to dress him for school, or when she asked him to run out and play? Would he have to study all over again, or did he carry inside him the mystical secrets of the Kabbalah and the contents of the Talmud? How much did we bring, indeed, if such a thing as past lives was true; how much did we bring with us from those experiences which, except for the little Indian children alluded to earlier, none of us ever recall? Was it true that the gifts and talents we develop in earlier lives stay with us, so that when we are born with what are spoken of as *natural* gifts, a born writer, composer, painter, poet, it is because those skills and talents are arduously developed and brought to a point of perfection in an earlier life?

The complications, it seemed to Anna, looking at the woman on line before her (she looked quite normal, as did all these people, in ordinary New England dress), for whom a seventeenth-century rabbi might appear quite exotic, especially if he was now six years old, the complications were enormous, for what did the woman do about the child's genetic hereditary lineage, in addition to his past lives? Was she blocked, as an adoptive parent, from knowing whether he was the son of a famous Congressman who didn't want to ruin his career, or a drunken mother, or a respectable matron who fell in love with another man, or a thirteen-year-old child, or someone in prison who had murdered his or her parents, or, indeed, a great artist or musician who had passed his or her gifts along genetically rather than through the Akashic network?

Ancestors again. Not only ancestors, now, but past lives. The problem grew ever larger. Even if one could trace, as

Bitsy Allingame's soon-to-be-completed crewel bedspread would, one's entire genetic heritage back to the Old Comers, how did one cope with the problem of past lives?

In the life just before this, Bitsy Allingame might not have been a member of a socially prominent New England Wasp family at all, but maybe a black man, lynched by the Ku Klux Klan in Mississippi. You didn't even necessarily have the same sex in former lives. Maybe that was a clue to some aspects of homosexuality. Maybe some of those characteristics of sex from an immediate past life remained. Maybe that's what caused the male/female mix that made men prefer men and women prefer women. It was surely, it seemed to Anna, just as logical as the hormone theory, or the anxiety-during-pregnancy theory, or the overbearing mother/absent father theory, or any of the other theories that had arisen, Anna always thought, a bit nonsensically to explain the reasons why some people, even great artists like Leonardo and Michelangelo, preferred boys to girls or girls to boys if such was the case. It had always seemed easier to her to say that God had made two sexes, had programmed in the possibility of infinite permutations of that. But, of course, the problem was: Whose real responsibility was it, God's or Nature's?

Tonight, in any event, was clearly God's show, and very soon the doors opened and the evening began.

The young girl stood on the platform. An organ was playing a hymn. The audience, mostly regular members of the American Spiritualist Church, filed into their seats and were presently directed, by ushers passing up and down the aisles, to put messages for loved ones in the other world on little white pieces of paper, with the name or names of the loved ones AND YOUR OWN NAME AND MESSAGE plainly printed and folded inside so as not to be visible to the already-blindfolded medium. There were white waxy flowers on the platform before her.

The young girl, the medium, was about to bring messages from the dead. Yet there was something very ordinary rather than extraordinary about the whole procedure, a casualness that was to be repeated on later occasions when Anna Bernstein accompanied Joanna Wilkens to a Spiritualist function. The ordinariness gave normality and credibility to the proceedings. For what, Anna thought, should contact with the dead be but normal? Everyone dies. To die is in itself normal. It would be abnormal not to die. To live forever. To be even older, as the saying goes, than Methuselah. To outlive the biblical age of six thousand years, and the anthropological age of five million years, and go back to the world age, which in the past hundred and fifty years or so had stretched from the biblical six thousand to almost five billion. Now *that* would be abnormal.

The spiritualists believed, Joanna Wilkens had told Anna on the way over, that your loved ones did not go up to heaven to sit with God in the stratosphere like golden Fra Angelicos. They were somewhere close by, on a very near plane, looking over your shoulder, so to speak, but of course you couldn't see them. Only the mediums could hear them, or read, through the psychic means mediums possessed, their communications.

— Do they hear voices? Anna asked.

— I'm not sure they hear them out loud, said Joanna. I think it's an internal hearing. When spirits speak to you in séances, you know, they use the medium's vocal cords. That's why they're called mediums, you see, it's quite literal. They act as mediums between the living and the dead. But anyway, in a billet reading, the medium will be getting very clear communications. Tonight, the medium is doing her first public billet reading. She just graduated.

— Graduated?

— God, Anna. You *are* dense. They're trained in a kind of spiritualist school. They're trained by other mediums, and when they're qualified they get a certificate. They're actually a form of clergy. They're called Reverend. It's the Spiritualist Church. I'll get you some literature on the way out. Come on, we're late.

The ushers were collecting the small white billets in wicker baskets and delivering them to the young medium.

The music stopped. The reading began. The medium dipped her hand into one of the baskets, fished out a paper billet, left it folded over, held it up and out where she could not see it anyway, blindfolded or no, but seemed rather to be feeling it, to be doing some kind of subtle finger test on its substance and texture. Tentatively, she started.

— Anderson. Mr. Anderson? Is there a Mr. Anderson here?

A murmured yes from the back of the room.

— Speak up, Mr. Anderson, I can hardly hear you. I have a lot of clamoring from the other side; you'll all have to speak up.

— Yes, said Mr. Anderson in a louder voice. I'm here.

— I have a message from Lily. Do you know a Lily?

— Yes. (Excitedly) My sister. She passed over just six months ago.

Under her blindfold the young medium smiled.

— She says she's fine, Mr. Anderson. She's getting along very nicely.

The medium frowned.

— She says you'd better get some more medical tests. It's not serious, but they haven't diagnosed you properly yet. Yes, said the medium more firmly now, get more tests.

Mr. Anderson settled back happily into his seat. He beamed at everyone around him and sat back with an audible sigh to watch his live companions get their calls through.

Anna, watching him, realized just then that that was it. Mr. Anderson was like someone who had been standing outside a phone booth, first on line, and had gotten his call through. This was a Spiritualist Long Distance phone she was plugging into, though the distance was, according to Joanna, not as long as she had imagined.

The medium, who had started a bit tentatively, was speeding up a bit.

— Mrs. Longhi? Do I have a Mrs. Longhi or Longho? I'm not sure of the name.

A short fat Italian lady near the front waved her hand.

— Mrs. Longho or Longhi? If you don't answer I'll have to pass you by. I haven't time to look for you, and — she stopped to laugh — I can't see you anyway with this thing on my eyes.

The lady's neighbor nudged her to speak up.

— She can't see you waving. Say something, say something or you'll lose your message.

Mrs. Longho found her voice.

— Here, she shouted, almost hysterically. Here, I'm right up front.

The medium nodded.

— I have a message from Dinny or Denny. He says the house should be sold now. Don't wait any longer.

Mrs. Longho nodded vigorously at the medium. Anna could see that Mrs. Longho kept forgetting the medium was blindfolded. The medium, after all, had extraordinary powers. She could hear Dinny, Mrs. Longho's own Dino, her husband gone these five years, and yet she couldn't see Mrs. Longho sitting in the same room very close by.

The medium's tempo was accelerating. She was hitting her stride, gaining confidence. She started calling out names quickly; one had to listen alertly not to miss one's turn.

— Mrs. Brenner? Mrs. Brenner, a Madeleine. Your sister? She says your daughter should not change her job. Stay where she is.

— Mrs. Johnson? Daniel, do you know a Daniel? Daniel sends love. Says not to worry.

— Ferguson, do I have a Ferguson? Mr. Ferguson, Mrs. Ferguson says you need a holiday. Go away and enjoy yourself, Mr. Ferguson, the medium teased with a light laugh now.

She was in command, the messages were coming through.

— Mrs. Honig, Mrs. Honig, have you been ill? It's not serious, Mrs. Honig, you can put your fear away. You're all right, my dear.

— Nordstrum? Mr. Nordstrum?

Suddenly the medium stopped and seemed to be addressing not the audience, but someone or something else not seen.

— Hold it, hold it. Take your time. I can't get to everyone so quickly. Please, please, I'll take you all. Just wait your turn.

The medium started to look harassed. Under her blindfold she was sweating, and shaking her head vigorously as though the pressure was growing too much for her. It was as though she were warding off a band of invisible bees.

— Ladies and gentlemen — she returned to her visible audience — please bear with me. There are so many spirits from the other side clamoring to get through, and I am only one person. I'm doing my best, but they're so impatient. I'm not sure I have the energy to do them all in this session. Bernstein? Do I have a Bernstein?

Anna couldn't believe her ears. She went mute. She couldn't believe she had gotten through. Especially when all those people were trying from the other side.

— Bernstein?

The call came again. The medium was annoyed and impatient now.

— Please, if you don't answer, I'll have to pass you by. I'm too busy. They're really overbearing today. I can hardly control them.

— Here! Anna screeched in a voice she didn't recognize, her heart pounding so loud she almost couldn't hear herself. Here! she shouted again.

— I have a message from Ellen.

— My mother. Anna gasped.

— Your mother says she's glad you're at Harvard.

A few people in Anna's row looked over at her with new respect. Harvard. Harvard intellectuals were usually too snooty and skeptical to come to these meetings, to believe in the spirit world or life after death. This Harvard intellectual was sitting in her seat with tears running down her cheeks. She had found her mother. Her mother was glad she was at Harvard. She had lost her mother when she was seven, and she had found her in this dreary auditorium with the white waxy flowers. The young girl with the napkin over her eyes had put the call through as easily as if she had deposited a dime in the phone slot.

The operator — Anna could only think of her as the operator after this — the operator clearly had a long line of spirits waiting to get into the booth. The spirits were harassing her. She grew more and more upset as they pressured her to get through, hardly letting her transmit one message before they badgered her with another. Though Anna could not see them, she could feel them, could feel them pressing their names and messages on the medium's thoughts so rapidly, buzzing, swarming around her mind, that she could not deal with them.

The session went on for another quarter of an hour. But the young medium was perhaps too young and new to last much longer. Had she been more seasoned, Anna learned from Joanna afterward, she would have kept the spirits in their place and gone on for the full session of an hour or hour and a half. But the spirits knew she was a novice, that they could take advantage and press their own causes on her. She had to stop the session out of sheer mental and psychic exhaustion. Many people, including Joanna, who was trying to reach Aunt Euphemia, left disappointed. But they were good sports about it. Spiritualists, Anna was to discover, were sweet-tempered people. The belief that we are all simply souls running around with physical shells covering our astral bodies somehow engendered an almost saintly tolerance for human foibles. They spent the rest of the session singing hymns, rather lovely ones, like Open my eyes, that I may see / Visions of truth Thou hast for me. Anna, having reached her mother, sang with lusty and triumphant pleasure. For the first time since she was seven, an essential loneliness had been assuaged.

The next morning, walking with Kurt Hahn and Andrew Hanson to Victor Allingame's class, Anna was full of the night before. Joanna had warned her, however, that most people either frown on spiritualist ideas or laugh at them:

— Either they'll think you're crazy and be impatient with you, or they'll think you're crazy and make fun of you, but either way they'll think you're crazy.

So Anna was reticent about revealing that she had found her mother. She found it difficult to believe, in the brightness of the new morning, that it had really happened. If she mentioned it, maybe it would never be repeated, her mother might never come back. They would doubt that it had really been she, and doubt itself would destroy the spirit of her mother through sheer disbelief and make her unable to return. But she could not bring herself to act as if nothing had happened. Omitting the account of her mother and the message, she chose only to mention the lady with the six-year-old seventeenth-century rabbi for a son. Both Andrew Hanson and Kurt Hahn burst into derisive laughter.

Anna was vexed with both of them. Her two closest friends, one of whom she loved increasingly with a growing sense of desperation and resistance, had not understood something central to her. She walked away from them quickly, angrily muttering about how silly and impossible they could be. Entering Victor Allingame's classroom, and finding a seat next to Joanna Wilkens, she was soothed by her presence, for Joanna was warm and friendly, and delighted that she had been able to initiate her new friend into the etiquette of the spirit world.

When Victor Allingame spent the entire session on Ruskin and God, Anna found herself wondering, suddenly, if her old friend Effie was too long gone to reach. She would love to hear the real story from Effie herself. Maybe there was something redeeming about Ruskin that only Effie would know. Maybe Anna could then relinquish her annoyance with him, which had prevented her, ever since reading the Admiral's book, from giving him the respect that Victor Allingame clearly thought he deserved. More disposed now toward the possibility of making it up with Ruskin (he had at least been kind to Joanna's Aunt Euphemia, and had, after all, been a rather lonely child, whose parents, in their overweening concern for and concentration on him, had made him unable to deal with real women, had obliged him to prefer pure and innocent children who did not threaten his sexuality, possibly more like her dear double friend Carroll/Dodgson than she was willing to admit), Anna lingered after class to discuss him with Victor Allingame.

Victor Allingame was overjoyed, for he read this as an indication that Anna was eager to repeat the pleasures they had shared together just a few days earlier. Though this had not been her intent, and though Victor Allingame could not discuss Ruskin and God without bringing the subject somehow back from God to Cotton Mather, with whom he was as much obsessed as Ruskin had been with Turner, Anna Bernstein decided to spend the rest of the day with Victor Allingame. Though there was no turkey that day, Anna was lured back to the large yellow house on Brattle Street, where, in Bitsy Allingame's absence, they spent the afternoon on top of the crewel spread, which already graced the bed, lacking only the addition of a few great-aunts.

Joanna Wilkens, however, had added another dimension, quite literally, to Anna's life, for the spiritualist concept that those who die before us exist on another plane quite nearby, easily within reach of the psychic's communicative powers, intrigued her. Anna felt her mother to be very close. Even God, God was not so high up in the heavens that He got mixed up with the constellations. God was not science fiction; He was made intimate by the idea of an invisible nearby level, on which all who had gone before rested as they watched the world go by. Anna, browsing in Melville's letters some few days after the billet reading, found him writing to Hawthorne:

> Would the Gin were here! If ever, my dear Hawthorne, in the eternal times that are to come, you and I shall sit down in Paradise, in some little shady corner by ourselves; and if we shall by any means be able to smuggle a basket of champagne there (I won't believe in a Temperance Heaven), and if we shall then cross our celestial legs in the celestial grass that is forever tropical, and strike our glasses and our heads together, till both musically ring in concert, — then, O my dear fellow-

mortal, how shall we pleasantly discourse of all the things manifold which now so distress us, — when all the earth shall be but a reminiscence, yea, its final dissolution an antiquity. Then shall songs be composed as when wars are over; humorous, comic songs, — "Oh, when I lived in that queer little hole called the world," or, "Oh, when I toiled and sweated below," or, "Oh, when I knocked and was knocked in the fight" — yes, let us look forward to such things.

But imagine if Hawthorne and Melville were somewhere close by, not guzzling gin or champagne up in the stratosphere, but still sitting in Cotton Mather's New England, worrying their Calvinist souls about the way the world was still going, waiting for it to become a reminiscence. Imagine if God Himself were conducting the affairs of the world right here, looking over one's shoulder with ease, to pick up every murmured prayer, every Oh God help me, every God damn it, uttered by everyone, for He was clearly omnipresent, no matter what plane He existed on. Anna, talking to Andrew Hanson about it, argued her concept of God with that earnest Darwinian while Kurt Hahn watched with amusement.

— Come off it, Anna, said Andrew Hanson. God, if He did exist, wouldn't let all these lousy unspeakable things happen in the world. Pestilence, apocalyptic destructions — it's all biblical myth that He did it all. One omniscient, omnipresent, omnipotent superbeing, even one with such a great beard, couldn't possibly control all that. Remember, if He's that powerful, and as good as He's supposed to be, He's supposed to be able to prevent it. No merciful God would let the things happen in human life that happen, not even the small personal deaths, the children killed, the people dying in fires because a goddamned electric socket, some ten-cent article from a hardware store, malfunctioned. No, He's just not there. It's all chance nature and the big bang. We may all just be a natural mistake. Maybe our os coccyx wasn't meant to disappear. Maybe we were all supposed to remain apes, like Roddy McDowall in that movie.

— Andrew, please. I can't believe you're so — so unbelieving. I'd be willing to drop the idea of God if the world were rational, but it isn't. It's the irrational aspect that makes me believe He's there. All those ironies, all those so-called coincidences, I just don't believe in them. Someone or something's controlling it, and if He doesn't have a white beard, and He isn't He but some earth mother or some invisible thing, or some Taoist force, He-It is still doing it. Psychics can see past and future, time itself is not what it seems to be. We float along on relativity bands and we're always in flux anyway. I don't know how we manage to think we're standing still and that things are solid but they're not. Read Martin Gardner's *Relativity for the Million*. He'll tell you. We're all inside a cubist painting all the time. And God is somewhere. I know it. And my mother is nearby.

Andrew Hanson and Kurt Hahn exchanged knowing and compassionate glances. Anna had not yet mentioned the contact with her mother. She didn't elaborate on it now, but Kurt and Andrew knew Anna well enough to know how deeply she missed and needed her lost mother. Anna Bernstein had to believe in the continued existence of God and her mother. She could not do without either of them.

Judging from one of the subcategory piles in her Widener carrel, Anna's reference to time should not surprise us. She had been trying to figure out Time.

⚜

In Anna's diary in the yellow room, in red and blue ink:

Alice sighed wearily. "I think you might do something better with the time," she said, "than wasting it in asking riddles that have no answers."

"If you knew Time as well as I do," said the Hatter, "you wouldn't talk about wasting it. It's him."

"I don't know what you mean," said Alice.

"Of course you don't!" the Hatter said, tossing his head

contemptuously. "I dare say you never even spoke to Time!"

"Perhaps not," Alice cautiously replied; "but I know I have to beat time when I learn music."

"Ah! That accounts for it," said the Hatter. "He wo'n't stand beating. Now, if you only kept on good terms with him, he'd do almost anything you liked with the clock."

Time was a strange substance to Anna. If it were not an it, but a him, it was stranger still. Time in the yellow room had nothing at all to do with clocks. The whole world regulated itself by all those little marks between the numbers on a disk. Except for those different time zones which made things go back and forth so that if you didn't change your watch after arrival you were early or late for lunch or dinner or an appointment or your hotel reservation or what have you. To Anna in the yellow room, time was closer to its own original reality, before the clocks had tampered with it. Time simply *was,* and flowed according to its own inclinations. The patients in the yellow room didn't bother it or him, and vice versa. They had no schedules to keep, they ate when given food, there were no appointments outside the hospital agenda for treatments and visits, and if the staff was aware of the marked-off disks with the relentless hands, the patients were spared this anxiety. Time for the patients seemed so removed from what was going on outside as to have fallen asleep from sheer boredom. It had, however, simply gone its own way. When Anna did think about it in the yellow room, it was closer to what the early American Indians had had. Just sunrises and sunsets and many many moons.

❧❦❧

Anna was not, however, beating time, either in the yellow room or earlier, in the days between Thanksgiving and Christmas. That space of time was rapidly foreshortening, and it was getting very close to Anna's trip to Nevada to visit Kurt's family and also, Kurt promised, a Paiute reservation at a sacred lake site nearby.

Cambridge, though, continued to exercise its own New England charms, and Anna delighted in wandering about the brick-paved streets, stopping occasionally to sit in the yellow Longfellow House. Once she prevailed on Andrew Hanson to drive her to Concord, where they walked up and down beside a small willow-lined stream, with Andrew Hanson murmuring about how crazy it was in the frigid December cold, and Anna affectionately wrapping her scarf around his neck while she chattered on about Emerson and Margaret Fuller, in whose relationship to her nephew, Buckminster, Anna took particular delight. Poor Margaret had recently become the focus of a number of feminist books, all designed to prove that she had had a brain in the nineteenth century. Her *Woman in the Nineteenth Century* had become a paperback classic, her life in Rome as a supporter of the revolution and as mistress of Count d'Ossoli a model for Betty Friedan and Gloria Steinem.

But Anna remembered very clearly that Betty Friedan, founder of NOW, author of a revolutionary book on the feminine mystique, which had however nothing to do with the mystical and everything to do with which sex took out the garbage at night, had relented and written an article for the *New York Times* on chicken soup. Jewish mothers never changed. Such was the lesson of Concord. And Margaret, who had never been able to penetrate Emerson's cool interior, had had to find herself an Italian, and any American woman tourist could tell you what *that* meant, as Katharine Hepburn had discovered with Rossano Brazzi. And since she had heard that Katharine herself had had enough of a brain to get a Ph.D. in anthropology or some such thing, it all meant that romance was possible for women with brains, and didn't Andrew know that?

Andrew, looking over at Anna trudging happily beside him, her golden hair spewing out under a knitted cap, her nose red, her heavy sweater only the top layer of three she was wearing to shield her from the New England cold, knew all this only too well. He had already begun, however, since hearing of Anna's projected trip to Kurt Hahn's home, to suspect that Kurt Hahn had gained the inside track.

This Kurt had, and it became even clearer in the week before the Christmas break, when Kurt Hahn and Anna, having asked their friend Andrew to join them at the Fogg Museum for a special opening of an exhibition of German and English nineteenth-century drawings, introduced him to a fat, unattractive girl with greasy hair who specialized in Holman Hunt and who was "very nice." Then, having ascertained that Victor Allingame was engaged in greeting the heads of the committees at the Fogg and the local historical society on which Bitsy served, they took their glasses of white wine and situated themselves on the top landing, above the thronged courtyard. Andrew Hanson could see them from below, silhouetted in the arcades, Anna's blonde head bobbing up and down in animated conversation, Kurt Hahn, still incongruous in his patinated hat, which more and more he refused to relinquish under any circumstances.

It was a busy week. Seminar papers due, lecture courses accelerating to cover material, endless images passing before the glazed eyes of Kurt and Anna, great masterpieces reduced to small colored slides or even black-and-white reproductions, from which proxy surfaces they would signal their existence and remind the world that some master or other had slaved to paint or sculpt this or that image, which (from an iconographical or iconological point of view) registered Renaissance or Baroque or Ancient Culture to be read by all succeeding civilizations if they knew how. If they did not, there was still the language of form, which, like the language of flowers, could speak to both the prepared and the unprepared eye.

That eye, however, was, as suggested, confronted for the most part by the vicarious masterpiece of the reproduction, not the flesh-and-blood weave of canvas, or the soft gauzed stroke of actual paint carrying the master's hand, traversing the surface with love, delicacy, power, artfulness, to offer an image of something he or she cared about enough to forsake all else. Those aspects were lost to the student, unless the specific work was in an available collection, and here, of course, is where the Fogg had many advantages, for its students could also deal with choice examples of art in the flesh, so to speak, and practice on "the real thing."

The roundup of courses had them bleary-eyed. The bustle of Christmas preparation even more so. Shoppers thronged the streets of the snow-lined townscape, turning Boston Common into Currier and Ives, though the rest of the city darkened quickly with soot and slush. Anna, Kurt, and Andrew, sometimes accompanied by Joanna Wilkens, went over to Boylston Street to buy small mementoes mainly for one another. Anna chose something special to send to Grandma, who would, of course, take it as a Hannukah gift, but no matter.

Anna had always celebrated Christmas with her parents, who as assimilated Jews would have considered it simply anachronistic to observe the older holiday. She still remembered the golden doll under the tree the year she was seven, the last year she had seen them alive. The doll had had golden hair, like Anna, and blue eyes with dark lashes, and china skin with red cheeks, and a pink lace dress, and removable pink socks and booties. Anna had slept always with the doll, whose name she could not now recall, not even when she tried to at night, alone in bed. The lost doll, like the lost mother, had disappeared after her parents were killed, when she was removed summarily to Grandma's house, never to see her own home again, nor most of her belongings, except for a few clothes and toys, among which the doll, for whatever reason, was not included.

II

❧ I ❧

PYRAMID LAKE is situated about fifty miles from Reno. It was Indian territory, Paiute territory, over a hundred years ago, when the famous American photographer Timothy O'Sullivan dragged his heavy glass plates and his photography van by mule across the Carson Desert and through the Carson Sink and over the great stretches of odoriferous sulphur and putrid water and malarial mosquitoes of the Humboldt Sink along the Fortieth Parallel in 1867 with Clarence King. When they crossed the Great Basin they found scorpions and rattlesnakes and spent most of their time fighting off malarial attacks; King, during a storm, was hit by a lightning bolt that numbed his right side and kept him immobilized in camp for a long time thereafter.

The Donner party passed through here around 1846, passed through the Humboldt Sink and the Carson Sink for days without water, on their way to getting stuck in the mountain pass where they ate each other. They ended up having the Donner summit of the Sierra Nevada named after them, and Donner Lake, but the cold fact of the matter still is they had to eat each other.

The recorded history of this Nevada area is short and recent, and, as Western history, shorter by two hundred years than New England history. It is post-Indian history as well. The geological history, however, can now be traced back two hundred million years, into the early Triassic, and has to do with terrains moving in from the ocean and colliding near Interstate 80, on which Kurt Hahn and Anna Bernstein were to do a lot of driving during the Christmas break of 1979. Timothy O'Sullivan met up with some Paiutes, fortunately friendly, when he photographed Pyramid Lake. The Paiutes were still there.

The weather was mild when Anna Bernstein and Kurt Hahn set down in Reno a few days before the holiday. This considerably displeased the local ski-lodge entrepreneurs, but not Kurt Hahn, who was delighted to be able to show Pyramid Lake to Anna in good weather. The house was about a hundred miles in the other direction, in Lovelock, near the Humboldt Mountains, and Kurt had spent a good part of the plane ride from Logan Airport in Boston talking about the great Alexander von, who had written *Cosmos* in five volumes in the mid-nineteenth century, and whose cosmic mind embraced the mineral, the vegetable, and even the stars. Humboldt was, after all, one of the great heroes of German nineteenth-century culture, and Kurt had been encouraged by his mother to know these as part of his ethnic heritage. Kurt Hahn started on Humboldt, intending to familiarize Anna with some aspects of Western geology and science. He soon realized that Anna had already been dealing with the nature philosophy of Humboldt's contemporaries as background to the paintings of Caspar David Friedrich, unearthing Humboldt in due course as a scientific counterpart to the great philosophers.

Anna had never visited the West before. Even on the short drive from Reno Airport to the lake, she was overwhelmed by the space. It was the kind of space that travelers since the very beginning have called awesomely sublime. Kant, she remembered, had found sublimity in the eye of the spectator, but for Anna more than the eye was involved. Anna felt her whole self permeated by vastness. It was as if universal vastness — of the kind we sense when we look up at the sky — had been floated down to earth and extended horizontally, and then somehow straightened out with a cosmic ruler across the surface of the earth. To one surrounded by it, as on a mountain top, it would read round, but it still read straight, like an Albertian perspective, from the surface on which Kurt and Anna were driving. The car was ploughing along a Renaissance line in that infinite space. In the near distance, mountains that Kurt said had pushed up "only eight million years ago" bumped up from the horizon line, but were still far enough away not to interfere with the space. *Nothing* could affect that space (Anna saw it as the most absolute of immovable objects) except the space itself — which she knew had its own organic life. That life had nothing to do with Kurt or Anna, but related to them, despite its indifference, in ways that she had not yet figured out. It had to do with life itself, and with the short, ephemeral, renewable existence of flowers, and the somewhat longer existence of people and animals, who might or might not be renewable, and the greenness of grass, and the endurance of mountains, which nonetheless, encysting themselves from the undercore of the earth, also existed in time but at a much slower rate. Eight million years versus Anna's possible eighty. Yes, a different rate.

— You see why I feel caged in New England, said Kurt, watching the road carefully, feeling himself and Anna zipping across its geometry in the middle of eight million years. You see why I can't be that impressed by all those goddamned New England snobs and their three-hundred-year history. I come from a really old place. New England lost its age when those tightassed Puritans came in and built their civilization. We haven't been able to erase time out here.

— I feel almost erased myself, said Anna, as the space invaded her.

Her eyes were adjusting to the sense of infinity on earth; they expected it in the sky. But here, where everything normally arid in the summer heat had turned even more lava-like in tone, she felt like a space traveler, with earth instead of air beneath her. They had exchanged the intimacy of Cambridge, its brick paths and wooden houses, its ghosts of Cotton Mather and Longfellow, for the Nevada Territory. Longfellow, of course, had had his Hiawatha, and Nevada had its Paiutes, and they were on their way to encounter the survivors of the original inhabitants of America, one of whom, in his position as head of the reservation, inspected them for malevolent intent and, discovering none, waved them on in as cursory a way as possible.

Then they were confronting the huge lake, and it was just as New England's Thoreau had said: Sky water. Blue, under a clear, cloudless sky that Goethe would also have called infinity. They were surrounded, then, by infinities, by the pure sky, unblemished by cloud, by the vast land space, contesting both sky and water, more solid, more resolutely claiming its place, but no less vast, no less infinite.

To be alone in that vast space together was to be alone in the universe and, more specific to that North American continent on which they found themselves, to be Adamic man and woman, beginning again, in the eye of Creation. Before them, in the azure pool, which stretched as far as the eye could see, were the strange tufa mounds that had earned Pyramid Lake its name when Frémont came through in 1844, even earlier than O'Sullivan, and noticed the resemblance to Egyptian monuments.

Timothy O'Sullivan, Kurt told Anna, had already been to Gettysburg with Matthew Brady when he arrived at Pyramid Lake, had already photographed the stark, stiff dead of America's Civil War. Then O'Sullivan, four years later, had exchanged the stench of decaying bodies for the stench of sulphur and dead vegetation, and headed for Humboldt Sink and found the tufa rocks.

His famous photograph, one of the greatest landscape photographs in America, had been taken from a tremendous height.

— How did he get up there? asked Anna with wonder.

— He climbed, said Kurt. Come on, let's see if we can do it.

He reached out to grab Anna's wrist, felt silky skin in his palm, and almost stopped the didactic discourse on which he had been engaged to lie down with her right there on the cold ground in the brisk sunshine.

— Let's see if we can figure out the spot. Just put your feet where I put mine, and hold on to me. It's not really dangerous, just awkward.

And then they were climbing up the strange rocks, described by O'Sullivan as resembling vegetable growths of vast size, climbing to about the height of a four-story building, watching out for insecure footholds, dislodging small rocks as they ascended, up up into the cloudless sky above the lake, which Thoreau at Walden had called molten glass cooled but not congealed. Timothy O'Sullivan, hardy son of Irish immigrants, had finished photographing the Confederate dead at Gettysburg, at Missionary Ridge, at Devil's Den, at Loser's Barn, at the pasture where the bodies lay in rows. Then he had taken a Civil War–type ambulance and two mules, and a small pyramidal tent of orange calico, and lugged his 20 x 24 camera and glass plates, along with tripods, lenses, several pounds of collodion, silver nitrate, alcohol, iron sulphate, potassium cyanide, nitric acid, and varnish, up and down the Fortieth Parallel, rushing back and forth with the collodion-coated plates to his ambulance or tent to fix and develop them.

O'Sullivan's glass plates had photographed the glass lake, glass unto glass like dust unto dust, though (Kurt told Anna) if the sticky collodion had picked up dust, O'Sullivan's precious images would have been lost. Anna and Kurt could imagine him scurrying back and forth with the heavy plates, up and down, up and down, mules waiting patiently below, losing his grip, almost dropping the glass, indeed, dropping some, surely, life being what it is. Which images never developed? Which masterpieces aborted? A still better photograph of Pyramid Lake that no one knew about, only O'Sullivan, long dead in a Staten Island cemetery? And finally they were at the top, standing where O'Sullivan must have stood to get the shot that lived to be a masterpiece.

How could they talk about blueness and silence, two things that can't be talked about? Blue is a color, and words can't describe that except by other colors, and metaphors. Blue as the sky, blue as the sea, blue as the lake itself was blue before them; to call it blue was to call it by its own name, which said nothing other than to name it. To qualify the blue was a help. Lapis lazuli, like the richest of cloisonné enamels, like the mantle of the Virgin Mary. A lost medieval blue. Or ultra-marine, like the river below van Gogh's bridge at Arles. They could talk of it as the art historians at Harvard did — highly saturated blue, as in Matisse's *Dance*, or, as was explained patiently to beginning students, a blue with maximum blue in it. Goethe, playing with color, had tried throughout the fifteen hundred pages of his *Chromatics* to justify his spiritual concept of organic and inorganic unity in the face of Newtonian physics, and ended up with his own pragmatic senses. Sense versus science. Blueness as light and life.

Anna and Kurt, standing precariously at the top of a laval eruption rounded like the edge of the world, looking over a synapse of lake water to yet another rock, bobbing phallus-like out of the soft wet blue womb that housed these volcanic erections, were on Goethe's side. Taking their senses across yet more blueness to the ultimate pyramid, which had named the lake, they were more conscious still of the properties than the names, but needed the names to identify them. What did mute animals do? Where were the words that said life, love, joy, for them? Bird songs, purrs, coos, rumbles — were they better than words? Blue silence.

No words for silence, which destroy it. No way to talk about Emerson's wise silence of the Over-Soul or Eckhart's central silence of the soul, attuned to God's word (again). Was God's word more silent than ordinary words? Was it the one word that could not destroy silence, indeed, embodied, defined it? Instinctively, both realized that silence, if not talked about, could be shared, because it would still exist. That they could preserve its central and fragile existence simply by an omission — of speech. That they could still their responses to embody it in their own selves. Immobile, then, in the face of this blue silence, in the belly of the world, they absorbed Goethe's blue light and Eckhart's centralness.

It was a long time before either of them spoke. When the silence was finally broken, it was Anna.

— This must be what Joanna was telling me about.

— Oh. Was Joanna here?

— No. Not here. But she was telling me where you go after you die.

Kurt, after the deep shared silence, was prepared to be playful.

— Has Joanna returned from the dead?

Anna tossed her head impatiently, and waved her arm in the direction of the pyramid.

— Kurt, please, don't tease me. I mean it. Joanna says the spiritualists believe you rest first on a wonderful island when you come out into the light after dying. It's on your way to the Summer Land. It must be like this — it's like what she described — blue peace. Ultimate peace.

Kurt, not wanting really to break the mood himself, could not resist his urge to tease Anna, lightly, but nonetheless seriously.

— Anna, please, we're here. Not there. I'm glad it'll be like this when we get there, but we're not running around in our astral envelopes yet.

Anna was hurt. Kurt, Kurt with whom she felt such rapport, Kurt with whom she could share this central moment, could come only so far with her. Joanna had warned her about this too.

— Most people will think you're nuts. Don't talk about it too much. We find each other, those of us who are capable of believing. Don't open yourself up to ridicule, don't let them spoil your hope.

But Kurt was beginning to become Anna's hope, and part of that hope, which stems from love, was feeling that he would feel what she was feeling, in exactly the same way, that there was no apartness, that he was not the Other, as they say, but part of her, a part, not apart, and that as a part of her, he would feel life and death the same way.

Anna, looking at Kurt in this blue place, had never loved before. She had no idea, as they stood on Timothy O'Sullivan's rock on the sacred site of the original inhabitants of America, of all the paradoxical frustrations of loving. Muffling her faint stirrings of disappointment at his disbelief, she roused herself to match his lighter tone and took refuge in a smile, transmitting her feeling through the glow of eyes and skin as much as through the smile itself, so that suddenly Kurt, looking at her, found her, even more than this magical place, the embodiment of life and beauty. Anna's golden beauty dazzled him as the lapis lazuli of Pyramid Lake dazzled him, and seemed only an extension of the universal plane on which they had landed, having taken what was only a rather ordinary plane, American or United or whatever, to get here. Man's machine had flown like a bird to nature's haven, only one letter away from heaven. If Kurt did not believe in Anna's spiritualist heaven, neither did he doubt it completely. His Indian heritage and his grounding in the nineteenth-century Germans were too strong for that. But Kurt was doing his doctoral research on Emil Nolde, a contemporary German, and Emil Nolde had made even flowers drip with angst (beside Nolde's sunflowers, van Gogh's were calm). Thus Kurt was torn between older values of a God or Great Spirit of peace, and contemporary doubt, aching perhaps to believe but unable to in the face of scientific evidence and human behavior, all of which served to refute God, as did God Himself, with all those catastrophes and chance disasters that people expected Him to prevent, if He could.

This was not, however, a contemporary moment, but a refuge in an earlier time. These were Timothy O'Sullivan's rocks, his blue water. This was the sacred site of the Paiutes, still so magical that they would not reveal its secrets to the white man who came to buy gas and even in milder weather to swim, and wonder what, beyond its natural beauty, was so special here. And Kurt, alone here with his golden angel, was as close to another time as he could ever hope to be. No sign of man's hand. No evidence that the world had ever been different from this moment. This was the seventh day of Creation, and all the world, and whatever God, were at rest. So Kurt and Anna, in this circumstance, were indeed Adamic, and they found, just a few feet down from where they had climbed, a small cave, half open to the sky, with some rather crude Indian drawings of fairly recent vintage on one wall, and warmed by the winter sun and lying down, as lovers do elsewhere and everywhere, with Kurt's jacket beneath them, they re-created the coupling of the original parents.

Much later, when they had achieved the illusion of oneness that such lovemaking offers, they climbed down to the wet blue jewel, the midday light glinting off its surface.

— My father, said Kurt, rolling over on the ground to look away from the lake to Anna, her heavy sweater open to the winter sun so that her body, having just contributed its share to their mutual warmth, could be replenished by the more indifferent solar rays, my father brought me here when I was a kid, maybe nine or ten, as soon as he felt it would mean something, and told me as much as he could about the Indians. He could tell stories about all the famous ones, Sitting Bull, Crazy Horse, Little Wolf, Roman Nose. I loved all the names. I would sit here with him, and make up stories of my own about how I would have befriended the Indians if I'd lived earlier, and gone riding with them, and hunting, and been a blood brother to them. My father always felt they'd gotten a rough deal. They *were* here first, after all, probably came over from Siberia or Alaska and down between the ice sheets thousands of years ago. And the whites pushed them out. My father's grandmother, remember, was half Paiute. Her mother was the one who was raped when their wagon was attacked by Paiutes. She was only fourteen. She lived with the tribe for years after that, and finally she managed to get away and marry my great-great-grandfather, and she took her three children with her. So my father's grandmother was raised like a white. But she never forgot what it had been like to live with the Indians. More important, to *feel* like one — in fact, to be one. Your spiritualists, he teased Anna again, aren't the only ones who believe in an afterlife. One of the most famous Paiutes was a member of my great-grandmother's tribe — Wovoka. He was supposed to be a Messiah. He brought back the ghosts of dead Indians to help the living Indians who were going through such hell with the white men. They all did some kind of ghost dance. Not only the Paiutes — all the other tribes. It made the authorities nervous and they arrested Sitting Bull and ended up killing him. Then they killed a whole bunch of his Sioux at Wounded Knee. That was the last gasp of it. By the end of the century, they had really wiped them out.

— You don't look like an Indian, Anna said lightly, glancing at Kurt's blond hair in the sunshine.

It always stood in small wisps all over his head, partly ruffled by the old cowboy hat, and partly because it grew that way.

— And *you* don't look like Anna Bernstein from Brooklyn.

— Oh? What do I look like? asked Anna, perplexed.

— Rapunzel, Cinderella, the Little Goose Girl.

Anna brightened. For some reason, Kurt's reference to Brooklyn had distressed her.

— I still read them, you know. Is that terrible? Considering all I still don't know.

Anna thought of the pile of scientific and philosophical books she had left behind at Widener. But beside her bed in the room at Trowbridge Street were her copies of Grimm and Andersen.

— They're so pure.

— The Grimms are bloody. Remember, my mother is from Germany. I was raised on them, sometimes in German.

— But they're about good and evil, and good always wins.

Kurt looked at Anna's golden hair, silhouetted against the lapis lazuli lake, and felt a surge of disquiet. Anna's strange innocence was so fragile.

— Let's hope so, sweetie pie, he said lightly. Let's hope so. Come on, let's go.

He pulled her up.

— Where?

— There's an island in the middle of the lake, out there, see it? About five hundred yards, I guess. And here's a rowboat. I want to stand out there on those rocks and look back here. Come on. In the summer I've gone swimming in this lake. The Indians won't. They think it's sacred. But for some reason, even though it's their sacred spot, they let visitors swim here, once they've admitted them at all. In a way, we're their guests, and they don't like to deny us anything. I know we're not supposed to go out there — it's a bird sanctuary, mostly pelicans. But O'Sullivan did. He photographed it. It's called Anaho. And I've always wanted to stand on it. Come on, before they stop us.

— Kurt. If they don't want us to, we shouldn't.

— Yes we should. It's forbidden. That makes it even better. Come on, Anna, don't be chicken.

Anna hesitated.

— You've got Paiute blood yourself. Doesn't that keep you from violating their rules?

— If I have Paiute blood, their rules are mine to violate. I'm not offending *them*, as an outsider. And if I don't, then their rules don't matter, and I'm just as bad as any white man who offended their beliefs.

— But you have — you said so yourself, said a now unhappy Anna.

— I also have German blood.

The voice was abrupt.

— And I was born in Lovelock, Nevada, to white parents. What does that make me?

For whatever reason, Anna Bernstein had upset Kurt Hahn. She climbed quickly into the boat. A mollified Kurt Hahn rowed, with Anna seated at the other end, over to the strange island in the center of the lake, which was dominated by one of the most peculiar of the tufa formations, volcanic eruptions that millions of years ago had deposited hot clay to create weird rock formations, like diseased flesh. To Anna, like noses afflicted with elephantiasis — bumps, fissures, and encrustations of rock making strangely organic sores.

— Kurt, she tried again. Maybe there's a practical reason why we shouldn't be out here. Not just a matter of sacred belief. I don't like it here.

— O'Sullivan got here. Come on, Anna, don't be silly. O'Sullivan photographed some of the members of his expedition sitting up there.

Kurt pointed to the center of the rock, which sectioned off to indicate a sittable ledge.

— I'm going to get right up there.

They were almost there. As they approached, Anna heard a strange hissing sound. It grew louder as they neared the shore.

— Kurt, Kurt, what is that?

Kurt listened a moment.

— It sounds like snakes. They'd be hibernating now. The rattlers hibernate in groups. Sounds, he said, more tentatively now, like a lot of them.

— Kurt, Anna pleaded. Let's go back. We've gotten a close view of the rocks.

Kurt Hahn was, indeed, descended from some Paiute warrior who had gone bravely into battle against the white invaders, who had taken a woman for his prize. He was also descended from a Western settler, one of the people who had survived to wrest the land away from the Indians. Kurt Hahn, born and raised in the State of Nevada, the Rattlesnake State, was not about to turn back. He reached into his pocket and produced something green that looked like a rubber egg with spines on it.

— Snake kit. Don't worry. You don't have to come.

Tying the boat to a nearby rock, he jumped out. Louder hissing. Rattles sounding. Kurt Hahn moved fleetly across the rounded tufa surfaces till he reached the ledge he had pointed out. More hissing and rattling. Closer to shore, to where the boat was tied, near the bottom of the rock, Anna caught the movement of a rattle, half emerging from the pustular encrustations. Then a snake head, from yet another crevice. Then another, just above.

— Kurt! she screamed. Kurt, they're all over the place!
Kurt, seated calmly on the ledge, grinned at her.
— I know.
— You what?
— Well, I thought they might be here. O'Sullivan ran into
them when he was here over a hundred years ago. They
inhabit this island. Diamondbacks. They're pretty lethal. I
figured if he ran into them when he hit this rock, we might
too. He called them "the serpentine tribe."
— So what are you doing there? Anna wailed.
— I am trying to impress you with my courage, pretty
golden girl.
— Oh God, Kurt, please. You'll never make it down
again.
— Anna, do you know the history of snakes? I'm not just
talking about fossil history — they go back at least as far as
the Cretaceous. I'm talking about mythical history. Not just
American Indian myth. World myth. They slough off their
skins and renew themselves. They're about rebirth. They
belong to the moon, and the womb, and time. The mystery
of birth and death. They're phallic. Part of the Eleusinian
Mysteries. Everlasting becoming. In the Buddhist legends
there's a cosmic tree very different from the tree in the
Garden of Eden. Muchalinda, a serpent king, saved Buddha
from a storm under the Tree of Enlightenment by coiling
himself around him.
Anna was hardly listening. Kurt Hahn, sitting on a weird
rock in the middle of the blue jewel, surrounded by the
hissing and rattling of deadly snakes, which thrashed and
moved, since they had been roused and threatened, in and
out of the rock crevices, was giving her a course in mythology.
— Do you know, he continued, enjoying Anna's distress,
do you know the many Indian myths there are of Creation?
This place. This place is the Beginning. The beginning of all
time. Genesis isn't the only version of the beginning. The
Paiutes could tell you about the Earth Mother, the Navajos
call her Naëstsán or Recumbent Woman, the Zuñis talk
about the four wombs of the earth. According to them, we

came up to the surface from the deepest womb of the earth, we thrust up from its hot belly, just like these rocks. The creation of man took place at the Center of the World, and this is the earth's navel. Right here. This is the spot of Creation. It has to be. You can feel it.

— Kurt, Kurt, please. Get down. We'll talk about all that later.

Paradise, the site of Creation, the navel of the world, Pyramid Lake, had more snakes in it than Anna had thought possible. Eden had turned dangerous.

A few of the snakes darted for Kurt's heels as he descended. Kurt, however, was wearing solid Nevada boots made to withstand just such encounters, and moving smoothly as any Paiute, he rejoined Anna in the boat.

Having known, or suspected, that the grandchildren of O'Sullivan's snakes (here for millions of years, probably, before O'Sullivan, and certainly for the hundred and twenty years since, on this one point of land that white America had not dug, cultivated, technologized, inhabited) would still be there awaiting their arrival at the Center of the World, Kurt Hahn was feeling triumphant. Like a child who had shown off his best tricks, Kurt Hahn chanted his version of a Sioux war song as he rowed them both back to the main shore:

> clear the way
> in a sacred manner
> I come
> the earth
> is mine

Anna Bernstein could not share his triumph. Had Kurt Hahn been bitten by one or more of the Western diamond rattlesnakes they had encountered, had one of them penetrated the boots in which he had so bravely descended the bulbous encrustations of Anaho Island, had they not been able to use the snake kit quickly enough or deftly enough (and all it contained, Anna discovered later, was a small razor blade, a suction mechanism, and no antitoxin), Kurt Hahn might have died. Paralysis. Difficulty in breathing. Hemorrhaging. Gangrene. Risking his life, Anna thought, to prove a point. It was not only that she had encountered the deadly realities that underlie the myths of existence. She had collided with a primal male need to exhibit superiority over the female through physical courage and daring.

✑ 2 ✑

ON INTERSTATE 80, after a night in Reno with a still somewhat smugly triumphant Kurt, Anna kept trying to put blueness foremost in her memory so that the rich peaceful color would block out the aroused fear. Was she being oversensitive? Kurt had not, after all, been harmed. But something else had entered, something to do with her growing feeling for him. And beyond this, beyond the specifics of the love relationship between one Kurt and one Anna, was the general problem of living in a world in which death and danger, life and joy, fate and chance, myth and reality, were so intermixed, so strangely tossed together, like a gigantic Salad of Existence, that one did not know, when one ate of it, which bit, tasty or bitter, would come to the tongue. They were heading once more into the Albertian perspective, threading across the kind of space Whitman had seen more than a hundred years earlier, when he had ridden the Iron Horse connecting Atlantic and Pacific, that Atlantic which had entered this area millions of years earlier. Whitman had been most impressed by the silently and broadly unfolding prairies and plains: *Even their simplest statistics are sublime.* Anna, however, had not yet gotten to Whitman, and it was Kurt who recited:

I inhale great draughts of space:

The east and the west are mine, and the north
and south are mine.

Kurt was exhilarated. Anna, the golden angel, was coming home to meet his parents. Kurt, their only child, was
bringing back to them another child, to become family, to
partake of their parentage, to be (he hoped) his other part.
Kurt Hahn's paternal great-grandfather, originally from
Germany, had come through this very route in the 1860s, a
cattle drover, pushing out in the direction of California,
though not interested in the gold that had drawn others a
few years earlier. Like so many others, he had gotten stuck
near the Humboldt Desert, described by contemporary
travelers, Kurt told Anna, as Dante's Inferno, where the
dead cattle and horses and mules lay about by the hundreds;
the Paiutes took the live ones, and the women as well, as in
the massacre that spared his future bride's mother. People
had abandoned all kinds of things in the Humboldt Desert,
trying to lighten their loads: clothes, kitchen goods, tools,
even law libraries and steam engines. Incredible flotsam and
jetsam greeted successive travelers on the trail, brooms and
beads, goldometers and horseshoes, lying side by side in
the desert sand, each a talisman of lost hope, or of, perhaps,
continued hope, for as long as they had life each traveler
had pushed on.

Now, finally, past the Humboldt Sink, there was the great
meadow, and modern irrigation had made it possible for
Lovelock, Nevada, to be the home of some of the leading
alfalfa mills in the country. Kurt Hahn's father, descendant of
pioneer and Paiute, owned part of one mill, which he had
bought into after returning with his German bride from the
war, starting the cycle again, so to speak, that Kurt's great-
grandfather had begun. He also had an interest in a small
cattle ranch some eighty miles away, often visited by the
young Kurt, cowboy-enthralled, boot-clad, wide-brimmed,
and swaggering like the figures who had ended up immor-
talized by Cooper and Wayne in America's most lasting
mythmaking apparatus.

Anna and Kurt, however, were heading not for the ranch, but for the town of Lovelock itself, for Kurt Hahn's mother had insisted on living as close to "civilization" as possible. Kurt Hahn's paternal great-grandfather had already built the perfect home for her, just at the edge of town, not knowing, when it was constructed in the 1870s, that it would be inhabited by a European determined to add something of Goethe, Schelling, and Beethoven to the fiddle music and Stetson hats of Lovelock's culture. In a town that, like so many Western towns, still bore the stamp of the frontier village — wide main street, low buildings, dust and dryness in the air — Charlotte Hahn's three-story white wooden house with its Southern-style veranda stood out. Climbing vines twined themselves around the porch trellis and, even in winter, stood as testaments to Charlotte Hahn's efforts to turn desert into garden, rehearsing in little the intentions of the Western settlers at large.

So Kurt Hahn was bringing Anna Bernstein, whose grandmother had come from Poland, to Lovelock, Nevada, where his family had settled when the long battle with the desert and the Indians had ended, and where his paternal great-grandfather had tried to re-create a small bit of German culture on the Western soil that represented in manners, customs, and mores the farthest point on the North American continent from that culture. When Great-Grandfather Hahn was able, he imported Tiffany lamps from the East, had local carpenters sheathe the interior of the house in dark wooden paneling, installed a tall stained-glass window in the parlor, and a mahogany staircase that circled gracefully up to the top floor. Kurt Hahn's mother, arriving from Germany some eighty years later, with her small treasures of books and a few paintings, was not interested in living at the ranch. The house was Culture to her, and stemmed a bit of the dry, raw sense she had, perceiving Lovelock, Nevada, in the early 1950s, of something not quite finished. Even now, if you go to Lovelock, Nevada, the sense of frontier, of beginning, will hit you. The most popular restaurant in town is a square, graceless room, overlit, glaring with light.

The raw surfaces of its tables are perfect foils for the raw faces of its patrons — sun-bruised, leathered, peering out from unremoved Stetson hats at dinnertime, cowboy heels clicking on the floor. None of the European cuisine Charlotte Hahn remembered from her childhood — no sauerbraten, no dumplings, no wursts, only the crude American hot dog, hardly competition. Surely not the fine pastries dripping with crème and buttery dough her father had brought back from his frequent trips to Vienna.

That father, however, had had to flee to Argentina, just as the war was ending. Left behind, Charlotte Hahn and her mother had lived through the Allied occupation of what is now West Berlin. When Charlotte met Kurt's father, he was part of the occupying army, one of those swarms of American soldiers streaming through the streets of Berlin on payday (many of them drunk), presenting their own hazards to any blonde German *Mädchen* they encountered. Kurt Hahn's father had a Western swagger even in uniform, and this attracted Charlotte Hahn. But when she finally arrived in the Land of Promise, she yearned for her European "Culture." Unfinished, she kept thinking. America was so unfinished.

The small corner of Germany created by Charlotte Hahn in Lovelock, Nevada, had a special grace of both inner and outer furnishing that set it apart. Charlotte Hahn tended her garden carefully, lest the desert reclaim it. Adding to the store of Victorian furnishings left behind by Great-Grandfather Hahn, she picked up bits and pieces in Reno whenever possible. Cut-glass windows lined the veranda, their floral designs chiseled by local craftsmen who had stolen some special time away from ranch tasks to etch them according to Charlotte Hahn's specifications. Not as graceful as those she had left behind in Germany, they still carried out Charlotte Hahn's primary intention: to cultivate this *foreign* soil.

For even now Charlotte Hahn resisted, in an odd way, the melting pot of Americanization. Anna's grandmother had more willingly accepted the New World. But then, Anna's grandmother had found the Old World much more painful to remember. Thus it was a thoroughly *German* Christmas celebration to which Kurt Hahn was bringing Anna Bernstein along Interstate 80 late in December of the year 1979, and Charlotte Hahn had been baking gingerbread cookies and küchen for days ahead.

Christmas showed all up and down Interstate 80, in the gas stations and rest stops holiday-wreathed and decaled with Santa Clauses, in the Muzak at Howard Johnson's bleating "Deck the Halls with Boughs of Holly" when they stopped for coffee. Yet Christmas was a holiday from which practitioners of Anna's religion had often felt excluded. Not to believe in the Christ Child or the Virgin Birth, not to take seriously the ox and the ass, not to sing "O Little Town of Bethlehem," had often proved painful for Jewish children in public schools. And if, indeed, their parents, more alert to the necessities of observing their own religious beliefs, tried to impose these on their young progeny, they had to give up — and it hurt — Santa Claus.

Anna's Jewish parents had spared her this. Fully assimilated Americans, they wanted Anna to have Santa Claus. She could remember writing to him. She could remember listening for him to come down the chimney and fill her stocking. She could remember stealing out that last Christmas morning, almost before dawn, before her parents died, to find the silken doll in the pink lace dress under the tree. Yet Santa Claus had died for Anna along with her parents in the accident that claimed their lives. She had gone to live with Grandma and helped light the Hannukah candles in the menorah. She had listened carefully to the miraculous legend of the Temple's eternal light, which lasted for eight days though there was oil enough only for one. The candles were placed in the window, where they shone like the solstice lights of earlier, more pagan peoples. Gifts were exchanged. But Santa Claus was dead.

Out in the world now, away from Grandma's house, Anna was on her way to reclaim Santa Claus. Driving along Interstate 80 in the great American West, she read in a Western guide that the celebrated Western hero Wyatt Earp had had a Jewish wife called Sadie, who hiked up and down the Rockies with him, and witnessed the famous Tombstone gunfight of 1881 at the O.K. Corral. Ultimately she buried him in a Jewish cemetery, the Hills of Eternity, in California. Wyatt Earp's wife Sadie had prayed, when things got rough, to her mother's *Lieber Gott*. Yiddish, not German.

But Anna did not really identify with Sadie Earp. She knew simply that she had been released, as it were, back to the anticipation of Santa Claus. She was once more, since Harvard, an assimilated Jew. Christmas belonged to her again, and she savored all the small nonsectarian touches that lined her way — the reindeer in front of the rest stops, the decals of holly and jingling bells. Never mind that in Cambridge, home of Harvard, and presently of Anna Bernstein, the celebration of Christmas in the year 1659 had been punishable by fine. (Her research had turned up this odd fact along with several others.) Never mind that Santa Claus, now living at the North Pole with his reindeer Rudolph, had originally been St. Nicholas of Myra, whose attribute was three bags of gold, with which he had saved three impoverished noblewomen from prostitution — those same three bags which, becoming three balls, signaled the pawnbroker all over the world, those same three pawnbroker's balls which often were thought to signal a Jewish proprietor behind the counter. Never mind that one could argue that the Jew had been forced into the position of usurer. Never mind even that the feast day of St. Nicholas had originally been December 6, and that this somehow came close enough to the fictional and initially unknown date of the birth of Christ (which was only established as December 25 by Pope Julius I around A.D. 350) for St. Nicholas's feast day to be merged with that date and become the official date of Christmas, though in Holland and even in some parts of Germany, December 6 was also celebrated, never mind any of that. All that was important to Anna was that she was on her way to Santa Claus, who had given her the lost pink doll.

Kurt Hahn, as they neared home, was filling her in. His mother knew he was bringing his golden angel home for Christmas. The only child of Konrad and Charlotte Hahn thought they would want very much for him to marry and bring his bride back to Lovelock, Nevada, where, having retrieved the land from the desert and the Indians, they grew alfalfa. Proud as he was of his Paiute blood, Anna always sensed some ambivalence in Kurt when he spoke of it, for he was just as proud of the white survivors who, usurpers or no, had founded these United States on the North American continent. Those survivors had joined the two coasts by the linkage of the Iron Horse tracks at Promontory, Utah, on May 10, 1869, just north of the Fortieth Parallel and the Humboldt Mountains, where Clarence King and Timothy O'Sullivan and all of Kurt Hahn's Indian and frontier ancestors had preceded the young couple now traveling on Interstate 80 in that direction.

A quiet town. Christmas decorations and lights strung across a main street. Low buildings with motel signs and shops. Pickup trucks, with heavy-duty tires, driven by cowboys in Stetsons. The house was at the other end, and Kurt and Anna had to drive clear through town to get there. Lovelock had been an overland stage station, traditionally known for its bad water supply. Yet despite the ranch fires for which the fire department kept a ten-thousand-gallon tank, and despite the dryness of the basin (which was still geologically threatened by the Mendocino fault, so that the ocean might come back, and water, maybe hundreds, maybe millions of years from now, maybe tomorrow, could flood back into Lovelock and give people more than they needed for their baths and showers), Lovelock, a town of many despites, endured. Charlotte Hahn's white-trellised house was another despite, indicating her yearning for the European culture she had abandoned. She had always stayed a bit aloof from her Lovelock neighbors, but her husband, Konrad, was one of them.

When Kurt and Anna drew up to the house and parked in

the round driveway, Konrad came running out in his Stetson and jeans. Leather-tanned. Round-featured. Small-eyed. Dark. Kurt did not resemble this medium-tall man with his paunchy belly who looked as though he could down ten beers and then go out and win a shooting match. The woman who stood behind him in the doorway, however, was white and fragile-looking, as though she never left the veranda for the Nevada sun. Her hair, a light mixture of gray and blonde, was pulled back in soft waves. Her eyes, light too, were a strangely luminescent blue-gray, laser-beamed onto Anna's face as soon as the car stopped. She came down the few steps of the veranda slowly and gracefully, with a measure of hesitation or reluctance.

— Lottie! shouted Konrad Hahn exuberantly. Here they are!

Long strides down to the car, with the same litheness now that Kurt Hahn had shown on the tufa rocks at Pyramid Lake. The warm greeting also that of the frontier settler with a reverence for community. Konrad Hahn and Kurt embracing.

— How are ya, you Eastern son of a gun? Have they turned you into a Harvard snob yet?

Konrad Hahn slapping his son proudly on the back. Konrad Hahn turning to Anna with quiet politeness:

— How d'ya do, young lady? Glad to have you with us.

— This is Anna (Kurt touching her shoulder protectively). My good friend from Harvard.

— You're very welcome, young lady.

Konrad putting one arm on Anna's shoulder and a bag of luggage under the other, ushering her back to where Charlotte Hahn waits quietly on the steps. Kurt moving ahead of them, embracing Charlotte Hahn. Anna diffidently waiting to be presented again. Charlotte Hahn hugging Kurt Hahn, who had gone off to Harvard to become educated beyond Nevada cattle and alfalfa, who had not been expected to return so soon with an Anna. Yet the right bride would surely be welcome.

The right bride for the mother of an only son who

represented some kind of cultural European-American dream, some vision of civilization of books and music, and not just any books and music, but the great *Kulturheroen* — Goethe and Beethoven. A special dream of America had, after all, brought Charlotte Hahn to Lovelock, Nevada, to the Fortieth Parallel near the Humboldt Mountains. Her own Alexander von had been a powerful culture symbol of that nineteenth century to which Charlotte Hahn owed her main allegiance, in a Germany which, long preceding the Nazi regime, stressed man's humanity to man.

Charlotte Hahn, beholding Kurt's golden angel, recognized Rapunzel. He had brought her a child out of Grimm. She offered a grave greeting, a how-do-you-do extended with a slim shake of the hand, and a lightly voiced, almost inaudible, You are very welcome, Anna, and led the way into the interior of her oasis.

Anna, tired, happy to wash and rest. The room's gauzed white canopy bed, welcoming after the drive, which had had about it a dry mountainous toughness, for all that they were on the straight highway. On the walls, family portraits — Charlotte's mother and father — the father a military man, perhaps some kind of Junker, Anna thought vaguely — young, erect, stern, and proper-looking. She came down to join the others in a front sitting room, dominated by a huge tree, glinting in the afternoon light. Between the fronds of fir leaves, small gingerbread men, lovingly baked by Charlotte Hahn days ahead. Under the tree — gifts. Santa Claus Land. Anna had not really been here since she was seven.

It was the day before Christmas. Kurt, eager to show Anna all over Lovelock, took her through town while it was still light. Lovelock, Nevada, was like any other small American town: *There* was the Howard Johnson's. *There* the bus stop for the Reno bus, over there, in front of that small hotel. *There* the Lovelock Motel, pool and all, with its vacancy sign blinking in broad daylight. *There* were the gas stations, with their little multicolored pennants, heralding the entry into town like Olympic decorations, welcoming with banners the Marathon road-runners, who had trekked clear across the continent to be here, in time for Christmas. Santa Claus and the Greeks.

Kurt Hahn and Anna were rehearsing Kurt Hahn's childhood together as lovers do. Kurt Hahn was offering to Anna those moments they had not shared, retrospectively but vividly, to fill her with his life so that they could partake of that mutual experience lovers feed upon. Anna Bernstein, whose life had been in many ways closed off, and opened each time only by the width of a book, felt herself suddenly stretching across a continent. She felt her body expand to match her spreading spirit.

That spirit, for Anna, encouraged by all the ideas of Christmas spread through the land, was filled with warm Peace-on-Earth-Good-Will-to-Men sentiment. It hardly included the idea of Christ, which was, indeed, part of the word itself, but had, perhaps more in America than elsewhere, been secularized, to the sorrow of millions of good Christians who wanted Christ returned to them intact. Christ had, she thought, chosen a rather awkward time to be born. For his birth, as Julius I had decided to place it, coincided with the pagan winter solstice, which already had people kindling lights and fires to help the sun god relight his lamp, so the days would get longer and spring would come, and the harvest would grow.

Food again, Anna mused. Just like the corn spirit. The Romans had turned it into a party for Saturn, god of agriculture. And the gifts of Saturnalia were accompanied by visiting friends and dancing. The Armenians had not at all liked a Christian birth date so close to those pagan dancers, which is why they let Christ be born on January 6.

But Christ, in Lovelock, Nevada, had been born on December 25, and if the Paiute Indians who captured Konrad Hahn's great-great-grandmother had not known about this, Charlotte Hahn, marrying almost a hundred years later into the family, did. Martin Luther had told her all about it. For Charlotte Hahn, devotee of Goethe and Schiller, of Alexander von Humboldt and Beethoven, was also a working member of the Lovelock, Nevada, Lutheran Church. Charlotte Hahn had brought Martin Luther with her to Lovelock, and the kind of Lutheranism she practiced (based on the beliefs of a still-earlier German immigrant, Carl Walther, who had studied at the University of Leipzig, who had been in America when Konrad Hahn's grandfather arrived) carried her, though she did not know it, very close to Cotton Mather's New England ideas of predestination and grace. Charlotte Hahn, who prided herself on being a rare intellectual in Lovelock, Nevada, had on her bookshelves not only Carl Walther's famous *Der Lutheraner*, but his *Proper Distinction Between Law and Gospel*, which was published after his death in 1887, and in her belief in grace got very close to ideas of the Chosen. She was still unaware that Anna Bernstein was also a member of a Chosen tribe, and though she might have heard somewhere that the Paiute great-great-grandparent of her own son was conceivably also a member of the lost tribe of that tribe, she paid no mind. For Charlotte Hahn, growing up in wartime Germany, had learned one thing, now best stated in Lovelock vernacular: Just pay no mind.

Thus, after a festive meal over a Christmas Eve goose (dominated mainly by Konrad Hahn telling the little lady Anna stories of how young Kurt had fallen over and over from a bucking bronco until he finally learned to ride 'em cowboy, as Charlotte Hahn, pleased at the golden aspect of Anna, observed her carefully from the other end of the table while ostensibly filling Kurt in on all the local news since he'd been away), Charlotte Hahn paid no mind when Konrad and the two young people elected to stay home and finish trimming the tree and watch *Miracle on 34th Street* on TV rather than accompany her to a special midnight service at the Lovelock Lutheran Church. But since she was head of the church Ladies Committee, the only community undertaking in which she had chosen to participate, Charlotte Hahn felt a strong obligation to go, even without the others, to give her best wishes to the little Christ Child on the grand occasion of His Saviour birth.

So it was that Charlotte Hahn was in the Lovelock Lutheran Church, listening to the Lovelock Lutheran Choir, beautifully bedecked in red and white gowns for the occasion, when a visitor knocked at the front door, which was opened by Konrad Hahn (wrested away from Edmund Gwenn just at the moment when he was filling everybody's dearest Christmas wish) to reveal standing in the doorway one Dude Holloway, the local cab driver, who had driven from the Lovelock bus station with a passenger he had never seen before.

— This fella, said Dude Holloway, pointing to his passenger, says he belongs here. You expectin' him?

Konrad Hahn looked at his visitor, whose telegram had never arrived, whose unexpected presence shocked. He recognized, from a photograph about five years back, the slim, slight, elderly gentleman who stood tentatively but erectly before him. Lottie's father from Argentina. Lottie's father, who had had to leave Germany and his wife and child for Argentina before Konrad Hahn arrived with the occupying army. Lottie's father, who had sporadically sent, over the years, the odd letter and photograph, who was now quite old and, judging from his pale skin and slight tremble, perhaps not very well. Lottie's father.

Konrad Hahn recovered himself sufficiently to take his visitor in hand, to usher him into the warm, Christmas-dressed sitting room, to help him with his one small bag, to present him to Anna and to Kurt. Whatever awkwardness accompanied the occasion came mostly from surprise. Lottie's father was welcome in Lottie's home. This, Charlotte Hahn made fully clear when she arrived home some few minutes later and confronted the father who had left her as a child, who had had, for whatever reasons Charlotte herself had never really questioned, to leave Germany when the war was lost. To what her father had done in Germany Charlotte had, as suggested earlier, paid no mind. Charlotte Hahn's dear friends in Germany were Beethoven and Goethe. To more recent figures and events, she had always managed a sublime indifference. That her father counted among his acquaintances some figures high in the National Socialist Party she had gathered as a young girl. But it was only afterward that some names had become unacceptable. At the time, they had the ring of celebrity, they betokened power in high places. By the time the names turned sour, her father was gone. His exit had been accompanied by a stern silence on the part of Charlotte's mother, who never discussed it with her. Goethe and Beethoven, however, had never abandoned her, and if sometimes at night young Lottie wondered what truly her father had done, by morning she paid that no mind either.

That Christmas morning, Charlotte Hahn awakened to the realization that her father had returned to her. The young people were still asleep. The old man, tired from his journey, slept too. The presents waited under the tree, some bits of clothing, a scarf, sweater, and wallet — plucked from the gifts for Kurt and Konrad Hahn — now were Christmas-tagged *Otto Dienes*. She had been Charlotte Dienes. The radio was sounding "O Little Town of Bethlehem" when Konrad Hahn came into the kitchen to help a joyous Charlotte Hahn prepare breakfast. After coffee and home-made küchen, they opened their gifts, Otto Dienes sharing a Christmas morning with his family for the first time in almost forty years.

— I am glad to be here, he said, nodding his head over and over again. I wanted — his sentences were in English with a heavy German accent, peppered liberally with German and Spanish words — I wanted to see again my little Lottie before I die.

His eyes misting over with sentiment, he reached his gnarled hands to undo the paper wrappings — all green holly-leaved and red-berried — on one of his gifts. Anna Bernstein watched those hands with fascination. They were shaking, but determined.

And what was Anna's reaction to the new addition to the Hahn household? This was, after all, a moving and intimate family situation — a long-lost father and grandfather, returned to his family after almost forty years of separation. Anna felt like an outsider. She would have preferred not to be present, though she was warmed by the sentiment that clearly united Charlotte Hahn and her father. Konrad, glad of his wife's pleasure, was all hospitality and concern. Kurt, she noticed, had closed off a bit, and though he made every effort to be polite and kind to the old man, his own pleasure in bringing Anna home to meet his mother and father had been somewhat subdued by this new and more compelling visitation. Though Anna sensed Kurt's feelings, she could not have known the nature of his thoughts, and if she had, she would have been distressed in the extreme. For Kurt Hahn had always harbored a terrible fear, never openly voiced, even to his parents, that Otto Dienes, his mother's father, who had had to flee Germany just as the war was ending, had had to leave for the all too obvious and onerous reasons, and that his choice of an Argentine harbor simply fortified all such suspicions.

Now, suddenly, as though Anna's consciousness of him had finally made him aware of her presence for the first time, Otto Dienes turned to Anna, his hands still tearing at the holly paper, and, holding a small bit with torn berries in one hand, smiled almost angelically.

— This *Mädchen*, this *Mädchen* is married to Kurt?

Charlotte Hahn moved in quickly to set him right.

— No, Papa, they are just friends. This is his friend Anna . . .

Charlotte Hahn suddenly paused, and realized that Kurt had never, in presenting her, offered Anna's last name.

— Bernstein, said Anna brightly, recognizing what Charlotte had been waiting for.

The old man looked up sharply, suddenly alert, his eyes momentarily narrowing.

— *Was für ein Name ist das?* Bernstein?

Leaning over to look at Anna, he thrust his face into hers.

— Bernstein?

.   .   .

In her diary for December 25, 1979, Anna Bernstein had written only one sentence, carefully lettered in red and appropriately underlined, given the date, in green:

Santa Claus is dead.

❦❧

It was something she had hoped to refute when she went with Kurt Hahn to Lovelock, Nevada, and now, gazing at the reproduction of the van Gogh sunflowers on the wall of the yellow room, she still wished it weren't so. Santa Claus, like Alice, was another kind of fairy tale. With her new faith in an afterlife (so carefully nurtured and supported by Joanna Wilkens), she did not want to believe that anyone really died. But though she could conceive of one spirit reaching that other plane, perpetuating the individual ego into eternity, she could not conceive of mass spirits. Thus the six million Jews of the Holocaust, stepping by the thousands into the showers at Dachau or Treblinka or Auschwitz — cleanliness is next to godliness after all, as was said — posed a problem for her because they entered the afterlife en masse, too rapidly. How could even an omnipotent God accommodate them — but why should an omnipotent God have allowed it to happen to begin with?

Dr. Gotthard was trying, she saw, as he often did, poor man, to penetrate her thoughts.

She looked up at him and smiled.

— I was thinking about the spirits. The Jewish ones.

— Only the Jewish ones?

— They were the ones who went all in a bunch. Hard for God to deal with them all at once.

Dr. Gotthard shook his head. Sometimes Anna seemed to be making progress. Then this.

Anna Bernstein felt sorry for Dr. Gotthard. There was no way to make him see. How could he know that she had just run across the Christmas entry in her diary, that even now, in her dreams, the wizened face of Otto Dienes pressed itself close to hers and asked, What kind of name is that? Only a Jew, and Dr. Gotthard was not that, could have understood the implications of the question.

For Jews that question is almost like being asked to wear a yellow star in the streets. And even American Jews knew very well that the question itself carried along with it all the answers: You are not a Wasp American; you are very possibly not even born in America; you are from some other stock; is that stock Christian? If she had answered only that Bernstein was a Polish name, thought Anna, it would align her poor dead relatives with the Polish perpetrators of the pogroms from which her grandmother had fled to begin with, pogroms that had continued even after most of the six million were already dead. Soap. They had gone into the showers and they had come out as soap. The recipes called for human fat, which then had to be properly cooled.

Somehow, it was all tied up with Jesus. Poor Jew Himself, He had tried so hard to redeem mankind on the cross. Anna did not know whether she believed this or not, but she was not Jewish enough in her heart to deny Jesus totally, nor was she in any way assimilated enough to embrace Him. But to be Christian meant something very special, enough for Christ to die for, enough for men to kill for. But did being Jewish mean that the individual Jews did the dying themselves, instead of having a celebrity like Christ do it for them?

Anna was confused. She got up and paced back and forth in the yellow room, aware that Dr. Gotthard was observing her intently, annoyed that he didn't understand, but then how could he, when she didn't?

⚜⚜⚜⚜

Charlotte Hahn had tried to be as nice as she could to Kurt's friend Anna. But once the question had been asked, the name established, and the label ascertained, Anna had felt a change. Or was she just being a paranoid Jew? But Anna, at that time, had not even felt Jewish enough to be paranoid.

Not even with Otto Dienes, who seemed to her, at that very first encounter, and apart from that devastating question, which he never asked again, and which never received an answer, a perfectly normal human being, a sentimental old man whose eyes misted over when they beheld his little daughter Lottie, grown into a woman with husband and son.

Only after her return to Harvard at the end of that week was the full impact of the Christmas Eve visitation of Otto Dienes felt. Kurt Hahn had spent the rest of the time they were in Lovelock introducing Anna to the few old boyhood friends still left in town, taking her up to the attic to show her his early paintings, primitive but promising, and out to the ranch to introduce her proudly to some of his cowboy cronies and to impress her with his bronco riding.

During that time Kurt Hahn also tried to make Anna see how much he loved and needed and wanted her. Konrad Hahn remained exactly the same, bluff and hearty, constantly suggesting to Kurt small outings he thought Anna might enjoy.

Charlotte Hahn had established, however, an almost imperceptible distance that nonetheless made it very clear that whatever else Anna might be, she was not the *right* one. Charlotte Hahn played German Christmas carols on the phonograph, and talked to her father constantly in German, and read Lutheran prayers in the evening. Martin Luther, Anna knew, had cared very much about St. Paul, another Jew, but that was not the point. (Martin Luther was hard on the Jews himself, as was St. Paul, with the convert's conviction.)

Anna Bernstein tried hard to be receptive to Kurt Hahn's tender words and deeds and forget the rest. But after she got back to Harvard she had more things to research. *Mein Kampf* came first.

♪ 3 ♪

FROM *Mein Kampf* Anna learned that her very appearance was a source of confusion for others. The blonde hair and blue eyes, the Rapunzel or Goose Girl look, were Aryan features, rightfully belonging to the master race. Any Jew bearing these had clearly chosen to deceive others into thinking he was ONE OF THEM, part of the larger international Jewish conspiracy to dominate the world. To present to that world the blonde hair and blue eyes not only of Hitler's Aryan Germany but even of the Wasp American heritage was to compound the crime. But there was much more. The most important thing was blood. Anna had never thought much about blood before. Now she immersed herself in its study.

To Adolf Hitler there was pure blood and impure blood. It all had to do with Columbus's eggs, for as Adolf Hitler said in *Mein Kampf*, Columbus's eggs lie around by the hundreds of thousands, but Columbuses are met with less frequently, and this is because, said Adolf Hitler, most people have not suitably observed the "most patent principles of Nature's rule: the inner segregation of the species of all living beings on the earth. The titmouse," said Adolf Hitler, "seeks the titmouse, the finch the finch, the stork the stork, the field mouse the field mouse, the dormouse the dormouse."

It was of course the Dormouse who played such a large part at the Mad Hatter's tea party, falling asleep, and talking of much of a muchness and treacle before being placed in the teapot — if indeed they had ever succeeded in placing him there — by the Mad Hatter and the March Hare. After reading *Mein Kampf*, Anna often wished she could ask the Dormouse about this herself. Did he, the Dormouse, prefer only dormice? That, after all, was a rather strict conservative adherence to the Great Chain of Being, which allowed for no mutability of species, something that Charles Darwin had gone far to disprove. It adhered, admittedly, to the Noachian accounts in the Bible, and it was true indeed that the world perpetuated a two-by-two, dormouse-to-dormouse point of view, making it difficult, for example, for singles to exist in present society, which is why, of course, there were singles bars.

But returning to blood: An average person, Anna had read elsewhere, had four and a half to six million red cells per cubic millimeter of blood. Goats had more, nine to ten million, and sheep more still, thirteen to fourteen million. But all people seemed to have the same amount of blood, which performed the same function in all living things: a great biological-chemical fetch-and-carry system to sustain life.

Yet who was to say that people were not sometimes sheep? The people who had followed Adolf Hitler might have been sheep, as possibly were the Jews who walked into the showers unprotesting, but did that mean that their red blood cells numbered thirteen to fourteen million? Not likely. All men had the same number. All men were equally red-blooded. And despite the evidence to the contrary, men were not sheep. How would Lewis Carroll, Master Logician, have put it? Anna wondered. She took a scrap of paper from a nearby table and scribbled with a red pencil:

> All men have 4.5 to 6 million red cells
> All sheep have 13–14 million red cells
> All men are not sheep.

Men were not sheep, and their blood, like all blood, was composed of plasma, red cells, white cells, and platelets, plasma containing 90 percent water, 9 percent proteins, 0.9 percent salts, plus sugar, urea, uric acid, creatinin, and traces. There were, of course, differences in blood types, depending on the kinds of agglutinogen your blood had. You could be various letters of the alphabet: A, B, AB, or O, thus designated because it was neither A nor B. And more recent research had isolated MNSs and Rh, the latter requiring sometimes whole transfusions of infant blood if you married the wrong Rh person. But marrying the wrong Rh person was not like an Aryan marrying a Jewish person. That, to Adolf Hitler, was defilement of one of the most patent principles of Nature's rule, because *she* (Anna might have known he would blame it on a woman) did not "desire the blending of a higher with a lower race, since, if she did, her whole work of higher breeding, over perhaps hundreds of thousands of years, might be ruined with one blow." That is why "the Germanic inhabitant of the American continent, who has remained racially pure and unmixed, rose to be master of the continent; he will remain the master as long as he does not fall a victim to defilement of the blood."

In North America, said Adolf Hitler, where the population consisted "in by far the largest part of Germanic elements who mixed but little with the lower colored peoples, there was a different humanity and culture from Central and South America, where the predominantly Latin immigrants often mixed with the aborigines on a large scale."

America. Indicted in *Mein Kampf* with no defense. An American population for which Adolf Hitler gave Germanic elements all the credit for humanity and culture. Adolf Hitler and humanity and culture. Adolf Hitler and humanity. The recipe for blood had included four and a half to six million red cells per cubic millimeter. The recipe for soap, according to a Danzig firm: "Take 12 pounds of human fat, 10 quarts of water, and 8 ounces to a pound of caustic soda and boil for two or three hours, then cool."

Kosher soap. Anna suddenly giggled wildly. Kosher soap. Dr. Gotthard, closed to Anna's inner world, did not understand and Anna did not care to enlighten him. When she became familiar with the Nuremberg Laws, passed by the Reichstag (in an action to which Kurt Hahn's grandparent Otto Dienes, then a member of that body, may have subscribed), according to which anyone with even one Jewish grandparent was deemed to have Jewish blood, she had realized there was no way she would be able to purify her blood sufficiently, all four and a half to six million red cells per cubic millimeter of it. There were, after all, almost five liters of blood in her body. No way, despite her Aryan hair and her Aryan eyes, that she could ever manage to undetile her Jewish blood, for the factor was not, as we have seen, chemical, but, like beauty, in the eye of the beholder. Chemical factors could be measured, but Adolf Hitler, dealing as he did with the irrational, had hit into levels of immeasurable absurdity that Carroll/Dodgson had also tapped. Carroll, however, had limited his aberrations to the benign pursuit of little girls unclothed in their mothers' presence. Only innocence, he had claimed, could stand naked and pure. But purity for Adolf Hitler was five liters of uncontaminated Aryan blood.

Anna Bernstein's head, since her first arriving at Harvard, had been filled with many noteworthy names: Charles Darwin, John Ruskin, Alexander von Humboldt, Lewis Carroll, Cotton Mather among them, but this was the first time she had added a notorious one: Adolf Hitler. Adolf Hitler, added to Anna's head after her encounter with Otto Dienes in Charlotte Hahn's white wooden house at the edge of Lovelock, Nevada, soon began to trouble Anna's sleep. Adolf Hitler, who attributed his development to the harshness of Fate and the Goddess of Suffering, both of which strengthened his will so that he could say, "I owe it to that

period that I grew hard and am still capable of being hard."
Adolf Hitler, who was rejected when he tried to apply to the
Vienna Academy because he belonged, said the rector, not
to the world of painting, but to architecture. This is, of
course, only Hitler's account of this encounter, and who
knows, maybe if we could get to the rector today, whether
or not killed when Adolf Hitler assumed the powers of the
Lord of Death, who knows what his version might be?
Maybe Adolf Hitler had no talent for architecture either.
Adolf Hitler, frustrated painter and architect, haunted
Anna's dreams.

He was not the first frustrated painter Anna had encountered. Nor the first neurotic one. Edvard Munch, shot in the
hand by a woman he had depicted surrounded by swimming sperm, would not walk into a room that was above 70
degrees in temperature and forever after had a thing about
hands. Van Gogh might not have been maddened by his
lack of success with women when he cut off his ear, but
simply angry, or even possibly epileptic. And Hieronymus
Bosch? Either a member of an Adamite sect or a sex fiend
who got his kicks out of sticking people in mussel shells (the
national dish, served with pommes frites, of Belgium). But
now to add Adolf Hitler to the list of those born under
Saturn, who did, after all, eat his children (although clearly
Adolf Hitler had assumed the powers of Saturn himself),
was to switch from benevolent to malevolent creativity. For
who is to say, Anna pondered, that it was not creative of
Hitler to try to make a Hell on earth, to reverse the physical
structure of the earth's anatomy, to take the hot bowels of
fire smoldering below, responsible for earthquakes and
volcanic eruptions, and bring the catastrophic heat buried in
the earth up to consume anyone with enough Jewish blood
to meet the requirements of the Nuremberg Laws? Cotton
Mather, witch burning in New England, had never thought
so big. But Cotton Mather, perhaps tinged slightly with the
notorious, remained for Anna, compared with Adolf Hitler,
still in the noteworthy category.

Now, back at Cotton Mather's Harvard, she was obsessed by Charlotte Hahn's Germany. In Charlotte Hahn's parlor, somewhat darkened by the large tree, was a reproduction of a painting that had been very famous throughout Germany: Arnold Böcklin's *Toteninsel*, Island of the Dead. Arnold Böcklin, though born in Switzerland, was claimed by the Germans. *Toteninsel* had hung in the chancellery of the Third Reich, from which it disappeared in 1945. Who took Arnold Böcklin's *Toteninsel*, only one, admittedly, of five versions that he had made (one of which Anna had seen in New York's Metropolitan Museum); who took it out of the chancellery of the Third Reich? Who hung it there to begin with? Why did Charlotte Hahn choose Arnold Böcklin's *Toteninsel* to hang in her parlor — the white shrouded figure, presiding over a garland-draped coffin, rowed by a mysterious boatman across a dark river to a rocky island dominated by cypress trees and funerary vaults? Death. Death. The Germans seemed obsessed with it. Arnold Böcklin had also called the Island of the Dead *A Still Place*, *A Silent Island*, and *Island of the Graves* and he told someone, "It shall become so quiet that you are frightened by a knock at the door." Whose knock would come at the door? Had Arnold Böcklin, painting *Toteninsel* in the 1880s, heard in the future Gestapo knocks at Jewish doors?

Continuing her research on Arnold Böcklin's predecessor, Caspar David Friedrich, in Widener Library, Anna realized that she had not noticed how many funerary ruins he had painted. His mother, like Anna's, had died when he was seven. When he was thirteen his brother Christoffer, one year younger, drowned, as Caspar David tried to save him. At the end of his life he had a stroke and, with a paralyzed hand, did a series of works in sepia in which owls perch on coffins, or in which lonely prehistoric dolmens, ancient cairns, sit like people for their portraits.

These dolmens, known as *Hünengräber*, giant graves, spoke to Friedrich's sense of infinite time and immortality. His biographers, Anna knew, especially Börsch-Supan, had seen in every element, every tree leaf, every shaft of moonlight, a specific Christian symbolism that drew on a pietistic North German Protestantism. Of the cross on Rügen, for example, Börsch-Supan had written: "The cross raised up on the rock shows the ship drifting on the troubled waters the way towards dry land (that is, the way to death) while the full moon, a symbol of Christ, illuminates the sea. The anchor suggests the hope of resurrection." Anna had always thought Börsch-Supan carried this to extremes. A ship on the high seas in full sail was interpreted by Börsch-Supan as "probably . . . a symbol of the Christian religion, the three masts making an allusion to the Trinity." Of *View of a Harbour*, Börsch-Supan wrote: "The harbour, with some ships at anchor and others returning to port as night descends, is an image of the security that lies in death. The crescent of the waxing moon represents Christ."

Anna simply did not believe Börsch-Supan. The moon, after all, was Robert Graves's White Goddess, the first member of the moon trinity, goddess of birth and growth. The moon trinity included of course the Full Moon of the red goddess of love and battle, and the black goddess of death and divination of the Old Moon, but the White Goddess was the New Moon of birth and growth. The moon was the Queen of Heaven, according to Apuleius' *Golden Ass*, giving off *feminine light*, and she wore garlands of flowers on her head, and a mirrored reflective circlet on her forehead, borne by serpents on either side, serpents such as Anna and Kurt had encountered at Pyramid Lake. It may have been the moon goddess, Pasiphaë, in the form of Ariadne, her younger self, who had Orpheus torn to pieces by a pack of drugged women, intoxicated, Graves said, by ivy, or sacred toadstools, because he was worshiping Apollo, the sun god. And Ariadne/Arianrhod, who appears in the 107th Triad as the Silver-circled daughter of Don, was the mother of the Divine Fish-Child Dylan, who becomes Llew Llaw Gyffes, who receives a name and a set of arms from his mother when, if it had been a patriarchal society, they would have come from the father. And as Robert Graves made very clear, Llew Llaw had no father.

So it was not too unlike the Virgin Birth, but still it was not

fair, thought Anna, for Börsch-Supan to limit the moon to
Christ. The moon did not belong only to Christ, nor was a
harbor, a simple harbor, to which Friedrich had returned
after a trip to the Baltic Sea, a death image of security. No.
Caspar David Friedrich transcended even Christianity. Caspar David Friedrich's landscapes were mystical images that
spoke to all human beings, Christian or not, as the moon,
source of magical and pagan rites since the beginning of
mankind, spoke to all human beings — the spinner and
weaver of Time knitting its silvery threads into the warp and
woof of existence. Anna had just returned, after all, from
Pyramid Lake, which, like Friedrich's paintings of the island
of Rügen, existed in the absolute time of perfect silence.

Given all this, it was not the moon as symbol of Christ
that had brought Anna to Caspar David Friedrich. It was the
silence. Surely it was not death. Yet Arnold Böcklin, only a
few years after Friedrich's visits to Rügen, had painted the
Toteninsel and called it *A Silent Island,* and the silence of the
Toteninsel had meant death to Arnold Böcklin. And where
did the connection lead, from Arnold Böcklin's knock at the
door of silence to the six million? How did the German
successors of Caspar David Friedrich and Arnold Böcklin get
to the apocalyptic fires of Auschwitz, compounding the fate
of Cotton Mather's witches millions of times over, lighting a
witch pyre that brought Hell up to earth?

Anna was looking for the thread. Her insatiable curiosity
made it necessary for her to find the thread, to comprehend
the incomprehensible. Joanna Wilkens had helped her to
find the plane beyond this world where all the souls were
standing. But she still couldn't comprehend this world, still
couldn't understand how one man, who (if she was to
believe the words of his valet in a movie called *Our Hitler* by
Hans-Jürgen Syberberg, just then playing at the Brattle
Theater) wore brown shoes with his black suits; how a man
who wore brown shoes with his black suits could exterminate human beings like vermin. Anna had to find out how
all those Germans participating in the Final Solution could
suspend humanity, could look at other human beings, who

after all had two eyes, two ears, one nose, one mouth, two arms, two legs, and one trunk, male or female, with suitably characteristic parts in between, and under that a spirit that could not be extinguished even by the hellfires and poisonous showers of Auschwitz, Anna had to find out how these other human beings could let it happen. Otto Dienes had looked quite human. But Anna had not noticed the color of his shoes.

The passion of Kurt Hahn and Anna Bernstein was growing. Denis de Rougemont, scholar of love, maintaining that no passion is conceivable in a world where everything is permitted, that passion presupposes, between subject and object, a third party constituting an obstacle to their embrace — a King Mark separating Tristan from Iseult — has given us the clue to the growing and expanding passion of Kurt and Anna. Adolf Hitler, in the specific person of Otto Dienes, blood relative to Kurt Hahn through his mother, stood between Kurt Hahn and Anna Bernstein.

Before this new unholy trinity, the trinity of Kurt, Anna, and Andrew had diminished. Kurt no longer made even a pretense at companionable friendship *à trois*. Maddened by his frustration at the barrier Anna had erected between them, his passion made ever more urgent by her withdrawal, Kurt now tried to find Anna alone, to charm and beguile her with wit and words, to impress her with intellect, to attract her with masculinity, to stifle her doubts with lovemaking. But Anna, though hopelessly in love with Kurt Hahn, felt a lump in her throat that had not, since Otto Dienes's rasping question, dissolved. Anna Bernstein could not perceive Kurt Hahn without Otto Dienes's shadow between them. She looked at Kurt Hahn, at his curved lips and Western languor, and yearned for him. She felt separated from Kurt Hahn as by an abyss that seemed primarily physical, for her spirit and psyche, after all, were already at one with him. Yet she could not join him over the barrier, for if she did, she would fall and sink, into the bowels of the earth, into the hellfires Adolf Hitler had brought up to the top, which had not yet perhaps fully subsided on the earthly level, for Otto Dienes had traversed from Argentina to Lovelock, Nevada, across that very terrain.

In Anna Bernstein's diary, some time around February 1980, we read, penciled carefully in red:

> For love is a perpetual flux, an anguish of the soul, a warfare, every lover a soldier, a grievous wound is love still, & a Lover's heart is Cupid's quiver, a consuming fire, an inextinguishable fire. As Aetna rageth, so doth Love, and more than Aetna, or any material fire. Vulcan's flames are but smoke to this. For Fire, saith Xenophon, burns them alone that stand near it, or touch it; but this fire of Love burneth and scorcheth afar off, and is more hot and vehement than any material fire; 'tis a fire in a fire, the quintessence of fire. For when Nero burnt Rome, as Callisto urgeth, he fired houses, consumed men's bodies and goods; but this fire devours the soul itself, and one soul is worth 100,000 bodies. No water can quench this wild fire.

All those fires. Anna Bernstein was consumed by the fire of her passion for Kurt Hahn, a fire much worse than the volcanic fire that so concerned Alexander von Humboldt, a fire worse than the fire of Aetna coming up from the bowels of the earth, which was itself not unlike the fires of Adolf Hitler at Auschwitz, which were worse than all the fires of all the volcanoes because they were the fires of hate. Anna Bernstein's passion fire was burning her up. Worse, she was separated from Kurt Hahn by the hellfires of Adolf Hitler. Fires all around her. Within her and outside her, waiting to swallow her up both ways. Anna Bernstein, in Cotton Mather's Cambridge, burning up with passion for Kurt Hahn, threatened by the hellfires of Cotton Mather/ Otto Dienes/Adolf Hitler, began to fear that she herself would soon go up in smoke. She would vanish like the Cheshire Cat, leaving only a wisp of smoke, rather than a grin, suspended in the cool Cambridge sky.

Kurt Hahn, if asked, might have admitted to feeling no less infected with the love disease, though less feverishly burned. For Kurt, love was at times Rilke's two solitudes, protecting and touching and greeting each other. In this, love for him was quiet and silent, like a painting by Caspar David Friedrich. But then, when otherwise moved, he was like Keats, writing: "Love is my religion — I could die for that — I could die for you. My Creed is Love and you are its only tenet — You have ravish'd me away by a Power I cannot resist; and yet I could resist till I saw you; and even since I have seen you I have endeavored often 'to reason against the reasons of my Love.' I can do that no more — the pain would be too great — My love is selfish — I cannot breathe without you."

Kurt Hahn and Anna, then; both were consumed in their own way, alternating hot and cold between estrangement and union. On certain days, when neither could survive separation, they would come together like two cells uniting and blending, to make love in Anna's sunlit room, to walk beside the Charles, to take the train over the Salt and Pepper Bridge into Boston. At other times — always at Anna's provocation — they separated. For though Anna carried Kurt Hahn's physical image, his blond wisps of hair, his Western hat and swagger, his tender hands, around inside her like a holy visitation, it weighed heavily and, like an unwanted pregnancy, terrified her with its daily growth.

Kurt Hahn's entire physical presence was so internalized for her that two beings, one with a visible and one with an invisible shell, passed under the gates of God and learning in the early days of the year 1980. Joanna Wilkens would have said Anna was transporting more than just a physical image; she had swallowed Kurt Hahn's astral envelope; he had, in a sense, willed her to, surrendered his being so completely to her out of his passion that he inhabited her. Two astral envelopes then, Kurt's and Anna's own, walked in Anna's body across Harvard Yard under the bare trees, zigzagging sometimes crazily across the paths, in the vain effort of one to displace the other. Anna wanted to push Kurt Hahn's astral envelope back over the gulf. The separation of his spirit from his shell was matched by her own.

Her body, doubly inhabited, walked around Harvard Yard always at the edge of the hellfire abyss, yet still another part of her own astral envelope had jumped over the gap, to be carried by Kurt Hahn himself. Four of them, each astral envelope doubled and exchanged, or perhaps halved and evenly divided (it is hard to be sure with astral envelopes), encountered each other on the walks of Harvard Yard, Anna in Kurt, Kurt in Anna, the gulf of hellfire separating them, Otto Dienes between. Yet the interchange of spirit and presence had taken place, and they were in thrall, as lovers always are, to that vision of oneness offered by the love disease. The virus of romantic love, most dangerous of illnesses, had seized them. Recovery was questionable — the negative prognosis compounded by the very existence of Otto Dienes and Adolf Hitler's brown shoes.

To all this Andrew Hanson bore troubled witness. It was not so much that he still harbored hopes of winning Anna's love. He had settled for what he knew he had — warm affection and companionship. For Anna spent more and more of her time with Andrew Hanson in her troubled double-presenced state, playing absent-mindedly with Celeste, walking Lucinda, sitting in the plant-filled bay window, and talking to him about Darwin.

— I think Darwin had the right idea, Andrew, she would say with the black rabbit in her lap. Maybe chance nature, chance nature is responsible for it all. Men invent their gods, gods didn't invent men. And look how many gods there have been. The Paiutes think we all came up from the bowels of the earth, and the Old Testament God sits on the Sistine ceiling with a white beard and creates Adam with one finger. Who's right? And there's the moon goddess besides, only Börsch-Supan says she's Christian. The Germans fuss a lot about Christians, it seems to me. Friedrich wasn't nearly as Christian as Börsch-Supan thinks. And then, no matter what religion you are, when you're an astral envelope, you sit on another plane. Everyone goes there. The occultists say evil people are simply punished by their thoughts. That's their eternal Hell. I wonder if Hitler took his brown shoes.

Andrew Hanson, in those early days of 1980, was beginning to worry about Anna. So kaleidoscopically did thoughts sometimes tumble out of her that if Andrew did not listen carefully he was whisked from Alexander von Humboldt and the Humboldt Mountains to Cotton Mather burning witches and back to the silence of Pyramid Lake or of Caspar David Friedrich without punctuation. Anna's mind seemed to traverse time and space, life and death, all at once. Like Emerson, who confronted angel and apple in the ether, and eating the apple, ate the world, Anna was trying to swallow all existence. God and Learning had been aptly named on the gates of Harvard Yard.

— Come, Anna, Andrew would say, you're working too hard. All these Germans. Let Caspar David Friedrich go for a while, and forget Effie and Ruskin (who appeared increasingly in Anna's self-bemused chatter, for Andrew was often now someone she talked at, rather than to).

Her sense of her own womanliness was tried too by this blocked love she felt. She wondered at her attraction to Effie and Ruskin, nor did she know why she was always so concerned with Charles Dodgson and Alice Liddell, except that Alice and Effie were *young* women, each still a child/woman, as she often felt herself to be. These others, however, were dealing with men who were surely afraid of women. Kurt was not afraid of Anna, that was clear. But Anna was afraid of Anna, and the fictional Alice's powers were ones she wished she had access to.

— Play chess with me then, she would tell Andrew.

And they would sit in the sunny window on Trowbridge Street with the animals romping about them, Celeste always looking for a hug and dropping tiny rabbit pellets on the floor. Anna would try to play chess as maybe Napoleon had, with Mälzel's automaton in Vienna, as hard as she could, but Andrew was better, and she usually lost. She did not, however, wrap a shawl around Andrew's face and chest, as Napoleon had the automaton, suspecting an opening for a hidden player. Andrew was real, but playing Napoleon gave Anna the sense of control she needed.

— I'm Napoleon, Andrew, and I'm checking your king. I'm capturing your red knight at move seven.

Entry in black and red in Anna's diary:

"I don't know," Alice said doubtfully. "I don't want to be anybody's prisoner. I want to be a Queen."

"So you will, when you've crossed the next brook," said the White Knight. "I'll see you safe to the end of the wood — and then I must go back, you know. That's the end of my move."

❧❦❧

Andrew could take Anna only so far. Andrew was the White Knight, but Kurt had progressed to King, and Anna wanted to be Queen. Yet she was neither Wasp aristocrat nor Aryan, and blood lines were a necessity for royalty, were they not? Unless, of course, she crossed the brook and found the golden crown.

There seemed to be no golden crowns available in the Boston/Cambridge area that winter, and the brook — as she walked restlessly along the Charles in the cold snow — steamed with hellfires, whether of Cotton Mather or Otto Dienes/Hitler she could not tell. It was Andrew who accompanied Anna, at her request, to Cotton Mather's grave early in February, and who stood with her on Copps Hill, looking out through the bare trees at the gray waters of Boston Harbor, floating with patches of ice and snow. Anna had waylaid him leaving class.

— Come with me to Cotton Mather, she said, wild-eyed.

The revelation of Cotton Mather's resting place in an ordinary Boston tourist guide had excited her urgently. Cotton Mather, said the blue book on which was printed

NEW ENGLAND, A Handbook for the Independent Traveller, was buried at Copps Hill Cemetery on Snowhill Street, not far from Paul Revere's Old North Church, where the one-if-by-land, two-if-by-sea lanterns had been hung. The Old North Church faces Salem Street. Salem Street, which, at the turn of the century, had housed the North End's immigrant Jewish section, pushcarts and all. But the North End had started out with Cotton Mather living (as if to prove there is no coincidence in this world, that all is laid out according to Providential design) on the very spot on North Street where Paul Revere's house now stands. Cotton Mather and Paul Revere — the one a horseman and silversmith, great patriot, savior of his country; the other a demonologist and smallpox physician — in the same spot (albeit about a hundred years apart) on the great continent of the New World.

And then, and then, Paul Revere finally got buried at the Old Granary Burying Ground on Tremont Street along with John Hancock and Samuel Adams and Benjamin Franklin's parents. And, of course, Elizabeth Goose, or Vergoose, or Vertigoose, the famous Mother. But Cotton Mather had been buried on Copps Hill, and when Anna and Andrew arrived, they had to look up and down all the rows of aged gray stones to find him. Pre-Revolutionary gravestones, like small irregular children's slates, each topped with a winged skull, each beginning Here Lies . . .

But then, when they found him,

— Oh. Poor Cotton Mather, said Anna.

For he had not even been able to claim his own bit of earth. No. Cotton Mather was buried in the very same tomb with Increase and Samuel, his daddy and son, all three together, in a red clay box labeled *Mather tomb*, to which had been affixed the irregular gray stone with which they had been marked when first they died, on which, again, all three names were carved, with appropriate dates, died 1723, died 1728, died 1785. All together, even at the beginning. Cotton Mather, who, according to a nearby plaque, had published 444 books, had entered Harvard at twelve, could at age eleven write and speak Latin (and had begun Hebrew grammar), who had proclaimed to visitors over his library door "Be short," Cotton Mather, whose father had presided over Harvard from 1685 to 1701, and who suggested that a competing college be named for Elihu Yale, who had judged who was and who was not a witch, who could light the pyres, Cotton Mather after death could not command room of his own.

✒ 4 ✒

WHEN the brown-paper-wrapped package arrived at Mount Sinai Hospital for Anna Bernstein, the nurse on the psychiatric floor checked it for possibly harmful contents, then brought it to Anna in the yellow room. Anna, for once, was not playing chess, but reading. Since things in this world are so remarkably arranged for coincidental effect, it was only fitting that she should be reading, in the copy of *The Grimm Brothers' Fairy Tales* she had brought with her to the hospital, the story of Rapunzel, for the package, once opened, revealed the portrait of a young girl with long blonde hair so titled by the artist, one Kurt Hahn. That the young girl strongly resembled Anna Bernstein was not strange either, since Anna herself only some months before, when she and Kurt Hahn were virulently infected with love, had posed for the picture in preparation for Kurt Hahn's March showing at his Boston gallery on Boylston Street.

There was no note, but then, a note under these circumstances would surely have been redundant. Kurt Hahn had said all he wished to say in the portrait itself.

Anna had posed for the picture on an afternoon late in February, shortly after she visited Cotton Mather, when winter snow covered the brick sidewalks of Cambridge and turned Harvard Yard into a Hallmark Christmas card. On that day, propelled toward each other by their shared illness, Anna and Kurt made love on a tiny couch before yet another fire, lit earlier by Kurt Hahn in the small fireplace of his studio apartment near Central Square, a welcoming, warming hearth of a fire, untouched by the dread associations of Anna's increasing fiery nightmares. There, melting into each other as though they could never again ungraft, they had a brief respite from their intermittent and chronic estrangements, the pattern of meeting and parting that was directly dependent on whether or not Otto Dienes's shadow had touched Anna that day or, more probably, on a restless night before.

Anna was, that February afternoon, Kurt Hahn's golden girl, and afterward she sipped hot chocolate foaming with whipped cream mixed lovingly with his own hand, turned into schlag, as Charlotte Hahn had taught him when a child in Nevada. While she was sipping the chocolate, after the lovemaking, after they had melted together with their passion, Anna had a look of utter contentment on her face — that of a woman satisfied to the full by her lover, that of a child delighted with an ultimate treat, double satisfactions for the child/woman that she was — and Kurt had painted her, quickly, before the expression changed, just her head and shoulders, draped in his white terry robe, and finished the painting afterward from a memory that fused her momentary expression with his own deep feeling for her.

It all showed. Anna sat and looked at the canvas, almost anachronistically painted in oils, rather than the more recent and popular acrylic, figurative, but touched with expressionist fervor, this part actually a style much in favor then in an art world governed more by fashion than feeling. She recognized on the face painted there all the interior emotions that had filled her up that day. For Kurt Hahn had indeed painted a vessel filled to the brim with contentment, and someone else, sitting in the yellow room observing the pale girl with the wild eyes, might not even have noticed, since that contentment was long gone, the resemblance between the harried figure whose world was now circumscribed by those yellow walls and the golden girl whose blonde hair streamed over her shoulders on the 12 x 16 canvas propped in her lap. It is hard to say how long she sat, almost comatose, in a manner familiar to those who knew her there, staring at the canvas, self-doubled through this pictorial counterpart, recognizing and then losing the image, as though this other person, that other part, had been owned and then disowned, and was now, distantly, reaching back for reclamation, much as the spirits had reached across that other plane when she had visited them with Joanna Wilkens.

Dr. Linnell found her that way and, after taking a blood test to readjust her medication, sat with her for a while. Anna preferred Dr. Linnell to Dr. Gotthard. Descended from the famous English artist John Linnell, of whose works Victor Allingame had spoken with feeling and appreciation, he did not have Dr. Gotthard's strange commitment to wholeness. Rather, Dr. Linnell accepted the imperfect with a tolerance and blitheness that was reassuring to those poor people whose difficulties, whether mental, emotional, physiological or psychological, chemical or cultural, had landed them, society never knew which or why, in places like the yellow room. To Dr. Linnell, madness was natural, and this simple *a priori* perception made it possible for Anna to relax with him. Unlike Dr. Gotthard, he expected nothing of her. Dr. Gotthard, true to his name, had come to symbolize the Alpine pass at the top of the mountain. She could never climb to Dr. Gotthard's heights of sanity, would always fall back down again from where he wanted her to be. Dr. Linnell made no such demands.

— Do you like it? he asked Anna. It looks a lot like you, I think, but there's a little too much paint in the way.

— No, Anna answered slowly. That's what gives it its character. He was writing about Nolde, you know. It's a bit Nolde-ish.

— Nolde?

— German. He got mixed up, I think.

— What do you mean?

Dr. Linnell was watching Anna and comparing her at the same time with her portrait, allowing the heavily painted likeness to make its own way, to let the paint have its say and tell him what Kurt wanted to say about the subject of Anna. Anna, the golden girl/child/woman, was revealed under the heavy globs of paint as an innocent visionary, wide-eyed and content but also, because Kurt Hahn was good enough to catch both the momentary expression and the fundamental one, with a strangely sober look, a white face with a slash of red across her mouth as though suddenly someone had just introduced her to reality.

— Well, the Nazis thought he was degenerate, and confiscated his paintings in 'thirty-seven, but he didn't understand why they did that to him, because he believed in a German soul, and liked Wagner and Nietzsche. Everyone says he was an anti-Semite himself, but so was Degas, and I like his paintings too. Degas, of course, hated flowers and women and dogs, so it wasn't just Jews. And Dreyfus, of course; he hated Dreyfus.

❦❦❦

On that same early day in February, after visiting Cotton Mather, Andrew had brought Anna to Copley's Restaurant at the Copley Plaza for a treat. Anna was unprepared for the multitudes of hanging plants, greenery trailing in the sunlight, and for the nineteenth-century paintings and prints hung salon-style one above the other, masking the color of the walls on which they hung. These rooms, and there were several, each bedecked with plants, paintings, and old weathered photographs, had a Victorian grace that made her feel she had stepped back into Henry James's Boston, and that he would enter soon, suitably dandified, chatting wittily with John Singer Sargent, just over from London or Paris or wherever, to paint the vaulting of the Boston Public Library across the square, where he would compete with Puvis de Chavannes, who was, in Anna's mind, incomparably superior. The hostess seated them on a banquette beside a wall that like all the others was montaged with art and artifacts of that earlier moment. They ordered snails, and relaxed and luxuriated in the warmth, for a fire was blazing nearby, and the dim grayness of the day had given way to that sunlight turning the ferns transparent all up and down the passageway between the rooms, all of which Anna could see from where she was seated. The arrival of the snails was cause for consternation, and the question was, Where were they? For Andrew and Anna were, after all, on student incomes, and for $6.95 it seemed too bad that the snails, served in small brown china crocks, the openings of which were sealed with bits of pastry, should prove, after the piercing of these doughy seals had taken place, to be scantily disposed at the very bottom of these vessels, with at least three inches of air or empty space, totally unoccupied by anything edible, between the small brown creatures (now dead and swimming in oil rather than butter) and the pastry lids that sealed their temporary tombs.

It was when Anna turned her disappointed face to the wall beside her that she discovered Captain Dreyfus, for he stood erect and proud before a tribunal in a *fin-de-siècle* print, hanging at eye level to her left. All the protagonists were labeled: Colonel Jouaust, Commandant Maxime, Commandant Carrière, Maître Demange, Maître Labori, General Billot, M. Cavaignac, General Zurlinden, M. Hanotaux, General Mercier, Colonel Picquart, General Roget, General Gonse, General Boisdeffre, in the lithograph by Vincent Brooks, Day and Son. Here, before her, was Captain Dreyfus, who had blue eyes and, according to one history of the Jews Anna had just read, "was a man of great personal wealth, a man always correct, a man without vice — in short, a bore," who was being demeaned and humiliated mainly because he was a Jew, and accused of something done by a charming Hungarian named Esterhazy, who was part owner of a house of prostitution that had not been sufficiently lucrative, so he had sold military secrets to the Germans. The Jews were happily accused by Edouard Drumont of conspiring against France. Colonel Picquart, there he was over on the right, had exposed Esterhazy, and someone had said to him, Why should you care about this Jew?

That someone had been a general, but looking over the names of the generals on the lithograph beside her in the plant- and art-filled restaurant on Copley Square, with I. M. Pei's Hancock Tower reflecting the sky in the square outside, Anna could not tell which one of these had made this remark. Zola, of course, was on Dreyfus's side, and had to run off to England before they arrested him for writing "J'accuse," which appeared in five hundred thousand copies of *Aurore* — still not enough, as the Parisians fought over them. Poor Dreyfus went through another trial and was again convicted, with a lesser sentence of ten years. Dreyfus, however, was such a snob, such an Uncle Tom Jew that, it is said, he would have convicted himself, had he sat on the court-martial board, to save the honor of the army. But anyway, after yet another review, he was set free and given the Legion of Honor. But he had been an early Jewish scapegoat. Scapegoat. Once the word came into Anna's head, she could not get it out. When she returned to Widener Library late that afternoon, she decided to research *scapegoat*.

The section on the scapegoat followed, in *The Golden Bough*, upon the section on the Propitiation of Wild Animals by Hunters, which in itself deals with the savage belief in the immortal soul or disembodied spirit of the animal, whose kin will resent the injury done to one of their number, and must be propitiated. Animal souls as well as human souls. Joanna Wilkens hadn't told her about that. Few Cherokee, said Sir James George Frazer, would venture to kill a rattlesnake unless they can't help it, and even then they must atone for the crime by craving pardon of the snake's ghost either in their own person or through the mediation of a priest. Otherwise the rattlesnake chief of the snake tribe would send an avenger of blood to sting the murderer to death. Thinking of Kurt Hahn (though to some extent a Paiute and not a Cherokee) surrounded by snakes at Pyramid Lake, Anna was glad he had not killed one.

This section was followed by Types of Animal Sacrament, which referred to instances in which the animal is not eaten because it is revered, and others in which it is revered because it is eaten. From this she went on to Processions with Sacred Animals, The Transference of Evil to Inanimate Objects, The Transference to Animals, employed as a vehicle for carrying away or transferring the evil, and The Transference to Men, by diverting to them the evils that threatened others. Witches, said Sir James George Frazer, cured diseases this way. Anna wondered if Cotton Mather, concerned as he was with the public dangers of smallpox, had been aware of this beneficial use of witches. Then came The Transference of Evil in Europe, often to trees and birds as well as animals, so if a scorpion stung you, you would, in ancient times, sit on an ass with your face to the tail, or whisper in its ear, "A scorpion has stung me," and the pain would be transferred to the ass. Chapter LVI of *The Golden Bough* dealt with the Public Expulsion of Evils and the Omnipresence of Demons, and told of attempts "to free a whole community from diverse evils that afflict it," and of "Annual expulsions of demons, witches or evil influences" that appear to have been common "among the heathen of Europe." Walpurgis Night, the Eve of May Day, was a good time for running seven times around the houses, yards, and villages of Central Europe and smoking out witches, with bells and pots and pans and dogs barking and yelping. This custom was very big with the Germans of Bavaria and Bohemia even in more recent times, especially in the Böhmer Wald Mountains. After saying all this, Sir James George Frazer finally arrived, in Chapter LVII, at Public Scapegoats and the Expulsion of Embodied Evils.

Anna was glad he had led up to it so logically. The soul, the spirit, Joanna Wilkens had *not* stressed, could also be evil or demonic. Joanna Wilkens had introduced her only to sweet and gentle spirits, who gave domestic advice about changing jobs and buying houses. But the belief in evil spirits, the savage belief in evil spirits, had endured elsewhere.

Sometimes the demons could be taken away in a little ship

or boat. On the island of Ceram (wherever that was) they filled a ship with rice, tobacco, and eggs contributed by all the people of the sick village. Then they hoisted a sail on the ship and someone called out to "all ye sicknesses, ye smallpoxes, agues, measles etc. who have visited us so long and wasted us so sorely" to depart on the ship. The ship would then sail away while the people beat on gongs. From the little ship, it was a natural step to the animal, or scapegoat. For cholera, in India, it was a goat or buffalo (which had to be both female and as black as possible) turned out of the village with grain and cloves and red lead in a yellow cloth on its back. Even the ancient Jews, on the Day of Atonement, the tenth day of the seventh month, would, through a high priest, confess all the iniquities of the Children of Israel over the head of a live goat, and having "transferred the sins of the people to the beast," send it away into the wilderness.

As it happened, Victor Allingame had shown such a creature in class only last week. Victor Allingame had shown *The Scapegoat*, painted by William Holman Hunt out in the desolate landscape, with his long wavy hair, each lock carefully delineated with Pre-Raphaelite accuracy, so that he did, indeed, resemble Botticelli's Venus, the tendrils of her hair winding around her in linear rhythms that pleased even Roger Fry, who hated line, as she rose from the sea.

Poor scapegoat, thought Anna when she saw him. Poor isolated, abandoned, expelled creature. Expulsion was a word Sir James George Frazer used a lot. Expulsion of the demons periodically, sometimes using not a ship or a goat but a person, so that at Onitsha on the Niger, the Reverend J. C. Taylor was witness, on the 27th of February 1858, to the sacrifice of a woman, about nineteen or twenty years of age. Someone like Anna. Someone almost Anna's age had been dragged alive along the ground face downward from the king's house to the river, a distance of two miles, with the crowd yelling Wickedness, Wickedness, so that in the merciless dragging the weight of all their own wickedness was carried away.

The scapegoat could even be divine, as Sir James George Frazer pointed out, thus combining two customs in one, that of the sacrifice of the god to save him from being weakened by mortal age, and that of the general expulsion of sins once a year. There was a further extension of the idea in the custom of Carrying out Death, which occurred in connection with death as the spirit of vegetation, slain in spring and then revivified to new youth. This Vegetative Death became mixed up with the Scapegoat Death, and Sir James George Frazer himself seemed a bit mixed up about these. But what was clear to Anna was that the use of the human scapegoat — in ancient Greece, for example, where a city suffering from famine or plague took an ugly or deformed person and beat him seven times upon the genitals with squills and branches of wild fig trees while they played flutes before burning him and casting his ashes into the sea — was a good way for people to get rid of what they thought was bothering them.

***

— Dreyfus was a scapegoat, Anna said now to Dr. Linnell. Like the six million. All goats, maybe even divine goats. God knows that, I don't.

— God?

— Whether they're divine or not. Maybe dying like that martyred them, made them divine. Or maybe, being blessed and chosen as they always claimed, they were always divine. Maybe I'm divine, Dr. Linnell. She looked at him and giggled with an edge of hurt hysteria. Do I look divine in that painting? Golden angel, he always said, golden angel.

— The artist?

But Anna had closed off, was lost in the picture, running her finger across the red slash of mouth that wounded the white face.

***

Kurt Hahn's exhibition took place in March, not long after
Anna sat for the painting of Rapunzel. The review that
appeared in the leading Boston paper is still folded carefully
into Anna's diary and reads:

> At the Apostle Gallery on Boylston Street the paintings of
> Kurt Hahn remind us that Expressionism, as practiced in
> 1980, can be not only chic but genuine. Hahn's use of paint
> recalls that of the German Nolde, whose works are the subject
> of the artist's Harvard dissertation, but there is also a gentler
> quality to them, as though something of the visionary Ryder
> or even the more dreamy Whistler had crept in from an earlier
> American tradition. After confronting so much neo-emotion
> in the current stylish Expressionist revival, it is a delight to
> find an artist who still *feels*. Despite his clear artistic forebears,
> Hahn's works are not son of anybody. He is much his own
> man. Until April 1.

Anna agreed to accompany Kurt Hahn to his opening at
the Apostle Gallery, and even spent a long time talking to
herself beforehand, scolding herself for holding Kurt Hahn's
ancestry against him. It's as bad, she told herself, as
someone holding your Jewishness against you, to hold his
German grandfather against him. It's group prejudice. It's
unfair. You never even *felt* Jewish until Grandma. You don't
practice it. You know very well that God doesn't distinguish
between spirits. Everyone ends up in the same astral
envelope.

As she told herself these things, the love she felt for Kurt
Hahn raised its clobbered head triumphantly, hoping she
would win the fight and take away the terrible obstacle so
that she and Kurt Hahn could reunite fully, without Hitler's
brown shoes between them. But if we are to believe Denis
de Rougemont, that love was also thriving on this very
impediment, which exacerbated the love pangs at the same
time as it separated the lovers by the hellfire abyss Anna
often felt between them.

By the night of the opening, Anna had stilled the fires
sufficiently to feel she could step over the gulf without
getting burned, could greet Kurt Hahn with true affection

and pride, as well as passion, on the occasion of this showing of his work, always an important moment for an artist, his soul bared, so to speak, to critics and friends, to enemies and well-wishers, to the cruel indifference of those strangers who wander in, devote thirty seconds or less to the labor of years, and walk away again, their faces unmoved, their feelings untouched.

Anna and Kurt started off early from Trowbridge Street to help set up the plastic glasses for the white California wine, to set out some fruit and cheese, to be there for the first arrivals.

Kurt Hahn's thickly painted images lined the walls of the small gallery almost to the point of overcrowding. Soon, however, enough guests arrived to make it difficult to see them, though their bright colors and large expanses were briefly visible through the interstices of the chattering and circulating crowd. It was Kurt Hahn's first show, and he found himself busy greeting and talking, taking compliments and good wishes modestly, almost sheepishly, with the ever-present Western headgear pushed back on his head.

Anna, dominated that evening by supportive feelings, watched his viewers nervously for reactions, acting in general as hostess, greeting newcomers, pointing to Kurt in the crowd, oh yes, he's over there, talking to the lady in the blue dress, there he is, by the big painting in the corner, yes, he just went back to get some glasses, he'll be right out, I'm glad you like them, Kurt will be delighted you came, don't you think they're very strong? Fellow students from the Fogg, with a proprietary pleasure in the actual accomplishment of one of their number — an art historian who could not only write and think about art, but knew how to make it — milled around in the crowd, exchanging pleasantries with the small group of Fogg professors who had also turned out, only those, to be sure, who believed in the *possibility* that a serious scholar could also be a creative artist, that Kurt Hahn, already acknowledged by his professors as a superb scholar, with unique insights and great theoretical gifts, could make real art — it was too early, of course, to say great art, but the first necessity was surely met, that it be real.

This crowd of milling chattering people was, in its way, jealously guarding the evidence of artistic achievement in the provinces, for Boston — whatever it had been in the late nineteenth century, when George de Forest Brush had lived on Brattle Street and breakfasted with John Singer Sargent, when Thomas Dewing had caused his dreaming ladies to hover in spaces filled with green air (weightless, bodiless ghosts who could haunt even the modern eye), when Winslow Homer, thwarted in his passions by yet another lady, one with whom he played croquet and swam at the beach, had gone off finally to Prout's Neck, a part of New England where one could forget all passions but that of the sea and rocks for each other, as well as he for them — Boston, whatever it had been still earlier, when Fitz Hugh Lane, a painter not unlike Anna's Caspar David, had done his first marine paintings in a studio at Tremont Temple, a good friend of Benjamin Champney, who told all about it in *Sixty Years' Memories of Art and Artists,* and Washington Allston, at Cambridgeport across the river, not far from the Fogg Museum, had rolled up his *bête noir,* his life's disappointment, his unfinished *Belshazzar,* and ten years later unrolled it, forcing workmen to enter backward, lest, Medusalike, the vision of it turn them to stone, and Margaret Fuller, chilled by Emerson's sangfroid, had run off to Italy to marry Ossoli, or not marry him, as the rumors go, only to drown with him and their newborn child off Fire Island coming back to see Boston again (Thoreau pacing up and down the beach, mourning her) — Boston was not the same, no longer the artistic center it was, though still, the intellect survived here rather beautifully. In this crowd were not only Victor Allingame, and Bitsy, who never missed any social opportunity (she had long since added those last ancestors to her crewel bedspread), but the geologist who had graced their Thanksgiving table and of whom Victor Allingame, for all that they had little in common, had become rather fond.

Anna, spotting his belly neatly sectioning off a painting with a ripe curve, made a mental note to introduce him to Andrew Hanson, who would arrive later, wistful but loyal, witness to the continuing passion of Anna and Kurt. Entering shortly after, Andrew found himself seized and propelled toward the fat god, who stood near the beverage table, imbibing the grapes of California.

This Silenus was not unknown to Andrew; indeed their contacts had been relatively frequent in the corridors of the various Harvard science departments. Andrew was writing his dissertation on post-Darwinian catastrophism for a close colleague of the gentleman who now appeared, slightly out of joint, in this crowd of milling art lovers, and who quickly launched a happy conversation about volcanic eruption and earth time, based on the recent events at Mt. St. Helens that had been filling the daily news bulletins. Anna, catching wisps of this, thought once more only of the hellfires that had been haunting her, and veered quickly away, over to the other side of the room, where she could recede into formal discussions of paint and color and prophecies about next year's art season (as much a point of discussion in art circles as are the off-the-rack versus *haute couture* speculations that dominate fashion).

When next she drifted by, for Andrew seemed now irretrievably glued to the spot on the floor beside the fat god (who had not yet found a satyr to carry him out of the gallery on his shoulders), the talk had shifted to the moon, which had somehow been more distant from us over four billion years ago. Anna wondered vaguely if Börsch-Supan knew this, or if knowing it could shift his certainty of Christian ownership. Christianity, after all, was only two thousand years old. A mere blink of the eye in earth and moon time. At her own next passing blink, it seemed, the conversation had shifted once again, initiated by the fat god, but quickly engaged by Andrew, who was happy enough to be talking fossils and paleontology to an older colleague while surrounded by aesthetes and humanists who thought the Renaissance happened a long time ago. Andrew's sense of time and history, so conditioned by fossil records and earth age, was something he had tried to transmit to Anna. It offered leveling perspectives to daily life. It made the genre events of the banal even more trivial.

If Anna, he thought, who seemed so impressed by Victor Allingame's ancestors, who seemed so disconcerted by Adolf Hitler's strangely chemical concern with blood, could only really understand ancestry, if she could only listen, even now. There she was, passing refreshments in the crowd.

— Anna, he called, we're talking about something that might interest you.

Anna, handing a glass to yet another fellow student from the Fogg, paused in her activity and briefly joined the two scientists, whose conversation was punctuated with words she had never heard before: prokaryotes, monera, methanogens — Fig Trees in South Africa. The Fig Trees, it seemed, were not however trees but primordial cherts, some of the oldest rocks on earth, about 3.4 billion years old. And the fossils in the Fig Tree cherts were probably prokaryotes, while earlier discoveries had been larger than some paleontologists would have liked them to be, and the wrong shape (spherical) as well. With C^{12}/C^{13} carbon ratios added, the Fig Tree evidence indicated rather conclusively to some scientists that the prokaryotes were indeed 3.4 billion years old. Anna, reading Darwin in her Widener carrel, had begun to understand the unisex fish. Now she was being pushed toward the consideration of a still smaller ancestral root, the prokaryote. She was descended not from an ape, or even a fish, but from a bit of blue-green algae.

Afterwards, when all had drunk their fill of California wine, the descendants of blue-green algae who remained behind — Andrew, Kurt, Anna, and Joanna Wilkens — found their way to the Wursthaus, Anna and Kurt to commune over their first meeting, memorializing it in their hearts over the iconic mustard pot, Andrew and Joanna to attend at the ceremony, Joanna, who had just emerged from yet another séance, and Andrew, always mourning the clear triumph of his rival for Anna's affection, stoically reminding himself that in the larger picture, which would embrace even the primordial cherts, his own unique and vulnerable love for Anna was, precisely in its local and specific character, of no importance to anyone or anything in the world save himself, just another aspect of a universal bonding instinct, cell to cell, chemistry to chemistry, as old as the rocks.

— I thought it went well, Andrew said to Kurt primarily and, as an afterthought, to the group at large.

— Hard to say.

Kurt, his hat pushed forward on his head, his cowboy slouch so exaggerated that he looked almost as though he had come down with stomach pangs (possible, since he had suddenly consumed four thick knockwursts, tenderly decorated for him by Anna in a rite of remembrance with thick globs of Dijon mustard), was feeling as any artist does after an opening, successful or not — let down. The works were there, on the wall, no longer in the studio, public not private, exposed, not protected. Any illusions he had about them, any rationalizations, were now vulnerable to critics, scholars, and collectors. Whatever happened, they were no longer his. Genesis had transpired. Now they were "works of art," for which his name, sprawled ungracefully along the bottom edge, became a label that, depending on the growth or diminution of his own myth or reputation, would offer additional associative insight, or perhaps oblivion. Kurt Hahn, never heard of him, they might sniff, and never notice the painting, any more than did the people who wandered through museums reading the labels of well-known masterpieces. Rembrandt van Rijn (1606–1669). Holland. *Portrait of a Man.* Altman Bequest. Paul Cézanne (1839–1906). France. *Artist's Wife.* Acquisition by Friends of the Museum, 1967. Giovanni di Paolo (c. 1403–1482). Italy. *Adoration of the Magi.* Museum Purchase Fund, 1975.

— I feel, he said finally, as though someone hit me in the belly.

Anna looked concerned.

— You ate too quickly. Or maybe too many.

— Hate the buggers, Kurt murmured, and everyone knew he was not referring to the knockwursts.

Andrew, however, pursued the subject with the happy unawareness of one not privy to the plight of the artist.

— I thought they looked at the paintings a lot, considering how crowded it was.

— I thought they drank a lot of wine, Kurt muttered gloomily.

Joanna Wilkens offered a toast:

— To Kurt.

Glasses of Wursthaus beer were lifted. Kurt Hahn took this a bit more gracefully, grunting and slipping yet further into a slouch, as if he would slide, if permitted, totally under the table.

— They're great, Anna whispered so the others couldn't hear. Don't worry, they're great.

And afterwards, alone with him in her bed, where she had allowed Kurt to spend the night in order to lengthen her reprieve from her own feelings of alienation from him because of Jewish blood and German blood and Otto Dienes and Adolf Hitler, because of Lottie Hahn's Lutheranism and somehow, also, Cotton Mather's witches, because of volcanoes and catastrophes and hellfires and holocausts, in that period of reprieve which was, perhaps, most understandably not really in her mind but in her heart, she could permit herself to show her love, and offer the support he needed for those extensions of himself which hung now abandoned in the darkness on the gallery walls, awaiting once more the responses they might or might not receive from the randomized and not so randomized amalgam that would make up their "public."

In Anna Bernstein's diary in blue and green ink, dated March 28:

> Kurt is a fine artist.
>
> Celeste is getting fat.
>
> Tried to reach Effie.

Anna Bernstein's obsession with Effie had been growing. Anna Bernstein had long identified with Effie for reasons that, as we know, are still hard to decipher. Effie had been, like Anna Bernstein, someone whose mother was, for all necessary purposes, unreachable. Effie's mother, locked into Victorian reticence and purity, had been unable or unwilling to tell her the facts of life. Anna's mother had been lost to her through death, Effie's through social inhibition, yet both Anna and Effie shared somehow, in Anna's eyes, that primal loss.

Sometime in mid-March Anna had prevailed upon Joanna Wilkens to bring her not to a billet reading, but to a séance. Though she had already received from her mother, *en groupe*, so to speak, the message that transmitted Ellen Bernstein's pleasure at Anna's Harvard residence and education, she was strangely shy about reaching her mother again in the privacy of a smaller séance. At a billet reading, as in a lottery, you sat in an auditorium or church building and hoped your number would come through — that the blindfolded medium (feeling your message through the small folded piece of white paper) would be able to connect you, by his touch, his ten fingers, and his mind, with a loved one who had passed over to that other level, invisible but near, generally thought of by laymen, when they believe in it, as Heaven. But a séance! A séance was more personal, more intimate. And a private reading even more so.

Anna felt she had to move slowly. She did not want to lose her mother again after having just found her. To rush in, to try to communicate without time to absorb her feelings, time to allow both Anna and her mother — now reconnected across death in a new relationship — time to get to know each other again, that could not be rushed even between two live people. But at this distance, as mortality and immortality met through, literally, a third party, a medium who had his or her spiritual counterpart, the child guide — often, as we know, of Indian origin, so that America's first inhabitants, the early victims of genocide, still had their role — at this distance it was best to go slowly. Anna asked Joanna Wilkens to bring her to a séance, but not, on this occasion, to try to reach her mother.

— Effie, she said.

— Effie? Joanna looked puzzled. My aunt?

— Well, maybe.

Anna and Joanna were sitting in One Potato Two Potato off Harvard Yard. Through the window she could see the students hurrying to class, their hair and clothes blowing in the March wind. Anna had stopped on the way to Widener, just visible over the Harvard gate opposite the restaurant.

— Ruskin's Effie, if possible. Your Aunt Euphemia knew him, didn't she?

— Yes. But she never knew her. That happened much later, after Effie was long gone and happily married to Millais.

— But the connection surely is there. Let's try. Can we?

— They're *very* long gone, you know. The thing is, they've probably reincarnated by now, or gone on to other spheres. There's a limit to how long they stay reachable. Arthur Conan Doyle sometimes comes back to address the spiritualists as a group, but I never believe it.

Anna looked at Joanna, her white face always drained of blood, as though she herself made the trip back and forth across the barrier between dead and living rather frequently, and asked,

— How can you tell when to believe it and when not?

— It's a sense of it. I think on some rare occasions they hoke it up, to boost attendance. They have no money, and they never capitalize on it. But I think they do like to theatricalize it a bit. I've heard Arthur Conan Doyle, but he's long gone too and I really don't believe he comes back. But the recent ones, that's something else.

— Let's try, can we?

Rising to leave, the two young women made a date for the following week. Joanna would call the medium and arrange for them to be included in a séance.

It was held the following Thursday at the home of the medium himself, this time not a young girl, but a fat man with sparse hair and a ho-ho manner. Anna thought he would have made a good Santa Claus. There were eight people present in the wooden house with the rambling porch on Walker Street in Cambridge. Rundown but homey. The séance participants gathered in the parlor, clearly most of them old friends, chattering about mutual acquaintances and local matters. Two tiny dogs, obviously at home, threaded in and out, greeting people. It could have been a ladies' quilting session, except that there were two men among them.

Then the medium, who had been animatedly greeting people, who had greeted Anna, the newcomer, with dignified formality and a reflective look, and Joanna with all the bluff hearty intimacy due the great-grandniece of a famous medium, summoned them all to a tiny room and seated them around a table, on which stood a trumpet.

The trumpet was tall, and Anna, seated in front of it, could not see the person on the other side. Blocked by the huge conical object, she found herself thinking about the way films handled séances. The trumpet, made of copper or cardboard (though seated so close by she couldn't tell), was like a Hollywood prop. She wanted to ask Joanna what it did, but the room had become hushed. Assistants to the medium, novice occultists, were plugging the door jamb with bits of cloth to keep out the light. Then suddenly they were all plunged into total darkness, and the jolly medium led them in song: Open my eyes, that I may see / Visions of truth Thou hast for me. The same song she had sung at the billet reading. She almost knew the words now. This was followed by several others she didn't know, and then, the medium having worked his psychic energies to a certain point, inspired by the singing and encouragement, like an athlete's warm-up period, began to transmit the voices. The room started to fill with a strange blue-white stuff, like wisps of floating gauze — ectoplasm, Anna learned later from Joanna, which flowed out of the medium's body, out of his mouth, eyes, ears, nose, fingers, but was offered also by the concentrated energies of all the people in the room. The voices boomed out, aided, Anna was told later, by the condensation of psychic energy through the trumpet, which increased their volume.

Anna sat very still in the darkness. They had not been asked to join hands, as they did in the movies, was it *The Ministry of Fear?* But the people in *The Ministry of Fear* were ominous spies. These people were homey New Englanders. Though her hands were free, she had been warned never to reach out to touch anything, no matter what she felt. She could hurt the medium that way, even kill him, because it was electrical energy and he could be burned. A colleague of his had been hospitalized for four months because someone had reached out to touch a spirit. Or maybe the trumpet, which was now flying around the room. Anna sat still. The first voices were those of Masters, carrying small platitudinous messages. Trust in thyself. Believe in thyself. We are all spirits together, each of us, in both worlds. Follow your energies. Trust. Faith. Belief. Inspirational talk. Then the loved ones started to enter, not as fast as they had at the billet reading. Almost everyone in the room had a personal visitation.

Anna sat in darkness, feeling the voices surrounding her, as well as hearing them. The darkness had an edge of gray to it, and a luminosity from the blue light, the ectoplasmic stuff which was by this time still thicker, a substance she wished she could touch, though true to command she kept her hands in her lap. Her pose was relaxed. There was nothing ominous here, nothing eerie, nothing that made her feel she was dealing with ghosts. They were not ghosts but spirits, and spirits were, she discovered once again, at least those who entered this room, gentle and good, simply the universal and immortal remains of human beings who had loved, and still loved.

She felt filled with wonder, literally wonder-full, with none of the ordinariness of the word as it was commonly used, and yet, as she thought of it, no matter who used it, or how, wonderful was filled with joy. But wonder-full, that was still something else again. Wonder-full. The word started resounding in her head, circling the darkness that paradoxically lit up her mind in this concentrated auditory bowl, almost blocking out the voices booming at her from one part of the room or the other as people heard the prosaic messages from their loved ones. Love you. Take good care of the kids. Glad the operation was successful. Don't worry, just take that job. Everyday things that mattered to the solid presences seated around the table. Assurances from those to whom these things were no longer pertinent. The spirits had lost their bodies, their families and friends, their jobs and money, their homes and habits; all the banal daily concerns had been erased and they had been left floating in their astral envelopes, more omniscient than those who remained tied to fleshly substance, able to look a bit into the future and give advice, but not too much, Joanna Wilkens had told her. They were only spiritual vestiges of human beings, hardly gods.

Aunt Euphemia came through. Anna, still thinking about the spirits, and hearing them, as it were, with only one ear, was suddenly alert as Joanna was summoned. But this Effie made no mention of Ruskin's Effie, just a cryptic comment to Joanna about continuing her own spiritual studies, and a soft welcome to Anna for her interest and belief. No Ellen Bernstein. Nothing more for Anna that day. Ellen Bernstein would not come till Anna was ready for her.

<hr />

Cambridge
August 10, 1980

Ms. Anna Bernstein
Klingenstein Clinical Center
Mount Sinai Hospital
100th Street and Madison Avenue
New York, N.Y. 10029

Dear Anna,

These people are really the end. I don't know how or why I put up with them. The book on Millais drags on and on, and production is now so far behind schedule that I probably won't be able to claim publication credit for it during the next academic year. The university loves all that, you know. The more titles one has after one's name the better; never mind the quality, I sometimes think. The old publish-or-perish refrain. I know that as a full professor I'm exempt from all that — I've much less pressure than the younger people — but I still would like to see it all put to bed, all the footnotes and illustrations and nonsense wrapped up, and the book between two covers on a shelf somewhere. You, dear girl, with your insatiable appetite for books, will appreciate my feelings. I remember so well how you seemed to eat them like popcorn.

Do please excuse me for not getting to the hospital. You must know how impossible it is to escape from Bitsy in the summer — she is so preoccupied with the sea and the Cape, and unless I really have a good excuse, as, if my publishers were in New York rather than in Boston, it's hard for me to get away. I must work on these book problems in town all week and then join her with the children on weekends at the Cape. But I know you, my dear sweet Anna, understand all too well, and I know you know I am thinking of you, and wishing you well, and seeing your sweet earnest face and intelligent eyes in my classroom, and hoping you will be well and back by fall.

My warmest affection,

Victor

P.S. Anna, my dear, I know what our relationship has been to you. Be brave, dear girl, and soon we will be back together again.

Cambridge
August 12, 1980

Ms. Anna Bernstein
Mount Sinai Hospital
Klingenstein Clinical Center, 7th Floor
New York, N.Y.

Dearest Anna–

As I told you when I visited the other day, I think you're getting along beautifully. You were right to start attending those crafts sessions they have there. I love the little clay pot you painted for me. I've planted a few bits of ivy in it and placed it in the sunny window where we so often sat together, and have sternly and irrevocably informed Celeste that she must not eat it. Anna dear, I wish I could convey to you some of the time sense I have, of a world so long and so old that we and all our small specific everyday problems cannot ever matter as much as we think they do, in the larger sense. I think it's knowing geological time that's always given me a perspective on things. When something really gets to me, I think of how unimportant it is, in terms of the world's life, how unimportant maybe even we ourselves are. Not that I mean to make less of man's achievements, but we live with such incredibly complex social pressures today. Maybe we should care a bit less about the rigmarole of systems we've created, and more about the *real* world, whatever indeed that is — nature's, God's, who knows? Ours, I think, is the artificial part, the man-made part, and that is coming apart a bit at the seams in this millennial moment. So here we are, like the medieval millennialists, awaiting the end of the world, whizzing toward the beginning of the 21st century, the completion of two millennia since Christ, and wondering whether our star, earth's star, will blow itself up and leave those astral selves you speak of floating around forever in the universe, with no earth to return to. Don't mean to depress you, Anna, only to say that you are someone with joy, and you should not let the systems and the pressures of the systems get to you, because men have made them all up, along with their cultures and civilizations, and sometimes, often, they've had the wrong end of the stick, so why should you temper your great joy because of their shortcomings? You're too valuable, sweetheart, and have too much to live for, and anyway, it's only 1980, so there is, I hope, still time.

Be well, Anna love, and remember that I'm looking forward to your return to Cambridge and to our morning breakfasts in the sun with Celeste, Samantha, Red, Bony, Lucinda, and even Lettie, all of whom send their warmest love.

As always,

Andrew

August 15, 1980

Ms. Anna Bernstein
Klingenstein Clinical Center
Mount Sinai
New York, N.Y.

Dear Anna —

Love love love love love love love love love love love love
love love love love love love love love love love love love
love love.

Kurt

Anna Bernstein, reading her mail on the seventh floor of the
Klingenstein Clinical Center, was waiting for Dr. Linnell to
appear. She had spent the morning recording in her journal
the following passage:

*"Come, my head's free at last!" said Alice in a tone of
delight, which changed into alarm in another moment,
when she found that her shoulders were nowhere to be
found: all she could see, when she looked down, was an
immense length of neck, which seemed to rise like a stalk
out of a sea of green leaves that lay far below her.*

*"What can all that green stuff be?" said Alice. "And
where have my shoulders got to? And oh, my poor hands,
how is it I ca'n't see you?"*

Interrupted by the receipt of the three envelopes, again
arriving (as if by Providential design on the part of the
United States Postal Service) in unison, she read each with
speculative interest and was about to record some more
when Dr. Linnell entered.

Anna's face, looking remarkably unharassed, much as she
had looked when she first arrived in Cambridge, elicited
several approving murmurs from the good doctor, to whom
she was beginning to transfer warm feelings, and for whom
she appeared as a wonderful example of the still useful

therapy, regardless of revisionist thinking in these areas, of electroshock treatment. Her mind, and her problems, had, in a sense, been cleared, and despite certain recent erasures, a new lucidity could be seen to emerge.

— You're looking very well today, my dear.

— Today's a good one.

— Mail?

— All of them.

Since Dr. Linnell still knew comparatively little about Anna's love life, this response meant not very much, but it was succeeded by some indications that Anna, for the first time, might soon be willing to talk a bit more volubly than before.

— None of them has changed, she continued.

— Have you?

— I'm not too sure about my neck, but I think going back to Grandma was in it.

— Grandma?

— Yes. For Passover. Victor had Thanksgiving and Kurt got Christmas. I had phoned Grandma a lot, but I hadn't been back to Brooklyn. Then I decided to give Grandma Passover instead of taking off for Easter, you see. It meant turning down Andrew, but I felt I owed it to Grandma. And I had to see how it related to Cotton Mather. Brooklyn, I mean. And Poland.

— Poland?

— Yes, of course. She shrugged impatiently.

Sometimes Dr. Linnell was not nearly as perceptive as she gave him credit for.

— Grandma was from Poland. Victor's roots are Cotton Mather, but mine are Poland. Maybe even nine hundred years. Only I have nothing to do with Zero Mostel.

— Mostel?

— He preferred to be an artist, you know, but still *Fiddler* was one of the best things he did. But I probably would have related more to his art. *Fiddler* was hard for me.

III

✿ I ✿

THE JEWS had been in Poland for over nine hundred years. This should have been long enough to set down roots, to Polonize, to assimilate, or whatever, before the Nazi occupation. A lot of them had arrived there as a result of persecutions elsewhere — Germany during the Crusades, Austria at the end of the fifteenth century. The nobles encouraged them and their banking activities. But the Church distrusted them, because the Church itself did not get to Poland until 966 and feared the Jews would set a bad example, keeping the still young Christian roots from grabbing hold. All this Anna learned shortly before leaving for Brooklyn, when in the course of her research on the Jews of Poland she ran into the canonical law of the Church Council of Breslau in 1267, which enjoined the Jews residing in the diocese of Gnessen to live "separated from the general dwelling place of the Christians by a hedge, wall or ditch." Under threat of excommunication, Christians were not to "invite Jews or Jewesses as their table companions or to eat or drink with them." And they had to wear specially shaped hats, and then, finally, to be sure they were still distinguished from the rest of the population, a red cloth sewn onto the left side of their clothes.

So the yellow star of Hitler had, in effect, been there for a long time. The Jews had been set apart, differentiated. Many people would say they themselves encouraged this. Once set apart, they kept to their own laws, their own religious and cultural traditions, their own moralities, their own sense of why we are on this earth, and what our role is, and what is God's role. And God, of course, held them together, and made it bearable to be set apart and special.

Chosenness, Anna thought, could offset the pain of the scapegoat, if he (the scapegoat) really believed in it. Anna read about blood-libel, in which the Jews were believed to have stabbed the Host and made it bleed. The first time this happened in Poland, in the fourteenth century, the Archbishop of Posen condemned the rabbi and thirteen elders to death by being burned alive. And this was earlier, she thought, than Cotton Mather's witches. Though the newly rising burghers and peasants hated and resented them, the Jews were often befriended by nobles and kings. One Polish fourteenth-century king, Kasimir the Great, was especially kind to them, restoring their rights, and living on in Jewish legend as a great and good king. Kasimierz, near Cracow, was named for him, and became a major Jewish center.

Depending on who was in power, the Jews fared better or worse in Poland. The massacres of 1648 were forerunners of the pogroms that brought the wave of immigrants to New York's Lower East Side from the turn of the century on. Anna's grandmother had come over during this exodus, a final admission that, after nine hundred years in Poland, the Jew had once again to move on.

Anna, sitting in Widener Library, with the histories of Polish Jews in her lap, visualized Harvard Yard outside and wondered if Cotton Mather and the Poles who burned the rabbi had had much in common.

— They all got burned and killed, she said to Andrew later that afternoon at tea.

— Who?

He was feeding Celeste first.

— The Polish Jews, in the fourteenth century.

— Are you into *that* now?

Andrew studied Anna carefully. Earnest, troubled eyes

looked out of the golden head. The slender body wrapped as always in a flowing Indian dress seemed now a harbinger of the approaching spring.

— I'm going home for Passover, Andrew. I'm sorry about Easter.

Andrew achieved something between a shrug and a sigh.

— I thought you would.

— How? How could you know?

— I just thought you would.

— I'll come visit your family some other time, Andrew, maybe during the summer. But I want to see Grandma. I must.

Anna, Andrew knew, had been building up like a volcano. The knowledge and ideas she devoured in Widener Library were piling into a combustible mass. She was overloaded. Kurt and Germany, he knew very well, were part of it. Now she was adding the Polish Jews. The conflagration that would result might touch on Cotton Mather but could exceed it a millionfold. Andrew could only think of it in terms of geology.

Kurt felt even more abandoned at Anna's plan to return home. For a few days after his opening there had been some sense of love acknowledged and recognized. Anna had tried to put Otto Dienes and Lottie Hahn inside a tiny closed box, one of the many she always imagined installed in her brain, some of which opened and closed at the most awkward and unexpected moments, so that she never knew what she would remember and what forget. It was worse than with most people — who often simply forget the name of someone they've seen every day for twenty years, and have to pause before making introductions. It was two or three boxes opening at the same time, when maybe they should or shouldn't, so that odd parallels, collisions, and alliances of information emerged.

Mind (brain) never ceased to awe Anna: here she might read something at Widener Library and then, as she was walking back to Trowbridge Street, it would connect with something she had read three months ago, in a totally different area, and then the two together would make yet another kind of connection, fusing past and present in a strange seesaw of time rhythms; world maps might change before her eyes (the present map of Boston would be superimposed in her mind on Cotton Mather's Boston), and the Hancock Tower, with its glass reflections, would appear and disappear beside Trinity Church, and Increase Mather would be running Harvard instead of Derek Bok. She tried desperately to file her thoughts properly, commanding her brain to be more orderly when filing, but somehow her brain did not feel organized these days. There were moments when even dear Victor Allingame, standing in his classroom lecturing on Ruskin, became Cotton Mather, and started scolding Ruskin, it seemed to Anna, for coveting young girls. Then he would become Lewis Carroll and ask them to take their clothes off, mothers present, of course. And then when their clothes were off, they were not Effie or Alice, but Anna, somewhere in Poland, being raped by a Nazi soldier before being burned as a witch by Cotton Mather once more. Or, like Kurt's great-great-grandmother, she was being stripped and raped, as an alternative to being burned alive by the Paiutes, or she was running, running as fast as she could, from a volcanic eruption in pre-history. Which fire would she prefer? This sometimes seemed her only choice. When her mind allowed her solace, she was sometimes just a simple bit of blue-green algae, without enough brain cells to be burdened by the terrible problems of humanity. But this did not often occur, and even the calm afterworld of the spirit to which Joanna Wilkens had introduced her came all too seldom, rarely bringing the sense of her mother's presence that might have soothed her. Anna needed Grandma.

She left for Brooklyn as soon as she possibly could, accompanied to the Eastern shuttle by both Andrew and Kurt, who vied to carry her one small bag, and refused to cede precedence in her affections even for a goodbye kiss, so that she found herself hugging and being hugged by both at the same time, with Lucinda, who had come along for the ride, barking somewhere between their legs, and winding them all up in her leash. She arrived the day before Passover was to begin.

Then she was being hugged by Grandma, high up in a tall building on Ocean Parkway near Cortelyou Road, in a neat little apartment that had an extra bedroom for her, filled with soft chairs she could sink into. Grandma felt soft, Grandma's bosom was so soft, it brought back Anna aged seven, nuzzling the cushiony vastness after her parents died. Grandma's voice too was soft, heavily touched with accent, and warm with Yiddishkeit, with the laments of synagogue prayer that she had brought with her from "the other side." What had that other side been like? little Anna used to wonder. Grandma had referred to "the other side" as though it were another world, and Anna used to sit, in those years after her parents died, with only Grandma's warmth to sustain her, and listen to Grandma sigh sorrowfully about the other side, about how it had been when she was growing up, in a village that had changed hands between the Poles and Russians so often that Grandma knew both languages, as well as Yiddish and Hebrew; in a village where Grandma's father, Anna's great-grandfather, had been the village blacksmith, a big man, Grandma said of her father, a big man with a red beard, and strong.

Anna now, feeling Grandma's warmth, having Anna aged seven slide back into her — and she wondered about that, whether our younger selves ever really leave us or are simply closed somewhere inside, so that year after year new selves, as it were, slide thinly one over the other, montaging us, as time and experience from without, and their effects within, play upon one another — Anna was glad she had come. Her nostrils were filled with the aromas of Grandma's baking: mandelbrot, rugelach, honey and sponge cakes wafting through the air as though they were waltzing, blending and then separating so that the different tastes touched her tongue even before she entered the kitchen.

— Come in, come in, *kindele*, Grandma was saying, ushering her into the kitchen, where the mounds of honey-covered taiglach sat like jeweled crowns on the table, rich with nuts and amber glow in the afternoon light. Come have a cup tea.

Anna, to Grandma, looked thin. Anna looked pale. Anna would have to be loved and fed in Brooklyn for a while. The air in Cambridge, Grandma had a feeling, had not enough Yiddish warmth for Anna. Anna had been out in the *goyishe* world for quite a while now. She needed this return to the hearth.

The taste of honey cake. Soft, crumbly, darkly sweet. And the hot draft of tea, rich with cream. And Grandma bustling around putting more riches before her, just sitting, sitting, and being cared for, all the luxury of Grandma's care, which had always had to replace her lost mother. And Grandma, somehow knowing this, had compounded normal compassion and warmth tenfold, so that she seemed to exude humanity like a small fleshly furnace. This was a different fire from those which absorbed Anna's thoughts before leaving Cambridge. This was the fire that came with life-blood, the fire of feeling that was part of the human apparatus, not perhaps readily available to algae. This was the "human" difference the philosophers spoke of, Kant's *humanitas*. This was the part that she had trouble reconciling with Otto Dienes and Cotton Mather. This was what made it impossible that Hitler too could have claimed human status.

Anna sat in the little kitchen, her nostrils filled with the aroma of holiday cakes, her body warmed by the hot liquid sliding down her throat, and by the warmth of Grandma's caring, and relaxed fully for the first time since her encounter with Otto Dienes.

— You had a good trip, *kindele?* You weren't afraid of the plane? I prayed *Gott shul helfen* all the time you were in the air.

— It's only an hour, Grandma. And the shuttle is really just like a bus.

— Not a bus. Grandma shook her head, her soft white

hair framing her round features, her blue eyes bright and disbelieving. Buses are on the ground, wheels on the ground. Planes, with wings, they shouldn't try to be birds. Birds are birds. Planes are making believe.

— Well. Anna laughed. The plane made believe it was flying in the air, and flew out of Logan Airport and waved to all the other birds, and landed at LaGuardia, and here I am.

— Thinner. Grandma eyed Anna accusingly. Thinner. You don't eat there? You think you can live on books? Books. Books maybe are not so good for young girls. Young girls maybe need other things more. Food. Love. You got a boyfriend?

Anna sat in the kitchen, with its white-and-red wallpaper the color of Valentines, and looked at the tiny hearts and flowers parading up and down the wall, each encased in a vertical column of two lines at either side, first a heart, then a flower (possibly a tulip, Anna thought), then a heart again. Why did Grandma have hearts and flowers all over the kitchen? Had they always been here? What had Grandma told her about Grandpa, long dead, probably sitting in spirit with Anna's mother, somewhere in Joanna Wilkens's afterlife, what had she said about her own romance with the man she had married? Grandma had told Anna stories over and over again when she was very young, but it seemed now to Anna as though she had never listened. If she had, surely she would remember. And even the stories Grandma had told her about Ellen, her mother, and about her mother as a little girl, as old as Anna when Anna had started her new life, her Brooklyn life with Grandma, what did Anna remember of all that?

Right now, it seemed to her as though her mind had been wiped out, that Memory had shirked all responsibility, was simply some crazy blackboard that listed all experience in chalk, and the chalk had been wiped away. What gave Memory the right to dispose of experience? The scientists talked of brain cells dying, of losing the keys to those little inner boxes, which, like the boxes of separate selves, sat inside people, specifically allocated to experience rather than self (though these were probably not nearly as easy to separate as they were in Anna's "system"), those brain cells dying, those continual small deaths, those deaths of experience that were, after all, the sum total of life. Anna had been adding so many new ideas to her head, maybe Memory had simply rebelled. Enough, enough, Memory was crying. How can I carry it all? And family history too?

Anna felt sorry for Memory. She had been overloading it. She must go slowly. She would start again, very gently, very tentatively, to ask Grandma the questions that would fill the boxes once more. If the memories were not erased but simply locked up somewhere, perhaps Grandma's answers would open them again. In all events, she had to try.

She answered Grandma's last question:

— Yes, I have a boyfriend.

Grandma smiled with satisfaction.

— Grandma, why did you leave Poland?

Grandma was taken unawares. Poland was oddly schizoid in Grandma's mind, like a strange globe halved down the middle, painted black on one side, white on the other, the line between them very sharp, but revolving slowly from one to the other, so that she never knew when white would turn black, sweetness sour, dreams of childhood nightmares, good evil.

Poland was where she had grown up, the eldest of eight children, only ten when her mother died. Grandma had had to tend the family, cook, care for the young ones, make a home for her father, who would come in sweaty and dirty from the smithy and not allow anyone to kiss him until he had changed and dressed, his yarmulke now fresh and new, his brawny arms, laced with red hair, embracing her — little Gittel, who had been enough woman at age ten to take on the responsibilities of someone three times her age. Poland was the *Jewish* village, separated from the *goyim* by over six hundred years of restriction, in which Grandma's forebears had held to the God who had chosen them, chosen them to be placed aside, to be put behind a wall, as it were, from the rest of humanity, not to be eaten with or danced with, surely not to be loved, except by one another, never by "the other." Grandma's people had always been small farmers, Grandma's world was the cows and the chickens and the goat, the small patches of vegetables, the somewhat larger fields of potatoes. Grandma's young world had been occupied by children and animals and growing things. Even now all over the Brooklyn apartment lemon and orange seeds had sprouted little trees in the clay pots she found at the five-and-dime. Grandma could see that early world sometimes in her mind's eye, could hold the little farm inside her head, could even see the family dog, a big brown happy stray she had welcomed one day and fed until he would never go away. Even in America, Grandma encouraged strays — all the Polish *landsmen* who landed in Brooklyn in the twenties had ended up on Grandma's couch, or even on Grandma's floor, suitably spread with down quilts, until they could find their bearings and become part of the American Dream.

But that was only one side of the globe. The other was black, or maybe more accurately red, with the broken heads and battered bodies of the pogroms, and red finally with the terrible fires of Auschwitz, where six of her seven brothers and sisters and a total of fifteen of their children had died, as well as all thirty members of her husband's family and all the friends who had inhabited the little village. But also, yes, black. Black smoke.

Anna's question remained unanswered. Grandma looked at her and decided that it was time for her to rest.

— Later, *kindele*, later, we have plenty time to talk. Tante Laitsche is coming this afternoon. Lie down *a bissel*, before she comes.

Anna lay on the narrow bed she had occupied since she was seven, surrounded by the small store of toys Grandma had lovingly provided her over the years, and by the few (minus the golden doll, ever mourned secretly as an image of her mother's loss) that had survived the devastation of her parents' death. She thought of the big white wooden house in Glen Cove, with its acres of ground running down to the sea, the children she had played with — children, she now understood, who were unghettoized, not torn by the sad or joyous memories of the "other side," of the place left behind for the American Dream. Their parents, or their grandparents or their great-grandparents, may have had those problems, but the children Anna had played with were simply "American," with no awareness of anything else. They all sang O beautiful for spacious skies at school in joyous unison as they saluted the Stars and Stripes and felt the feelings of shared patriotism kindle. They all recited the Lord's Prayer and the Twenty-third Psalm. Anna did not go to church as they did on Sundays, but then, Anna's parents did not belong to any church. They simply told her, when she asked, that God was good and belonged to everyone. That was her religion. She did not feel deprived of church; indeed, she hardly noticed it. God was always in her, her mother had told her, as long as she treated people with kindness and respect for their humanity.

— Humanity, Mommy?

— It's a big word, Anna. It simply means remembering that we are all human beings together. If you hurt, they hurt. If you cry, they cry. If you laugh, they laugh. And all the things that happen to you during the day, the good and the bad things, happen to everyone, but some people have more bad things, and you have to help them if you can. We all belong to the same human family.

And once Anna asked her father a question, the answer to which, she now knew, was untrue.

— What is Hell, Daddy?

— There is no Hell, Anna. Don't worry about it. There's only Heaven.

So Anna had grown up without an awareness of Hell, and without an awareness of Hell meant without an awareness of Evil, and without an awareness of Evil, an inability to comprehend how Auschwitz, how Hitler could have happened, how God could have let it happen, how there could, indeed, be a God.

Anna had not discovered Auschwitz until she moved to Grandma's, and then it only hovered vaguely in whispered memories of the family and friends who had never escaped, who had vanished without a trace, almost two decades before she was ever born. Anna had really discovered Auschwitz at Harvard.

Tante Laitsche was small and round, like Grandma, but with hennaed hair that contrasted oddly with Grandma's white, and tiny beady eyes. She was only two years younger than Grandma, and one could tell this despite the henna, because of the network of wrinkles that traversed her face, like small channels in a sand map, erupting around the circle of her mouth like tiny solar rays. Tante Laitsche was the taiglach specialist of the family, and though Grandma's taiglach already sat proudly on the kitchen counter, Tante Laitsche arrived with *hers* and unwrapped the gooey mounds with divine assurance. Gittel's taiglach were taiglach. Laitsche's were diamonds.

The diamonds uncovered, the tacit recognition of her status confirmed (Gittel had muttered her thank-you's, aggrieved as always by her sister's one-upmanship but fully cognizant of the justice of her claim), Tante Laitsche sat down to inspect Anna, who appeared, brushed and combed, at her summons.

— Where is Anna? What they did to her at Harvard? She's lying down, she's sick? The food there must be terrible. *Goyishe* food. Ach!

Then she started kissing and hugging her, clutching Anna and muttering endearments.

— *Kindele, kindele.*

Tante Laitsche, like Grandma, had a strong sense of commitment to Ellen's bereft child, whom, however, she had seen only occasionally since she moved to Baltimore and was, like Grandma, finding it difficult to travel, indeed, even to move around.

Grandma got out the *milchedig* dishes, and they all had tea, Anna as always watching with wonder as Grandma was careful to take spoons and forks, cups and saucers, from the separate cupboard reserved for dairy utensils — no mixing of *milchedig* and *fleishedig*, no mixing of milk products and meat. God would be offended if the kosher rules weren't met, if chickens were not bled when slaughtered, and oxen too, no matter how painful, their throats slit, the blood pumping down a gutter, to purify the meat, as Abraham would have sacrificed Isaac had the angel not stayed his hand. Jewish hygienic laws must be observed. Else, why had all the family died at Auschwitz? Respect for God, no matter what, because God had chosen them, and the Chosen had forever to pay for that privilege.

Weeks earlier, in Widener, Anna had found in *The Jewish Almanac, Traditions, History, Religion, Wisdom, Achievements,* Compiled and Edited by Richard Siegel and Carl Rheins, with Extensive Illustrations, Maps and Charts:

> When one wants to observe the *yahrzeit* (anniversary of the death) of a person who was murdered without records during the Holocaust, there is often a problem of the proper date to observe. An exact date of the death is usually not available. Jews who want to observe this Jewish tradition must, therefore, observe the date on which the town where the Holocaust victim lived was liquidated. It is at least an appropriate date on which to remember the Holocaust victim in a special, personal way.

There followed a list of towns: Baranowicze, Bendin, Bialystok, Bilgoraj, Boryslaw, Busk, Dobromil, Dovinka, Dubno, Dubrava, Frampol, Jadowa, Jaroslaw, Jedlinsk, Lemberg, Lipsko, Lomza, Lublin, Mielec, Minsk, Mir, Myslowice, Ostroleka, Oszmiana, Pinsk, Plonsk, Przemysl, Radom, Ropczyce, Skalat, Slonim, Sokolow, Sosnowice, Stanislawow, Tomaszow Lubelski, Wasowice, Wlodawa, Wolkowysk, Wyszkow, Wyszogrod; and beside each town a date: 12/17/42; 8/1/43; 8/19–9/15/43; 11/2/42; 2/1–5/30/43; 5/21/43; 7/29/42; 10/19/42; 10/5/42 . . . Dates on a calendar, when a town went, was gone, vanished, the people like wisps of smoke. No date later than 1943. Some dates several weeks long. Had the people who lived in those Polish villages — Bialystok 8/19–9/15/43; Boryslaw 2/1–5/30/43; Lemberg 6/21–27/43; Przemysl 9/3–10/30/43 — fought back? What happened during that span of time when they fought for their lives and their families and their God and their dietary laws? Or did they just take longer to exterminate, like some resistant strain of virus? Jews, the anti-Semites claimed, were a disease. The Polish Jewish population, according to the neat tables in *The Jewish Almanac*, numbered 3,250,000 in September 1939. Two million eight hundred fifty thousand Polish Jews died during the war. In the section on Nazi Concentration Camps and Extermination Centers: A Partial List, Anna read: Auschwitz, Belzec, Bergen-Belsen, Breendonck, Buchenwald, Chelmno, Dachau, Drancy, Gurs, Majdanek, Malines, Mauthausen, Natzweiler-Struthof, Ravensbrück, Sachsenhausen-Oranienburg, Sobibor, Stutthof, Theresienstadt, Treblinka, Westerbork. Some names were not known to her; Belzec, Mauthausen: "Of the 60,000 Jews who entered Belzec extermination camp, only one inmate survived the Holocaust. The commander of Mauthausen from February 1939 to May 1945, Franz Ziereis, is known to have given his son fifty Jews for target practice as a birthday present."

Was it the dietary laws? Anna wondered. Would it have made a difference if the Jews had not followed Leviticus 11 and Deuteronomy 14:3–21? Jews were permitted to eat antelope, buffalo, gazelles, goats, harts, ibexes, kine, oxen, roebucks, and sheep but not apes, asses, bats, bears, boars, camels, cats, dogs, elephants, foxes, hares, hippopotami, horses, hyenas, jackals, leopards, lions, llamas, mice, mules, pigs, rats, whales, wolves, and zebras. No boar hunts. No Moby-Dicks. No participation in the great indigenous hunt of Wasp New England. What if they had eaten whale meat? Would that have equipped them better to fight back? A photograph in *The Jewish Almanac* showed General Eisenhower at the liberation of Bergen-Belsen, the great General, ultimately President of Columbia University and of the nation, observing some bags of clothes strewn on the ground. In the clothes were skin and bone. Mortal remains.

Had General Eisenhower eaten whale meat? Should Grandma have abandoned her two cupboards? But Grandma was in America now, wasn't that enough? In the land of the brave and the free, in the land of Cotton Mather, surely she could feel safe.

Tante Laitsche's family joined them the next evening for the first Seder. Grandma was hostess, and the small dining area was carefully laid out, both table leaves extended, lace-clothed, cut-glassed, and warmly wine-glassed and candled for the ceremony. Tante Laitsche had one daughter, Tania, who had, therefore, been Ellen Bernstein's first cousin. Tania, married to Sheldon Schreibman, a Brooklyn lawyer, had three children, the eldest, Linda, just a bit younger than Anna and a senior at Hunter College. The two younger children, a boy and a girl, were in high school. Anna had played with Linda when they were children, and with other, more distant cousins she met when she came to Brooklyn, after leaving Glen Cove and America behind. For Brooklyn, as Anna knew it through Grandma, was not America, but some *other place*, where many people spoke in accents and where, despite increasing ethnic mixes, the East European Jews still clustered together in a community as close-knit as any European ghetto. Within this community there was even a royalty pattern, and though Anna had not recognized it at the time, Tante Laitsche had given to the world a line of Jewish Princesses, first Tania and, after her, Linda, the college student.

Observing them now, entering and kissing, exclaiming over Anna, my you look so thin, the big Harvard girl, how are you enjoying yourself there, are you meeting any nice Jewish boys or is there no one to go out with? Anna felt a spontaneous recoil, and then shame for the feeling. Tania Schreibman had kept her figure. There were, after all, plenty of Jack La Lannes in Brooklyn, and whenever Tania got two pounds heavier on the scale, she went on an all-liquid fast. This was necessary, for example, after every small excursion she and Sheldon took to La Sammana, on

St. Martin in the Caribbean, where they would eat three- or four-course meals, expensive as the diamond she wore on her finger, and sun and bask, away from the stresses and strains of keeping up an active social life (Tania) and business life (Sheldon) in Brooklyn and its suburb, New York. Tania and Sheldon were actively involved with the Brooklyn Museum, the Brooklyn Academy of Music, the Library, the Brooklyn Jewish Guild for the Blind, the United Jewish Appeal. Tania was on the board of Hadassah. They no longer kept the kosher home in which Tante Laitsche had raised Tania, but then, princesses by royal decree could modify tradition. And they kept the faith, so to speak, by their involvement in Jewish causes, their strict and scrupulous commitment to the perpetuation of the Jewish people — no marrying out, no, not even dating out, for that could lead to marriage, and then another one would be gone in an assimilation feared by the rabbis even more than Hitler, homogenization, Americanization, erasure of the Jewish identity through blood mixtures, Jew and Goy. Contamination. As in *Mein Kampf*.

Tania Schreibman's cone-shaped figure was big on top, narrow in the hips and bottom. Tiny, dark, not unlike the Great American Sex Goddess of film, herself a converted Jew, Tania clothed her cone in garments from Bergdorf's and Bendel's, descending on these Wasp establishments fortified by the mink and diamonds Sheldon had promised her when she accepted him. He had been what the girls in her crowd called "a good catch." She met him while she was a student at the University of Miami, where she improved her suntan and figure in the "unparalleled climate" to which old Jews so often repaired, establishing their own tiny ghetto in the Art Deco hotels that rented rooms and kitchens, supported by small pensions and savings and welcome checks from the children who had "moved up." Sheldon Schreibman was a blind date, visiting his mother in one of these establishments, with glass blocks on the curvilinear façade and old Jews ornamenting the porch like fading light bulbs. His mother had a friend who was a friend of Tante

Laitsche's, and the minute she saw Sheldon she envisaged a *shiddach*. In the old days, everyone got their mates this way. No dating bureaus. No computer matching. No singles bars. Simply the *shadchen* or matchmaker, using intuition, hope, and optimism. Sheldon could not withstand the pressure. A nice Jewish girl, smart. Like Liz Taylor, I'm telling you, a regular beauty.

Sheldon was impressed. When Tania met him at the appointed time in the lobby of the Fontainebleau she was a real knockout, down to her carefully lacquered toenails. And nice. He could get nowhere beyond the good-night kiss, and even this was bestowed with great virginal reluctance. The true Jewish Princess, Tania knew that there could be no sexual compromise of her regal status. Lorelei Lee had made it clear that even for a *shiksa* diamonds were a girl's best friend. Tania wanted hers on a wedding band.

The house in Brooklyn Heights, the full-time maid, the lovely holidays and special gifts: a mink after the first five years of marriage, a Cartier diamond watch when Linda was born — Sheldon certainly knew how to keep a princess happy. A willing courtier, he considered himself blessed. In America especially, true princesses were hard to find, though actually the Jews did produce an inordinate number of them, a special gift, perhaps, to the democracy in which they had enlisted.

Bitsy Allingame, encountering Tania, were such an unlikely confrontation ever to occur, might have considered her a bit ostentatious. But if she fit the cliché of Jewish materialism, she did so with such good taste that, though far from the ethic of the Republican cloth coat, she was virtually indistinguishable from the Wasp wives of many corporate executives. Within the Jewish hierarchy, she was not only a princess, she had real class. It is possible, in fact, that in her heart Tania felt in no way less privileged than the Bitsy Allingame who was descended from Martha Washington. She was a Jewish American Princess, and if Tante Laitsche's forebears, like Grandma's, had been simple Jewish farmers in a tiny Polish village, this had very little to do with Tania, who was the child of American privilege, an impression that Tante Laitsche had, through every motherly action, reinforced daily.

Tante Laitsche spoke broken English, colored by the mix of Russian and Polish, Hebrew and Yiddish, that marked her earliest utterances. But Tania was an American, born by definition to privilege and, in addition, a Jewish American Woman, a special class within the Chosen People. Jewish American Women never fucked before marriage. Jewish boys might do this with *shiksas*, but never with the princesses, who were not as loose in their morals as *goyim*. Tania, rarely venturing out of the Jewish ghetto, never dating out, had maintained an aristocracy of demeanor that came from knowing she was "special." The "help" did all the unpleasant chores. Unlike Bitsy Allingame, Tania would never break her fingernails raking garden leaves, nor would she concern herself with the labeled genealogies of the bedspread. Tania knew who she was partly because she spent so much time never letting Sheldon forget it.

Now, sitting with her consort and progeny at the Seder table, Tania radiated the confidence of one who had achieved her purpose in life. She had instilled in her two daughters, Linda, and Elaine (four years younger), a full and proper sense of their own royal status within the Jewish hierarchy. Princesses outranked all contenders. Linda, also cone-shaped, with long black hair worn with a side part and barrette that attested to her craze for forties movies, tapped her lacquered fingers on the table in boredom. Princesses rarely did what they did not want to do. This was special, a command performance for Grandma Laitsche and Tante Gittel, and once a year, a Seder was bearable. Even if it did involve eating matzoh, which she had hated since she was a child. So dry, ugh. Even with salt and butter, as Tania had tried to make it more palatable, Linda could not get it down.

She had had instruction. She knew very well it was the unleavened bread the Jews had eaten in the desert after the exodus from Egypt. But that was over three thousand years ago. Why did she, Linda Schreibman, sitting in an apartment on Ocean Parkway in Brooklyn in 1980, have to eat unleavened bread? Even prisoners in jail got better bread than that. But she was, after all, Jewish, and that privilege, the privilege of being Chosen, had its obligations. She would eat the matzoh, and she would not marry out. Looking over the table at Anna, she felt even more special. Anna was dating *shgutzim*. She had wormed that out of her before they sat down. Anna never observed any of the Holy Days, not even Yom Kippur, for her own parents. Anna really was a lost soul, and Linda Schreibman felt sorry for her. Linda Schreibman might be a modern, enlightened, somewhat unobservant Jew, but she was still Jewish. What, after all, was Anna Bernstein?

Anna Bernstein, engaging Linda's eye in return, was wondering the same thing. In Cambridge, at Victor Allingame's Thanksgiving dinner, God had taken the face of Cotton Mather. In Nevada, it was Martin Luther. Now, there was a Jewish God, and she could not read His face. Older, white-bearded, like Michelangelo's God creating Adam in His own image. Weren't we all in His image? Did it really matter whether she was feasting in honor of the corn spirit in Cambridge, or the barley harvest that was part of the calendar of the Exodus? Hadn't Christ too attended a Passover feast? Wasn't that what the Last Supper was all about? And hadn't Christ too been a Jew? What would Cotton Mather and Martin Luther and Otto Dienes say about that?

The image of Otto Dienes, thrusting his beady eyes close to hers and questioning her name, made her shiver suddenly, so that Grandma, solicitous, said, If there is a draft, *mamale*, maybe you should put on a sweater. Naming the Jew. The label of separateness. The distinction between the adherents of the Old Testament and those who had accepted the New. But Cotton Mather had always liked the Old Testament, hadn't he?

The reading of the Haggadah was beginning, a ceremony with which she could barely feel a connection. She was Jewish because born to it, she could not be otherwise, and though she did not reject it, neither did she understand it.

That was why she had come back to Grandma now. The Passover feast would perhaps explain it to her. Explain to her why she must identify more with Linda and Tania Schreibman than she did. She kept trying to see them as people, but they kept reasserting themselves as types. They did not merely accept their Jewishness. They embraced it. Linda, she could see, was bored with the trappings. But not with the state itself. For Jewishness bestowed on Linda a distinction she could not have otherwise. How else could she be a princess?

Even the scapegoat, Anna remembered, had special powers, often kingly or religious and magical powers. The sacrifice of the scapegoat meant the saving of the community. Sir James George Frazer had seen the killing of the *divine* scapegoat as an "opportunity to lay upon him the burden of their sufferings and sins." The divine scapegoat. Christ. The Jews. Even the Jewish Princess. Chosen.

Someone was nudging her.

— Anna, where are you? Grandma was saying. You are far away, *mamale*. Come, *mamale*, pay attention. Sheldon is reading the Haggadah, listen, *mamale*.

And Anna listened to the voice of Sheldon, now no longer in a courtroom, but reading in a Hebrew she did not understand, like music, with a small plaintive cry at the edge of each sound. She knew that the Haggadah dealt with the Exodus — the Jews liberated from Egyptian slavery. The youngest child, in this instance Tania's fourteen-year-old son, would ask the questions. But first the wine was blessed, and the prayer said to God: Thou selected us from all other people, Thou didst love us and was favorable unto us above all nations, and Thou sanctified us with Thy commandments, and brought us near, O our King, unto Thy service and by Thy great and holy name Thou called unto us and granted us, O Lord our God, this day of the feast of unleavened bread, the time of our redemption.

Anna followed this in her grandmother's Hebrew-English prayer book. Small, bound in black suede, with gold-tipped pages, it was a prayer book Grandma had had for a long time, though she couldn't read the English parts: *The Form of*

Daily Prayers According to the Custom of the German and Polish Jews, published in Vienna in 1857. Where had Grandma gotten such a prayer book? Anna wondered. Why were these people thanking God for their redemption? In 1857 perhaps this was possible. But in 1980? Forty years after the Holocaust? Still chosen? Still selected for the role of divine scapegoat? Each Jew a Jesus on whom others could lay the burden of their sufferings and sins? Anna would be happy when the ceremony was over.

It was a beautiful ritual — the vegetables dipped in salt water, the matzoh eaten, the bitter herbs commemorating the sorrows of slavery tasted, the Paschal lamb shank displayed, the drops of wine spilled in mourning for the Egyptians themselves, the drops for the plagues:

> *Dam*, Blood
> *Tzfardeyah*, Frogs
> *Kinim*, Lice
> *Arov*, Wild Beasts
> *Dever*, Blight
> *Sh'hin*, Boils
> *Barad*, Hail
> *Arbeh*, Locusts
> *Hosheh*, Darkness
> *Makat B'horot*, Slaying of the First Born,

but Anna could not connect with it. She could not tie it to her own experience. She was supposed to come from Egyptian slavery into Redemption, she was supposed to watch for Elijah to come and drink the glass of wine — the door was left open for him to come and drink the wine of endless promise — and at the end, Sheldon would sing again: *Baruch Atah Adonai Eloheinu Melech ha-olam borei p'ri ha-gafen*, We praise Thee, our God, Sovereign of all Existence, Who has created the fruit of the vine. They would sing the Hallel, and everyone would say, Next year in Jerusalem, and she would be freed from Egyptian bondage, but then what?

Anna had been at many of these Seders in her years with Grandma, but they had always felt alien. Grandma had not insisted that she learn Hebrew. Anna had always followed in translation, or had someone else, one of the many instructed boys, distant cousins or neighbors fresh from their Bar Mitzvahs, tell her what was happening. Anna had not learned anything but English in Glen Cove. Removal to the Hebrew of the Jewish festivals in Brooklyn had been like a journey to a foreign land. Perhaps today the informal feasting would feel better.

It began with a hard-boiled egg, symbol of new life. As at Thanksgiving and Christmas, the main course was the blessed bird chosen for the slaughter. Now a goose. Anna's mother had read to her from Mother Goose when she was a child. But when Anna transferred her life from her mother's house to Grandma's, the children's books, she remembered, had gone mute. Now, when she was ostensibly past the age for them, they filled her head like a cerebral security blanket, wrapping themselves in and out around her nerves and feelings. The outside world would have to get past Alice and Rapunzel to reach her, and Alice's ability to adjust her size had great evasive utility.

Anna, hearing Grandma's familiar chant, *Ess, ess, kindele,* and cutting into the sacrificial fowl, was lured back from her own thoughts to Linda's chatter about clothes and men. The younger children were beginning to get restive; having participated proudly and quietly in the ritual that reinforced their faith and identity, they were now released back to the prerogatives of Jewish adolescence, smaller versions of Linda, to whom Tania and Sheldon catered with indulgence and pride. Live for the children. Die for the children. In Tania's hierarchy, Sheldon loomed as the great provider, one notch below her on the ladder and handing up to her the material gifts her special status commanded. But the children were higher still, and Tania joined Sheldon in handing up to them the royal gifts endowed them at birth. The table conversation suddenly began to revolve around the children: their grades at school, their gifts of art and music, their special projects, their plans for summer camp and trips and colleges, even for professions. Their whole lives telescoped back to be deposited on the table at Grandma's Passover feast, and Anna, listening, wondered at the prophetic powers possessed by Tania and Tante Laitsche, who sat like court astrologers, reading the future backwards.

Anna's future seemed suddenly to her like a vast hole, one of the black holes, perhaps, now being turned up by astronomers or, perhaps even worse, the steaming hole at the tip of a volcano. Anna did not feel like a princess. She was not Jewish enough to be a princess. Her identifications, such as they were, were not so much with royal rights as with the scapegoats — the six million, the ashes. But she was not so sure that these identifications were more Jewish than simply human. Who would not identify with the six million? Didn't all human beings feel for the six million? Were her feelings for the six million a part of her solidarity with them as a Jew or as a person? And if her feelings were simply human, could not Kurt Hahn, only part German, also feel these? But the Germans had run the camps, ordinary Germans had run the camps. There must have been many Germans running the camps, to kill the six million. How many Germans to kill how many Jews? Where were the statistics in *The Jewish Almanac* for this? Anna had not found them. How many Germans? How did she erase the German part of Kurt Hahn, and if she did so, would she also erase Goethe and Caspar David Friedrich?

For, sitting at Grandma's Passover feast, surrounded by Jewish royalty, Anna had to admit that she loved the enemy's earlier historical and cultural self, that she was passionate about Goethe, that she adored Beethoven, that she was transported by Caspar David Friedrich. How had they aged into Adolf Hitler and Otto Dienes? And even around the time of Goethe and Friedrich, admit, admit, even then, Heinrich Heine had had difficulty in Germany as a Jew. Why was she drawn by the philosophy and art of a people who detested her? Why was she trying to erase the barrier that separated her? Born Jewish, she had to accept her identity. She did not want to deny it, because she couldn't deny or forget the six million and live with herself. But how could she accept her identity and marry Otto Dienes's grandson?

Later that evening, when everyone else had gone, Grandma, moved to reminiscences of earlier Seders, had talked finally of Poland. Of the forest to which she retreated after the day's work was done, the smaller children fed and clothed, the house cleaned, the meals prepared, the cows milked, the chickens fed, the work in her small vegetable garden, one of her real pleasures, ended for the day. Grandma could still remember the smell of the forest, the pine needles, the sky through the trees, under which she would often lie, to think a little, and to dream. She had also loved the wooden smell of the small synagogue in the village, with its straight simple lines, but she had not loved being separated from the men, a thing apart, almost an untouchable. In the morning service at the synagogue, the men prayed: Blessed art Thou, O Lord our God, King of the Universe, Who hath not made me a woman. The women prayed: Blessed art Thou, O Lord our God, King of the Universe, Who hath made me according to Thy will.

Grandma, a strong woman, had not understood why men would pray to God with thankfulness that they were not women. Grandma liked being a woman. Grandma used to brush her long golden hair for a long time at night before going to sleep. Grandma had Rapunzel hair, like Anna's. Grandma had especially liked one of the young Polish peasants who sometimes came into the village for her father to shoe his horse. Her father was the best blacksmith for miles around. Even the *goyim* preferred him to anyone else. The young man was not a Jew. He was *treif*, untouchable. But sometimes Grandma would see him leaving the smithy as she was coming with her father's lunch, and he would wish her good day, and they would look into each other's eyes and wonder why they should not walk together in the forest. The young man, Janos, found Grandma very beautiful. One day he had come upon her in the forest, alone, strolling under the pine trees, the needles crackling under her feet, and singing like a nightingale. Grandma had the most beautiful voice in the village. Grandma loved to sing, and Anna remembered now that when she first came to Grandma, Grandma had sung her Yiddish lullabies to help her sleep. But when Janos met Gittel in the forest, singing, he did not dare to walk with her, though he wanted to, and she wanted to, and they had stopped and greeted, and just passed on. Sometime soon after that, Gittel's father had arranged for her marriage to a young man, Ephraim, from the next village, a delicate sweet young man who was a tailor. But before the marriage could occur, there was a pogrom.

Grandma, telling Anna all this, shuddered. Anna did not press her, but Grandma somehow, catching her breath, wanted to go on. All of a sudden, the peace of the village night had been broken by loud shouts and cries and sounds of screaming people. All of a sudden some of the houses were aflame and people were dashing and crying. Grandma had been alone in the house with some of the younger children, and Ephraim had just come to call. He was not in the house five minutes when the peasants broke in, brutish, drunk, with clubs and pitchforks. Grandma's father was nowhere around. Ephraim stood up to them, but they cracked his head with one blow. Grandma felt herself being grabbed by a smelly, fat peasant, reeking of vodka. He had started to tear her clothes off. And then, suddenly, he was wrenched away from her, and Janos was there, and Janos said no, leave her alone. And in that moment, as the peasant yelled Jew-lover and went for Janos, Grandma escaped out into the forest with the children.

The next morning, when they dared to return, Ephraim had a concussion, ten houses had been destroyed, twenty killed, and double that number injured. As soon as Anna's future grandpa recovered, he and Grandma were married. Soon after, they left for America. Grandma never knew what had happened to Janos, but her husband, who was very frail, died shortly after Anna's mother, Ellen, was born, and Grandma was left alone in America to raise her American daughter.

Grandma had come to America in 1926. The rest of the village was destroyed by the Poles and the Nazis in 1942. The people became smoke at Auschwitz some time around then. Grandma was crying now. Grandma cried whenever she thought of the family left behind. She was alive and they were dead; the younger children (all but Tante Laitsche, who had taken Grandma's place for a while until the children were older and she too left for America) had grown and married and stayed in the village. Two of the girls were married to Talmudic scholars. One of Grandma's brothers had also become a Talmudic scholar. He had puzzled over the ways of God until the fires came. What had the fires to do with the ways of God? The Seder was a way of praising God for each Jew's freedom after the Egyptian bondage. But when the Haggadah was written there was no Adolf Hitler. Even Grandma, raised in Orthodoxy, had trouble with God after Auschwitz. But not with being Jewish. Never with being Jewish. The only way a Jew could keep faith with those who had died was by being Jewish. To cease being Jewish was to deny the six million. Or, to take it even farther away from the abstract, to cease being Jewish was to deny her dead brothers and sisters.

— Isaac Singer, Grandma said to Anna the next morning, placing before her a delectable matzoh brei, made of matzoh and eggs and milk. Isaac Singer you should read. Translated from the Yiddish. Translated maybe it will not taste the same, but some idea, it will give some idea.

Anna had come home to Grandma for warmth and support. She had found a tradition that claimed her, to which she was a stranger. That afternoon she scoured the bookshops for Isaac Bashevis Singer, and departed for Harvard the next morning carrying a two-volume paperback of his writings under her arm, bearing Isaac Singer back to the land of Cotton Mather.

ℐ 2 ℐ

IT WAS Dr. Gotthard again. Anna was impatient and annoyed. Dr. Gotthard never understood. Dr. Gotthard always expected her to be normal, and seemed disappointed when something made it clear that she was not. How could she tell Dr. Gotthard that she would never be normal, that it was impossible to be normal if you had discovered what Anna had discovered about life and God?

— It's God's fault, she said, knowing this would upset him.

Dr. Gotthard looked at Anna and wondered how this pretty little post-nymphet, still all too desirable to him, should have gotten to this.

— Do you care about God?

— I'm not sure who He belongs to.

— Doesn't He belong to all of us?

— The Jews say He likes them best, but that's hard to figure. In Warsaw they had to pay taxes to get through the gates.

— The gates?

— In the nineteenth century. Isaac Singer said so. I don't read Yiddish.

— Did you try to read him in Yiddish?

— I read him in translation. When my grandmother reads him in Yiddish she says it was like that. When I read him in English I can't believe it.

— Believe what?

— That God really wanted the Jews to be so separate, so apart.

— Do you feel separate?

— Not really. I didn't at the beginning. I've only felt separate since I've been Jewish.

— Are you a convert?

Anna was becoming increasingly impatient with Dr. Gotthard.

— I've been Jewish since Passover.

— Passover?

— Yes. I have no choice. No Jew has a choice.

— Does this upset you?

— It made it hard with Goethe and Otto Dienes.

— Oh?

— I had to give them up, you see. I hated Otto Dienes, but I loved Goethe.

Dr. Gotthard, knowing full well by now that there was a more recent love behind Anna's madness, waited.

— And?

— That's it, she said abruptly. I loved Goethe.

∾⟨⟨⟐⟩⟩∾

When Anna returned to Cambridge bearing Isaac Bashevis Singer under her arm, both Andrew and Kurt met her at the airport. Lucinda, sulking, had been left at home, and Anna was embraced by the two young men without the leash that had so symbolically encircled them at their original parting. Struggling to claim her baggage — Let me, no let me — glowering at each other, for they were becoming now more rivals than friends, they drove her back to Cotton Mather's Harvard, where she gratefully breathed the springtime air of New England after Jewish Brooklyn.

— How's your grandmother? both asked solicitously and almost simultaneously.

Anna found suddenly that she did not know what to say. The few days with Grandma had been like a visit to another land. Initially, she had come from that land to Cambridge, but Cambridge had changed her, altered her so that she could never go back, yet having gone back, she realized too that she could not ever be a true part of Cambridge either. That she now knew too much and too little, and would be obliged to go in one direction or the other, and since it was unlikely that she could erase her new realizations, she could only go forward, in a desperate attempt to rock herself out of the limbo in which she found herself.

— How's Celeste? she asked. Grandma says to feed her more cabbage.

— Celeste is eating carrots and waiting for you. Andrew laughed. Celeste thinks she's Peter Rabbit, or maybe Beatrix Potter. She's been putting on airs lately.

— Digging in the garden?

— Two Trowbridge has been besieged.

Anna suddenly couldn't wait to see Celeste.

. . . Alice felt so desperate that she was ready to ask help of any one: so, when the Rabbit came near her, she began, in a low, timid voice, "If you please, Sir —" The Rabbit started violently, dropped the white kid-gloves and the fan, and scurried away into the darkness as hard as he could go.

Alice took up the fan and gloves, and as the hall was very hot, she kept fanning herself all the time she went on talking. "Dear, dear! How queer everything is to-day! And yesterday things went on just as usual. I wonder if I've changed in the night? Let me think: was I the same when I got up this morning? I almost think I can remember feeling a little different. But if I'm not the same, the next question is 'Who in the world am I?' Ah, that's the great puzzle!"

Celeste jumped into Anna's lap as soon as she was seated in Andrew's breakfast nook, making it clear that she had missed her perhaps almost as much as the two young men who scurried around, arranging things for tea.

— We'll take care of it, you sit. Here's the pot.

— Andrew, where do you keep the bloody teabags?

Kurt was elated. Anna had been gone only a few days but

it felt as though his heart had been torn out. Damn. How had he gotten into this? Andrew — involved less through passion than affection, and propelled into more energetic action by pangs of jealousy — watched Anna and Kurt with a vague sense of his own simultaneous omission and inclusion. There were three of them, and there were two and one. Yet he knew, or sensed, that things were happening inside Anna that threatened the love match, and might make him, Andrew, the possible heir to the princess's hand. For if Anna was not a true Jewish American Princess, she was, in both men's eyes, a princess all the same. Seeing her in the sun-flooded nook, her golden hair spread about her, her white gauze dress covered lightly with a flowered shawl, who could possibly doubt this?

In bed that night, alone, Anna, who had (on separate occasions of course) discouraged both Andrew and Kurt from sharing her sleep under pretext of special fatigue, turned back to the copy of Isaac Bashevis Singer she had begun on the plane that morning. Isaac Bashevis Singer's Polish Hasidic Jews inserted themselves into the house on Trowbridge Street like Old Testament Prophets come to haunt Cotton Mather's Puritans. They danced and sang behind their wall of separateness, and beneath their earlocks and skullcaps or high-crowned hats were minds that spent all the hours and minutes of each waking day intent on piercing the wall of God's intentions. The "mansions of Paradise" must be claimed, and could only be claimed through the volumes of exegesis of the Talmud and the debates that would clarify God's Will. After all, what better use for one's time while awaiting the Messiah, who would abolish evil, slavery, exile, and bring heavenly joy and salvation?

Isaac Singer's Hasidim were soon amplified by Widener Library, where Anna's pile of books received several significant additions. A new layer of knowledge was deposited on top of the original ones: the Torah, the Talmud, and the Kabbalah. It was in these books that Anna discovered the true magic of numbers, and in the Talmud itself "seven" was amplified for her as never before: "Seven classes will stand before the Holy One, blessed be He, in the Hereafter." They would get to Gan Eden after suffering the privations of the poor and despised in this world. Gan Eden and Gehennah, Heaven and Hell. There were, of course, seven heavens, corresponding to the seven strata of the earth, and now Anna could even name them: Vilon, Rakiya, Shehakim, Zebel, Moan, Makom, Arabot. There were seven paths in the knowledge of the Torah. The seventh was the special path, the Holy of Holies again, fit only for prophets, the seventh class, who would know the seventy-two letter names of God, and such holy names of God as Adonai, El, Eloah, Elohim, Shaddai, Zevaot. But most especially YHWH. All the holy names are part of YHWH. To know YHWH is to know the Torah. To know the Torah is to know God.

All these things Anna tried to comprehend without the *rebbe* or leader of Isaac Singer's Hasidim to help her to interpret them. The Talmudic scholars spent day and night pondering the meaning of the Torah and the Talmud. Every word of the Torah had 600,000 faces, or meanings, one for each Jew who stood at the foot of Sinai. Six hundred thousand. What was the magic connection between 600,000 and the 6,000,000? Simply a zero, another zero, simply the multiplication by ten, simply the symbolic addition of the pure absolute, and the 600,000 souls of the Exodus become the unspeakable 6,000,000 of the Holocaust. Had the Holocaust been awaiting the Jews ever since Sinai? Had God, YHWH, known when He gave Moses the Tablets that a simple zero over three thousand years later would cause the lives of 6,000,000 human beings to end, and not only to end — that would be too simple — but to end in degradation and suffering beyond human capacity to understand? Had He done all this to test their optimism, that optimism which caused those who were left, especially the American Jews, and those European Jewish survivors who had made their way to America, to hold Passover services in which they thanked God for their redemption from Egypt *forty years* after the Holocaust? Egypt? God had sent plagues to torment Egypt. How had He plagued the commanders of the death camps? How had God kept His covenant? Why did He choose the Jews? The Jews were chosen, for what? The Puritans too were chosen, for what? The Americans who developed a culture out of Cotton Mather's beginnings praised God for giving them the bounty of American land, American mountains and rivers, and waterfalls, and hills and plains, and rocks and rills, America, America, God shed His grace on thee / And crown thy good with brotherhood, from sea to shining sea. Everyone, it seemed to Anna, was chosen. She did not know if she wanted, as an American or as a Jew, to be chosen. To be chosen was not necessarily a fate she relished.

✿❧✦❧✿

Spring had come to Cambridge. The air was no longer biting but balmy, Anna's Indian dresses required now only a light sweater or shawl, in which she could stroll across Harvard Yard with Kurt or Andrew or Joanna Wilkens, looking more like a blonde Isadora Duncan than a carrier of the fate of the Chosen. The gardens of Brattle Street began to bloom. Bitsy Allingame's crocuses and daffodils were up, and Victor Allingame, observing Anna in class, noticed that though she seemed more distracted and wan she was lovelier than ever. It was some time since she had visited the crewel bedspread.

— Anna?

They were standing in the great courtyard of the Fogg, the arcades piling story upon story above their heads.

— Yes, Professor Allingame. (She called him Victor only when their "other" relationship was in progress.)

— How is Mr. Ruskin these days?

— He said God was in the still small voice.

— Yes of course he did, my dear. One of his most brilliant insights.

— Not in the earthquake, you know. I'm not sure he was right.

Victor Allingame looked at Anna more closely. Since her return from Brooklyn there was something a bit strange about her. Several times in class she had raised the question of Ruskin and God, though this was not her paper topic.

— How will any of us ever know, my dear? Victor Allingame summoned his most soothing voice. How will any of us ever know?

— Cotton Mather thought he knew.

At mention of his ancestor's name, Victor Allingame straightened his neck. Cotton Mather always made him stand taller. To be descended from Cotton Mather was as much an obligation as an asset. One did not carry such an ancestor lightly. Victor Allingame's erect head extended to receive the crown of the ascendancy. Cotton Mather had upheld good against evil. He might have gotten a bit carried away with the witch business, but Victor had just seen *Some Like It Hot* replayed at the Brattle Theater and, as Joe E. Brown had said, nobody's perfect.

Norma Jean. Victor sighed at the thought of her wondrous legs. Bitsy's legs, if truth be known, were totally straight, athletic, and muscular, the result of all that walking and bending in the garden. No ankles. Norma Jean had ankles. Anna had ankles. Victor Allingame had first noticed them peeping out under her long gauze skirts, and had verified their perfection at Thanksgiving. Victor Allingame, standing in the courtyard of the Fogg Museum, momentarily forgot his illustrious ancestor and thought of Anna's ankles. He had a sudden desire to lift Anna's skirt to see if they were still there. Too long. It had been too long.

Victor Allingame asked Anna to come by the house at her earliest convenience to discuss Ruskin and Millais.

Anna, wanting to be fair, not wanting, in fact, to discriminate against her two friends/lovers in favor of her own true love, visited Victor Allingame's Brattle Street house that same afternoon and brought about for the first time the confirmation of Bitsy Allingame's long-held suspicion, since Bitsy Allingame found the bedroom and the crewel bedspread sufficiently disarrayed after Anna's departure to confront Victor Allingame with her hurt, envy, and wifely despair. This encounter, however, had little effect on Anna, who hardly knew of it, except for Victor's furtive recounting upon their next meeting, furtive though there was no one in the Fogg courtyard who might have heard them anyway, a recounting followed by Victor Allingame's resigned comment that they must be more careful in the future, and Anna did of course understand, didn't she? This meeting had also little effect on Anna, who had gone right back from Victor Allingame's to satisfy Andrew's desire, rarely requited since her true love had taken her heart. This Anna did the same way she had originally coupled with Andrew, out of friendship, compassion, and a real inner wish to feel more for this good and dear friend than she actually did. For her passion for Kurt Hahn was becoming an obsession, as was his for her.

The two lovers were separated by a five-thousand-year-old wall that Anna, as she drew more deeply upon her Jewish roots, felt increasingly obliged to respect. She felt sometimes as though she were the oldest tree in the forest, one that had endured through millennia, fossilized and mineralized back through time to the Jewish slaves under the Pharaohs, and time was the earth, so that she could visualize this fossilized tree, herself, with genuine roots, plunging deep deep down, so that maybe beyond the five-thousand-year level she would, as she had thought as a child, reach China. Dig a hole to China. Dig a hole five thousand years deep and hit the Pharaohs in Egypt. Dig a bit higher and hit the plagues. Dig higher still and hit the medieval blood-libel. Dig farther back and find the Polish wall of separateness. Dig just near the top of time, and there, right at the surface of the soil, are Otto Dienes and the six million. How were she and Kurt Hahn to deal with the 600,000 souls of Mount Sinai and the 6,000,000? How could she make Kurt Hahn understand that his Aryan blood, albeit mixed with Paiute, separated them, without sounding as though she too were a racist? Sleepless, one night at Trowbridge Street, she turned on the television and watched

Joel Grey singing in *Cabaret*. He was singing and dancing with an ape. He was asking his German audience to see her as I do, she doesn't look Jewish at all.

The Jew as animal. How could Anna marry Kurt Hahn, when Otto Dienes was there? Yet Anna loved Kurt Hahn with a rare passion. Anna's love for Kurt Hahn was of the sort that made it impossible for her to imagine the world, life, without him. A world without Kurt Hahn was inconceivable, lusterless, undifferentiated, limbolike, lacking in sensation, numb. Anna's erratic self-imposed separations from Kurt Hahn could be tolerated only for limited periods, and then she would allow him back into her life, to walk with her along the Charles, to lie together on the grass and watch the golden dome of the State House glinting in the sun on the opposite bank, to make love in his studio, where the new paintings leaning against the wall seemed even more violent, more Germanic, more testimonial to the very quality in him that was, for his art, most advantageous and, for his love, most threatening, or in her own small apartment on Trowbridge Street, where Andrew, ever knowing, lay painfully next door, unwilling witness, sad rival, and compassionate friend to both. Kurt would whisper urgently,

— Marry me.
— Kurt, please, she would beg.
— Let's talk about it, please.
— No, let's not talk. Please.

Kurt in his frustration would spring out of bed and walk up and down. Anna, knotted up, once the pleading and questioning began, would rise too and make a cup of tea. Sometimes after making love they would start separating themselves out with words, they would talk about everything other than themselves, about matters of the intellect rather than those of the heart. Anna, especially, would talk about Cambridge and America, and history and evolution, and ancestry, though she was clever enough not to bring it back, not after they had just made love, to Jewish ancestry or German ancestry. Those unvoiced ancestries, however, draped themselves over the wall of words between them, amplifying and toughening her meaning so that the coatings of significance were nonetheless there, to be noted by each of them in the small hours of the morning.

Such evenings became more or less the rule for Kurt and Anna after her return, roughly paralleled by a pattern of changes in her diary, which began to take on a still more incoherent appearance. The lettering on the page became ragged and unevenly spaced. A large printed word would be followed by a very small one, calligraphically shaped, or by an almost formlessly written one, whose legibility required careful deciphering. The entries were now sometimes violently printed.

The first page on which this change was evident was dated April 4, Good Friday. On that date, Anna wrote in her diary:

And when the sixth hour was come, there was darkness over the whole land until the ninth hour.

This was written in rather large calligraphic sweeps, with a wide-nibbed purple marker, at the very top of the page. There was a huge space left empty below, and then, at the very bottom of the page, in yellow, in letters so small they were almost illegible:

Cotton Mather likes seven. Cotton Mather says the greatest of the prophetic visions go successively by Sevens. Cotton Mather thinks the seven trumpets of the Apocalypse will sound in America for the New Jerusalem.

All around the margins of the page Anna drew bunnies and Easter eggs, richly colored and decorated with little flowers.

Shortly after Anna had returned to Cambridge from Grandma's Passover Seder she had found herself confronted with Good Friday. Christ too had gone to a Passover feast. As St. Mark, Chapter 14, told her quite clearly, it was the feast of the Passover and unleavened bread. The priests and scribes were out for him, said St. Mark, but they decided not to take him on the feast day, because the people might cause an uproar. Finally, they had to take him to Pilate, after Judas had betrayed him, and then he was clothed with purple and crucified as King of the Jews. And when he was on the cross, according to Mark, Chapter 15, he cried at the ninth hour: *Eloi, Eloi, lama sabachthani?* My God, my God, why hast Thou forsaken me?

Anna found this hard to deal with. Christ had been born a Jew. Christ had attended a Passover Seder and eaten of the unleavened bread. Christ had eaten matzoh. In Leonardo's *Last Supper*, the Christ without a face, whether for chemical reasons (deterioration) or for aesthetic ones (not even Leonardo could visualize the face of Christ), the Christ without a face had been eating matzoh. She hadn't ever really thought of this. Whatever one might say about the Jews and the Romans and the Crucifixion, wherever the blame was fixed, Christ was indeed a Jew. Insofar as the blood within him was human blood, it was Jewish blood. All the chemical differences in blood that Hitler had premised were incorrect. Christ, born according to Christian belief, of Mary and God, which mixed in some Godly blood as well, Christ's blood was Jewish blood.

Anna was depressed by the darkness she felt on Good Friday. The whole world seemed to her to have lost its light. She hoped Cotton Mather was right about America and the New Jerusalem. But she couldn't wait until the day was over. She didn't want to think of Christ as yet another dead Jew. She had had enough of dead Jews, and of Jewish blood as well. The Passover feast had begun with an egg, symbol of redemption and life. She would spend Saturday decorating Easter eggs and making a costume for Celeste — for whom, in Andrew's absence, she was sitting — a special

bonnet, with fan and gloves like the White Rabbit's. Only
Celeste was a black rabbit, and Anna, on Good Friday, was
torn by the sharp contrast between dark and light, between
the sixth hour and the promised Resurrection.

It was Joanna Wilkens (coming upon Anna with her eggs,
many of them broken and squashed, valiantly trying to
drain them through a tiny hole, instead of taking the easy
way, and hard-boiling them first, covered with paint and
brushing her hair out of her eyes with paint-stained fingers
splayed outward) who reminded Anna that the spiritualists
considered Easter Sunday and the Resurrection a special
holiday that testified to their belief in life after death.

— Every day is Easter Sunday for the spiritualists, said
Joanna.

— When can we go to a séance? asked Anna, mixing
some red and blue for a purple egg (the purple paint having
been upset by Lucinda).

— In about two weeks, or ten days. I think I can get one
scheduled.

— I must talk to my mother.

— I hope she comes through.

— She must. I must find out about the Jews.

To Joanna Wilkens, looking sharply at Anna with her eggs
and paint, her friend seemed more distracted than usual.
There was a kind of desperation that Joanna's instinct told
her had to do with Kurt Hahn, and with something else as
well. Anna, as all her friends had noticed, had been different
since her return from Grandma's. Joanna sat down with
Anna and helped to decorate the eggs.

On that afternoon, with the light gradually dimming
about them as it retreated from the sunlit nook at Trowbridge Street, as the light must have dimmed for Christ at
the sixth hour, as the light had dimmed for those other six
million, and for all who had been murdered and crucified
throughout time, Anna and Joanna, Joanna especially who
believed in the light, and in the light of the hereafter, and in
the eternal light of Summer Land, and in the light of the
daily resurrection, practiced the art of decoration upon the

symbol of life. Circles and spirals. Rectangles and squares. Zigzags and dots. More circles. Worringer, Anna remembered, had said that primitive man used geometric forms as absolutes. An absolute circle could push away all the chaos, all the stuff out there that piled up and made her head ache. Classical man, Worringer said, was at home with his world. His knowledge of the world gave him a kind of calm. Primitive man existed in a pre-knowledge state, and only geometries gave him solace.

Anna was looking for solace. No matter how much knowledge she acquired from the books at Widener, she could not find it. Rather, her senses and intellect proceeded together at a dizzying pace, zigzagging, like the zigzags she now drew, through her head; no matter how much she decorated the eggs with circles and squares, all the geometries that should, if Worringer was right, have pushed away the chaos, she felt no peace. She was always in a pre-knowledge state, but that state, looking to geometries for solace, received none. When would she ever know enough to achieve calm? When would everything she was stuffing into her head come together, so that in some glorious synthesis she would understand existence? For understanding, she might be able to forgive, and forgiving, she might be able to marry Kurt, and marrying Kurt, she might consummate her love forever. And even further, even beyond Kurt, she might, through understanding, begin to know who she was, Anna Bernstein, child of Ellen and Robert, granddaughter of Gittel Cohen, descendant of the 600,000 at Mount Sinai and of the 6,000,000, American citizen, heir to Cotton Mather's New Jerusalem, child/woman, cousin to Effie and Alice, human being, cousin to blue-green algae, soul, reaffirming, through her decoration of the egg, her belief in life, and its continuation in the hereafter, ardent spiritualist, reaching out into the beyond.

The eggs were very pretty. Anna, coloring them, felt much as Kandinsky must have, when he spoke of the aliveness, the humanness, the personality of colors, each with its own special quality, bubbling up: "A pressure of the fingers and jubilant, joyous, thoughtful, dreamy, self-absorbed, with deep seriousness, with bubbling roguishness, with the sigh of liberation . . . came one after another these unique beings we call colors — each alive in and for itself."

Widener Library had reaffirmed for Anna the connection between Passover and Easter. She had gone home to Grandma for Passover, the Hebrew Pesach. The name for Easter in many European languages (though not in German, significantly enough) was derived from Pesach: Pascua in Spanish, Pâques in French, Pascha in Greek, Paaske in Norwegian. So the Jews had Pesach and then there were Pascua, Pâques, Pascha, and Paaske. Lewis Carroll, Anna thought, could do a nonsense rhyme on that. But it wasn't nonsense, though there was indeed something of Carroll's mad illogic about it. The Jews held Passover. Christ was a Jew. Christ was crucified. The Jews were crucified ever after for continuing to be Jews, like Christ. Then, when Christ rose again, the Christians celebrated Pesach and called it Pascua, Pâques, Pascha, and Paaske. The Jews had celebrated Passover partly as a barley feast. Easter too was the result of a long tradition of celebration of spring: the old Norse Eostur, Eastar, Ostara, Ostar, season of new birth and the growing sun. Before there had been Christians and Jews there had been spring fire ceremonies for the sun god. Then there were Easter fires. In Germany there were bonfires, and flaming straw wheels were rolled over the ground.

Sun symbols — like the swastika. Originally, like the Easter fire, a symbol of light and life. The symbol of life converted to the symbol of death. Fire, the stuff of creation, burning people up. Anna's head ached again. Here she was, coloring Easter eggs, lovingly fashioning a bonnet for Celeste, the black Easter bunny, symbol of life and procreation, for who, after all, is more procreative than a bunny, here she was doing all this and she found herself back with the swastika. Like Grandma's Polish globe, good and evil revolved faster and faster before her eyes, so that they ran one into another, were part of the same globe, the same world, the same existence, no way to Heaven without Hell, no white without black, no sun without darkness.

Celeste seemed to love her bonnet. It was worthy of Wonderland, baby blue, covered with pink crêpe-paper roses, carefully folded by Anna with Joanna's help, into remarkable lifelike simulacra. Anna had bought a small straw infant's sunbonnet the day before and dyed it. Then she stapled the paper roses all around the lid, and built the crown still higher with white lace doilies. To this confection, which began rather quickly to assume the aspects of a birthday cake, she added blue satin streamers, at least a dozen of them, which, when the bonnet was settled on Celeste's head, made her look, Anna thought, like a black bunny with blue satin hair, styled a bit like that of Veronica Lake in an Alan Ladd movie. Wasn't there one, in fact, called *The Blue Dahlia*?

Celeste, parading in this extraordinary confection, had an infallible sense of occasion. Lucinda, Anna was sure, would, in a similar situation, have shrugged the bonnet off. Celeste, on the other hand, kept her head gently balanced and moved more slowly than ever, as if she knew in her tiny rabbit mind that the crown she wore was fragile and commemorative, that she was indeed the Easter Bunny, Eostur, Eastar, Ostara, Ostar.

Anna did not, however, dare to give her the fragile Easter eggs to carry.

Joanna Wilkens returned on Easter Sunday to carry Anna off to a spiritualist service. Anna was glad to go. Easter confused her. How much could she participate in the real meaning of Easter? Despite the American celebration of Easter as yet another national holiday, with chocolate Easter bunnies and chocolate eggs, Anna Bernstein, American, was supposed to eat matzoh and observe Passover.

But now Joanna Wilkens offered spiritualism. All souls, under the fleshly shell, all astral envelopes, were the same. There was no reason why Anna could not go to an Easter service at the Spiritualist Church and feel like another soul.

Just another human soul. From the very first time Anna had accompanied Joanna Wilkens to one of these gatherings, she had started to look at people as souls. All the fleshly shells were different, but they were all simply souls, and the envelopes, the fleshly ones that is, did not matter nearly as much as *Vogue* and *Harper's Bazaar* suggested. Pretty or ugly, fat or thin, tall or short, all were souls. This ecumenical unity, this soulful oneness, Anna tried to keep with her as she went through her daily encounters with people. She found it made her better-tempered. It was hard to get angry at people for being rude, or ill-mannered, or arrogant, when you realized that they were all simply souls, thrust into their bodies by whatever powers at the moment of birth, souls chosen from a heavenly pool, to which they had returned, and from which they were now recycling again, earth to Heaven, Heaven to earth, in an eternal round in which God never wasted a single soul, though a lot of disposable bodies turned to dust.

Several of those souls were happy to be present at the American Spiritualist Church in Cambridge on Easter Sunday. The sermon that day was especially joyous, the meeting room decked out with lilies, the atmosphere filled with hope. The medium, the Reverend Anstrom, reminded the convocation, as Joanna had reminded Anna the day before, that for spiritualists, souls were resurrected every day. That much of the Christian world, celebrating Christ's Resurrection on Easter Sunday, this day, was unmindful of this. That many, for all that they were Christians, did not really believe souls survived and were resurrected after death into the Summer Land. That the spirit photographers had managed to capture them, at the moment of death, still attached by the cords of their astral envelopes, floating above their fleshly bodies, watching the mourners beneath them, the mourners weeping, weeping when they should have been smiling, with joy at the triumph of the spirit. That death, to the spiritualists, was a joyous entry into a better world. That it was the reward for having lived, for having tolerated the misfortunes of this place, this earthly place with all its hazards and sorrows. That spirit, as Andrew Jackson Davis, the great nineteenth-century seer, had written, was substance, and obeyed a higher law than gravitation. That Paul himself had said there is a terrestrial and a celestial, a natural body and a spiritual body. That Paul, the converted Jew, believed this strongly: we are sown in corruption, but raised in glory. Then the Reverend Anstrom started talking about sevens. Anna listened even more carefully, already buoyed up by the sense of joy that surrounded her in the room. Everyone was smiling and looking as though they could see the Summer Land even there, see each spirit in the gleams of sunlight that filtered through the windows.

There are, said the Reverend Anstrom, according, again, to Andrew Jackson Davis, seven spheres in the universe, and the Seventh Sphere is Beauty, blooming, as Andrew Jackson Davis said, with an immortal fragrance: "It is the Tree of Immortal Life, because there is no death. It is the Tree of Divine Perfection, because nothing is imperfect. It is the Tree of Goodness, because nothing is evil." The Seventh Sphere is "the Infinite Vortex of love and wisdom and the Great Spiritual Sun of the Divine Mind which illuminates the spiritual worlds."

The Seventh Sphere was filled with Deity. There was no evil on the Seventh Sphere. No Adolf Hitler, with his brown shoes. No Otto Dienes. Anna felt suddenly, surrounded by voices singing celestial hymns in high-pitched unison, as though all her earlier preoccupations had been unreal. This was reality, this room filled with light, these people affirming spirit. She drew closer to Joanna Wilkens. She never wanted to leave.

The billet reading began. The Reverend Anstrom took the small, carefully folded bits of paper out of the wicker baskets one by one. He did not bother, on this special day, to blindfold himself. There was no question of tricks to disprove. He kept each paper at arm's distance, fingered it to sense its message, and started calling out:

— Mrs. Henderson? Mrs. Henderson, where are you?

Like the other medium, he could identify the spirits but not the locus of the earthly in the room.

— Mrs. Henderson, your husband says something will change soon, be patient. It will be all right.

(Smiles from Mrs. Henderson.)

— Mrs. Quinn, Mrs. Quinn, have your doctor check those reports again, it's not terrible, but just have him check them, dear. Mr. Armstrong, Mr. Armstrong, oh yes, there you are over there, Mrs. Armstrong says she loves you, love, Mr. Armstrong, the message is love. Mr. Bailey, Mr. Bailey, change that job as soon as you can, start looking now, it's not going to work, I'm sorry.

(Compassion on the Reverend's face.)

— Miss Wilkens, Miss Wilkens, your aunt says she is glad you are keeping up. She is grateful for your loyal faith, Miss Wilkens.

Anna was about to poke Joanna, to whisper how glad she was that Joanna's Aunt Euphemia had come through, that Aunt Euphemia who always brought to mind Anna's friend Effie, that Aunt Euphemia who had brought spiritualism and hope not only to Joanna, but also, in some way she did not yet understand, to Anna, hope that her mother was really there, and that God had really, difficult though the accommodation might have been, welcomed the six million into the Summer Land, where there was no evil, no Otto Dienes, no pain or suffering, only a golden light. Anna was about to poke Joanna, but as she leaned over to whisper to her, the Reverend Anstrom called clearly:

— Miss Bernstein? Miss Bernstein?

He looked over to her solemnly and with a strange expression on his face as she raised her hand.

— Anna Bernstein, your mother says to remember you are Jewish.

All eyes of those attending the Easter Sunday service of the American Spiritualist Church turned to Anna. The Reverend Anstrom, for the first time since he had been calling out the billet messages, fell silent. All eyes contemplated Anna. Christ had risen and Anna was still a Jew.

The Reverend Anstrom, after his short silence, continued reading billets, and the loved ones kept responding across the line of living and dead. But Anna felt suddenly marked, in a way she had never been before. Even Joanna Wilkens, with no rent at all in the fabric of her friendship for Anna, seemed chastened, and for some of the less faithful, it was clear that this identification of Anna brought problems that caused them to avert their eyes when passing out of the church. Only the most devout of spiritualists really believed we are all souls under the earthly flesh.

Not long after Anna's mother had reminded her to remember, Kurt Hahn prevailed upon her to walk with him in the early morning sunlight along the Charles. Lying on the grass, beside the river that fronted Cotton Mather's Boston from the Cambridge side, looking over yet again at the golden dome of the State House, and the outscale glass of the Hancock Tower, Kurt Hahn asked Anna yet again to marry him at term's end. Anna, watching an ant tug at a tiny blade until he had loosed it from its moorings and tottered away under his burden, felt the weight of her own responsibilities upon her.

— Anna, look, it's so easy.

The old hat was pushed over his eyes to keep out the sun's rays. All Anna could see was his mouth, kissing the words to her. It was as though, by masking himself from her, it was easier to ask, easier to accept the expected no, easier to persevere — yet again.

— Kurt, please.

— Anna, please. Let yourself say yes, that's all, just yes.

— Your mother.

— Fuck my mother. *She's* not marrying you.

— *My* mother.

— What about your mother? Your mother's been gone since you were a kid.

Kurt Hahn was baffled. What other obstacles, what other impediments to the Path of True Love was he to encounter in his quest for the golden maiden? The ghost of Anna's mother, what was her name, Ellen, Ellen Bernstein? What did Ellen Bernstein, dead for fourteen years and, from Anna's earlier accounts, not religious anyway, have to do with it? A shade? A spook? A ghost? Of course, Joanna. Joanna had taken Anna with her to the spiritualist meetings. Now, clearly, he was to do battle with a spirit. Okay. Let it come. He wasn't going to be undone by some damned spirit. He slowed down now, now that he recognized the tripping stone. Gently. Gently. He pushed his hat back, and sat up, and took Anna's golden head in his hands, and stroked the long Rapunzel hair.

— Your mother's gone, sweetie. I know you still miss her. But I'll take care of you. Let me. Please let me.

— I'm Jewish.

Kurt Hahn heard the words with dread. Fuck the Jews. Fuck them for keeping Anna away from him. Couldn't they ever forget? Did he have to be punished for Lottie Hahn, who could never forget Martin Luther, or for Otto Dienes, God save his damned soul, whatever he might have done? Kurt Hahn, American-born, of ancestry mixed between German and Indian stock, was no one but himself. And Anna was no one but herself. Kurt Hahn loved Anna Bernstein. Fuck Jesus, fuck God, fuck Adolf Hitler and Martin Luther, fuck them all. Kurt Hahn loved Anna Bernstein. Why wasn't that enough? What battles did he have to fight, what spirits engage in mortal, or immortal, combat?

— I'm part Paiute as well as part German, you know. Don't I get some points for Indian blood? That makes me very Native American. (Trying to tease her into an affirmative, into a one-word yes from which he would never release her.) They were victims of genocide too, doesn't that count? Don't I get some points for that genocide? For the Indians who were murdered, and forced to walk the trail of tears, and treated like animals, and deprived of their homes and their lands and their immortality? What good white Americans did to the Indians was like what the Nazis did to the Jews. They wiped them out. They won't admit it of course, they don't even want to think about it. That's why they took Indian history and Indian myth and tossed them out the window, divorced them from our heritage as if they had never happened — all those great Creation myths, the bowels of the earth, the four corners, the Sky People. They even knew about the Ongwes. Swedenborg wasn't the only one, Anna, or your spiritualists after him. The Ongwes lived in Heaven on the other side, and they lived in houses in the sky, just as we do. So much for your Theosophy and spiritual correspondences, so much for the advanced knowledge of your civilized world. And who learns those things in American schools? No, it's just cowboys and Indians. John Wayne. Good guys and bad guys. The world isn't so black and white, Anna. It's not just good Jews and evil Germans. There were some good ones, too, you know. They also went to the camps, or got out and came here. Goddamn it, they founded the way we're taught art history in this country. They're our teachers! All the great names are German, some Jewish, but some not. The Jews weren't Hitler's only victims.

Anna heard Kurt's voice at a muffled distance. Indians. The Indians had, at least in some instances, fought back. With dignity. Like the Warsaw ghetto. But the Jews in the camps. The Indians had suffered from illness, and dread epidemics, and starvation, like the Jews in the camps. But they had had a better chance at fighting back. Somehow, they had managed to preserve more dignity. So it came down to dignity, not to numbers, not to annihilation, not even to death. It came down to dignity. The Jews had not really had a chance to fight back. It was a question of dignity, Anna thought.

She was lying on the new spring grass beside the Charles River, her head caressed gently by Kurt Hahn's hands stroking each golden strand, Kurt Hahn talking about marriage, and Indians and myths and Sky People, and, in every intonation of his voice, about love. Anna could feel Kurt Hahn's love for her emanating from his hands, as healers emit rays that stroke — so the occultists would say — the astral envelope, not even touching the body, and hoped that the unseen forces that permeate all of being would heal her with love. Anna wanted Kurt Hahn to heal her, to remove the nightmare of memory and of separation, to make her feel not like Anna Bernstein, Jew, heiress to the legacy of the six million, but like Anna Bernstein, part of the American Dream, open to all Utopian optimism, which had begun here in the cradle of democracy not too far from the State House dome, gleaming like the mosaics of Byzantium in the crisp spring sun of Boston. Anna Bernstein wanted to wipe out the genocides in her head, to wipe out the Polish towns the Nazis had wiped out, so that she wouldn't cry, as she had begun to do, in the middle of the night for the six million, so that she wouldn't feel, as she had begun to do, the Wasp supremacy of Cotton Mather's America, that America which had virtually eliminated the red man, enslaved the black, been hostile to the yellow, had even sensed beneath her own white skin blood that was not Christian. Anna wanted to erase all that so there would be in the world only Anna and Kurt, free to choose each other without memory or obligation. Wasn't that true American liberty? Wasn't it only in America that this could happen, as the saying went? Anna willed her heart to triumph, for those few moments at least, over memory, and at that early hour of the morning, like some glorious white swan, extended her lovely neck so that her lips joined those of Kurt Hahn, followed naturally by a very discreet and rather beautiful coupling, under Anna's long gauzy skirt, as the two lovers reclined along the banks of the Charles, with only a passing group of scullers to notice them, and since they were, in the naturalness of their love, really not much different from any two birds mating, even the scullers remained totally silent as they glided past.

Thought, however, does not idle long in heads inclined to that activity. Thought, for Anna, once Kurt Hahn had gone to his studio to paint out his frustrations (Anna, after their union, having as always withdrawn once more, claiming that an answer to his constant question was not yet possible, suggesting, still in the glow of their fusion, that maybe, maybe, who knew, when she had it all straightened out), thought, for Anna, and with it memory, returned as she climbed the steps of Widener Library, and vexed her even as she researched some of the Creation myths, for she found in a general book on myths that Adam, according to the Kabbalists, "was as big as the world" and also "contained in him all the souls of all human beings who ever existed — namely 600,000." The magic Kabbalistic number again. The ancient sum of the 600,000, which had only to be tenfolded to be the 6,000,000.

Anna turned the pages of the book rapidly, almost feverishly, looking for some other source, some other Creation, not out of Jewish myth, of which she had had enough, but from the Indians Kurt Hahn had spoken of, and found the Ongwes in the Iroquois cosmogony, and the concept of the earth deposited, along with a pregnant Sky Woman, on the back of a tortoise. On the next page, she discovered that in Indian legend supernatural pregnancies could come from fleas or lice. Was that how the Virgin Birth had been conceived? The author, Marie-Louise von Franz, referred to this as louse symbolism: "The louse in symbolism," said Marie-Louise von Franz, "usually carries the meaning of a completely autonomous thought; something that sticks in your mind, though you don't want it, and sucks your blood." Thought obsession could even be responsible for Creation: "Creation begins by a completely accidental little event — a woman combs her husband's hair and perhaps has eaten a louse." Then the pregnant Sky Woman fell on the tortoise and became the earth. What would Andrew say about this? Anna wondered. What would Andrew say about the extraordinary Creational possibilities of thought? And didn't she remember, yes surely she did, that Louis Agassiz had confronted Darwinian science with the assertion that species had been created by a thought of God? But hadn't that idea, of thought so potent that it could create world, been used by Louis Agassiz as justification for racism, for the God-intended immutability of the white, red, black, and yellow races?

Yet it was a lovely idea, it seemed to Anna, that Mind could be all powerful. It was just that, as with all things, it could be good or bad. There was that problem again, the good and the bad. Were these dialectical opposites the only reality? Could one ever manage to separate the pairs, save the positives, discard the negatives, turn all no's to yes, all hate to love, all murders to births? Here Marie-Louise von Franz began to draw on Jungian philosophy, but Anna's head had begun to tire. Jung was too much for now. She opened her copy of *Alice* and read instead:

"Would you tell me, please, which way I ought to go from here?"

"That depends a good deal on where you want to get to," said the Cat.

"I don't much care where ——" said Alice.

"Then it doesn't matter which way you go," said the Cat.

"—— so long as I get somewhere," Alice added as an explanation.

"Oh, you're sure to do that," said the Cat, "if you only walk long enough."

3

WIDENER LIBRARY suddenly felt very confining. Anna's small carrel, with its books cantilevering out over the desk, unsteady and precarious ziggurats on the floor, began to press in on her.

Anyone seeing Anna Bernstein's exit from Widener Library on that sunny spring afternoon might have speculated whether she was fleeing an unseen terror. Anna half ran out of the tall building, through the columned portico, down the steep stone steps, onto the crisscrossed greensward of Harvard Yard, and then stopped at the center, as though at the center of the world, at the omphalus of Creation, bewildered as to which direction to take, which path to follow. Randomly, without really knowing why, she struck out finally toward Brattle Street, tracing the red bricks to the yellow-and-white mansion of Longfellow, the verses of Hiawatha dimly chanting somewhere in her head:

> By the shores of Gitchee Gumee,
> By the shining Big-Sea-Water,
> Stood the wigwam of Nokomis,
> Daughter of the Moon, Nokomis.

The moon again. Here it was a nice, sunny spring afternoon, and here was the moon again. Börsch-Supan's Christ figure. Anna's head could not stop making connections. The Moon Goddess and Christ, and Börsch-Supan attending him, jostled in her head, and the afternoon sky suddenly looked dark and threatening.

> Many things Nokomis taught him
> Of the stars that shine in heaven . . .
> Showed the Death-Dance of the spirits,
> Warriors with their plumes and war-clubs . . .
> Showed the broad white road in heaven,
> Pathway of the ghosts, the shadows,
> Running straight across the heavens,
> Crowded with the ghosts, the shadows.
> At the door on summer evenings
> Sat the little Hiawatha.

Ghosts. Spirits. The whole universe peopled with spirits. All those souls who had ever lived, all the souls of the original 600,000 tenfolded by Adolf Hitler into the six million. It was all ghosts. Even Longfellow and Hiawatha had known this. And Hiawatha, sitting at the feet of Nokomis, sitting at the feet of the moon-daughter, that moon who was to become Christ, in whose name the Indians were to be exterminated, for they were not Christians, and therefore, said the American settlers, could not be entitled to the bounteous lands of America, could not be allowed to sing My country 'tis of thee / Sweet land of liberty, as Anna Bernstein had done in Glen Cove, Long Island, as a child, Hiawatha, sweet Hiawatha, about whom she had also learned as a child in school, reciting with her class, By the shores of Gitchee Gumee, / By the shining Big-Sea-Water, sweet Hiawatha, nestled in the arms of wrinkled old Nokomis, rocked in his linden cradle, bedded soft in moss and rushes, sweet Hiawatha of the Longfellow classic had grown up, according to revisionist history, to be a cannibal. Had he eaten only Christians? Would he have eaten Anna, a Jew? Kurt Hahn too was part Indian. There she was, there she was, back to Kurt Hahn. Back to ancestry. Back to genes and blood. Back to genocides and cannibalism, back to hate, when all she wanted was to love

Kurt Hahn. Anna stood outside the yellow-and-white home in which Longfellow had written "Hiawatha" and found her face wet with tears.

— Anna? Anna Bernstein?

It was Bitsy Allingame, coming along Brattle Street with a small cart full of bushes and plants. Bitsy Allingame, who was wary of Anna, who suspected the worst, who had debated with herself (having recognized the distinctive figure of Anna Bernstein in her gauzed white costume) whether to stop or just pass on without recognition, and then decided, since Anna seemed distressed, indeed, on closer observation, to be crying, that it was more charitable, indeed more *Christian*, to stop. Anna, with tears streaming down her face, and the Indian spirits mixing in the heaven of her head with the six million, hardly recognized Bitsy Allingame at Hiawatha's gate.

— My dear, said Bitsy Allingame, who had, as she trucked along, been wondering how she was going to get all those plants into the ground and still make a meeting of the Boston Daughters of the American Revolution. My dear, she said, stopping and releasing the handles of her small carrier, so that the plants pitched forward and shifted precariously as they rested on the sidewalk. My dear, may I help? Have you failed one of your courses? Is there bad news from home?

Anna Bernstein, perceiving through a shimmer Bitsy Allingame's athletically trim figure dressed in a lean wrap skirt and tailored blouse, composed herself.

— No, she said, beginning to avert her eyes and then straightening up and confronting the good Christian head on, her long neck erect and proud. No, I'm fine.

She noticed Bitsy's burden.

— May I help you with those?

Some of the plants, having continued to pitch slowly forward, were indeed sagging on their stems, their heads unable to straighten as Anna's had.

— They seem to be losing their balance.

— Oh, said Bitsy Allingame, now distracted by Anna's sudden composure. Oh. Would you? It's two o'clock, and I must get them in by three.

Bitsy Allingame had not quite understood, but it hardly mattered. Anna was happy not only to assist her with the plants to the gate of the Allingame residence, but to kneel on the cool spring earth, irretrievably brown-staining her white dress, as she dug small holes in the ground into which Bitsy Allingame, with a rare indication of supreme knowledgeability, deposited the roots of each budding bush.

Anna, feeling the earth in her hands, felt a sudden grounding there. Anna had been too much in the ether lately. Now she was back to earth, away from the spirits. Plant. Grow. Water. Bud. Flower. Die. Bud. Flower. Die. Bud. Flower. Die. No. She was not that far from the spirits. Nature recycled and renewed. Bud. Flower. Die. Bud. Flower. Die. What was the real difference? Resurrection was everywhere. Resurrection did not belong only to Christ. Resurrection was universal. Bud. Flower. Die.

— Will you hand me the pink azalea, my dear?

Bitsy Allingame was extending her long thin arm. Bud. Flower. Die. No budding without dying. No life without death. Dialectics again. Anna stopped suddenly and, to Bitsy Allingame's surprise, instead of complying with her request, simply sat back on her heels and began to examine the azalea. Gently, as though making love, she parted the pink petals to reveal the organs of reproduction, the inner parts. Bitsy Allingame, standing behind her as though transfixed, recognizing that Anna was not hearing her, absorbed as she was in her examination of the plant's growth and sexuality, stood there quietly, waiting.

Anna, for her part, began to stroke the petals as she parted them, gently, gently. The stuff of life was there. She could hardly remember the botany course she had taken in that other life in Brooklyn. But she remembered Goethe on the floor near her desk at Widener, Goethe who had searched for the *Urpflanze*, the perfect archetypal plant, the blueprint, the diagram for all existence. Like the perfect Aryan? Had Goethe himself held the seeds of Otto Dienes and Adolf Hitler? Not her friend Goethe. Not he too.

Bitsy Allingame finally grew impatient.

— Anna, my dear, she repeated briskly. Anna, I'll take the azalea now.

Anna Bernstein returned from Goethe searching for the *Urpflanze* in the gardens at Padua to the garden on Brattle Street, to Bitsy Allingame. Anna's mind, flashing back to the high school in Brooklyn, had begun to catch botanical terms that might be pertinent to the pink azalea plant, actually quite beautiful, which had been transferred, albeit with some difficulty, from Anna's hands to the more seasoned gardener's fingers and palms of Bitsy Allingame. Protoplasm. Nucleus. Phylogenesis. Cytoplasm. Cellulose. Photosynthesis. Osmosis. Transpiration. Tropism. Chlorophyll. Megaspore. Microspore. Meiosis. Sporophyte. Zygote. Chromosome.

Anna could not remember which came first, nor could she differentiate at this moment, watching Bitsy Allingame put the azalea into the earth, between the terms, could not assign meaning to any of them. They were simply words stored in those little brain boxes in her head, randomly released by some trigger from their storage bins. She knew that in some way, designed by nature or God, they had to do with life, and that her cells, Bitsy Allingame's cells, the azalea's cells, were all related. Everything living was cellular, and sexual, just as Bitsy Allingame had reluctantly (to herself) observed, and had she voiced this idea to Anna, Anna would have agreed. Did flowers propagate through love? Anna wondered. Had each azalea found its own Kurt Hahn? Was love necessary for life to continue, or was sex sufficient, and if it was, why must one be trapped in love, or if trapped in love, why did one's cells and heredity have to matter?

Mendel. The storage bin in Anna's head had turned up Mendel. Mendel had worked with garden peas. Had Bitsy Allingame planted any garden peas? Mendel had worked with hybrids. Kurt Hahn was a hybrid, an Aa instead of an AA. According to Mendel, Anna now remembered, the Mendelian storage bin suddenly widened to its ultimate state, in the second generation both grandparental types always reappeared in the same constant proportion, three-fourths dominant, one recessive. How would Kurt Hahn's Aa operate? How would Lewis Carroll/Charles Dodgson have reasoned it out? If A equals Otto Dienes and a equals Paiute Indian, did Otto Dienes win? Kurt Hahn had more Germanic genes. There was only a little bit of Indian there. According to Mendel, in the next generation one-fourth might be pure Indian, one-fourth pure German, and one-half would resemble the first-generation hybrid. Suppose Kurt Hahn was already AA instead of Aa? And Anna was surely BB. In the next generation, what chance would she have of having a child who was not AB, a child whose German and Jewish halves might hate each other, might tear each other equally in two? Would the genes of Otto Dienes, reinforced by Lottie Hahn and Martin Luther's AAAA, be more dominant than Anna's BB, watered down admittedly from Grandma's Yiddish by Ellen Bernstein's Glen Cove and finally now by Cotton Mather's Harvard?

Bitsy Allingame was calling to her. The planting was finished. Bitsy Allingame was offering tea in the home of one of Cotton Mather's descendants. Bitsy Allingame was opening the door to one of Boston's most distinguished social residences, if one were to go by ancestry and blood. The blood and the genes were the problem. Blood and genes. Anna followed blue-blooded Bitsy into the house, and asked for her tea with milk, please.

When Victor Allingame returned home a while later, he was surprised to find Anna Bernstein and Bitsy having tea. Bitsy tried hard not to reproach Victor for his little conquests. She knew very well that she could not push her wifely rights too far. She could only suggest to him that his associations with his young and beautiful students made her uneasy, especially when she suspected they surpassed the proper boundaries, when Victor inserted his blue-blooded "thing" (Bitsy never knew quite what to call it) into the *strange,* and that was the real point of it, strange, and possibly unclean receptacle of one of these young creatures. It made her ill to think of him even contemplating putting it thereafter into *her* private part, under an invisible PRIVATE sign reserved for Victor and only Victor for all time. But she couldn't nag him about it, for Victor Allingame wasn't the descendant of Cotton Mather for nothing. Victor Allingame, though he had never revealed this to Anna, was a bit of a martinet, a small kind of tyrant, and one could conceivably say that this was because he was, in Mendel's terms, AAAAAAAAAAAA. All Wasp New England. All royalty out of the Old Comers. All pure Cotton Mather. And Cotton Mather was not a man to tangle with. And he, and this Bitsy knew perfectly well (for the truth of this had entered history), he was also very fond of young girls, and had a great and loyal following of them, and is, indeed, purported to have used this following according to his necessities. So Bitsy Allingame, for all her own AAAAAAAAAAAA ancestry, could not push her disapproval of Victor Allingame's activities too far, though Victor knew very precisely how she felt. He was therefore surprised to find her sitting in his parlor having tea with Anna Bernstein under the portrait of Lucinda Allingame by Gilbert Stuart.

— Anna, my dear. Victor rallied quickly. What a lovely surprise. You've come, of course, to talk about your Millais paper!

Victor Allingame, his dark hair barely thinning or graying, was looking very fit. Hardly like someone who had been teaching for twenty-five years. Considering the spectacle of Anna and Bitsy sharing a civilized tea, with the afternoon sunlight dappling their heads, he had a profound feeling of well-being. Civilization really was a comfort. That one's wife and one's lover (for there was no doubt in Victor Allingame's mind that he and Anna were lovers; they had, after all, several times coupled in this very house) could indeed hold pleasant discourse together — how very *civilized* of Bitsy. He was inordinately proud of Bitsy right now, for he knew full well that she knew full well. Good stock. Stock, in the final analysis, was all. Blood would tell, as the saying goes.

Anna, starting to explain that her encounter with Bitsy

Allingame was a chance one, thought better of it and simply nodded a kind of affirmation. Victor Allingame amiably joined the domestic tableau, adding his tall frame to the shorter angles established by Anna and Bitsy as he completed the triangle.

— You are really almost morbidly concerned with Effie, are you not, my dear? Even after she was happily married to Millais, you held it against Ruskin.

— Ruskin was insensitive, Professor Allingame. She had six years of torture with him.

— But she was exposed to genius, my dear. Surely that was worth something. Ruskin was very supportive of Millais, after all, both before and after Millais went off with Effie. He thought Millais's *Ophelia* was a masterpiece, made Millais's reputation for him. And he was nice enough to invite Millais to Scotland with him in the first place. How could he know Millais would run off with Effie?

— Professor Allingame, you know very well they didn't run off together just like that. Poor Effie didn't even know what was expected of her as a wife. All she knew was that nothing (an eye to Bitsy's delicacy here), nothing *happened*, and nothing would have happened, once the five years she waited were up. And if Lady Eastlake hadn't found out, and told her what her mother had never told her, that it was not the way it was supposed to *be*, it was just *wrong*, very *wrong*, she might even have stayed, and anyway she left Ruskin and went home to her family *before* she and Millais got together. And I'm sure she was very nice. She looks nice in Carroll's photograph.

— My dear young woman — Victor Allingame was warming to his subject — did it ever strike you, in your admiration for Lewis Carroll, that he and Ruskin were really very much alike? They both loved pure young girls. Ruskin wanted to keep Effie pure. Carroll would photograph little girls in the nude only as long as their spirits were innocent.

For Bitsy Allingame, the conversation was taking on overtones that made her uncomfortable. All this business about pure young girls. What made the young so special?

What was so pure about youth? Anna Bernstein (Bitsy was now beginning to feel old resentments once more) was far from pure, despite her gauzy white gowns and Rapunzel hair. Anna Bernstein took up, it was quite clear, with married men. And Millais had taken up with a married woman. Thou shalt not commit adultery. It was very clear. What others? Honor thy father and mother. Why was Bitsy Allingame thinking that one? Victor did, indeed, often seem like a naughty child, and she his mother. Bad boy. Putting his thing into Anna Bernstein, even on the crewel bedspread of his ancestors. Bad boy. Bitsy remembered she was already late for the DAR meeting.

Even in the yellow room, Anna could not get Effie and Ruskin and Lewis Carroll right in her head. Dr. Linnell tried to talk to her about them, but it never came clear. They were giving her more electric, she knew they had just given her some more, but she couldn't quite remember when. She tried to push her head beyond that, back to the Bitsy Allingame day with the azaleas, but she kept coming up with Effie and Lewis Carroll.

— Do you identify with Effie, my dear?

Dr. Linnell was trying again to be helpful, or maybe, maybe, despite the fact that Anna liked Dr. Linnell much better than Dr. Gotthard, Dr. Linnell was being nosy.

— Identify? I-dent-ify?

Anna could talk the word and make it look as if she (I) were becoming a tooth. I — dent. Or a brand of toothpaste. I-O-Dent. Anna started playing with I-Dent-Ify. Anna found this amusing. Dr. Linnell waited. When Anna had stopped playing he asked her again:

— Do you?

— I'm not nearly as good with words as Lewis Carroll, you know. 'Twas brillig is a lovely poem, I like the slithy toves. I guess I-Dent-Ify is rather banal compared with slithy toves.

— Do you?

— Effie is my friend.

— Why?

— I don't know. I think when I found out about her, I felt sorry for her. Ruskin hurt her.

— Do you feel friendly toward everyone who is hurt?

— I feel friendly toward the six million.

— All of them?

— All or one, it's all the same.

— But why are Effie and Alice your friends? Alice wasn't hurt.

— That's what's so nice about her. Alice can't get hurt. And Victor was right, you know. Carroll and Ruskin were alike. They both liked young girls. But Carroll didn't hurt them. He gave them powers.

— Powers?

— Alice could be any size at all.

— What advantages are there to that?

Anna was puzzled.

— Some, she answered slowly. Some, I think. And Alice and Effie were very alike, only Effie got hurt.

— Are you a young girl like Effie and Alice, Anna?

— No, Dr. Linnell. I'm almost four billion years old. Andrew says so.

— Andrew?

— The one who comes sometimes. The problem is, I'm not sure I can be an alga and a garden pea too.

— A garden pea?

Anna shook her head. She was the one who was in the yellow room. Dr. Linnell was supposed to be the sane one.

— Mendel, you see.

— Mendel?

— *You* know. AAAAAAAAAAAAAAAAA. Victor and Bitsy Allingame are straight AA's all the way back to the beginning of America. But if they don't really start there, if they're algae too, then maybe billions of years ago they weren't as straight. Maybe there were no garden peas at the beginning. Then Cotton Mather wouldn't be so pure after all.

— Cotton Mather?

— He liked young girls too. But he had a tendency to burn them.

— Burn them?

— Well, some people say that in Salem they only hanged them. But I prefer to think of them as burned.

— You prefer to?

— Because then it ties up with the Apocalypse, you see, and the six million. It's much neater. It's the ends that got to me.

— The ends?

— The loose ends. I've been trying to figure it all out, but it was the ends that got to me.

Dr. Linnell could get no more from Anna that day, but felt he had begun to make progress. Had he been able to find the entries in Anna's diary for the weeks preceding her arrival at Mount Sinai, it might have helped even more, for there she had written:

> Ruskin had a terrible dream about a Cobra with a woman's breasts running after him. Ruskin told Effie he imagined women were very different and when he saw her that first evening, April 10th, he was disgusted. Ruskin had another dream about a little girl who died in a box. He had put her into it while she was alive. Ruskin hated his mother and Sundays. Ruskin lectured at Oxford and talked about the English as a still undegenerate race mingled of the best Northern blood.

Here Anna's diary changed abruptly. Anna enlarged the letters, writing,

BLOOD BLOOD BLOOD BLOOD
AAAAAAAAAAAAAAAAAAAA
AAAAAAAAAAAAAAAAAAAAA
AAAAAAAAAAAAAAAAAAAAA

continuously, till she had filled up the remaining space.

The dilemma of the algae had preoccupied Anna for several days after her encounter with Bitsy Allingame. For if she were indeed descended from a simple cell, a prokaryotic cell, a blue-green alga, if she were indeed, genealogically speaking, made up of a bacterial colony, if her real ancestry could be traced somehow from the blue-green algae and from those prokaryotic cells into the acoeles, or marine flatworms (which, the scientific books assured her, even had penises), then according to these books she was as much related to a sponge as to Grandma, and the whole human race, everyone, was so interrelated through cellular amalgamation that no prejudice, no bias, no human differentiations of skin, nationality, group, or color, least of all religion, could possibly apply. It was all DNA no matter how you looked at it.

And, in fact, if you wanted to go further, away even from science and evolution, you could go to Madame Blavatsky, so venerated by Joanna Wilkens's spiritualist friends, you could go to the Great Madame, whose Theosophist followers could link the *universal life force* between men and stones. Some of them could even (as Joanna Wilkens had informed Anna) preach the idea of each of us progressing through various forms of existence before reaching the human state. We might have been stones, or trees, or flowers, or birds, Joanna told Anna.

Anna, suffering her way through the convolutions of Blavatsky's mind, flanked in her carrel at Widener by flatworms and DNA on the one hand, and Blavatsky's *Cosmic Evolution in Seven Stanzas, Translated from the Book of Dzyan* on the other, read in Stanza One of this last that "the Eternal Parent . . . wrapped in her ever invisible robes had slumbered once again for seven eternities. . . . Time was not, for it lay asleep in the infinite bosom of duration. . . . Universal mind was not, for there were no Ah-hi . . . to contain it. The seven ways to bliss . . . were not. The great causes of misery . . . were not, for there was no one to produce and get ensnared by them. . . . The seven sublime Lords and the seven Truths had ceased to be. . . . Naught was. . . . The causes of existence had been done away with;

the visible that was, and the invisible that is, rested in eternal non-being, the one being."

Sevens again. Either Anna could be descended from an alga, or she could be part of the eternal non-being, the one being. Madame Blavatsky knew about sevens, about the Kabbalah. Had she known also that only fifty years after the publication of *The Secret Doctrine* in 1888, the 600,000 of the Kabbalah would be tenfolded? Had she looked into the "Mirror of Futurity" in the Secret Books and found the cycles within the bosom of Sesha or infinite time written down, recorded, so that she knew all about the 6,000,000? What if Anna had a mirror of futurity, what would it reveal to her? Was there peace out there? For her mind felt ever more tortured, more tormented by the endless boxes opening simultaneously in her head, endless collisions of Kurt Hahn and Hitler's brown shoes and Alice and Grandma and Brooklyn, and Cotton Mather firing the pyres of white supremacy, with his clone, Victor Allingame, guiding little girls to the flame. To be an alga or a stone. To be part of the eternal non-being. To be anything but human, with nerves and feelings, and little boxes in one's head. She was grateful when Kurt Hahn arrived, carrying a bottle of white wine and some pâté, and took her off to the Charles for some respite. She was beginning to feel very strange in her head. She hoped Kurt Hahn wouldn't notice.

Kurt Hahn, as it turns out, was so preoccupied with getting Anna to marry him that he hardly noticed at all. Like Goethe's Werther, he was berserk with love, and unsure that it could ever be reciprocated in kind. If Anna really loved him, how could she hold his blood against him? How could he be responsible for his blood? He didn't for a moment accept Anna's remonstrances, that it was *her* blood, her Jewish blood that stood in the way. No. It was his blood, his Germanic blood, the blood not only of Goethe and Nietzsche but of Hitler, more specifically, the blood of Otto Dienes, the blood of his grandfather, who, while Anna's people were being murdered at Auschwitz, had been an Important Person in Hitler's Germany; who, a few years after Anna's people had been turned to soap, fled to Argentina, for what crimes Kurt Hahn still did not know.

But having finally seen an old and withered Otto Dienes, Kurt Hahn had felt neither compassion nor kinship, but rather, as he watched Otto Dienes's beady regard of Anna Bernstein, a sinking feeling that all his worst fears were true. Had Otto Dienes remained in Germany, he would have had to account for actions that Kurt Hahn dreaded ever knowing. Not knowing kept Kurt Hahn pure. Not knowing, he could live with himself, could acknowledge with some pride the German blood in his veins. That blood mixed with American and with Native American made him what he was, gave him, perhaps, his special artistic talents, sensitivities, passion, his ability to love Anna Bernstein. And in feeling passionate love for Anna Bernstein, it was only natural to Kurt Hahn that he should want to marry her. He rejected the idea of his ancestral countryman Nietzsche, who had skeptically pronounced, "The institution of marriage stubbornly maintains the notion that although love is a passion, it is still capable of *lasting* as a passion." This "noble superstition," to use Nietzsche's term, Kurt Hahn indeed sustained. His passion for Anna Bernstein would never, could never die. Marriage — bourgeois, ordinary domestic marriage — could not kill it. Anna Bernstein was his Rapunzel, and his love for her was ever a fairy tale, and reality, that reality which applied to everyone else, did not apply to them. Kurt Hahn was, in this sense, both Indian warrior and German Nordic god. He would claim his maiden, his fair princess out of Grimm. Nietzsche's misogyny, his tortuous connections to Nazi mythology, did not sit well with him anyway.

Kurt Hahn believed with a true romantic heart that Anna Bernstein had been intended for him since Creation, that each had drifted through the ages waiting for their souls to meet. Given Anna Bernstein's obsession with ancestry, he would have settled for the algae she was always talking about. No blood. Just the beginning of life. Common ancestry. No man-made differences, no organized religion, no ethnic twaddle.

Anna Bernstein, equally absorbed in her own thoughts, shared with Kurt Hahn a silence that was for each of them alternately peaceful and tortured. She spread her gauzed skirt about her on the river grass like a wide-petaled camellia, and thought of madness. For Anna's head felt, as Alice might have put it, stranger and stranger. She had begun to research this last subject with the same intensity given to all the others.

So she had read Sebastian Brant's *Ship of Fools,* the *Narrenschiff,* and could visualize now Bosch's painting of this eternal subject. The medieval mad had been sent not to institutional asylums, but to the sea, where they would wander on the wet plane of space, seeking the asylum of infinite oblivion. Anna would not, at this moment, have minded such oblivion. She was finding it increasingly hard to sleep, and the idea of the soft roll of the seas, of the flat endless horizon was, right now, as close to Madame Blavatsky's eternal non-being as she might find in this world. Madness, she discovered with distress in a book by Michel Foucault, was directly connected by Tissot to the "life of the library."

The "perpetual agitation of the mind without the exercise of the body, can have the most disastrous effects." Reading this, making her careful notes in the small carrel at Widener, Anna, feeling stranger and stranger, had to agree. "Among men of letters," continued Foucault, again quoting Tissot, "the brain hardens; often they become incapable of connecting their ideas. . . . The more abstract or complex knowledge becomes," said Tissot via Foucault, "the greater the risk of madness."

This claim was fortified by Anna's discovery, in the rare-book room at Widener, of a richly tooled leather-bound copy of *The Anatomy of Melancholy,* printed from the "authorized copy of 1651" and signed Democritus Junior (the author's true name: Robert Burton). This Democritus Junior/Robert Burton also stated that "many men come to this malady by continual study and night-waking, and of all other men, scholars are most subject to it." Too much study, Festus told Paul, according to Democritus Junior/Robert Burton, "hath made thee mad." And not only mad, but melancholy. And not only melancholy, but otherwise ill. (Hard students were, in addition, commonly troubled with "gowts, catarrhes, oppilations, vertigo, winds, consumptions, and all such diseases as come by over-much sitting.")

Now, lying on the springtime grass beside her love, Anna had begun to feel some of these things — wisps of melancholy, and a kind of giddy vertigo. But Democritus Junior/Robert Burton had not mentioned the thought boxes, had not spoken of the battle of ideas and feelings. Anna Bernstein's mind and heart were suffering from overload, and Widener Library, all the books overloading the space of the carrel, were feeding this, but it was not the ideas and feelings per se, but the battle between them, the pulls and tugs of the specifics, each with its claims upon her, that was causing this strangeness. Love/hate/ego/race/eternity/present/God/self/memory/oblivion. It was not simple knowledge, not just student overstudy, not the old idea of the active versus the contemplative life. Not a matter of running for two miles a day, as some of her friends at Harvard did, as Andrew had begun to do. No. It had to do with choice, and with conflicts so old that Democritus Junior/Robert Burton should have known of them.

For he had known, for all this, about love, had described Kurt Hahn's feelings quite accurately: "Most part of a lover's life is full of agony, anxiety, fear and grief, complaints, sighs, suspicions, and cares . . . full of silence and irksome solitariness . . . except at such times that he hath *lucida intervalla*, pleasant gales, or sudden alterations; as if his mistress smile upon him, give him a good look, a kiss."

Kurt Hahn and Anna Bernstein were enjoying a brief *lucidum intervallum*. Kurt Hahn was enjoying some small relief from his agony, simply by being in Anna Bernstein's presence. Anna Bernstein too was feeling some relief from

the great indecisions that were tearing at her, for the
moment did not demand choice. Kurt Hahn, in this instant,
was not pressing her. He was absorbed in his own thoughts,
and she in hers. She was, for this brief time, with the
springtime sun on her skin and the grass between her toes,
feeling surcease from pressure. Maybe it was indeed simple.
Maybe, like Andrew, she should run for two miles each
morning. Maybe then the thought boxes would stay closed
and the "humid, heavy" world of melancholia would not
advance on her. Tomorrow she would ask Andrew if she
could join him. She breathed a sigh that almost startled Kurt
Hahn with its dolorous extension. Then she smiled at him,
as though released from some terrible constraint, and the
rest of that day would have been described by Democritus
Junior/Robert Burton as an exceedingly long *lucidum intervallum*.

Andrew Hanson was delighted to have Anna's company for
his morning run along the river, though the sight of Anna,
still in her gauzed dress, incongruously attired in running
shoes and struggling to keep up, awakened in Andrew
Hanson further feelings not only of love but of tender
protectiveness. For Anna had confided in him, and in him
alone, that she was beginning to feel strange in her head,
and maybe Democritus Junior was right, and she needed
some exercise, some relief from the sedentary state of the
scholar.

She continued to research madness. Maybe if she knew
enough about it, it would go away. Experience, however,
was teaching her that this was not the way things developed, that the more research she did, the less she really
knew. Knowledge brought only the realization of the im-
possibility of knowledge. Learning was an endless pit, a
forever-receding horizon that kept unraveling the universe
at a rate no single human being could ever catch up with.

But she had to try to save herself. Thus to the impossible
mound of books in Anna's Widener carrel (which had
already overflowed into two nearby spaces, with notes and

signs appended to them attesting to Anna Bernstein's proprietary claims) were added the medical books on depression that introduced Anna more intensively still to DNA. Anna had not known very much about this stuff of life. Now, suddenly, she discovered that if she had a defective strand of DNA, it would affect the neurotransmitters in her brain. These so-called chemical messengers were supposed to be signaling one another inside her head, controlling her feelings and thoughts. Were they even responsible for the inner battles of the thought boxes? Was she missing some neurotransmitters? Could she be missing something called norepinephrine? If her norepinephrine was inadequate, this would explain why she felt so strange. She felt all the symptoms described in the books. She was developing what the books called anhedonia (loss of joy). This anhedonia was accompanied by insomnia and loss of appetite. Anna was becoming still thinner, and her long neck, always elegant, was beginning to look decidedly bony. Anna would lie in bed at night and her eyes would refuse to close. She would will them closed, and they would pop open again quickly, and when they did, the thought boxes popped open as well, as if they were all on the same latch. Anna never knew which thought boxes would open, and she was suffused with anticipatory dread, for too often the Otto Dienes box would open, and the painful list of eradicated Polish towns would parade with totally clarified recall down a screen in the darkness. Anna's mind assumed more clarity than ever at night, and the simultaneous eruptions of the thought boxes began to resemble the graves of the souls on Judgment Day. Here is Otto Dienes. Here a devil to cart him away in the air. Here is Cotton Mather. Who gets him? Angel and devil struggling. Here is Lottie Hahn. Limbo. Where will she go? Here is Anna, strung from a harp in a segment of Hell. Here is Kurt Hahn, wearing his cowboy hat, being weighed on the scale of justice.

If Anna indeed had a defective DNA strand, which was causing her to have insufficient norepinephrine, how was she to deal with this? For she would get up from these terrifying nights, dominated by ever more active thought boxes popping open, commanding her attention and wakefulness, and then, overstimulated and at the same time exhausted from lack of sleep, drag herself through her days, half dozing in her carrel at Widener, where now she spent most of her daylight time, unless specifically routed by Andrew or Kurt or Joanna, trying to decide whether her strangeness was indeed chemical, or, according to Democritus Junior/Robert Burton, the result of overstudy. Only one of the books dealing with madness had pointed to the problem of choice and indecision as a factor. This was buried in a footnote so tiny she might have missed it. What *is* sure is that Anna did not know the real cause of her growing strangeness to herself, and was now growing madder worrying about it.

Though she did her best not to communicate her anxieties to her friends, it was clear to them that something was wrong. Madness, however, was not something they readily considered; indeed, how often do the rational admit the existence of the irrational anyway? Joanna Wilkens, with due respect for spirit, did not find her own belief in the world beyond in the slightest way irrational. Madness would have been something else again. As for Kurt, to discern madness in his beloved would have been to admit a flaw in her perfection, compromising the wholesomeness of her beauty. Kurt preferred to think simply that Anna had been studying too hard, that she was just overexhausted and should have more fun. Andrew was the only one who was capable of considering the idea of a growing illness that, if it reached a certain threshold, could be called madness. For Andrew, with his scientific background, his knowledge of such mysterious body substances as DNA, could indeed premise that Anna's chemistry was disturbed, that something in her inner balance, her blood, her metabolism, her neurotransmitters even, had gone wrong. Anna clearly was becoming ill. Though he hoped that, as some medical authorities believed, the jogging along the river might release some necessary norepinephrine, and even some serotonin, Andrew was afraid that Anna's illness was already too far along for this. Her insomnia, she admitted to him, had grown worse. Her mind (her thought boxes, as she put it) would not stop. Dark circles were appearing under her eyes. She was losing weight to the point where her grace was giving way to a certain ungainliness.

— Anna, he said to her one morning, when she appeared merely more exhausted, not exhilarated from their river running, let me get you to a doctor.

— Don't need one, Andrew. She threw her headband off and untied her shoes.

— He can at least give you sleeping pills.

— Don't believe in them.

Her speech too had lost its grace, as though even the niceties of language were too much for her.

— Anna, this is not good. It can't go on this way. You're getting sick.

— Yes, Andrew. I am.

She changed her shoes and went off to Widener, where, despite her chronic exhaustion, the words on the printed page continued to exert their spell. Somewhere in Anna's racing mind was the idea that the books at Widener held the answer she was looking for. When she found it, she would get well.

Entry in Anna Bernstein's diary, undated, near end of volume:

The Adventures of Chess, Edward Lasker, p. 273, Diagram 36:

In reply to 2. . . . . K-Kt1, White has a forced mate in six moves as follows: 3. Q-R5, R-K1; 4. QxP ch, K-R1; 5. Q-R5 ch, K-Kt1; 6. Q-R7 ch, K-B1; 7. Q-R8 ch, K-K2; 8. QxP mate.

Black cannot escape his doom with 2. . . . . K-Kt3 either. 3. P-KR4 would threaten to win the Queen by forcing the King to R3 with P-R5 ch and then giving a discovered check with the Knight, as shown above. Black must therefore move his Queen to a square which the Knight cannot attack, for example, Q-K2. However, after 4. P-R5 ch, K-R3 (Diagram 37), White has again a forced win. 5. Q-Q3, threatening mate through Q-R7 as well as KtxBP dbl. ch., would compel Black

to answer P-KB4. Then 6. PxP e.p. renews the threat, and this
time there is no defense.

Anna was feeling blocked. Anna was feeling that there was
no defense. Among the books at Widener were some
directly connected with the thesis on which she was ostensibly engaged, that thesis which represented her early
intention, so long ago, in her first days at Cambridge, to
write about Caspar David Friedrich, Goethe's near contemporary from that early Germany she still found difficult to
surrender. That early Romantic Germany had as its
heroes — her mind made its usual run of connections —
Jakob Böhme, a Christian mystic not unrelated to the
mystics of the Kabbalah, and Meister Eckhart, who had
written of the central silence, like Emerson's wise silence,
like Madame Blavatsky's eternal non-being. Anna wanted to
get to the calm inner place of the eternal non-being, to find
the peace of the wise silence. Could she close the thought
boxes in her head by substituting images for words?
She stopped reading for several days and just sat leafing
through reproductions of Caspar David Friedrich's paintings
over and over again, ignoring Börsch-Supan's text with its
relentless emphasis on Christian iconography — no moon
without Christ, no rock that is not symbolic of the faith, no
light without the light of Christianity, no rising sun without
Resurrection. Anna especially liked Caspar David Friedrich's painting of *Moonrise on the Sea*. It was smooth, and
brownish purple. No hard edges. All delicate curves. On the
curved rocks sat three figures, silhouetted against the sky;
light emanated from some celestial core beyond the material
surface of the painting. The figures watched the sea on
which two ships were sailing. The sea of Caspar David
Friedrich's painting was the sea of eternal non-being. It was
where one could find the wise silence. It was also the wet
plain on which the *Narrenschiff* had set sail. Peace and
madness all together. Anna sat for a long time with the three
figures and watched the ships. She knew very well that
Börsch-Supan thought the ships were concerned with the

brevity of life, with journey's end, that Friedrich himself probably was, as Börsch-Supan contended, preoccupied with death. But what was death but a final consummation with eternal non-being? What was death but Summer Land? Despite Börsch-Supan, Friedrich's Death was accessible to Everyman. Why should only Christians have a priority on the blessings of death? Why should the peace, calm, and fulfillment of death be blocked to the unbaptized? Anna's God could not have let the six million die and forbidden them peace in death, at the very least. Nor could Caspar David Friedrich have painted his mountains and rainbows, his mists and his silences, only for the initiated.

Anna hung a reproduction of Caspar David Friedrich's *Moonrise on the Sea* opposite her bed. When the thought boxes waked her, she did not turn on the light. She lay there in the half darkness, the light from the street lamps below filtering past the tree leaves into her room, and watched the barely visible silhouettes of the three people watching the sea, which alternated in her mind between the universal peace of the eternal non-being and the wet limbo of the fools.

It was Joanna and Andrew who suggested the picnic at Walden, which they saw as an opportunity to get Anna away from Widener. Widener, clearly, was becoming lethal to Anna. Her eyes were overbright, she continued to lose weight, and seemed increasingly removed from her friends, absorbed with an inner battle to which they had no access. Kurt saw the trip as a rare opportunity to spend some relaxed time with his love, as well as another chance, if he could be alone with her, to convince her that marriage between them was a necessity, that once married to him she would lose her fears, that she would be a part of him, and he of her, no longer alienated by ancestry, whether German, Paiute, or Jewish, but producing children whose mixed homogenized blood would proclaim the American Dream.

Had anyone told Kurt Hahn that this glorious ideal was simply another way of eliminating Jews, that rabbis trembled at the thought of intermarriage, that this was the subtlest and most insidious of all mass exterminations (for Anna to "marry out" was to contaminate her pure Jewish blood — which despite the suspicious signals of her blonde hair and blue eyes, ran BBBBBBBBBBBB, just as Victor Allingame's ran AAAAAAAAAAAA), he would not have understood. For Kurt Hahn this was the one sure way to eliminate religious and racial differences — to mix it all up, to scandalize those who thought in terms of "pure breeding," to mongrelize all participants so that hate and prejudice could finally vanish because everyone's blood ran through everyone else's blood and there was no point in trying to sort it out.

Anna was happy enough to go. She threw herself into preparations for an elegant picnic feast, spending hours reading through cookbooks for appropriate cold salad recipes before arriving at chicken and walnuts in tarragon mayonnaise, arugula salad with basil and watercress, strawberries, a Thermos full of Häagen-Dazs ice cream in everyone's favorite flavor, and chilled white California wine. There was much debate as to which animals should go, but finally only Lucinda made it, and proudly exited with the humans, so to speak, while the black rabbit and the cats sat and watched the leave-taking, each with that expression of wistful reproach so well known to departing animal owners.

Walden, that day, was Paradise.

Anna left 2 Trowbridge Street clutching a copy of the famous book, as well as a volume on the thoughts of Thoreau, while Andrew and Kurt struggled with Lucinda and the picnic things, Joanna calling for them all in an old open car, just then becoming fashionable again. Anna and Kurt sat with Lucinda in the back while Anna recited bits of Thoreau aloud to her friends. The measure of love all felt for her was indicated by the indulgence with which they accepted still more text from the reader on a day in late spring that required no words, not even Thoreau's:

Walden is a perfect forest mirror, set round with stones as precious to my eye as if fewer or rarer.

— Lucinda, stay still, you're upsetting the food.

Nothing so fair, so pure, and at the same time so large, as a
lake, perchance, lies on the surface of the earth.

Her listeners, chattering about trivia and watching for
road signs, denied to Thoreau the rapt attention Anna felt
he deserved; so Anna read silently for a while, retreating to
her own familiar word-entranced state, turning the open
sky into the carrel at Widener:

When a new country like North America is discovered, a few
feeble efforts are made to Christianize the natives before they
are all exterminated, but they are not found to pay, in any
sense. But the energetic traders of the discovering country
organize themselves, or rather inevitably crystallize, into a
vast rat-catching society, tempt the natives to become mere
vermin-hunters and rum-drinkers, reserving half a continent
for the field of their labors. Savage meets savage, and the
white man's only distinction is that he is the chief.

Thoreau, thought Anna, had known not only about
Nature, but about genocides:

We survive, in one sense, in our posterity and in the contin-
uance of our race, but when a race of men, of Indians for
instance, becomes extinct, is not that the end of the world for
them? Is not the world forever beginning and coming to an
end, both to men and races?

Anna and her friends were on their way to Walden, Thoreau's "earth's eye." Anna recalled another lake, visited not
in springtime but in the winter of the American Southwest,
when the sun still had some warmth in it, when Kurt had
brought her to the sacred lake of his own Paiute people.
Kurt Hahn's German blood was for the moment put aside
and now his smaller Native American part, his Indian part,
could find rapport with her Jewish fate.

"This life we live is a strange dream," Thoreau wrote to
his mother on August 6, 1843. Thoreau, whom she had not
sufficiently befriended during her year at Harvard, was
someone with whom Anna could communicate. Thoreau

could sound like Lewis Carroll. Anna arrived at Walden feeling as if she had acquired a new friend who would walk with them beside the lake filled with blue angels — beside the Sky Water. For the first time in a long while, Anna felt calmed. Thoreau had calmed her. His serene philosophy had changed, for the moment at least, her inner pace. Now that she knew he knew about genocide, Anna could share with him the peaceful serenity of Nature.

Nature that day might have achieved this miraculous calming effect upon Anna even without Thoreau, or with some other, nameless lake. For water, that gentle day, seemed to Anna to quench her inner fires, dousing the multiple holocausts, and even the harsh fire of her passion for Kurt Hahn. So she could contemplate him without anguish, could run with him as in the psalm in the woods beside the still waters. Water entered Anna's soul through her eyes, and cooled her fever.

Anna's three friends were delighted with the effect of Walden Pond on Anna Bernstein. Lucinda, sensing their happy mood, ran through the woods in wild circles (called back by Andrew every few moments — it was not a day for leashing either man or beast). Thoreau at Walden, Anna knew, was not really in the wilderness; with his mother's house only three miles away, a good family meal was always at hand. But now, even marred by fame and tourism, the lake still radiated a primal light. As Fitz Hugh Ludlow, a nineteenth-century writer, explorer, and dope addict Anna had discovered in a footnote, might have said, Anna and her friends had entered into the "sacred closet" of Creation.

Genesis at hand, crystalline light casting sublime rays upon translucent water, they walked clear around Thoreau's deep green-and-blue well, so carefully surveyed that he knew it to be half a mile long and a mile and three quarters in circumference. Along the way, Andrew Hanson pointed out pitch pines dropping sulphur-scented pollen all over the pond and shore (perfect, said Thoreau, as Grecian art, one of Nature's *later* designs). Time, indeed, registered for all of them much as Andrew always took it, measured in transcendent geological spans. The day hung suspended, without arbitrary markers. Heady and oblivious, they ate when hungry.

It was in such circumstances that the two lovers, by tacit agreement among all the friends, parted from the others, to wander off into the woods and lie quietly together, Anna clutching a bit of fern that Andrew had told her went back to the Carboniferous period, actually known as the Age of Ferns, about 280 million years ago.

— It's very old, she said to Kurt, tickling his nose with it as they reclined under a large maple tree.

— And life is short, he answered, sitting up and looking into Anna's eyes, which this day gleamed with a lighter light, reflecting her lifted spirits.

— That depends on how you look at it. Thoreau was a kind of spiritualist, you know. He thought we just pass on to another form of life after death.

— Anna, stop fooling around. I'm only interested in one life, or two. Our lives, together. This is the only life we'll ever know, even if there *is* something more afterwards, even if we reincarnate. This is the only one *we'll* ever know. Please, Anna.

— Thoreau thought it was a dream, just like Lewis Carroll.

— Anna, come on.

Kurt pressed his body against her.

— Feel me. I'm no dream, and neither are you. I love you.

Anna felt Kurt's body against her, and feeling flesh, felt also a surge of spirit, and feeling spirit felt also a surge of love, that love she had tried so hard to deny, that love she found impossible to repress under this tree, near Thoreau's pond, with the sunlight filtering through the leaves and the earth beneath her. Anna felt heaven and earth coalesce in this one moment beside the earth's eye. Anna, for the first time since her encounter with Otto Dienes, laid aside all apprehension. Anna for the first time allowed herself to feel her total love for Kurt Hahn.

Afterwards, after the two spirits had joined in an act that mimicked the bonding of heaven and earth, when Kurt asked Anna for the hundredth or maybe the thousandth time to marry him, Anna wordlessly nodded, in that simple gesture taking upon herself the awesome prospect of mixing her BBBB with his AAAa, in that single moment allowing herself to hope that the small *a* would triumph over Otto Dienes and Lottie Hahn, that the Paiute in Kurt Hahn could match the Jew in her.

♪ 4 ♪

Cambridge
September 1, 1980

Ms. Anna Bernstein
Klingenstein Clinical Center
Mount Sinai Hospital — 7th Floor
New York, N.Y.

Dear Anna—

I was delighted to see the way you have improved.
Almost my old Anna again. I know you will be coming
back to 2 Trowbridge any day now, and we are all waiting
for you. Celeste, especially, has missed you, and Lucinda,
though she won't admit it, is dying for you to get back
and walk her. Everything here is beginning again, and I've
seen to it that your carrel at Widener is still reserved for
you. Except, honey bun, I'm not going to let you overdo it
this time. You're going to get much more fresh air and
exercise. I'm becoming a real jogging champ, and if you
want to keep up with me, you'll have to go some. Will
try to be back in New York by next week. Maybe by
then your treatments will be over, and I can take you
home with me. As you know, I am always here to care for
you, dearest Anna, so don't be afraid to come home. I've
spoken to your grandmother, who's feeling much better

after her high blood pressure attack, though the doctors still won't let her travel. She loves you very much, and she told me I'm a good boy for caring so much about you, but then, we all knew that, didn't we? She would like you to come home to Brooklyn, but I think if you can, Cambridge would be healthier. You belong here. See you soon, dearest friend.

Ever your
Andrew

Anna Bernstein, reading Andrew's letter in the yellow room, smiled. She *was* feeling better. She didn't quite know whether she could face Widener again, but she certainly couldn't face Brooklyn, though she loved Grandma more now, as some things began to come clearer for her, than ever before.

Dr. Linnell, entering at just the strategic moment, was in time for her comment:

— I don't know where to go.

— You're not quite ready to go anywhere yet, Anna. Leave it alone.

— I feel ready.

— That's good, my dear. You're getting along fine. But don't worry yet about where you'll go. It's still premature. Take your time. I'll let you know when.

— I like this room. I feel safe here. You don't have too many books.

— Do too many books upset you?

— The books had too many answers. I couldn't deal with all the answers. There were so many answers, there *were* no answers.

— Must there be answers, Anna?

— So many people expect there to be, I just felt obliged to keep looking.

— Do you care so much about what other people think?

— I didn't think I did. But responsibility. Where does responsibility go?

— Which responsibility, Anna?

— Oh, you know. The six million. They were all mixed up with the sevens.

— The sevens?

— Yes, of course. The sevens.

✺✺✺✺✺

It was only natural after Anna accepted him for Kurt Hahn to share his joy with the others. It had never occurred to Anna to tell him not to, to wait until she, especially, had time to absorb it, or indeed, at the very least, to consider the feelings of Andrew Hanson, Andrew Hanson who had never given up hope, Andrew Hanson who might really be crushed at this announcement, Andrew Hanson who loved Anna, in his own way, as deeply as Kurt. When they rejoined the others, Kurt, grinning broadly, so that his smile almost transgressed the limits of his face, simply said:

— We're getting married.

All proper joy was projected by the two friends Anna and Kurt had rejoined, hugs and kisses were properly exchanged, Lucinda, sensing pleasure, ran in and out of the small embracing group. Andrew Hanson withheld any signs of his distress from the happy couple. To his question, When? the reply was, As soon as possible. All this from Kurt, with Anna standing beside him in a rather dazed state, thinking only that she must let her mother know. Thus it was that when she had a moment alone with Joanna Wilkens, on the way back to the car, Anna asked if Joanna could arrange for another séance. Anna wanted Ellen Bernstein's blessing on her union with Kurt Hahn.

The séance was soon scheduled for a week hence. Anna, despite Kurt's impatient prodding, refused to set a wedding date quite yet.

— Two weeks, Anna, he said firmly. No more. Two weeks, that's it. Then we can go back to Nevada for the rest of the summer. I'll make a cowgirl out of you yet.

Kurt Hahn, who had always felt out of step with New England, would bring Anna back to Pyramid Lake. Knowing Anna's reservations about Otto Dienes, and even Lottie Hahn herself, he was instinctively drawing closer to his Indian forebears. If Anna wanted him to, he'd turn full Indian, wear a war bonnet, dance and whoop in Harvard Square, anything, anything to keep that total offering of self he had felt under the maple tree at Thoreau's pond. He would, if necessary, become a rabbi or a Kabbalist. Anything. So long as Anna would marry him and live with him for the rest of his life in *this* world, fuck the next one. Anything.

Anna, for her part, seemed, in the week following the picnic, to swing erratically from one state to another. She was going to marry Kurt Hahn. She had done it, committed herself. Their two futures would go teleologically in the same direction, into middle age, into old age. They might even be buried together, not necessarily as Increase and Cotton and Samuel Mather were, but side by side, maybe with the same headstone: Here lies Kurt Hahn with his wife Anna Hahn, *née* Bernstein, daughter of Ellen. With whom she must talk as soon as possible. Whose permission Anna felt desperately she must have.

The thought boxes had intensified the pace of their odd openings and closings. Anna slept now almost not at all, tossing and turning in the half darkness lit by the street lamp, joining Caspar David Friedrich's three figures on the rocks, but unsure of the nature of their companionship. In the middle of the night she was led by the three figures into thought, but not into the serene contemplation she sought. Rather, it was a strange mix of pleasure and doubt, of ambivalence and pain worse than any she had ever known.

Anna Bernstein pursued her research at Widener, still convinced that somewhere in the books was the necessary clue to the strangeness she continued to feel. That her pain was not unique, that other lovers had also experienced pain in passion, was clear from Novalis: "When pain is being shunned, that is a sign that one no longer wants to love. Whoever loves must everlastingly remain aware of the surrounding void, and keep the wound open." According to Novalis, she must endure this pain or she did not love. But also according to Novalis, "The intoxication of the senses may be related to love as sleep is to life. It is not the better part, and a man of strength must always prefer waking to sleeping."

Torn between waking and sleeping, Anna felt a pain generated both by passion, by her desire for Kurt Hahn, and by something more abstract, by the conflict of that personal desire with her obligation to other souls and other spirits who had shared her genetic composition, her blood. All blood, it seemed to Anna, looked the same. Just red. Regardless of the skin that covered it. When anyone was cut, they bled red. All blood was red. Couldn't she make some sort of Lewis Carroll logic out of that? Opening her copy of Lewis Carroll's *Symbolic Logic*, she found in Book VIII, Chapter I, 5: Pairs of Concrete Propositions, proposed as Premises: Conclusions to be found: 7.

Some Jews are rich:
All Esquimaux are Gentiles.

This appeared just above 8:

Sugar-plums are sweet;
Some sweet things are liked by children.

and 13:

No Frenchmen like plumpudding;
All Englishmen like plumpudding.

Was Lewis Carroll just using the Jews like the French and English? Was it a simple proposition of logic, a way to make his point? But Lewis Carroll was drawing, was he not, on

precisely the kind of stereotypical comment about Jews that
had brought upon them the enmity of the Polish peasants
and the hatred of the Nazi regime. And worse, in the section
following, under Examples, No. 14:

(1) No Gentiles have hooked noses;
(2) A man who is a good hand at a bargain always makes
    money;
(3) No Jew is ever a bad hand at a bargain.
Univ. "persons": a = good hands at a bargain; b = hook-
nosed; c = Jews; d = making money.

And in Book VIII, Chapter III, under Solutions:

> 21. *No Jews are honest;*
>   *Some Gentiles are rich.*
>   *Some rich people are dishonest.*
Univ. "persons": m = Jews; x = honest; y = rich.

Anna had to accept it. Tears running down her cheeks,
she had to admit it. Lewis Carroll expected her to have a
hooked nose, be greedy for money, make a shrewd bargain.
Lewis Carroll, who knew, like Thoreau, that life was a
dream, Lewis Carroll shared the world's prejudices about
Jews. Lewis Carroll.

In Anna Bernstein's diary, again very close to the end of the
volume:

I still love Kurt Hahn.

And beneath this, in very erratically spaced letters, in
red:

I still love Lewis Carroll.

Anna needed her mother. Ellen Bernstein had to tell her if it was all right for her to marry Kurt Hahn, all right to dilute her BBBB blood with AAAa that had some genes from Hitler's Germany; had to explain to her why even Lewis Carroll isolated Jews, even he. Ellen Bernstein, who had assimilated in Glen Cove, Long Island, who had raised Anna in her first seven years simply as an American, singing My Country 'Tis of Thee with all the other children, saluting the flag like any other American, who would answer, if someone had asked her, I am an American, not I am an American Jew. Ellen Bernstein had to explain to her why she had told her, on their last encounter, that she must remember she was Jewish. Did that affirmation of her Jewish identity negate all possibility of her marriage to Kurt Hahn? For she would not only be "marrying out," in Cousin Linda's terms, starting that process of genetic assimilation in the line that would end in wiping out a people who had endured longer than Christianity, she would be marrying someone whose genetic ancestors hated Anna's people to such a degree that they had eliminated them in a way so merciless and degrading that it was still, to many people, unthinkable, so unthinkable that some still claimed it hadn't happened, so unthinkable that Anna herself to this day had great difficulty, when the thought boxes sprang open in the middle of the night, comprehending how it could have happened, or why God had let it, for if she believed in God, she had to know why.

Waiting for the night of the séance, Anna Bernstein spent the time in Widener pressing God to tell her why. She went to the stacks and started pulling out books on religious theory, which brought her rather quickly to sevens. Sevens became a fugue of sevens. Gershom G. Scholem, the great expert on the Kabbalah, told her that God had offered the commandments on Mount Sinai in seventy languages, that seventy was the traditional number of the nations inhabiting the earth, that seventy could stand "for the inexhaustible totality of the divine word."

That, according to the Talmud, the complete Torah contained seven books. That each of these was related to seven *sefiroth*, which govern the seven cycles of aeons. That the *sefiroth* in turn were related to the seven *shemittoth* or cosmic cycles, that the complete series of seven *shemittoth* constituted the Great Jubilee, and that each of these cycles endured for seven thousand years and then, according to Gershom G. Scholem's interpretation of the doctrines of Sefer ha-Temunah, or Book of the Image, "the whole of Creation returns to the womb of the third sefirah, named 'return' or 'penitence' or even, in the opinion of some of the later Kabbalists, to nothingness."

Kabbalists, Anna realized, could add up all those sevens and end with nothingness! Infinite sevens could become infinite nothingness. Then, too, there were the seven holy forms of God, the seven potencies or archetypes of all Creation, the seven first days of Genesis.

Anna had God's number. It was clearly seven. God made the world in seven days, and if He wanted to, after the seven thousand years of each of the seven *shemittoth*, He could take it all back, to the nothingness out of which it came. That was if you were interpreting the Torah and the Talmud, that was if you were a Kabbalist. But, she remembered, her mind racing, if you were Cotton Mather, if you were reading the New Testament, if you were reading in the Revelation of St. John the Divine, there were the other sevens. There were the seven stars and the seven seals, and the seven angels and the seven trumpets, and every time an angel sounded, hail and fire mingled with blood and blood-red seas: "and the third part of trees was burnt up, and all green grass was burnt up. . . . And in those days shall men seek death, and shall not find it." Finally, when the seventh angel began to sound, according to St. John, "the mystery of God should be finished." God would finally show Himself. God — Anna's thought boxes could hardly deal with all this — would come out of the fire and the seas running with blood and take the Chosen back with Him to Heaven. God, according to St. John, had already marked some of the tribes of Israel for favor, for some of the 144,000 elect seem to have been members of those tribes, but these, in a manner not quite clear to Anna, were included among the loyal martyred Christians and were known to some interpreters as "Jewish Christians."

Anna's head was spinning with numbers. The God of Revelation had 144,000 elect. The original souls on Mount Sinai numbered 600,000, one for each meaning of the Torah. The 600,000 could very readily become, as she had known for some time, the 6,000,000. And underlying all of it was seven. Seven was in some way the key. What was the connection between the Jewish seven and the Christian seven? Why did God like seven so much? Because she discovered, with rising excitement, that what had always been claimed about the relation between the Old and New Testaments was true. That the Old Testament prefigured the New. That all the sevens of the Torah and the Talmud looked forward to the sevens of Revelation.

If this was true, was it true that the 600,000 of the Torah, becoming the 6,000,000 of the Holocaust, were also a prefiguration? That the six million became once again, in this circumstance, the martyred Chosen for God's purposes? They had been retrieved by God, taken back to nothingness as in the third *sefirah*, returned to the womb of Creation, as a signal to the world that the seven angels might soon sound.

Nothing, nothing, seemed to Anna so familiar as the description of the trees and grass and mountains burning up, of men seeking death and not finding it. Nuclear holocaust would be the seven angels trumpeting. The unthinkable return to nothingness already signaled by the unthinkable Holocaust of the Chosen. Prefiguration by the 6,000,000 — the Chosen beloved of God (hard though this was to believe). Six million martyrs, just to warn the world what it was like to return by fire to nothingness, to smoke?

Anna's question now raised itself in all its magnitude: What was her obligation to the 6,000,000? Must she sacrifice Kurt Hahn? Must the fire of her passion be subsumed by the larger collective fire of the Holocaust? The séance was urgent. Ellen Bernstein had to be reached, had to cross the line from eternity to tell her daughter, who had been orphaned at the age of seven, God's number, what to do. Ellen Bernstein had to come through, because time was running out, and Kurt Hahn would soon come to bring her back as his wife to Lovelock, Nevada, and Lottie Hahn, who felt about Jews as Martin Luther had, and whose father, for all Anna knew, might still be sitting there, having decided to live out his days with his daughter. Otto Dienes. Ellen Bernstein had to tell Anna what to do about Otto Dienes.

On the night of the séance, Anna was ready two hours early, desultorily playing with Celeste and Lucinda in Andrew's apartment. Andrew, worried about the dark circles under her eyes and her new gauntness, was trying to tempt her with food, and even, though this was painful to him, to talk to her about her future plans with Kurt.

— Are you and Kurt going to Nevada right after you're married?

— Don't know yet, Andrew.

— Kurt tells me you're getting married next week. He asked me to stand up for him.

— Don't know yet.

— Is Joanna standing up for you?

— Haven't asked her, Andrew.

— Anna, for God's sake. If this is what you want I'm happy for you, but if not, don't do it. For a prospective bride you don't seem happy to me.

— I'm happy, Andrew. Anna tried a weak smile. But I have to talk to my mother first.

— Oh God, Anna, you're not still into that. You really expect someone to produce your mother?

Anna looked at Andrew with the patient compassion of the believer for the unbeliever.

— Of course, Andrew. She'll come. I'll know later tonight what my plans are.

— What if she doesn't come?

— She has to come, Andrew.

— Has to?

— Has to.

When Joanna arrived, Andrew Hanson stole a moment alone with her.

— I hope you know what you're doing. Anna's nutty enough already.

— Her mother will come through, Andrew. Don't worry. She's got to talk to her.

— But what if she doesn't?

— Let's deal with that when the time comes. If she does talk to her mother, maybe she'll feel better.

— Look, Joanna, I didn't say this to Anna because I didn't want to upset her any further. She's on the edge of freaking out as it is. But her mother, goddamn it, her mother has been dead since she was seven. And you and your nutty friends are not going to bring her back.

— We're late, Andrew; see you later, was Joanna's response. She ushered Anna quickly out the door. We have to hurry, Anna. They won't wait for us.

The two young women arrived at the Reverend Anstrom's house just as the door jambs were being plugged to keep the light out of the séance room. Anna, from her earlier session, was prepared for the trumpet on the table and the blackness of the room when it was finally readied. Anna sat in the dark, patiently awaiting her turn, singing Open My Eyes with the others to usher the spirits gently into this world, back into contact with material, physical reality; the Reverend Anstrom went into trance and began, as before, getting his messages as though he had placed a long distance call. Departed relatives started coming through, and all about her, in the circle around the table, Anna heard happy family members talking to their loved ones.

— Glad you like your new job, Eleanor. You're going to enjoy it.

— Don't buy that house, Bill. The children won't like it. Wait. You'd better wait.

This went on for about twenty minutes.

And then, and then, after a very long silence, a space in the proceedings that seemed itself like eternity, the Reverend Anstrom as medium, using his vocal cords for the spirit voice, called Anna's name.

— Anna Bernstein?

— Yes.

— Anna Bernstein?

— Yes, here I am. Mother?

— Anna Bernstein.

Yet again. And then:

— Baranowicze, Bendin, Bialystok, Bilgoraj, Boryslaw, Busk, Dobromil, Dovinka, Dubno, Dubrava, Frampol, Jadowa, Jaroslaw, Jedlinsk, Lemberg, Lipsko, Lomza, Lublin, Mielec, Minsk, Mir, Myslowice, Ostroleka, Oszmiana, Pinsk, Plonsk, Przemysl, Radom, Ropczyce, Skalat, Slonim, Sokolow, Sosnowice, Stanislawow, Tomaszow Lubelski, Wasowice, Wlodawa, Wolkowysk, Wyszkow, Wyszogrod.

The recitation of this list was followed in the darkness by a heavy thud. The séance was abruptly terminated. When the Reverend Anstrom came out of the trance, some members of the party told him what had happened. He had recited some names that sounded Polish, and Anna Bernstein had fainted. After they revived her, Joanna Wilkens took her away.

Anna Bernstein and Kurt Hahn were arguing. On the morning after the séance, Anna Bernstein told Kurt Hahn she wouldn't marry him.

— I can't, Kurt.

— You can, Anna, you *must*.

— She doesn't want me to.

— Fuck it. How do you know your mother was ever there? These charlatans, these fucking charlatans. The dead don't come back, Anna. I don't want to make you feel bad, I know you'd feel better if you felt we could make contact, if you could really believe in something that goes on, but this is it, our one crack at it, our only life, and after that, it's down into the dark, and we've had it, and that's why, that's why, said Kurt Hahn desperately, that's why you've got to marry me. I love you, Anna. You've got to marry me.

— I can't, Kurt.

— It was just a bunch of fucking Polish towns, for Chrissake.

— It was the towns they wiped out. The towns I've been dreaming about.

— But don't you see? Kurt Hahn's face showed the hope of a new insight. That's it. *You* projected the towns. The medium didn't get them from your mother. He got them from you. He probably has some kind of telepathic knack, and he read your mind and gave you those places, because you've been thinking about them.

Anna *had* been thinking about the Polish towns, obsessing about them, not so much dreamed about them as seen the list of names in the darkness behind her eyes when she was trying to sleep. The places from which all the Jews had been eradicated, shipped to those other places, Auschwitz, Treblinka, those other places to which, had her grandmother not left Poland when she did, her grandmother and mother too would have been taken, and Anna Bernstein would never have been born. Because of Otto Dienes.

— Kurt, I love you. You know I love you. I love you so much it's killing me. But I can't break faith with my people.

— What people, Anna? For God's sake, what people?

— I'm Jewish, Kurt.

— Anna, you don't even go to a synagogue. You've been

going to spiritualist meetings and singing Protestant hymns. You hardly know anything about Judaism, except for all that reading you've been doing in the Kabbalah, and that's something else again. That's mysticism. It's not so different from Böhme, or Eckhart. And they were German Christian mystics. It's all the same, Anna. It's all the same. We don't even know if God is sitting up there with His fucking white beard. Men make these things up, you know. Because it suits them. Everything is made up to suit them. The Paiutes have a totally different system of gods.

— They killed *them* too, said Anna morosely, but beginning to hear Kurt Hahn.

— Anna, look. When you boil it all down, it comes down to you and me. To individuals. Not to groups. I love you. You love me. I can't help it that my people were German. You can't help it that yours were Jewish. I can't help it that there have been centuries of anti-Semitism. Why the hell must I — we — be punished for someone else's hate? I don't blame all the white Americans for what they did to the Indians.

— You should, Kurt, Anna said solemnly. You should.

— Anna. Love. Love is the only thing that matters.

— But what about remembering, Kurt? What about obligation?

— Love, Anna, he said, taking her in his arms, for he felt that he had begun to get through to her. Only love. Tomorrow, Anna. I'm not waiting any longer. I'm coming for you tomorrow morning. I'm booking us on the plane to Reno. We can get married very easily in Nevada, hardly any wait at all. And then we'll go on to Lovelock.

Anna tried not to see Otto Dienes and Lottie Hahn in her mind's eye. Anna tried to see the blue jewel of Pyramid Lake, the serenity of that other earth's eye, the sacred place of the Paiutes, even more beautiful than Thoreau's pond. Anna's silence was enough to give Kurt Hahn hope.

— Tomorrow, Anna. I'll pick you up tomorrow about nine-thirty. There's an eleven o'clock flight out of Logan.

He fled before Anna Bernstein could deny him again.

In purple ink. Inside back cover of Anna Bernstein's diary:

"... the Seventh Square is all forest ... one of the knights will show you the way — and in the Eighth Square we shall be Queens together, and it's all feasting and fun!"

... Alice began to remember that she was a Pawn, and that it would soon be time for her to move.

Anna Bernstein spent the rest of that morning walking all over Cambridge. She crossed Harvard Yard and stood for a while looking up at the columned portico of Widener, without climbing the steps. She walked past Bitsy Allingame's garden on Brattle Street. Anna spent a long time down at the river, looking across at the golden dome of the State House. Then, since she had all the time in the world, she walked very slowly across the Salt and Pepper Bridge into Boston and found her way to Cotton Mather's grave. Cramped, poor man. No. She would not feel sorry for Cotton Mather. He did not deserve a grave of his own.

Anna Bernstein returned home well after dark and very tired. She threw herself on her bed and slept for a while. About midnight, she found herself wide awake. The thought boxes, series of them, began to open in her head.

It was the blood that was the real problem. It was the blood that carried the genes, the BBBBBBBBBBBB blood that was in the way. Once the blood had drained out, she was free of her responsibility to the 6,000,000. All she had to do was slit her wrists. Then by the time Kurt Hahn arrived in the morning, she would be pure for him. A pure Aryan bride. Rapunzel.

November 1, 1980

Anna Bernstein
Klingenstein Clinical Center
Mount Sinai Hospital — 7th Floor
New York, N.Y. 10029

Dearest Anna–

   The doctor says you will be out next week, and I want you
to know I will be waiting. I'm so glad you will finally be out
of there, and back with someone who loves and cares for
you. Lucinda, Bony, Samantha, Red, Celeste, and Lettie are
all waiting too, so be prepared for an onslaught of affection.
Your grandmother has asked that I bring you to Brooklyn to
spend a couple of days with her before we go on to
Cambridge. Please say yes. Cambridge is where you belong
now. We're halfway into fall semester, and you can rest and
read and catch up before you register for spring classes.
Nothing and no one will hurt you, and whatever it was, I
know it is gone, and I will be there to protect you. Don't
disappoint me, dearest Anna. Please say you will come.
With love always,

                        Andrew

November 2, 1980

Anna Bernstein
Klingenstein Clinical Center
Mount Sinai Hospital
New York, N.Y.

Dearest Anna —

   I have heard that you are coming home. I will be waiting,
my darling love.

                        Kurt